EXTRA INNINGS

SEATTLE CASCADES
BOOK 1

C.M. KANE

COPYRIGHT

owners of various products referenced in this work, which have been used without permission. The publication/use of these trademarks is not authorized, associated with or sponsored by the trademark owners.

～

Editing & book design by Maggie Kern @ Ms.K Edits
Cover art by Golden Czermak @ FuriousFotog

BOOK ONE

SEATTLE
CASCADES

DEDICATION

For my father, who instilled in me the love of the game.

PROLOGUE

*L*ucy...

It wasn't supposed to be like this. Ten years ago, when Ryan was in the middle of his FBI career, I could see him being killed. It wasn't like he had the most dangerous job, but still, it wouldn't have come out of the blue like this did. He'd retired from the bureau three years ago, though, and this was supposed to be our safe and secure future. Our happily ever after. Instead, I was sitting in the front row at our church, looking at a box that held what was left of him, and I was crushed.

Rayne was pissed at the world, and I didn't blame her.

"Why didn't he tell us goodbye?" she'd shouted when I'd told the kids. "He told us we should always say goodbye, 'cause we never know when it'll be the last time we see each other."

How do you tell a thirteen-year-old girl that her daddy didn't want to wake her up for a simple trip into the city? He wasn't going to be gone long, either. Just a run into the field office to discuss an old case. But I should have insisted. It was one of the things we'd promised to always do. He said goodbye to me, but not the kids, and now they would never get that final one.

Thomas was upset, too. His was just the opposite of his sister,

1

though. Where Rayne raged, Thomas was silent. Oh, he cried, but he didn't blow up like his sister. Her torrent flooded through the house, but he simply sat at the table and let the tears fall. Once she was in her room, though, he really let go. The sobs were heart-wrenching and racked his body violently. He was small for his age, looking more like an eight-year-old than the eleven that he was. The sorrow he felt was fierce, too. Much bigger than anyone his age should have to endure. Now, he was silent, sitting stoically in the front row with his sister and me.

Rayne's fury was boiling again, and I could feel it coming off her in waves. It was like she couldn't turn it off at all. I was thankful Mom and Dad were here and that Mom was going to take the kids home shortly after the service. Honestly, I wasn't sure what Rayne would do if someone gave their condolences. It was a coin flip whether she'd blow up or brush them off, and I wasn't sure which would be the better option.

Ryan had done a good job of keeping his private life and his working life separate. While I knew many of his colleagues, both from the community college where he currently worked and the bureau, the kids had been kept out of that connection. Today would be about shaking hands and accepting condolences on behalf of the family. It would be rough, but I knew I could get through it somehow. I could always compartmentalize my emotions. Showing grief without letting it get out of hand was what I would do today. Tonight, after the kids were in bed, I'd let go and cry until I couldn't see. Then, tomorrow morning, I'd get up and figure out how to get through the next day. One day at a time, isn't that the saying?

"Please rise," Pastor Glen said. "Join me in a prayer for the family as they find their way to the social hall."

Standing, I looked at my kids. Rayne with her fury, and Thomas with his sadness, each looked to me to lead them. How was I supposed to do that without Ryan? He was the rock, the solidity of our lives. Now we were just left to drift in the endless river of pain.

"How long do we have to stay?" Rayne scowled as soon as we were out of the sanctuary.

"Not long," I replied. "Grams wants to thank some of her friends who came, then she's going to take you guys home."

"Good," Rayne snapped. "I can't stand this. I don't even know why we had to come."

"Because we're family," Thomas said. "We need to be here for Mom."

"Mom's fine," Rayne lashed. "She isn't even sad. She's probably glad Dad's gone. This way, she can find another dude and just move on."

"Rayne," I barked. "That is enough."

"Whatever," she said, rolling her eyes and stomping off, Thomas following in her wake.

Turning to find my mom, I ran right into George Warde, or as Ryan called him, 'Captain Clueless.'

"Sorry," he said, grabbing my elbow in a guise to steady me. "Didn't see you there."

"No problem." I cringed. "I've got to find someone."

"I'm here to help," he said. The tone was saccharine, and it set me on edge.

"It's quite all right," I countered, trying to move around him.

"If you ever need anyone to talk to…" he continued, moving in front of me once more. "I'm happy to be your shoulder."

"I appreciate it," I replied, once again trying to navigate around him.

"There's a coffee shop just around the corner," he said, gripping my elbow harder. "Why don't I take you there and get you away from all of this?"

"Lucy," my dad said, and I'd never been more thankful to see him in my life.

"Hey, Dad," I replied, pulling my arm from George's grip.

"I'll catch up to you later," he said, walking away.

"You okay?"

"Yeah," I replied. "I'm really glad you came by just now."

"Where are the kids?" Dad asked.

"I think they went into the family room they set up for us," I said.

"I was just going to look for Mom and see when she wanted to head out. Rayne's really eager to get out of here."

"Mom's just talking with Faye," Dad said. "She was pretty sure the kids wouldn't want to stay long."

"I'm not sure about T," I said. "But Rayne is beyond done."

"I'll go check on them," he replied. "You sure you're good?"

"Yeah," I said. "Just tired and ready to be done."

"You've got a ways to go." Dad smiled. "I'm really proud of you, though."

"Why's that?"

"You're holding up so well under all this pressure," he complimented. "You will get through this."

"Thanks, Dad." I hugged him, then sent him to find the kids.

"Hey," Andrea said when I turned around.

"Oh, geez," I whispered. "I didn't see you there."

"Sorry," she replied with a hug. "You holding up?"

"As well as can be expected," I replied.

"Anyone you want me to run interference with?"

"Actually." I smiled. "That guy over there." I pointed with my head. "He's Captain Clueless."

"*The* Captain Clueless?"

"That's the one." I smirked.

"Ew," she sneered.

"Right?"

"I'm on it," she said, hoisting her baby up on her hip and sauntering over to the man.

I watched as she struck up a conversation. From the way he looked at me over her shoulder, I could tell she was telling him in no uncertain terms that she was keeping an eye on him. That was her. No fear whatsoever. God, I loved her in that moment.

"Mrs. Fallon," a man said, and I turned to him, ready to do my duty as the bereaved widow. It was the role I knew needed to be played, and I relished the fact that I could shut down and just exist for a couple of hours.

~

JONATHAN...

"I can't believe Meg's gone," Kate said. "How's Grant holding up?"

She looked at my boy, asleep on my shoulder, completely oblivious to the rest of the world for the moment. God, I wished I could do that —just forget, even for just a few minutes.

"I mean," I began, then cleared my throat. "He doesn't really understand what's going on. Keeps asking for her, and I keep having to tell him she's gone."

I sniffed, trying desperately to hold my emotions in check.

"Are you doing okay?"

"Not really." I barked out a laugh. I mean, what else could I do?

"I'm so sorry," she said, and hugged me.

Kate and I had always been close growing up. Even when we hated each other, we still found a way to stick together. It was her and me against the world from the time we were little. Not like anything was ever against us, but still, it was nice to have a comrade-in-arms.

"Not your fault," I replied.

"But it sucks," she said, and I nodded. "You going back to the team?"

"Yeah," I replied.

I played for the Seattle Cascades, the Major League Baseball franchise north of us. It was one of the closest teams to where we grew up in the middle of Oregon and had been 'our' team. My dreams came true when they drafted me out of college. Kate was almost more excited than me, actually. I was drafted from high school, but at such a low level, it didn't make sense to go pro at that time. The scholarship from the University of Oregon helped to make that decision easier.

"What are you doing with Grant?" Kate asked.

"He's gonna stay with Mom for the next three weeks," I replied. "She said it would be easier for her to do it here rather than uprooting herself and coming to Seattle."

"You gonna be good up there by yourself?"

"I'm sure I'll be fine," I lied.

Nothing was going to be fine again. How was I supposed to go on without my other half? My better half?

"Mama," my baby said as he stirred on my shoulder.

"I'm sorry, baby," I replied, letting the tears fall as I pushed the hair from his face.

While Grant had my eyes, the rest of him was all Meg—blond, wispy hair, fair features, and the most adorable pushed-up nose. Even his tone was like hers.

"Dada," he mumbled, rubbing his eyes.

"Yeah, baby," I said, kissing his head.

"Hungy," he said, and I couldn't help but laugh.

At almost two, he was nearly always hungry. Meg told me he was going through a growth spurt, but I had laughed, asking when it started. That little boy seemed to eat nonstop.

"Nana has snacks," Kate said, reaching out and taking him from my arms.

"Nana," he called as my sister set him on the floor, and he toddled off to find my mom.

"Thanks," I said as I watched my sister follow him.

I'd held it in through the service, but it was all starting to hit me. She was gone. Forever. And nothing I could do would bring her back. The only person who could give me a boost when I felt off was gone, and being stolen from me in such a meaningless way was almost more than I could bear.

Going back to Seattle was going to be tough. The condo was full of memories, and I didn't know whether it was a good idea to stay there, or if I should find a hotel and book a room for the rest of the season. After all, it was only three weeks, with only two in the city itself. We were so far out of the playoff picture that I didn't have to think beyond the regular season, which was a blessing in disguise.

I'd take the off season and spend it with family and friends in my hometown, forgetting for a little while about baseball and everything Seattle held—the memories, the happiness, the experiences. They were all tied to the woman who I put in the ground today. A woman who was the center of my existence, even more than baseball. Maybe after the first of the year I could think about next season. I might be ready to move on after that. Or maybe this was meant to be the end of my career. I honestly didn't know, or care, anymore.

"Hey," Dad said as he came up to me. "What can I do?"

"Bring Meg back," I said.

"I would if I could," he replied. "Have you set up an appointment with someone to talk?"

"I don't have time," I replied.

"You need to make time," Dad insisted. "I can talk to you, and you can talk to me, but you need to seek someone who can give you proper tools to get you through this. Promise me you'll call someone."

The pointed look he gave me brooked no argument, and I nodded in compliance.

"Good boy," he said, squeezing my shoulder.

He turned and walked back to where my mom, sister, and son were. There were a few others here still, but it was mostly just family now. Meg's mom had wanted to come, but it just wouldn't work to get her up here, and it killed me that she had to miss it. Her sister fixed it so that we could stream the service and her mom could watch, but it wasn't quite the same. She'd lost her husband earlier this year to cancer, and while we'd known it was coming, it didn't make the loss any less. Meg had gone to stay with them for a month or so at the end. It was the last time they'd seen her, and now she was gone. They didn't even get to say a proper goodbye.

CHAPTER ONE

*L*ucy...

"It's not gonna be the same," Thomas complained.

"But we can remember the past," I tried. "And make new memories. You'll see, it'll be all right. Not easy, but we can do it together."

"We should just skip it this year," Rayne commented.

"Which part?" I asked.

"The whole thing," she barked. "It's not the same, and it won't be the same, and it's gonna be stupid and horrible and I don't wanna do it."

She shoved back from the table and stomped off to her room, slamming the door. I sighed and looked at her hardly touched dinner and wanted to cry.

"It'll be okay, Mom," Thomas offered, placing a hand on top of mine.

"Thanks," I said, trying desperately to put on a brave face.

"Maybe we just go to Grams and Gramps on Christmas Eve," he suggested. "I know Rayne likes that, so she would probably be fine with it."

"Since when did you become such a grown-up?"

"Since I had to become the man of the house," he said.

He'd made the statement before, about having to step up and be the man of the family. I'm not sure who put that thought in his head, but it was too much weight to put on his little shoulders.

"You don't have to do that," I said.

"It's okay," he replied. "I can do it."

My heart broke right there for the thousandth time or so. No child, even one who was an adult, should ever be put in the position of having to take on the responsibilities of an entire family. But an eleven-year-old? That was just ludicrous.

"Finish up," I encouraged, changing the subject.

The night went on, Rayne storming in her room, playing all sorts of melancholy music too loud, and Thomas being extra helpful with cleanup and the like. Honestly, I felt like all I wanted to do was have a drink and sleep for a week. It'd been almost three months since Ryan died, and it wasn't getting easier. We were growing accustomed to the way things were, but it wasn't easy.

I'd kept the kids out of school until after the funeral, but then sent them back. Rayne fought me, but Thomas seemed to excel in a way he hadn't before. December came in cold and dreary, as most winters in the Pacific Northwest, with lots of rain and cool temperatures. It almost felt as if the world was mourning with me at times.

Mom and Dad had been great, giving me a day here and there to just unplug. I found myself going for a run more often now than before, even in the rain. Andrea would come with me on days when it wasn't actually raining but couldn't bring Noah during the downpours. Because I ran when the kids were at school, she didn't have Bret to watch him. I was fine with it, though. It gave me a break from having to be put together. The rain allowed me to cry and hide it, so there was a benefit to it in some ways.

"Mom," Rayne said as she came into my bedroom.

Her hesitancy was unusual, and I didn't want to shun her, even though it was nearly midnight.

"What's up?" I asked, trying to sound cheerful.

"Can't sleep," she said, climbing onto the bed with me.

"I get that way, too," I said, hoping to give her a chance to talk things out.

"How come he didn't say goodbye?"

"He didn't want to wake you up," I said. "And I know it was dumb, but he really thought he'd be back before you were home from school."

"But he wasn't," she argued. "He promised, and he broke the promise."

"I know," I cooed as the tears fell.

"I hate him," she sobbed, and I gathered her in my arms, letting her get it all out.

We sat like that for a while, her sobbing and me just carrying the burden for her. Finally, she gave a big sigh with a hiccup and pulled away.

"I'm sorry," she said, wiping her face.

"You have nothing to be sorry for," I replied, handing her a tissue for her nose. "There is nothing wrong with being upset, or angry, or any other feeling you have."

"But I shouldn't hate him," she said on a sob. "He's gone, and I shouldn't hate him for not being here."

"But you do, don't you?"

"Yeah," she said, tears streaming from her eyes once again.

"It's okay," I said. "I think he knows he screwed up. God knows I've told him so many times."

"Really?"

"Yeah," I confessed. "I was so mad at him, that he would leave me without any warning. We'd promised that once he left the bureau, we'd be able to grow old together."

"Then he had to go and have a brain aneurysm," she said.

"The nerve of him." I smiled.

"Sucks, though," she said. "He's not gonna be able to threaten any of my boyfriends."

"You think I won't?"

"Pft," she spat. "You're hardly intimidating. Besides, you're too nice. Dad had that FBI threat of knowing how to hide a body going for him. What do you have? Baking them too many cookies?"

"You don't think Dad gave me some pointers?"

"Mom!"

The shock on her face was comical, and I laughed. I couldn't help it. She laughed, too, and it was cathartic.

Maybe we'd be okay.

~

"WE'RE GONNA KEEP IT LOW-KEY," I SAID. "JUST DINNER AND GIFTS at your place on Christmas Eve."

"I guess it would be too hard to do the whole festival you usually do at your place," Mom replied.

I'd called her the next morning to let her know we were going to tone down our celebration. Ryan was the push for Christmas to be big every year. He'd dress up as Santa and, even the last few years, when both kids knew it was him, he would hold on to that spirit of Father Christmas, just to give a little bit of magic to them.

"That, and the kids are a little overwhelmed," I replied. "I don't want to tax them too much. I think it'll be nice to do some things that are new, you know? Something different from what we've always done. I don't want to forget the past, but I want to try to give them some memories that aren't wrapped up in what we're missing."

"Makes perfect sense," Mom said. "I'm surprised you aren't canceling everything."

"I can't do that," I argued. "I don't want to forget, but I don't want to dwell on it, either. I have some ideas of things to do that will make this year special and remind them of the good times we had while Ryan was here. They need to learn how to move forward. Honestly, so do I."

"You've been really brave," she said.

"How do you mean?"

"I don't know if I could have held up as well as you have," she explained. "Holding the family together, keeping the kids going forward. You really should be proud of yourself."

"Thanks, Mom," I said. "Honestly, I have no idea how I've done it. There are days I don't even want to get out of bed. That I hope the ground will swallow me whole. But I just keep going. I'm afraid if I stop, I won't be able to start again."

"Is there anything I can help you with?" she asked. "Anything you want Dad and I to do to make it easier?"

"If I think of something, I'll let you know," I replied. "Right now, just plan for dinner and gifts. Let me know what you want to cook, and I'll bring something."

"You don't have to," she said. "I can get it all done. Dad is learning some pretty amazing dishes to try out. Do you guys want to experiment?"

"Depends." I laughed. "How crazy of food combinations are we talking about?"

"He's on a Mexican kick right now," she said. "I think I've eaten more beans and rice in the last week than I have in the two years before it."

I laughed, and we talked about all the things Dad had begun doing since his retirement. It was good to hear, but once I hung up the phone, I lost it. My kids wouldn't have that in their dad. No learning new things or finding some hobby to keep him busy while we grew old. I would truly be an empty nester once Thomas left, and I wasn't sure how I felt about that.

CHAPTER TWO

*J*onathan...

"No Santa! No Santa! No!"

"You love Santa," I tried.

"No, no, no," Grant shouted.

"You sure you don't want to tell him what you want for Christmas?"

"Want Mama!"

And there it was, the only thing he said he wanted, and the one thing I couldn't give him.

"Mama's an angel now," I offered.

"No angel, want Mama."

He broke down in tears, sobbing on my shoulder.

"Maybe you should try again later," the girl dressed as an elf in the mall suggested. "There are way fewer people here during the week, so if you can come in then, it might be easier."

Honestly, I think she was just trying to get rid of me. Not that I blamed her. Who wanted to deal with a toddler in full meltdown with a line a mile long behind them?

"OK," I said. "Let's go."

The relief on the little elf's face was palpable, but it did nothing to ease my son. He continued to cry as I made my way to the food court.

"Oh, baby," my mom said, rubbing his back when we caught up with her.

"Nana," Grant called, pushing away from me.

"OK, little man," she said, taking him from my arms. "You want some pizza?"

"Pizza, pizza, pizza," Grant chanted, his sorrow forgotten for the time.

The one thing that could distract my son was food. I swear that kid ate more than some of the players on my team. I was worried about what he'd be like as a teenager. I would probably have to work both during the season, and in the off season, just to keep him fed. If only it were that easy for me.

I'd spent the last three weeks of September in Seattle, with a road trip to Sacramento and Los Angeles in the middle, and it was a struggle every day. The condo was a reminder of everything I was missing while I was there. Meg being gone was bad enough, but it was cold and empty without Grant as well. Solitude was not something I was built for, and the time I spent there just solidified that reality.

"You should bring him every day," my mom said after we'd settled with some food. "That way he could get used to the man, maybe warm up to him."

"You think that will work?"

"It worked with Kate," she said, cutting a slice of pizza up for my son.

"Kate didn't like Santa?"

"That's an understatement." She laughed. "We tried everything we could think of, but she didn't want anything to do with him. Why do you think I was in some of the pictures with you guys?"

"I just figured you wanted to be with us," I said.

"Not hardly." She laughed again. "You, on the other hand."

"What?" I asked when she didn't elaborate.

"I was worried you'd wander off with some stranger all the time," she said. "No fear in you whatsoever. Although, you did shy away from a few people. I guess you just had a gut feeling about who you could trust."

"You mean strangers?" I asked, taking a bite of my own lunch.

"Yeah," she replied. "You were also a talker. Man, did you talk. To most anyone who would listen. Complete strangers would be standing next to you in the store and you'd strike up a conversation with them, talking about whatever was on your mind. Whether it was something you saw on the shelf, something you watched on TV, didn't matter. If they were willing to listen, you'd chat 'til they cried mercy."

I laughed, and it felt good.

"I don't remember that at all," I said.

"You and your sister were polar opposites," she said. "But you were thick as thieves, too. I don't know how many times I'd come into one or the other of your rooms and you'd be plotting and scheming some shenanigan or another. Planning on taking over the world or deciding the best way to get extra dessert."

"Now that I remember," I said. "Dessert is always the best part of the meal."

"I have 'sert?" Grant asked, his mouth full of pizza.

"Eat your pizza first, baby," Mom said.

He nodded, chewing away, humming his own little tune. He reminded me of Meg, always dancing around the condo, humming some tune or another. Whether it was a song she'd heard earlier, or something that just came to her, there was always music coming from her. She'd even make up songs when she was putting Grant down for bed. I wondered whether that was the reason he was humming now as I watched him yawn. Maybe, subconsciously, he was comforting himself with the music.

"I think someone's tired," my mom said. "Maybe we should head home after lunch."

"Probably a good idea," I replied. "Maybe we'll both get a nap this afternoon."

"Still not sleeping well?"

I shook my head. It'd been like this for a couple of weeks. I'd get a good night's sleep but wake up feeling tired. That, or I wouldn't sleep at all. My doctor had given me some sleeping pills to use, but I didn't want to take them for fear of not hearing Grant during the night.

"You should take those—"

"Mom," I interrupted. "I don't want to take them."

I'd seen what they did to some of the guys on the team when they were prescribed. It wasn't something I wanted to tempt.

"Fine," she replied. "But you aren't sleeping, and that's not good for you, or for Grant."

"I'll see if there's something else I can try," I conceded. "Maybe something natural that will help me sleep."

"Good," she said.

I knew she meant well, and only wanted what was best for me, but she'd never seen what happened when someone has a bad reaction to those sleep aids. I had, and I wasn't going to go there, not if I didn't absolutely have to.

~

"Don't wake him," Santa said.

"Are you sure?" I asked.

"Absolutely," the jolly man replied.

We'd been to the mall every day for the last week and a half, and every time we came up to Santa, Grant would lose it—crying, screaming, running away. You name it, he did it. I was exhausted and had pretty much given up the idea that we'd get a picture this year. I shifted him from my shoulder and he didn't even stir.

"He's had a rough go," Santa said as he settled Grant in his arms.

"You remember?"

"Sometimes," the man said. "It's the little things I remember. His wispy hair reminds me of my kids when they were little."

"That comes from his mom," I said, looking at him, resting quietly.

"I take it she's not around," the older man said.

I shook my head, unable to get past the lump in my throat.

"It's all right, son." He smiled. "Just take it one day at a time."

"You, too?" I asked, though I knew the answer before he said it.

"Seven years now," he said as he looked at my sleeping angel. "Some days it feels like it was just yesterday that I kissed her goodnight."

The smile he held was a bit sad, but I think I only recognized it because I'd seen the same look in my own eyes when I looked in the mirror.

"At least you had a long life together," I said, and couldn't quite keep the bitterness out of my tone.

"Doesn't matter," the man said as he looked up at me.

We were nearly alone, there in the middle of the mall. The lunch rush hadn't started, and the early morning group had dissipated. It was just me and Santa having a conversation about loss while my son slept in his arms.

"How do you do it?" I asked, unsure why I felt the need to get guidance from this stranger.

"I remember," he said.

When he didn't elaborate, I asked, "Remember what?"

"The joyful times," he said. "The tiny little moments when everything was perfect. Whether it was when she was holding my first born for the first time, or when she was smiling right before she went to sleep for the last time. The moment I knew I would marry her, to the moment I knew she was going away. From the first kiss to the last, there are a million moments to remember."

I pressed my fingers to my mouth, unable to stop the tears from spilling over my lashes.

"It will get easier," he consoled. "You won't ever stop hurting completely, but you will learn what to do in those moments in order to get through."

"I'm just afraid I'm going to forget her," I confessed. "That I won't be able to tell him about her when he's older."

"Doesn't matter," he said, stroking my child's hair back from his closed lids. "Whatever you remember, he'll love to hear."

"My job keeps me away," I said, unsure why this moment was granted to me.

"So, you make the most of the time you have together," he countered. "Many parents are away from their kids for long stretches. Doesn't mean they love them any less. Doesn't mean they're terrible parents."

"But he's so young—"

"Nope," he interrupted. "Stop trying to find something wrong. You are you, and you are the best person to be his parent. If you have to spend the rest of your life trying to learn that, you'll miss out on all the wonderful things that are still to come."

"How…" I began but paused.

"How, what?"

"How do you know so much?"

"I'm Santa," he said, and there was a sparkle in his eye. "I know a great many things."

"Santa," Grant muttered, and the look of sheer joy on his face was exactly what I had been missing.

I stepped to the side as the camera operator snapped several pictures of my boy waking up in Santa's arms. The moment was magic, and I couldn't help but think Meg had something to do with it.

CHAPTER THREE

*L*ucy…

"I can't believe Rayne didn't want to come," Thomas said. "She doesn't know what she's missing."

We were standing in line for the fan festival put on by the Seattle Cascades, our local major league baseball team. It had been a family tradition for a few years. Ryan found out about it and made a day of it several years ago, getting us all up early to go get autographs and enjoy the stadium before Spring Training even started for the season. They'd bring in a handful of players, plus the announcers, and they had all sorts of fun things going on within the stadium.

"She wanted to do something else," I lied.

"No," Thomas replied. "She wanted to be a butt."

"T," I scolded. "Let's not call her names."

"I'm just saying," he countered.

We walked into the stadium after having our tickets scanned and looked up the big staircase that led to the main level of the concourse. The sections were divided by caution tape, only allowing you to go up one row.

"Looks like we need to pick which autographs we want to get," I said.

"I don't see the Guardian," Thomas said, looking over the choices.

"Are you sure he's even going to be here?"

"He should be," T said. "He's the best player on the team, so he should be here."

"My guess," I offered, "is that he isn't signing autographs because of him being so popular. I think there would be a stampede if he were up there."

"It's not fair," Thomas whined. "I want his autograph."

"We can go to that one," I suggested. "That way we could get two autographs instead of just one."

"I guess." He sighed. "Better than nothing. I just wish we could meet Ichigo."

I tried to think of what Ryan might say in this moment. It was times like this that I really missed his insight. He'd have known what to tell Rayne to help her get over her anger, and he'd know how to encourage T with his disappointment.

"We still might see him," I tried. "He's probably here, just not signing autographs."

"I hope so," he said. "Hey, can we do the zipline?"

"Really?" I asked. "I thought you were afraid of heights."

"Well," he hedged. "Dad said it looked like fun, so I thought I'd try it."

Just like that, he was over his disappointment and on to the next big adventure.

"Let's see what we have to do," I said. "We need to make sure we're done early enough to make it to our signing, though."

Walking along the mezzanine, we found the line for the zipline.

"Hi," the attendant said. "Are you interested in going on the zip?"

"Yeah," Thomas said.

"Just him," I confirmed.

"Perfect," the bubbly girl said. "Here's the form. Please read it over as you stand in line. When you get to the front, you'll need to complete and sign it before he can go on the ride."

"Thanks," I said, taking the piece of paper from her.

It was your typical release, holding the company and the team at no fault for any injury that was not caused by a malfunction of the equipment itself. By the time we got to the front of the line, I'd read it over and felt a little nervous about letting my son climb the monolith and strap onto a single rope rushing him down to the bottom. His excitement, however, eased my concern.

"This is gonna be epic." He beamed. "You need to take video of me doing it. I wanna show all the guys at school."

"I think Grams and Gramps are gonna be pretty impressed, too," I said.

"Who is gonna fly across the Cascades?" the attendant asked as we came to the area where the equipment was put on.

"I am," Thomas said, bouncing on the balls of his feet.

"Let's get you geared up," the attendant said.

It didn't take long for my son to get the contraption around his body. The harness looked sturdy and was snug, even on Thomas's small frame. Once he was strapped in, the young man placed a helmet on his head, tightening the strap around his chin. He also gave Thomas a quick tutorial on what to expect when he went down the rope, explaining where he would hold on now that he's strapped in, and what he shouldn't do when coming down.

"Mom," Thomas said, turning to me just before hooking up to the rope for the climb up the tower. "Get a picture of me with all this on first. Then video me going up and coming down and everything."

"Have fun," I said after I took a picture.

His climb seemed to take forever, and the further up he went, the smaller he became.

"It'll be fine," the young man who'd helped him strap up said. "We've been doing this for years. It's perfectly safe, as long as he follows the instructions. From what I saw, he'll be just fine. If you want to step over there," he continued, pointing toward the landing area, "he'll be down soon."

"Thanks," I said, and it didn't sound nearly as nervous as I felt.

I turned back to him, switching my camera on my phone from pictures to video and waited for him to get hooked up to the line coming down. I caught him every time he came back to the front of the tower, waving each time he could see me. The smile, even from this distance, was clear that he was enjoying himself to the fullest.

There were enough people in front of him that I had plenty of time to get to the landing zone where another attendant was stationed to unhook the straps from the line itself. I turned around, and he was on the last landing before heading to the back of the tower for the rest of the climb.

Watching other kids, as well as adults, slide down the line and laugh the entire way eased my nervousness quite a bit, and made me a little sad I hadn't decided to go with him. I saw him come up to the gate at the top, lines leading from him to the wire at the top. I turned the video on and was set to catch this moment in time. The gate opened, and he and another boy looked at each other with big grins on their faces, then stepped off the ledge.

The shout of joy that came from him made my heart leap to my throat, but then his grin and giggles followed and I laughed as he turned round and round while floating slowly down to the platform.

"Oh my gosh," he said as he landed. "Mom, did you get it?"

"I did," I said, stopping the video.

"That was so much fun," he said. "Rayne is gonna be so mad she didn't come. She totally missed out on an epic flight."

The attendant helped unstrap both boys from their harnesses, and the other boy's parents gathered him up and walked away. My heart gave a little skip when I realized Ryan would never see this moment.

"Hey," T said. "It's okay. He saw it, just not from here."

"How did you know what I was thinking?"

"Come on," he muttered, rolling his eyes. "What else would you be thinking?"

"I'm just so proud of you," I said, pushing the tears back and swallowing the lump in my throat.

"What's next?"

I pulled out the schedule and figured out where we needed to be in order to do the autographs.

"Looks like we have just enough time to get to our signing

session," I said. "Says we're in the clubhouse. Do you know how to get there?"

"Mom." He laughed. "Do I look like I work here?"

"I guess you're right," I replied. "We'll go up and ask someone the fastest way to get there."

~

"I CAN SEE THEM," THOMAS SAID AS WE STEPPED THROUGH THE DOOR to the actual clubhouse.

We were late in getting in line, so ended up near the end of it. That didn't seem to deter my son, however, as he was just excited to be doing anything related to baseball.

"We've still got a way to go." I sighed.

"I know," he said.

Once we got into the room, they had those stanchions with lines between them marking where we were to stand. There was just enough room for two smaller people to stand side by side. It made the line go back and forth a couple of times before they opened up to the table that had the two players at it.

"Tell me who these guys are again?" Thomas asked.

"Here," I said, handing him the card we'd picked up when we first came in.

"Says it's Jonathan Bridge and Beckett Hennings," he said. "I don't know either of them."

"Let's look them up," I suggested, pulling my phone out and pulling up the app for the baseball league.

It took a bit, but I was able to find the team on the app, and finally, after many wrong clicks, found the list of players.

"Says that Jonathan Bridge has been playing with Seattle for a long time," I said once I found his profile. "He was drafted by the Cascades and came up through the minor leagues."

"He looks kinda old," Thomas said.

"Says he's younger than me," I replied. "Guess that makes me old, too."

"I mean..." he stopped before actually agreeing with me, but the sentiment was there. "What about the other guy?" he asked.

"Let's see," I said, backing out of the profile for the first player. "Looks like he's new here. I think we got him in a trade in the off season and he was a minor league player before that. There really isn't much information on here about him."

"Great," Thomas grumbled. "We get an old guy and a rookie. I think we should have picked someone else."

"Just because you don't know them doesn't mean they're bad players," I offered. "Who knows, maybe they'll be exactly who the team needs to make it to the World Series."

"We're gonna need a lot of help if we're gonna get to the World Series, Mom," he chastised. "Have you ever seen the team?"

"Don't you remember that one team?" I asked. "The one that was really bad, and then one year they just weren't?"

"That was a fluke." He laughed.

We continued to look at the information on the players we were getting autographs from, and the more Thomas looked at the information that was on the app, the more and more excited he became. Apparently, the rookie was some kind of superhuman player who did amazing things in the minor leagues the last couple of years. For some reason, he'd never really made it up to the major league, though.

The older player had quite the record as well. He played a bunch of positions, and it looked like he was pretty good with a bat. I wasn't sure why he wasn't someone we knew, though. We'd been watching the team, even coming to a bunch of games throughout the years, and we'd probably seen most, if not all the players at one point or another.

Thomas said it was probably because he never played the same position that we didn't recognize him, and the logic made sense. In what seemed to take hours, we finally made our way through the back-and-forth of the lines to get close enough to the players.

"Here," I said, having pulled a couple of balls from my bag. "You get a signature on each ball, and I'll do the same."

"Oh, yeah," he replied. "That way we can keep one and sell one, if they're any good."

"No," I countered. "That way Rayne can have one set as well. She may not have wanted to come, but the least we can do is bring her back something from the day."

"I suppose," he said.

We were finally in front of the players and we each handed them a ball.

"How you doing?" the older one asked Thomas.

"Good," he said. "You know Ichigo?"

"Thomas," I scolded, but the player just smiled.

"Yeah," he said. "He's a great guy. He's still in Japan right now, though."

"Oh," Thomas said.

"Come to some of the games this year," the player offered. "You'll probably see him do amazing things. He is the Guardian after all."

"I know," Thomas said, then moved to the younger player.

"Good kid you got there," he said to me.

"Thanks," I replied. "He really is a great kid."

After we got the autographs, we went out the door and into the press room. People were in there taking pictures of themselves up at the podium, pretending to be interviewed. Thomas really wanted to do it as well, so we spent a good half an hour there, goofing around.

Honestly, it was a great time. We did the walk around the bases, taking pictures the whole way. There was also a place where you could get your photo taken as if you were part of the crew that did the announcing, so we had to do that as well. After everything was said and done, we'd spent nearly the whole day at the park, and had more than enough pictures and video to keep the memory with us for years to come.

Was I sad that Rayne didn't want to come? Absolutely. But Thomas got a day with just the two of us, enjoying things we loved. The memories were what I would treasure forever.

CHAPTER FOUR

*J*onathan...

"Sorry, man," Huffman said. "Better you than me, though."

I'd been stuck with the rookie that we'd picked up on a trade in the off season for the signing portion of the fan festival the team put on. Most of the time, rookies weren't at these events, but this guy was supposed to be some kind of modern marvel. From what I saw, though, he hadn't spent any time in the big leagues, so it was going to be a trial-and-error kind of year. Huffman was right in that it was better that I was stuck with this kid than him. He had this sort of menacing vibe when he was annoyed.

"Yeah," I replied. "But then again, it might be better if it were you. Maybe you'd be able to knock some sense into him."

"I'd likely knock the fucker's head off," Huffman mused.

The best and worst part of these events every year was that we got to spend time with the fans. They could come in, get some autographs, take pictures of us from behind the tables, and even get the chance to ask a question or two in the Q&A sessions of the event. Huffman was set up to be in one of those sessions, but I was just slotted for the one autograph session.

I think the team wasn't quite sure whether I'd even be at the event, so wanted to keep my schedule short just in case I wasn't able to make it. They'd been overly generous with my time, giving me whatever I needed to be able to come back. It was refreshing to be employed by such a great organization, and I wanted to do what I could to show them I really was a team player and a value to the club.

"You met him, yet?" I asked.

"Nope," the guy said.

Just then, the door to the room they were using for us to congregate between sessions busted open and the kid in question blasted through.

"Party can officially begin," he bolstered, louder than was necessary for the smaller space. "This year's Rookie of the Year has arrived."

"Pretty sure you're gonna do a whole hell of a lot of pine riding this year, Rook." Huffman laughed.

"Laugh it up, big boy," the kid said. "You just mark my words."

"Sure, sure," I said, shaking my head. "You ready to do this thing?"

"Ready, willing, and more than able," he boasted. "Can't wait to meet all my eager fans, especially the young and female variety."

"You know you can't hook up with fans, right?" I asked.

"What the boss don't know, won't hurt anyone," the kid said.

"Best read your contract, kid," Huffman said. "Pretty sure there's a clause in it about fraternizing with the crowd. You could end up flipping burgers with no chance at all to play in the show if you don't follow the rules."

"Nah," he replied. "I'm way too valuable. This guy," he said, jerking his thumb in my direction, "could use some time on the bench. He probably needs the naps he'll get in when I'm on the field."

"This guy," Huffman said. "He's been there, done that, got the damn trophy to prove it. Best be checking that privilege you think you've got. He's got more experience, better clout, and honestly, he's got a shit ton of height on you. I think the little boy better sit down and shut up when it comes to what's a good idea in this game."

I snorted a laugh, but the kid looked, I don't know, annoyed, maybe? He wasn't happy, and it was probably the comment about his height. To be honest, he wasn't much taller than my sister. Before either of us could say another word, the kid turned on his tail and stomped out of the room. If Grant had thrown that big of a tantrum, he'd probably have gotten a good talking to at the very least.

Huffman let out a bark of a laugh, slapping his knee and everything. I was laughing myself, but also wondering what the kid was thinking. Guess I'd find out soon enough, since I was gonna spend an hour signing autographs with him.

"Seriously, though," Huffman said as he headed out the door. "Keep your eye on him. He's gonna screw something up. I can just feel it."

～

"I AM A GOD," BECKETT BOASTED AS WE STEPPED BACK INTO THE cordoned off area set aside for the players. "I think I got at least a dozen phone numbers from some pretty hot chicks."

"Slow it down there, Romeo," I said, following him into the room. "You can just toss those numbers right into the trash."

"No fucking way," he said. "I worked hard for this, and I deserve it."

"I'm telling you, kid," I began.

"I'm not a kid," he shouted. "I'm a fucking adult and you better start treating me like one, too."

"Soon as you start acting like one," Huffman said as he stepped from behind one of the lockers in the space.

"Ooh," Beckett said. "Think you scare me because you're big and dumb?"

"Nope," Huffman said, popping the last part of the word.

"Good," the kid said. "'Cause you don't. I ain't afraid of any of you stupid players. I've been at the top of my game since I was in T-Ball, and nothing you old fucks are gonna say will change the fact that you're a dying breed and I'm the best thing to come along."

He shoved the papers he had numbers on into his pocket, then stormed out toward the stadium and where he was set to do the next Q&A session.

"That little shit is gonna get himself so deep into trouble he won't be able to find a way out," Huffman mused.

"Ain't that the truth," I replied.

There had been nothing on my schedule prior to the autograph session, and I was pretty much free now. While I didn't have to, I went to the dugout where they were setting players and announcers and the brass up to do the question sessions with the crowd. It wasn't that I had to be there but thought it might be nice to get out there and go the extra mile. Besides, there was a chance I could watch Beckett fall on his ass and make an absolute fool of himself, and that was worth the price of admission right there.

"Hey, J," Jenn, one of the announcers, said. "Thought you were done for the day."

"Thought I'd stick around and see what else was going on," I replied. "Can't miss these moments. Gotta give the fans what they want, too."

"You're all in on this aren't you?"

"Bet your ass I am," I said. "This is my life, my livelihood, and what I need to do."

"How are you doing?" she asked, and I could tell she really wanted to know.

"Not gonna lie," I said. "It's been a struggle. My family has been amazing, though. They've really come together to help me out. I couldn't have done it without them, that's for sure."

"I'm really glad to hear that," she said, patting my arm. "I know it was a big hit last fall, and I was honestly surprised you came back then. Not that I'm complaining, mind you. I'm happy you're back. You're one of my favorite players. Don't tell anyone I said that, 'cause I'll deny it to my dying breath, but you are probably the most professional and personable of the whole team."

"Thanks," I replied. "That's really nice of you to say."

"I mean it," she insisted. "I've probably interviewed almost every player on the team for the last several years, and you are honestly the easiest to talk with, and the most willing to put up with our questions. I really do appreciate it."

"Jenn," the coordinator of this part of the event said. "You're up."

"Gotta go," she said with a smile.

"Kill it like you always do," I said as she made her way around the end of the dugout and up on top of the roof.

I hung out in the dugout, waiting to see if they wanted to bring me up to answer questions, and was there when Beckett came in. He took one look at me, then glared before moving past me up to the steps to the top of the dugout.

The crowd cheered when he came up, and the dude had the nerve to smirk at me before disappearing from my view.

"What do you say we bring up an extra player this session?" Jenn asked, and the crowd cheered loudly again. "Since we've got the rookie here in Beckett Hennings, I thought we could bring up someone who's been with the team for years. What do you say?"

Again, the crowd cheered, and I made my way to the end of the dugout, ready to climb the steps to the roof.

"How about we give a big Seattle welcome to our very own Jonathan Bridge?"

As soon as she said my name, I moved to where I could be seen and climbed my way up to the top of the dugout. One of the guys who was helping to coordinate the event brought a chair over and I sat down next to Beckett. The guy handed me a mic, and I laid it in my lap.

"Say hello to Seattle, Jonathan," Jenn said.

"What's up?" I asked, and they all cheered.

"For those who may not know," Jenn began. "Jonathan has been with the club for, wait, what is it? Ten years?"

"Twelve," I replied. "Fifteen if you count my minor league time."

"That's why we all call him 'Daddy'," Beckett said, and some of the crowd laughed.

I glared at him, knowing that he was going to make this as uncomfortable as possible. Apparently, I had stolen his spotlight. This was going to be a one-on-one session where the newest phenom was interviewed about his great and wonderful self.

Without bringing the mic to my mouth, I said, "My toddler is better behaved than you."

Jenn must have heard what I said because she stifled a laugh. There were a few people right in front of us that also laughed, which just served to piss Beckett off even more.

"So," Jenn said, hoping, I'm sure, to make this session a little more respectable. "Beckett, tell us about your career so far."

"Absolutely," he replied, then began to regal the crowd with stories of his time at the Little League World Series, which he participated in twice, and won both times.

The amount of bragging on this kid made me realize he thought he was better than damn near every other player on the field. It was an attitude that would get him swiftly labeled as a prima donna on the baseball team. Everything that came out of his mouth was just one more thing that he was the best at. Little League, high school championships, college baseball World Series; you name it, he'd done it, and better than anyone else.

By the time he'd worn his mouth out, Jenn turned the questions to me.

"Jonathan," she said. "What's it like having such an accomplished player join the team?"

"Since I haven't seen him play," I began, looking directly at the punk. "I can't really give an opinion. If he's as good as he says, he'll be a great asset to the team. The trick is to not play as an individual, though. It takes teamwork to get to the championship. There are nine guys on the field on defense, and while each player has his position and needs to play at the top of his game, one player can't, by himself, beat another team."

When Jenn had first asked the question, I thought she was trying to make me look bad. But looking at the smile on her face after my answer, it was clear that she was showing Beckett that even the announcers knew he was full of shit. I gave her a head nod in thanks as she turned another question to the newest player on the team.

CHAPTER FIVE

*L*ucy...

"You're sure?" Andrea asked for like the hundredth time.

"Look," I said. "My choices are stay here with Noah and let you two enjoy Valentine's Day or stay home alone with my memories and cry all night. I'm choosing the better option."

"Where are the kids?" she asked.

"They're staying with Ryan's parents for the week," I explained. "Mimi and Papi missed them and offered to take them for the midwinter break, so I jumped at the chance."

"What are you going to do with the rest of the time?"

"Spring cleaning," I grumbled. "It's been a while since the house has had a good cleaning, so I thought I'd take this time to do it. I also have to figure out what to do with all of Ryan's clothes."

"You sure you're ready for that?"

"Not at all." I laughed. "Now, get. You're never gonna make your reservation if you two don't get out of here."

"Come on," Marco said, pulling his wife out the door.

"Bedtime at eight," Andrea called over her shoulder.

"Got it," I replied, then turned and looked at the little bundle sitting on the floor in the living room.

Noah was an angel, a delight in every sense of the word. I'd watched him several times over the almost year of his life, mostly when Marco and Andrea wanted a night out. His birthday was coming up in a few weeks, and I hadn't figured out what to get him. Not that he needed anything, really.

"Well, kiddo," I said to him. "Looks like it's you and me tonight. Shall we find some trouble to get into?"

He giggled and laughed, that deep belly laugh, then promptly flopped onto his belly to crawl over to me, pulling himself up on my pant leg.

The night was easy, with him already having eaten dinner, so I just played on the floor with him, building towers to have him knock them down. His giggles were so infectious that I couldn't help but join him. He was excellent therapy for my weary soul.

Before long, he was yawning and fussing, and I knew it was close to him going to sleep. Climbing the stairs, I took him to his room, changed him, and put his jammies on. We went back to the kitchen where I made a bottle for him, then returned to the room so I could rock him.

Andrea had this amazing gliding rocker that was super comfortable, and I sat down to let him drink his bottle before putting him in bed. Honestly, he was easier to deal with than either of my kids had been. Rayne was super fussy and wanted to be rocked a certain way, while Thomas didn't know what sleep was.

Bottle finished and snuggling done, I kissed his head, set him into his crib, stepped out into the hall, and pulled the door so that it was just cracked open. Then I made my way down to the kitchen with the empty bottle and set about cleaning up.

With the baby down, I clicked on the television, looking for something to keep me occupied until Marco and Andrea came home. I found some ridiculous comedy show and just let it play for some background noise. By the time they got home, I was ready to be in my own bed, so I wished them a good night and headed back to my house, walking the small walkway from their door to the sidewalk, then back up my own walkway to my door.

Sitting next to the door was a small box with a vase with tulips in it, a note tucked into the blooms. I pulled out my keys and opened my door, then picked up the box to bring in with me. I'd been getting little things like this—flower arrangements, small gifts—and each time I delighted in the fact that Ryan had thought ahead to plan these to come. It wasn't that he'd known he would be gone, but he was a planner, and would often set up deliveries in advance.

None of the previous items had a card, so I wondered what this one would say. Probably something ridiculously mushy that would make me cry my eyes out. I set the flowers in their box on the counter, then pulled out the card, opening it.

Now that you've had a few months to grieve, I'm here to help you move on.

George Warde

I dropped the card and stepped back, putting my hand to my mouth. Gagging, I raced to the bathroom by the front door, barely making the toilet to lose the little dinner I'd had earlier. I continued to dry heave for what seemed like an eternity.

Finally, feeling like I could actually move without losing it, I stood and washed my face, rinsing my mouth out several times. Feeling like a fool, and knowing I was weak, I went back to the kitchen and picked up my phone, staying far away from the offending blooms. I sent a quick text to Andrea.

Me: *If you're up for it, I could use some help.*

Andrea: *What's up?*

The fact that she responded at all was amazing, but that she was also wondering about me was even better.

Me: *I could use a friend, if you and Marco don't mind.*

I pressed send before I chickened out and just told myself not to worry about it. I wanted to follow up with a text that said I understood if she needed to stay home, considering it was Valentine's Day and all, but she responded before I got a chance.

Andrea: *Be right there.*

And she was. It took only a couple of minutes before she was knocking on my door.

"What's up?" she asked when I opened the door.

I couldn't speak, just let the tears flow. She stepped into my foyer and reached out, encompassing me in a hug that was meant to make everything better. The fact that she was actually younger than me showed just what an awesome person she was.

Once I'd gained a bit more composure, I stepped back and just headed into the kitchen. I walked through the portal, then stepped aside, letting Andrea come fully into the room.

"Did Ryan set up flowers for you?" she asked.

I shook my head, the lump in my throat too much to talk around. She went to the counter and picked up the card, reading it over.

"What the actual fuck?" she asked. "Who the fuck is this?"

I choked on a combination of a laugh and a sob, then tried desperately to clear my throat. It took a minute or two, but I finally was able to breathe again.

"Captain Clueless," I replied.

"Someone's about to die," she said, and there was a seriousness in her voice that almost scared me. "Who the actual fuck does he think he is, sending this to you. And on Valentine's Day? The audacity!"

"He hit on me at the funeral," I said.

The look of shock on her face was so much that I giggled, which turned into hysterical and maniacal laughter. Before long, we were both roaring with tears rolling down our cheeks.

"Let me get rid of these," she began, but I said, "Wait."

"Why?" she asked. "What in the ever-loving fuck do you want with these?"

"I mean," I began. "It's not the flowers' fault that an asshole sent them out. Besides, they're pretty."

"But—"

"No," I insisted. "I'll accept the gift and reject the giver. He'll never get the satisfaction of knowing that he upset me. Never know that this was so beyond horrible that it..." I stopped, realizing that there was only one way for him to have been able to send these to me. "I'm calling the school in the morning," I said. "Somehow he's gotten into the personnel records and got my address. He needs to be fired for this."

"Holy shit," she barked. "I didn't even think about that."

"Yeah," I replied. "I'm gonna call the florist and see if all the other things I've gotten in the last few months have been from him as well."

"Wait." She was shocked. "You've gotten other things, and you're just now telling me?"

"I thought Ryan had done his annual scheduling." I shrugged. "He did that from time to time, so it wasn't out of the ordinary."

"Tulips are your favorite, right?" she asked.

"Yeah," I replied. "Why?"

"How did he know?"

"I don't know," I confessed. "They're blooming right now, though, so it was probably just—"

"Nope," she said, holding her hand out in front of me. "*We* are calling the florist in the morning, and we're gonna see if this was specifically requested or if it was a fluke. Now, what else did you get?"

"I got flowers, mostly," I said. "I did get a little stuffed teddy bear at Christmas, though. Here, I'll show you."

I went to the stairs, mounting them two at a time to my bedroom. Beside the bed, on Ryan's side, I had placed the small teddy bear with the little heart in his hands. I picked it up and went to go back to the stairs, but Andrea was right behind me.

"This is what you got?"

"Yeah," I said. "Just before Christmas. Ryan knew I loved little things like this, so it was obviously from him."

"Or," she countered. "It was from that freak show Captain Clueless who has somehow hacked into your life or something and is working to control you and bend you to his will."

"That's a little farfetched," I argued.

"What was Ryan's specialty?"

"Forensic science with a bend toward cyber security," I replied, then realized what she was getting at. "You don't think…" I let the sentence trail off, not wanting to voice the reality that was slowly sinking in.

"Yeah," Andrea said, grabbing my hand. "You're staying with us tonight."

I protested, but when she got something in her head, there was no arguing with her. She was a powerful force, determined to get her way, and she would not be deterred. We packed up an overnight bag with my toothbrush and some pajamas, then I followed her down the stairs, grabbing my phone and the charger, my purse and keys, and stepped out of my house, locking it behind me.

"This is ridiculous," I protested.

"Nonsense," she said. "Tomorrow, after Marco goes to work, we're gonna make some calls and get things rolling. We need a full forensic assessment done on your laptop, phone, and any other smart device you have in your house. Speaking of which," she continued, then grabbed my phone, turning it off.

"What if my kids—"

"They'll be fine," she argued. "It's just for tonight. Everything will be better in the morning. I promise."

From her phone, she sent a text to Rayne's number, letting her know my phone was on the fritz and that if anything was needed, to contact her.

"Satisfied?"

"I guess," I said. "I just think this is just a little too much of a reaction to a simple vase of flowers."

"It's not about the flowers, and you know it," she argued. "This has gone way beyond anything a normal person would do. This is not just not okay, but it's bordering on dangerous. I'm not comfortable with how much this guy has decided to invade your life and push himself on you."

"It's not that bad," I countered.

"You're not seeing it because you're in the middle of it," she said. "Rest tonight, for tomorrow we hunt."

"Isn't that some saying from one of those shows you watch?"

"Just because I didn't invent it, doesn't mean it isn't true."

Her snark and sassiness were overflowing with this new and

sudden need to help me. I wasn't sure whether I should be impressed or terrified.

CHAPTER SIX

*J*onathan…

"You have got to be kidding me," I barked.

"Look, J," Coach Johnson said. "I know babysitting this kid isn't your job—"

"Damn right it isn't," I argued.

"I just need someone to take him under their wing for a bit," he said. "Show him the ropes of what it means to be a major leaguer and not the shit he's been doing already."

"And you picked me because…" I left the word hanging, knowing he knew what I was asking.

"Couple of reasons," Coach said. "First, because you're about the most levelheaded guy we've got on the team. You've been there, done that, and I know he could benefit from having you help him out."

"And the other reason?"

"You wanna coach, right?"

"Not yet," I returned.

"Of course not," he agreed. "But the thing about coaching is, you kind of have to know a few things before they'll give you the responsibilities that come with it. You know that saying about great responsibility comes with great power?"

"But I'm at least five years away from coaching," I said. "And that's at the earliest. I may be able to make this thing last another decade."

Coach looked at me because we both knew that a decade was a pipe dream at best. I was already thirty-two. That I was still relevant and able to perform my duties like I have been was a miracle in and of itself. Even if I moved to the Designated Hitter role, there was no guarantee that I'd even be around by then. He looked at me and waited for me to realize the truth.

"Fine," I finally acquiesced. "But I'm not gonna wipe his ass when he gets his arm broken by some dude who didn't like the fact that he was hitting on his girl."

"That's one of the first things I want you to make him understand," Coach said. "He needs to know what is and isn't allowed up here."

"I tried that at the fan festival," I argued.

"He didn't have the shit that happened between then and now to realize what he was doing was wrong," Coach said. "Now that he's had a taste of reality, I think you can get through to him."

"How long is this gig supposed to last?" I asked, hoping he'd say a couple of weeks at most.

"However long it takes to get it through his thick skull that the games he's played thus far stop here and now," the coach replied. "I've got a meeting with him in a few and will let him know what is what, and that you're his sponsor for the duration."

"Gotta say," I said. "I'm not wild about this whole thing, and honestly don't know whether I'll be any good or not."

"Hope you can get through to him," Coach said. "He's a great player, but he needs to work on his off-the-field activities. This shit doesn't fly with the big boys."

"Don't I know it," I replied, then ducked out of his office and made my way to the locker I'd been assigned for Spring Training.

It wasn't long after that I saw the kid in question walk into the locker room. He gave a chin lift in greeting, then stepped into the office with the coach. Not too much time passed before I heard raised voices, mostly the kid's, about how unfair it was and that he was an adult and other such nonsense. I definitely needed to remind him that the coach was the authority, and raising your voice was a good way to ride the pine in this league.

"Fine," I heard the kid shout as he stepped out of the office. "This is some serious bullshit, though. Don't think I won't say something to some people about this shit. Like, I'm not a kid, so stop treating me like I'm twelve."

When he turned to look at me, there was nothing but animosity in his eyes. This was going to be a long spring, that's for sure.

∾

"WHATEVER YOU SAY, DAD," BECKETT SAID BEFORE WALKING INTO the clubhouse after practice that afternoon.

"What the fuck is up his ass?" Huffman asked me.

"Coach has him on a short leash," I replied. "And I'm the lucky bastard who gets to hold it."

"Glad it isn't me," my teammate said. "That shit wouldn't fly with me."

"Well," I replied. "Shit's about to get real for him in just a minute."

"Uh oh," he said. "Don't piss off daddy or he'll ground you."

"Shut up." I laughed, knowing he was joking.

Honestly, I was close to the oldest person on the team right now. All the rookies looked younger this year than any year in the past. Besides the coaches, I think there were two other players who were around my age. Matsui was our first baseman, and he was maybe a few months older, and Kelly, the DH, was a couple months younger. Everyone else was under thirty, with most of them closer to twenty.

"I'm too old for this shit," I muttered as I stepped into the club-house, about to have a throwdown with a kid who thought he was the best thing in baseball, and everything else, apparently.

The moment I stepped into the clubhouse, the rest of the team got quiet, obviously knowing shit was going to go down. *Might as well get to it,* I thought.

"Hennings," I called, looking right at him. He stood there, back to me, pulling shit out of his locker. "Hey, kid," I shouted again. "When your sponsor calls you, you answer."

"Fuck you," he said, taking his shower kit to the stalls.

There were a few "oohs" and "ahs" from the other players, but no one really said anything. I marched over to the shower area, pissed at him, as well as the coach for the role he had thrust me into. I was not his father, not his coach, and the kid didn't respect me at all. This was either going to end in blows or someone crying, and I wasn't gonna shed a tear.

"Listen here, punk," I said, quieter than I thought was possible. "When I say something to you, you had better listen. Or did Coach not tell you about the deal he made to keep you here?"

"The fuck are you talking about?" he shouted, clearly wanting an audience.

The rest of the team stayed in the locker area, but I knew they would hear any shouting that came from back here. I didn't want to embarrass the kid, but I would do whatever it took to keep this team on the level and keep chaos out of the locker room.

"That shit you pulled after the fan festival," I said.

"Old news," he said. "Just like you."

"Except it's put you on notice," I said, holding my temper as best I could. "You are on such thin ice, and you have no idea."

"Nothing is gonna happen to me," he boasted. "I'm the best thing this team has seen since that run in '94 when they actually knew what the fuck they were doing."

"You weren't even born in '94." I laughed.

"There's this little thing called the internet," he said, glaring daggers at me. "And they did have film back then, so I've seen the run, watched the players, and learned their history. Which, by the way, is something you are about to become."

"I'm less likely to become history than you." I laughed. "I follow the rules. I know what my contract says. Unlike you, I don't screw around with fans. That's a line you don't cross."

"Maybe you should," he said, turning his back to me once again.

"What's that?"

"Screw the fans." He laughed, looking over his shoulder at me. "Maybe then you'd finally get laid and get that shitty attitude taken care of. At least a blow job would loosen you up some."

Gritting my teeth, I counted to ten slowly in my head, trying with every fiber in my being to keep me from walking over and knocking the smirk right off the kid's face.

"Oops." He laughed again. "I didn't realize you were the one giving the blow jobs. My bad."

He'd barely gotten the final words out of his mouth when I punched him square in the jaw. Watching his head spin on his neck was a satisfaction I didn't realize I needed. He crumpled to the ground and several players raced in. Huffman held me back from doing further damage.

"Fucking psycho," the kid sneered, blood trickling from the corner of his mouth.

"What the…" Coach Johnson came in to see what was going on and saw the kid, the up-and-coming star, sprawled on the floor with a growing bruise on the side of his face.

"You," he barked at me. "My office. Now!"

Huffman turned me around and shoved me toward the office, following close behind to ensure I didn't go back for more. Truth was, I felt awful. I'd never punched anyone for any reason. This kid just riled me up something fierce and brought out the horrible things I never wanted to be. Shaking my hand from the sting, I made my way to the office and threw myself into a chair next to the desk.

"What in the hell were you thinking?" the coach growled as he came into his office, slamming the door behind him. "I told you to keep an eye on him. Keep him in check. Make sure he didn't do anything stupid." He was pacing back and forth in the small space, his face getting redder with each step. "I thought I could trust you, and you go and pull this stupid stunt? How is anyone going to take you seriously if you can't even keep your emotions in check during something like this?"

"Look, Coach—"

"No," he seethed, cutting me off. "I don't want to hear it. There is absolutely nothing you can say to make this better. I would have expected Huffman or Cote, but not you. You're a seasoned veteran. Someone who has been around long enough that fights within the clubhouse do nothing but distract from the reason we're here."

"Hey," I began.

"J," Coach said. "I know you have a big heart, and I know you've been through some shit, but you need to keep everything on the field and in the clubhouse about the game. Everything that happens outside of this space is not to be brought in here. You get me?"

"Tell that to Beckett," I said.

"Oh, I will," Coach replied. "He's going to get his ass chewed out just as soon as we make sure you didn't break his jaw."

"It's not broken," I said. "Trust me. That little shit deserved the punch. He honestly deserved a bigger ass whipping, but I didn't want to hurt myself."

"Your hand good?"

"Yeah," I said. "Just stings."

"Ice it tonight," the coach said. "And tomorrow—"

"I know," I said. "I'll apologize for getting out of hand, but I expect an apology from him about the shit he said to me, too."

"What'd he say?"

"Said I needed to get laid," I replied. "That a blow job was probably what I needed, then indicated that I was the one who would be giving it, not getting it. I snapped."

"Yeah," Coach said. "He's gonna apologize. He needs to know that we don't talk shit to our team. That we're in this together, and if we can't trust each other, then we can't win. Go home to shower. I'm gonna yell when you leave, so if you could look at least a little put off, that'd be great."

I laughed, then stood up and opened the door.

"And don't you forget it," Coach shouted. "We're a team, damnit, so you better start acting like it. Now take yourself home and come back tomorrow with a better attitude."

I did my best to look put out or annoyed or something, but I couldn't suppress the small smile of satisfaction that the coach knew the kid deserved what he got, and that I was getting off very light. Since it was just the first week of Spring Training, I had plenty of time to get my game in the shape it needed to be in before we started playing for real.

CHAPTER SEVEN

*L*ucy...

"Mrs. Fallon," Katie Neubauer, my son's teacher said. "I'm so happy to see you."

"Thanks," I replied. "I'm really glad to be able to help out with this field trip."

"You're sure you're up for it?"

"Absolutely," I replied. "Thomas has been looking forward to this trip all year and was very insistent that I come as a chaperone."

"Because if it's an issue," she began.

"No, no," I replied. "It's totally fine. In fact, I think it's just what I might need right about now."

"As long as you're sure."

I could hear the concern in her voice, but I knew I was ready for this and said as much. She handed me a manilla envelope that held the kids' passports for the trip, along with a schedule for the entire outing. Rayne had stayed with my parents because the trip was going to take the full day. Having to be at the school at such an early hour, it was more convenient for her to stay with them.

"Kids," the teacher called. "Let's all get our belongings together and get ready for the bus. Each of you should have your lanyard with your names, your chaperone's name, and phone numbers for everyone, including me. If you don't have it, please raise your hand."

I watched as the kids checked their tags and took a moment to check mine as well. It included the six kids I was to be in charge of, as well as the other parent who would be working with me on this trip. The Gardner family was new to the school, having arrived just after the new year. Thomas had talked about Aidon, but I hadn't met the parents.

"Are you Lucy?" a woman asked.

"I am," I replied. "You must be Paulette."

"Pleased to meet you," she said, shaking my hand. "Aidon has talked so much about your son that I feel like I already know him."

"Thomas has mentioned Aidon as well," I replied.

"I'm sorry," she said. "I'm so new to this whole area that I'm not really sure what we're doing or what's going on."

"Thomas said you just moved here?" I asked.

"Yes," she said. "My husband was relocated right at the end of the year. It wasn't in our plan to move until the summer, but it worked out that we could actually do it, so we made the leap."

"Well," I said. "Welcome to Washington state. I hope Thomas has been kind to Aidon and helpful in his transitioning to a new school."

"Oh, he's been wonderful," she gushed. "I don't know what my little guy would have done if he hadn't found a friend in Thomas. He tends to be a little on the shy side, so the fact that Thomas made the first move was a delight."

"Thomas was shy when he first started school, too," I said. "He's found his voice in the last year or so, though, and has really excelled in becoming quite the popular kid. I was worried that the popularity would tarnish his gentle heart, but it seems that isn't the case."

"Okay, kids," Mrs. Neubauer said. "Coats on, let's get on the bus."

The kids all stood up and headed toward the door. Mrs. Neubauer opened it, and we all followed her out to the parking lot where two buses were waiting.

"Chaperones," she called, and all the adults looked her way.

"Would you mind heading to bus number two? Once you're there, we'll load the kids up in pods so everyone is accounted for, and the kids get to know who their adults are. Mr. Tate's class will be in the first bus, so we won't mix during the drive, but after we're to the ferry, we'll be able to connect with his class."

Paulette and I walked to the second bus, along with the rest of adults. Once we were there, the kids lined up with their respective groups so each of us knew who we were responsible for, and the kids knew who to go to if they had issues. After that, we climbed aboard our respective buses and found seats in the same area for each group. We ended up in the middle of the bus, which wasn't my preferred place to sit, but wasn't horrible, either. At least we didn't end up in the back.

"All right, kids," the teacher said as she stepped on the bus. "The ride is long, so if you're tired, you're free to sleep. Also, if someone is sleeping next to you, do *not* bother them. I expect you to be excellent students and role models for your parents. They're not used to behaving, so make sure you set a good example."

The kids chuckled, some even laughing outright. The tactic she used to keep things light while maintaining order was remarkable, and I was thankful, not for the first time, that we'd chosen this school for our kids.

The first length of the trip was short, since we were heading into downtown Seattle to pick up the ferry to take us across the water to the peninsula. While on the ship, we were instructed to keep our group together, but that we were free to walk about the vessel to explore. Fortunately, our kids were pretty mellow and found a puzzle they all worked on for the quick trip across the Sound.

Once we'd boarded the bus again, the kids settled into a quiet lull, some chatting, but most dozing off on each other's shoulders. I never could sleep on a bus, so I pulled out my notebook from my purse and began to write my thoughts. It was something I had done for years, but with the hustle and bustle of kids, it had slacked off. Once Ryan died, however, I found myself taking the time to jot down some feelings and thoughts, just to get them out of my head.

"Journaling?" Paulette asked when she stirred from her nap against the window.

"Reminiscing," I replied. "Might write something down, but for now, just rereading what I've been dealing with for the past while."

"I tried journaling," she continued. "Never could quite get the hang of it, though. I was never really good at sharing my thoughts with people in person, let alone getting them down on paper."

"It's something my therapist suggested," I said. "After Ryan died, I needed an outlet for my feelings. I didn't want to do it but found it to be actually really helpful. I could tell him all the things I was upset about, and all the things I missed, and it wasn't stuck inside me, building and building."

"Ryan was...?" She left the question hanging, and I remembered she hadn't been around then.

"He was my husband," I said. "He died suddenly last September, so six months ago now."

"I'm so sorry," she said. "I didn't know."

"I understand," I comforted. "There's no way you could have known, but I appreciate the sympathy."

"I'll leave you to it," she said, patting my hand sympathetically.

"Thanks," I replied, then shifted so I could read the words without having to worry that she'd read them over my shoulder, so to speak.

This was a journal I had started at the beginning of the school year. I'd started doing that each year when the kids started school. Though I hadn't filled up many notebooks, this one was fuller. Of course, this year had been especially difficult, and had so many more emotions to get out that it wasn't surprising. The first few pages were all about how excited the kids had been to start a new school year. I was pleased to have time during the day to do things that hadn't happened over the summer. Oh, we'd done plenty, but there were just some things that I couldn't do with the kids at home. The overhaul of closets was a first-week-of-school project every year.

Once I'd gotten to the day before Ryan's death, I stopped. I wasn't sure whether I wanted to reread the turmoil I'd gone through. Taking a deep breath, I flipped the page. My thoughts, though jumbled and chaotic, were actually cathartic. I read the words of mourning and sadness and realized that I had come so far in such a short amount of time. I continued to grieve, but it wasn't as all-consuming as it had been initially. There were days when I didn't even notice Ryan not there. It was the nights that were the hardest.

"Psst, Mom," Thomas said from across the aisle.

"What's up, T?"

"You got anything to drink?"

"We'll get something when we get on the ferry to the island," I replied.

"But I'm thirsty now," he complained.

"Well," I began. "How long does it take for someone to die of thirst?"

"Three days," he whined. "But that doesn't mean I'm not thirsty."

"No," I replied. "But it does mean that you can wait. We're more than halfway there, so just shut your eyes and try to rest."

"Fine," he grumped and shifted away from me.

"That was brilliant," Paulette whispered. "I never would have thought of that response."

"It was something that my husband would do," I replied. "He'd often give a reason for them not needing something, and when they'd whine, he'd explain the logic behind waiting. Sometimes it went over their heads, but things like this," I indicated, waving my hand in my son's direction, "were a quick way to educate them and give them something to think about when things didn't go their way."

"I feel like you're a better mother than me," she said, and it was a bit of a shock.

"Why do you say that?" I asked.

"I mean," she started, then stopped.

"Seriously," I urged. "Let me know how I can help you be a better parent than you think you are."

She looked down at her hands in her lap, then up at me, and there were tears gathered on her lashes.

"I-I," she stuttered, then stopped.

"Hey," I said, reaching my arm around her shoulder. "How can I help?"

She sniffled, then said, "Things aren't great at home."

"Been there," I replied. "What can I do to help?"

"I just..." she faltered again. "Brock and I are struggling. We thought the move away from our families and to a new area might help us with the boundaries we've been trying to set. It was great to begin with, but his parents just sent him an email saying they were thinking of moving up here to be close to us."

"And you moved to get away from their invasiveness?"

"Yeah," she replied. "I mean, they're fine in small doses, but we lived on their property when we first got married, and his mother became accustomed to popping in whenever she felt like it. I'd told Brock that I wanted to have some space, a place that was ours, where we could set the rules about who came and how often. At first he balked, but he finally saw what the issue was when we were—"

She stopped talking, looking around the bus to see what the students were doing.

"I get it," I said. "You were enjoying each other's company."

"Yeah." She laughed a little. "So, we were hanging out in the living room, which is right where the front door opens to. His mom opened the door and got an eyeful of us together. I was embarrassed and ran to our room, holding clothes over me, and cried. She lit into him like he'd just burned puppies or something. He sent her packing, and we were looking for an apartment the next day."

"That's good," I said. "Setting boundaries is hard."

"Anyway," she continued. "Once we had Aidon, she got worse. She was insistent that she be at the house when we brought him home. She promised that she'd be helping us, but I didn't want to have anyone there. Not even my mom, who is another story in and of itself. Brock felt bad that I didn't want her there, so went behind my back and gave her the key to be there when we came home. She had ruined my safe space, done some 'cleaning' and threw out a bunch of stuff that I really wanted."

"I'm so sorry," I comforted. "No one has the right to throw something out that doesn't belong to them."

"Exactly," she exclaimed a little louder than before.

She put her hand over her mouth, realizing the volume she'd used, but the kids around us were either ignoring her or napping.

"Sorry," she said.

"No worries," I replied. "They honestly probably don't even care."

"When I couldn't find something my great-grandmother had given to my grandmother, and had been passed down through each generation, that was the last straw," she said, and she started to tear up again. "I told Brock that she had to go, and that she was never allowed to be in the house when we weren't there again."

"Did that work?" I asked.

"Ha." She barked a laugh. "She'd made a copy of the key, so when I took Aidon to the doctor for his first checkup, I came home to her sitting at my kitchen table, smirking at me."

"Oh, no," I said. "That would have been the end of it for me."

"Yeah," she replied. "I called Brock and told him to get home and get his mother out of my house. She sat there, drinking her coffee, *my* coffee, and glared at me the whole time. She kept saying that she was there to help, that she knew how hard it was to be a first-time mom, and that since I'd never done it before, she was there to show me the right way to do things."

"Pardon my language," I said. "Nothing pisses me off more than someone saying there is a right way to do something. Like, yeah, there are some things you shouldn't do, but there is no absolute right way for most anything."

"And her way was dangerous, too," she said. "Like, yeah, you were a mom, and you didn't kill your kids, but that was a quarter of a century ago. Things change, bitch."

"So much so," I replied.

"Anyway," she continued. "I told him I didn't want to be around her, didn't want Aidon around her, and if he wanted to be around her, that was fine, but I needed a break. He was cool with that for a while, but when it came time for Aidon's birthday, he insisted that she be invited to the party. I didn't want to, but he was so insistent that he would keep her reined in that I gave in."

"Let me guess," I said. "Horrible results?"

"It's like you know." She laughed. "It was awful. They brought a bunch of Brock's old stuff with them and insisted that we *had* to keep it because it was an heirloom. Seriously, this shit was gross, and there was no way I was going to let my baby have any of that."

"Ugh," I said. "Nothing worse than using the heirloom term to get their way."

"Right?" she agreed. "Like, it was trash when my husband was a kid. It's still trash, now."

"Don't get me wrong," I said. "We had the cradle my husband's great-granddad made for their first baby. That thing was made to last through damn near anything, and we loved that we could put our babies in something so precious."

"That's an heirloom," she declared.

"For sure," I agreed. "It's the other stuff that was so *not* a quality-made item that they feel like it has to be handed down because they had it. Some things are meant to stay in the past."

"Did your mother-in-law ever pull out pictures of your husband's ex?"

"What?"

"Yeah," she added. "She said that her husband's high-school girl-friend was *so* pretty. They would have made beautiful babies and would be the perfect couple and on and on and on."

"God, no," I said. "That's awful. What was her plan?"

"No clue." She shrugged. "I guess to just make me go away so she could have her baby boy all to herself or something."

"That's gross," I said. "No, my in-laws are pretty decent. They were a little overbearing when we first got together. I think they thought I was too young for him or something."

"How old were you?"

"I was almost twenty," I said. "But he was twenty-six, so there was an age gap between us. I think they thought he would find someone closer to his own age. We got engaged, married, and had

Rayne less than two years after we met. But the thing was, we were perfect for each other. There were so many things we had in common that we just clicked. Don't get me wrong, he did things that were weird to me, but he let me do my thing and he did his, and we just worked that way."

"Yeah," she said. "I don't really have a thing. I mean, Aidon is my thing. He's my whole world."

"What do you do for fun, though?" I asked.

"I don't have time for anything fun," she replied.

"Sure you do," I argued.

"Between the house staying clean and keeping up with everything for Aidon, there really isn't time for me to do anything," she said.

"But," I began. "Do you like to read, or write, or garden, or paint, or anything?"

"I mean, I love to cook and bake, but I just do that for us," she said. "Aidon's got so many extracurricular activities, and Brock does so many things, too, I just don't have time for anything else. I'm always exhausted."

"Girl," I said. "That has got to change. You need time to unwind, to rejuvenate yourself. You can't survive just doing for others. There has to be something that you love that you can squeeze in there some-where. Maybe pull Aidon from one of the extra things. Or, have Brock keep him for a weekend while you go away with friends."

"He wouldn't go for that," she said.

"Why not?"

"Because my job is as a wife and mother," she said. "Everything has to revolve around those two things. Anything else is unnecessary and just frivolous."

"Bullshit," I said. "You are not just a wife and mother. You're also a human who has needs and wants and deserves to be your own thing outside of the other things you do. I'm a mom, sure, but I'm also me. If Ryan tried to pull some sexist misogynistic bullshit like that on me, he'd have found himself sleeping in the guest room until he apologized for it."

"I'd never do that to Brock," she said, horrified.

"Why not?" I asked. "Are you less than him? Do you not deserve to be treated well?"

"Well, sure," she said. "But being a wife and mother are important jobs and—"

"Nope," I cut her off. "Just because you have other things you do, that does not negate the need for you to be well. You can't fill someone else's cup from your empty pitcher."

"I don't get it," she replied.

"You need to fill yourself up with good things in order to pass them on to someone else," I explained. "Take me, for instance. I run. It's something that I did when I was in school, and it's what fills me up. When I first had Rayne, I didn't do it. I found that I had to spend so much time on her and doing things she needed that I just couldn't add it to my day."

"That's me," she said.

"But, my husband saw the state of my mental health," I countered. "Rayne was about two months old and I was struggling. I remember him getting up with her, taking her to the living room, and letting me sleep in. Then, when I got up, he sent me out to go for a run. I tried to argue, it was raining, I was sore, or the baby needed me, all of that. He said that she was fine, he wanted to spend some one-on-one time with her, and that I looked like I could use the endorphins I got when I ran.

"I didn't want to do it," I continued. "But once I was out there, and once I started, it was the best thing in the world. I didn't go far, because I was still recovering and hadn't run in forever, so I only went a few blocks. When I got back, he sent me to a hot shower, then brought up some breakfast for me to have in bed. It was the most amazing thing he ever did for me. That afternoon, we went out and bought a jogging stroller for her, and I realized I wasn't in a good place and needed to run. It was a gift he gave both of us, as well as our kids."

"That's amazing," she said.

Just then, the bus driver came over the speakers.

"We're coming up to the ferry terminal," the driver said. "If you've pulled anything out, now's a good time to stuff it back into your bag. Do not get up but do what you can within reach."

"Guess that's the end of that," she said.

"We can talk later," I replied. "It was really good to talk to you."

"Yeah," she said, but turned away from me.

I wondered whether she actually heard me, or if what I'd said was more difficult for her to listen to because of her own situation. I guess time would tell.

CHAPTER EIGHT

*J*onathan...

"This was such a brilliant idea," I said as I buckled Grant into his car seat.

"You're sure it won't mess up his sleep schedule?" Kate asked.

"He'll be out in no time," I replied. "He's good about sleeping in the car."

"I just didn't realize we'd have to leave at the ass crack of dawn." She laughed.

"Ass crack," Grant said.

"Not cool." I glared at Kate. "He's mimicking everything anyone says. Didn't Mom tell you that?"

"Well," she hemmed.

"Just watch your mouth around him," I said. "The last thing I need is for him to be swearing in front of Mom. She would lose her mind."

"Yeah," Kate said as she got into the passenger seat of my car. "Do you remember the first time you swore in front of her?"

"I don't think I ever have," I replied, buckling my seatbelt.

"Oh, man." She laughed, clicking her belt in place.

I started up the car and heard Grant babbling away in the back seat. He was still facing backward, but I could see him in this little mirror thing that Meg had gotten for each of the cars. I could look in the rearview mirror and see the mirror facing his seat. It was a pretty nifty device, and very handy to have.

"I think the first one I said was—"

"Don't," I interrupted.

"S-h-i-t," she spelled.

"I tee," Grant mimicked his aunt.

"Like I said." I looked at her pointedly before putting the car in reverse and heading out of my parking spot.

The trip to the waterfront was quick, and we really didn't have much of a chance to talk before I was purchasing a ticket for the ferry to take us across the sound. The ferry ride itself was less than an hour, but there would be another couple of hours drive between when we got off the ferry here and when we could board the ferry up in Port Angeles.

"You been to the island recently?" she asked once we were in the line waiting to board the first ferry.

"Nah," I replied. "I think the last time I was there was something with Mom and Dad."

"I haven't been there since college," she replied. "I told you about that trip, right?"

"I don't think so," I said.

"It was when I was dating Alex," she said.

"Don't think I ever met him," I replied.

"And you never will." She laughed. "He was an absolute tool. Problem was, he didn't know what he was getting himself into when it came to dating me."

"Oh," I said, rubbing my hands together. "This is gonna be good."

"Hell yeah, it's good," she said.

"Hell," Grant called from the back seat.

I glared at her and she actually looked like she wanted to eat the words back without saying them.

"Sorry," she muttered. "Anyway. We had this plan that a bunch of us were gonna go up to the island and stay at those little cottages that Mom and Dad went to when they first got married."

"Oh, yeah," I said. "I remember those. They were cool little places. Each one was separate from the others, so it was like you had your own little space. I think Meg and I went up to them a few years ago, just before we got married. Oh, wait. I think that's where I proposed to her. Man, that was forever ago."

"Okay," she said. "So, you definitely know the place. They have this larger space where a group of people can rent it out. Me, Alex, and a few other people planned to go up and rent the larger space to hang out and spend the weekend. Might have been Memorial Day or something, don't remember. Doesn't matter. We had it all planned out, and he picked me up from my dorm and we headed north."

"Where were you?"

"It was like sophomore year or something," she said. "I was at SPU, so Seattle. Anyway, we headed up, and he said that everyone was driving up as couples so we could each have cars to get around and do stuff if we wanted to. We go to the border, go on through, hop on the ferry from Vancouver and get to the place. He said he'd go in and get the key and everything since it was all on his credit card."

"Why do I feel like this is not going to go the way he thought it would?"

"You know me so well." She laughed. "He comes back and we head into the area. I notice he passed the bigger lodge and is heading over to one of the smaller cottages. I ask him what's up and he said that everyone else backed out and that he got a smaller place because he didn't want to disappoint me."

"Please tell me you kicked his ass," I said, keeping my voice low enough to not let my son hear me.

"You're getting ahead of me." She laughed. "We get to the small cottage and I've been texting Bethany asking her what was up with canceling and not telling me. She's like, we didn't cancel, Alex said you changed your mind."

"Oh, I bet you were pissed," I said, anticipating the cruelty she would do to this kid who thought he could pull something over on my sister.

"Worse than a cat trying to be baptized," she said. "I'm pretending to not notice that we're sneaking way back to the back of the property, as far away from the office as possible. He puts the car in park and turns it off and says, 'We're here.'"

"And you said…" I left it hanging, knowing she'd fill me in on all the details.

It was one of the things we shared a lot of that others didn't quite get. Sure, we were siblings, and we were opposite genders, but we loved to root each other on in good ways and be angry when things went south.

"I looked him straight in the eye and asked why he thought it was a good idea to lie to me," she replied, smug as all get-out. "He said he didn't lie. He knew I wanted to go away, just the two of us, and he knew I wouldn't say anything to my friends, so he decided to be a gentleman and make the decision for me."

"Oh." I laughed. "He's a gentleman, now, is he?"

"But wait, there's more," she said, using the terms those infomercials used all the time.

"Does it cut a can, then cut a tomato?" I asked.

"He also said that there was something very special in the cabin for me," she continued. "Said that he had it set up early so it wouldn't waste time, knowing our trip would take us all day. He didn't want to delay any of the fun."

"What was the surprise?" I asked after she left me hanging for a minute.

"I played along with him, went into the cabin, and there, right on the table, was an enormous bouquet of roses," she said, painting the picture with her words. "In front of the flowers was a note that said, 'Congratulations,' on it. I turned around and looked at him and he was on a knee on the ground, just outside the door, holding a ring out."

"What?"

"Yeah." She laughed. "I looked at the ring, looked at him, then shut the door in his face."

I blinked, then realized she wasn't kidding and began to laugh.

"He brought you all the way up to the island…" I said. "Proposed to you on the spot, and you shut him out?"

"You better believe it." She laughed. "This was not the kind of rela-tionship we had. We were friends, sometimes with benefits."

"Ew," I said. "Not something I need to think about."

"We were not at all in a committed relationship," she continued, ignoring my obvious discomfort. "When he realized that I wasn't going to open the door again, he pulled out the key and came in. I was sitting at the table, had pulled out a piece of chocolate that was also part of the display, and was munching away on it."

"What did he say?"

"He asked if I was going to answer his question," she said.

"And..."

"I said, 'nope,'" she replied. "He was like, 'Nope, as in you aren't answering or...' and I was like, 'Not marrying someone who lies and cheats.'"

"Wait, he was a cheater?" I asked, felling like I had whiplash from all the back-and-forth of the story.

"He was dating a girl at school," she said. "He thought I didn't know, but I did. We were actually in a couple of classes together and I'd seen her with him in some serious conversations and such. When I'd asked who he was, she'd said her boyfriend. I asked how long they'd been together and she'd said a couple of years. Mind you, this dude and I hadn't met more than a few months earlier. So, he was a cheater, and he thought proposing in the first year was a good idea. I finally just said that he should go back to the office and rent another room for himself because we were not now, nor ever in the future, sleeping in the same bed."

"But he drove you up there," I argued.

"And I told him that my daddy knew where I was," she said, the smirk clear in her voice, even if I hadn't seen it on her face. "Told him that if I wasn't home tomorrow, early, that he should probably not bother to go back to the States because he wouldn't survive the next week."

"You didn't even need to bring out the karate," I said.

My sister was a black belt in several martial arts, but she loved her karate. I blamed it on our dad insisting she watch that movie with the wax-on, wax-off bullshit. She loved it and would rewatch it with him every summer when she was home from college. Even now, after she'd graduated and had her own career, she still loved to sit with Dad and watch that stupid movie.

"He tried to argue," she continued. "But I simply put up my hand and said, 'talk to the hand, cause the rest of this chick ain't listening.'"

"Dang, girl." I laughed. "You took that way back."

"Don't you know it," she replied.

Just then, the cars in front of us started moving, so I started up my own car and followed the line to get onto the ferry. Once we were on and parked, I popped the trunk and pulled out the stroller while Kate got Grant out of his seat and picked up the diaper backpack. With Grant strapped in, we moved to where the elevator was for the upper decks. The trip was short, and my boy was obviously tired, but still interested in what was going on around him. He held his little Freddy fox in one hand and had his thumb in his mouth.

"You ready to see the boat?" Kate asked him when we stepped from the elevator.

"Boat," he parroted, mimicking his aunt.

We found a quiet corner that had a window view of the water and waited for the boat to start up and begin the first leg of our journey.

"You've got his passport, right?" Kate asked me when we sat down.

"It's in his bag," I replied. "Along with mine. You got yours?"

"Sure do," she said.

"Hungy," Grant said, looking at each of us in turn.

"I mean, he didn't eat breakfast," Kate said.

I laughed and pulled out some snacks from his bag and set them on the little tray at the front of the stroller.

"Fish, fish, fish," he chanted as he ate his snacks.

"He is such an easy kid," Kate said, watching the little tyke eat his snacks.

"I think Meg did that," I said. "She was so patient and willing to help him learn but was also strict in certain situations. Not sure how she did it, but she was a miracle with him. God, I miss her."

"Hey," she said, placing a hand on my arm. "You're doing amazing. I know it's not the same, and it is more complicated than it should be, but you're a really good dad, and I think he is in amazing hands."

"But the season is starting," I argued. "He's gonna be with Mom for most of the year, with very few moments with me at all. How is that the best way to raise a kid?"

"Knock it off," she admonished. "There are a ton of single parents out there who have to work really hard and rely on their families to help them out. Be thankful that you got this off season to spend with him. That was a big deal, and I know Mom appreciated you being with her as well. Also," she continued. "You need to trust that you're doing the right thing. Grant loves you and is going to love you for a long time. Let us help out where we can. You can't worry about everything all the time and still function."

"I just feel like I should take a year off," I said. "Spend more time with him."

"You know that if you take this year off, you won't go back," she said.

"But he's just a baby," I replied, and could feel the emotions welling up inside me.

"Exactly," she replied. "He's so young that this is the perfect time for you to stay with the team. In five years, he'll be in school and you'll be able to either retire or move to something with a little more home time. Who knows, maybe the high school will hire you to coach the team there. That would be cool."

"I guess you're right," I conceded.

"You know I am." She laughed. "I'm right about so many things it's ridiculous. I don't know anyone who has ever been righter than I am right now."

"Right," Grant said, and we both laughed.

CHAPTER NINE

*L*ucy...

"Before we disembark from the buses, I need to make sure that each student knows who their adults are," Mrs. Neubauer said. "You each have two adults who you need to keep track of. Their phone numbers are on the back of your nametags. While we're waiting for the ferry, you need to be sure to program their phone numbers into your phones so you have it at all times. Parents," she continued. "Take a look at each of your six students and make sure you know what they're wearing. You should also plan to put the student's phone numbers into your phone, as well as your chaperone partner's number. I'll be back in a few minutes once we're given the go-ahead to load onto the ferry. Any questions before I go?"

There was mumbling on the bus from the kids, some complaining that it was too early to be doing anything, but mostly it was quiet. I'd already put the kids and Paulette's number into my phone, but double-checked just to make sure. It didn't take long for her to come back to the bus and give us the green light to line up and be ready for boarding the ferry.

Paulette and I were in charge of six boys, her son and mine, plus four more that I knew from earlier in the year, or from previous years.

Paulette didn't seem to know anyone but her son and mine. We walked to the waiting area for walk-on passengers and were at least warm. March was cool in the Pacific Northwest, so the kids were all wearing jackets and hats. Some had gloves as well.

Once we had everyone in our group together, we were allowed to board the ship. It was almost as difficult as herding cats to get these kids in line and on the ship, but once we were there, we were allowed to travel in pods to go to different areas. Paulette and I took the kids up to one of the higher decks where we commandeered a table for the kids to leave their backpacks and such. Everyone was allowed to head to the bathroom that was near us but were warned to not leave until everyone was finished.

"Mom," Thomas said. "Do we really have to wait for everyone?"

"Would you want to be the one left behind when everyone else was done?" I asked.

"I guess you're right," he said, then they wandered off to the facilities.

"There you go again," Paulette said once the boys were gone.

"What?" I asked.

"Giving them enough information to come to the right answer without telling them what to do," she explained.

"I guess it just comes naturally," I replied. "Don't get me wrong, the kids will do shit they know they're not supposed to. But often times it's not done with malice, but simply because of their age."

"Well," she said. "You're still a great mom."

"Thanks," I replied.

The conversation lagged, and I wasn't sure whether I should broach the subject we'd been speaking of before the bus ended up stopping. I decided against it, knowing I'd put enough information out there for her to think about, and giving her the space she may need to process it. From what she'd said, it sounded like she'd never really thought of herself as an individual, someone who had autonomy outside of her role as a wife and mother. I desperately wanted her to know that I was a safe person to come to with questions or concerns, but not someone who was pushy and demanding her to do things my way.

Once the kids were back, we gave them a little bit of leeway to roam the area we were sitting in but demanded that they not break off in groups smaller than two. I suggested they pick up some fliers for the attractions on the island from a kiosk that was set up on the ferry. I didn't tell them why I wanted them to grab them, just that they should try to find at least two each that were different from the others they had. My plan was to ask why they chose those, whether one that someone else chose first was one they would have picked up instead, and why they wanted to pick the one they didn't get. It was something I always did with my kids that gave them something to do on a long ride and also taught them something about the area we were traveling to. We did it when we checked into hotels on our travels, or when we were in new cities.

It was fun to watch the kids see what was available on the island, to see what they chose, and to discuss each attraction and what they thought was great about it. By the time we'd finished all our discussions, it was getting close to the time the ferry would be pulling into the terminal in Victoria, BC. I pulled out each of the kids' passports and ensured that they could answer the questions likely to be asked when we got off the ship.

"Next group," the border agent said.

"That's us," I said, herding the boys toward the desk he was at.

"What's the purpose of your trip?"

"To study your government system," Thomas said.

"It's a field trip," Aidon added.

"And we're learning about governments from around the world," Parker added.

"Very nice," the guard said. "How long will you be with us?"

"Just for today," I offered. "We're heading back on the last ferry from here to the Washington peninsula at the end of the day."

"Good for you," he said.

He swiped each of the passports through his reader, confirming everyone matched their pictures. "What school do you guys go to?"

"East Side Prep," Parker said.

"Yeah," Thomas added. "We're a private school."

"I see," the agent said. "And are you the teachers?"

"We're two of the parents," I offered. "This is my son," I said, indicating Thomas.

"And Aidon belongs to me," Paulette offered, indicating her son.

"You seem to be all in order," he concluded, handing the stack of passports back to me. "Enjoy your day and learn lots."

"Thank you," the boys replied in unison.

We stepped out of the customs area and waited in the lobby on the other side for the rest of the students, chaperones, and the two teachers.

"We're all here," Mrs. Neubauer said. "Let's head out to the capitol."

"But stay with your groups," Mr. Tate added.

CHAPTER TEN

*J*onathan...

"What's with all the kids?" Kate asked after we'd settled on one of the upper decks of the ferry.

We'd made the drive from Bainbridge Island, where the first ferry dropped us off, to Port Angeles, with Grant sleeping most of the way. After parking the car in one of the lots designated for those who were traveling on foot onto the ferry, we'd packed up everything we'd need for a day of sightseeing. Looking around the ship we were on, I realized that there were several kids of school age wandering around.

"No clue," I replied. "Maybe it's some sort of field trip or something."

"To a foreign country?" she asked.

"I mean," I began. "It's Canada. I go there a couple of times a year with the team."

"But that's your job," she exclaimed. "And you're an adult. I wouldn't want to send Grant to some foreign country without me going."

"You do realize you sound a little crazy, right?" I laughed.

"You're saying you'd be okay sending him off?"

"He's two," I argued. "He isn't going anywhere without someone he knows with him. Besides, who's to say they aren't part of a family or something."

"This many kids?"

Her concern was escalating higher and higher, and I was worried that Grant would become anxious because of it.

"Kate," I said firmly. "Look at me."

She finally did, and I just looked at her, trying to give her my calmness.

"Don't you Jedi mind trick me," she said, but I could see she was beginning to relax.

"I see the kids interacting with lots of adults and other kids," I explained. "My guess is it's a field trip of some sort. Nothing to worry about."

I waved my hand in front of her face like they did in the *Star Wars* movies and she finally relaxed and laughed.

"You know I hate it when you do that," she said.

"What?" I asked, trying to appear innocent.

"Daddy funny," Grant said, and both Kate and I busted up laughing at him.

"Out of the mouths of babes," I said.

"Truer words have never been spoken," she concurred.

"So," I said, becoming serious. "What have you been doing lately? We never seem to connect much."

"I met a guy," she said, blushing deeply.

"Oh," I cooed. "Do tell."

"God, you're awful," she mumbled.

"What?" I asked. "I need to know whether I need to protect my baby sister."

"Ha." She barked a laugh. "Since when have I needed you to protect me?"

"I seem to recall an incident with Jacob Wheeler," I began.

"I was eight," she argued. "And I hardly needed your help. He tried to kiss me, so I punched him in his big, stupid mouth."

"Stupid mouth," Grant said, and I glared at my sister.

"We don't call people stupid," she said to him. "Auntie wasn't being nice."

"Be nice," Grant parroted.

"That's right," I agreed. "We always want to be nice when we can."

"But sometimes we have to be firm," she said, pointedly looking at me.

"We can still be nice, even when we have to be firm," I countered.

"Be nice, be nice, be nice," he sang in his sweet little sing-song voice that melted me every time I heard it.

"You got it," I said, holding my emotions in check.

"Anyway," Kate continued. "Jacob Wheeler was no match for me, as displayed by my perfect right cross. He ended up losing one of his baby teeth from that punch, though, so I kinda feel bad about that."

"But not too bad," I added.

"No," she agreed. "Not too bad."

"So," I offered. "About this boy…"

"He's not a boy," she said. "He's a year older than me."

"I don't like him already," I said. "Why is he robbing the cradle?"

"You're how much older than Meg?"

"Touché," I replied, knowing that we were actually three years apart in age.

"Yeah," she gloated. "He's a year older than me, but in the same field I'm in."

"You don't work with him, do you?" I asked, hoping that she hadn't done something dumb like hooking up with a work colleague.

"Not on your life," she said. "I don't eat where I—"

"Don't," I said, knowing she was going to finish that statement up with the word shit, and I didn't need to try to keep Grant from copying any more swear words.

"You get my drift," she said.

"Yeah," I replied. "So, how did you meet?"

"You remember last month when I was hiking up near Jawbone Flats?" she asked.

"Not really," I replied honestly.

"So," she continued. "I was up there hiking with Kenzie, doing our thing. She's totally into that whole ghost town thing, so she wanted to see the one up there. She knew that since I'm a hiker, I could help her get through it and find the way."

"Where is this?"

"Like an hour and a half east of home," she replied.

"Like, in the mountains?"

"Dude," she said. "I hike in the mountains all the time. It's no big deal."

"Pretty sure Dad told us not to get lost in the mountains," I replied. "Can't get rescued that easily up there."

"There is literally a reserve right near there," she countered. "Besides, I have a sat phone that I take with me when I go hiking."

She stuck her tongue out at me and Grant giggled at it, then copied her.

"Be nice," I said, more for my sister than my son.

She continued, "We were almost to the ghost town and there was some dude shouting on the trail up ahead of us, like really freaking out. When we got up to him, he said his friend had fallen over an edge or something and pointed out where he was."

"You believed a stranger in the woods about someone being lost?"

"It was real," she said. "I know fake when I see it. So, I check out over the ledge and this dude is lying down by the creek at the bottom with his leg going the wrong way. I hand my phone to Kenzie to call in some help and she looks at me like I'm nuts. I dial the number, tell them that there's a man over a cliff with a broken leg, that I'm gonna climb down and investigate, but that Kenzie will give them details on where we are and such. I hand the phone off to her and the other dude and throw my rope around a big-ass tree and start my descent."

"Big-ass tree," Grant says, and I look pointedly at my sister.

"Sorry," she said.

"Why did you have rope with you, anyway?"

"I always bring it on hikes that have cliffs or potential places to fall over," she explained. "Never can be too careful when out in the wilderness. I head down the side of the cliff, and sure enough, dude has a broken leg. Thankfully it wasn't near his artery, 'cause that would not have been a good thing. I kept him company, tried to keep him calm, and we waited for S&R."

"So," I began. "You rescued him after he fell down a cliff. That's a sweet story."

"What?" she asked. "Oh, no, that wasn't him. That was just the dude that got us together. If he hadn't fallen, and if Mason hadn't been the one to come on the call, then we'd never have met."

"Mason?"

"Yeah," she said. "Oh, he's a physical therapist, too. How crazy weird is that?"

"The search and rescue guy is a physical therapist?"

"Yeah," she replied. "He works in a clinic over in Fruitland. It's just such a small world when you think about it. I mean, what are the odds that I would run into someone who does the same thing as me, lives less than an hour away, loves the wilderness and hiking, and is amazing at repelling and such?"

"Probably about the same as the odds that caused Meg and I to meet," I replied.

"True," she said. "You guys were from completely different places, and yet, there you were, the perfect couple, with the perfect son."

"Until it was all taken away," I said.

"But you got some happy times," she tried. "And you got the most amazing little guy in the world, right Grant?"

"Right," Grant said, not understanding what he was agreeing with.

"Just sucks that we didn't get our second," I said. "That we didn't get to grow old together. We had so many plans, Kate. There were so many things we still wanted to do."

"Hey," she said, putting her hand on my arm. "You can still do amazing things. Grant needs to do amazing things with you."

"But I can't do that if I'm not here," I argued.

"You're here for the important things," she said.

"Not if I'm on the road half the year," I countered. "I just keep going back to the thought of taking the year off and giving it all to Grant."

"You know you'll regret it if you do that," she said.

She was right, too. I knew that my love of the game would cause me to resent having to give it up. I loved my son, too, but knowing that he was in good hands with her, my mom, and my dad, should be enough to get me through.

"He's fine," she said. "He's not gonna miss having you around. I mean, he'll miss you, but in the bigger picture, it isn't that big of a deal."

"I know," I agreed. "It just sucks that he has to be stuck away from me for so much time."

"But in the end, having a happy daddy is going to be more important for him," she said. "You'll spend the off season next year with him. After that, you just need to see what happens. Who knows," she continued. "Maybe you'll meet another Mrs. Right at some point."

"I don't think there will ever be another one," I said. "Meg was absolutely perfect."

The rest of the ride was spent simply watching the water go by and listening to Grant babble and sing to himself. It was almost peaceful, even with the crowd of kids rambling around the deck.

CHAPTER ELEVEN

*L*ucy...

"Let's stay close together," Paulette said as we came down to the waterfront after our visit to the Parliament building as well as a couple of other stops on the way.

"Come on, Mom," Aidon complained. "We've been inside all day. Can't we at least run a little bit?"

"Tell you what," I said. "You are allowed to *walk* anywhere between where we are, that post over there," I pointed, indicating a place a few yards away, "and that sign over there," I concluded, pointing the other direction at a signpost. "But," I added, making sure all the boys were looking at me before continuing. "If *any* of you run, run over someone, or hurt someone, you are gonna be planted like these flowers right here. Got it?"

"Yes, ma'am," Thomas said. "Guys, it's better than just sitting here."

His encouragement helped the others agree to my terms, and they were off at a fast-walking pace, toward the bush at the far end of their space.

"See," Paulette said. "There you go again, giving them limits and making it seem like it's freedom. I really need to learn from you."

"They really should run off some of the energy they have from being cooped up so long," I counter. "I know that making them sit here for the next however long, waiting for the rest of the class, as well as the ferry, is just going to make them more nuts. This way, they get their wiggles out and we get a little time to enjoy the rare sunshine and relative warmth and not have to worry too much about them getting into trouble."

"True," she said. "It isn't a huge space, and we can see them all, so this is probably perfect."

"Exactly," I replied. "Between the both of us, we can see the entire area."

It was true, too. The space wasn't very big but had enough space to at least move some. They could do lots of things in the small space, and I wasn't worried about them getting lost or anything. While it was early in the year, it was unseasonably warm for March. That meant that more people were out on the waterfront, but not to the point where it was extremely crowded.

"What time is everyone supposed to be here?" she asked after a couple of minutes.

I looked at my lanyard to see what time we were supposed to meet for the ferry, then checked my watch and saw we had about fifteen minutes until that time, so I told her.

"Good," she replied. "Today has been a long day, and I'm ready to head home."

"Same," I replied.

"Aidon," she shouted, looking over my shoulder.

I turned just in time to see the boys in a game of tag and watched in slow motion as Thomas tumbled over a stroller with a toddler in it.

"Thomas," I scolded. "What did I say about running?"

"Sorry, Mom," he said, standing.

"Are you okay?" I asked the couple, looking at the stroller that had fortunately not tumbled over.

"I think we're good," the woman said.

"We're fine," the man said, tussling the child's hair. He looked up at Thomas and asked, "You good?"

"I am," Thomas replied, looking sheepish.

"And…" I prompted.

"Sorry," he mumbled without looking at them.

"Thomas," I warned, and he looked up and again said, "Sorry."

By this time, Paulette had arrived and gathered the rest of the kids. She took Thomas with her as they went back to where we'd been sitting.

"You're sure you're all okay?" I asked, wanting to make sure they weren't actually just being polite.

The man had kneeled next to the stroller and was checking out the child, but turned up to me and said, "I think Grant is just fine. He's a tough kiddo."

"I'm glad," I replied, looking a little too long at the man.

"Thanks for checking," the woman said.

"Again," I said, breaking eye contact with the man. "I am so sorry."

"Accidents happen," he said, standing. "But thanks for making sure."

"Absolutely," I replied, then turned and went back to where Paulette had the kids sitting on the edge of the planter we'd been resting at.

"I didn't see them," Thomas said when I got close enough.

"Because you were running," I replied hotly. "Which is something that was not allowed in order to have your freedom, correct?"

"Yeah," he mumbled.

"So," I continued. "Maybe you should apologize to the others because you caused them to lose their freedom as well."

"I'm sorry, Mrs. Fallon," Parker said. "I started it, so it's really my fault."

"Then you should probably apologize, too," I admonished.

"Sorry, guys," Parker said, and he sounded sincere.

"Yeah," Thomas chimed in. "Sorry."

The rest of the boys looked uncertain but decided to not voice their thoughts. We sat against the planter for the next ten minutes or so, even when other groups showed up. While others were playing around, our group sat on the ground, knowing they'd thrown their chance to be up away. Finally, after what to me seemed like entirely too long, and what was probably unbearable for the kids, Mrs. Neubauer and Mr. Tate showed up.

"Looks like we had issues?" Mrs. Neubauer said when she greeted us.

"Just not following rules," Paulette said. "But I think they've learned their lessons, haven't you, boys?"

They all grumbled their agreement, while standing with their backpacks.

"Glad you got it all worked out," the teacher said. "We're coming up on the time the ferry should be ready for us to load up, so let's all meet over at the building so we don't lose anyone."

Following the teacher, we went back toward the building we'd left when we first got to the island.

～

THE FERRY RIDE BACK TO WASHINGTON WAS MUCH MORE SUBDUED, AS the kids who were in our group knew they hadn't behaved, so were simply sitting at one of the tables on the level we were on, putting together a puzzle. This gave Paulette and I more time to talk.

"You doing okay?" I asked once we'd all settled into an area.

"Just thinking about how you handled the kids today," she said. "I mean, you were really good with them. Gave them room to grow and gave them consequences that they knew were coming should they disobey. That's what I have a hard time with."

"Which?" I asked. "The room or the consequences."

"The consequences," she replied. "Brock hates to discipline Aidon, so I end up being the bad guy all the time. And even when the punishment is just, he lets Aidon slide by without actually feeling the results of his actions."

"Yeah, that's not how parenting works," I said. "You have to be a united front, especially when it comes to discipline. Ryan and I would always tell the kids that they can ask either of us, but we're going to check with the other one before giving them a yes. If we find out that the other parent already said no, then they were going to be in bigger trouble. It's like lying. If they do something wrong, they'll get punished. If they lie about it, tell us they didn't do it or something, then not only will they get in trouble for what they did, but they'll also get a punishment for lying about it. Sort of a double whammy kind of thing."

"Oh, man," she said. "That lying thing always pisses me off. Aidon is a notorious liar, always telling his dad that he didn't do something I *saw* him do, and then Brock gets mad at me for punishing him. Why is he like that?"

"Honestly," I said. "It sounds like you guys could benefit from some counseling, individual, couple, and family counseling."

"Nope," Paulette said. "Brock has told me he will never go to counseling. I tried to get some before we moved here, but he was adamantly against it. He also told me that no son of his would do some pussy thing like that, and that if I tried to get him into counseling that he'd take him away from me and I'd never see him again."

"Babe," I said. "That's abuse. He's weaponizing your love against you. It sounds like you should get some counseling, maybe while Aidon is in school. It would help you learn to stand up for yourself at the very least."

"Brock won't let me," she said, and I could see the defeat in her face.

"Then we need to figure out a way to make it happen," I said. "Would he let you hang out with a friend a couple times a week? We could make it happen at my house, that way he wouldn't know about it."

"How would I pay for it?"

I could hear the desperation in her voice, and I wanted to have all the answers for her, but I wasn't sure whether I could.

"Tell you what," I said. "Why don't we plan at least one day a week where you come to my house for some girl time. I'll find a few ladies who love to hang out and help each other out and we can chat. Maybe one of them will have some ideas."

"I don't want to just tell strangers about my miserable life," she said.

"Nonsense," I said. "We'll get together and get to know each other. Maybe we'll do a book club kind of thing, where everyone reads the same book and we all get together to talk about it. Would you be interested in that?"

"As long as we're not talking about me," she said. "Oh, and it can't be anything smutty. Brock doesn't want me reading any of those trashy romance novels."

"You do know that those are the best kind of books, right?" I asked.

"Not in our house," she said.

"Okay," I agreed. "Let me talk to a few of my friends and see what we can come up with. I'm sure there's something out there that doesn't fall into the 'trashy romance' category that will get past Brock. At least then you could meet some other moms."

"I really would like that," she said.

"Me, too," I agreed.

The rest of the ride was pretty uneventful, and by the time we got through customs in Washington, got the kids on the bus, and started our trip back to Seattle, I was worn out. Since it was Tuesday, I would normally be worried about getting the kids up early the next morning, but they had the day off from school. I also had a surprise scheduled for them, but I wouldn't be telling them until we got to where we were going.

CHAPTER TWELVE

*J*onathan...

"That was a little crazy," Kate said once we were on the ferry.

"What?" I asked, pulling a snack out for Grant.

"That kid running over Grant," she said. "I mean, the mom could have kept control of her kid."

"It was fine," I said. "Kids are rambunctious, and he didn't hurt Grant, so all's fine."

"But he could have," she insisted.

"Kate," I said pointedly. "Grant is fine. The kid felt bad that he'd bumped us, and he apologized. So did the mother. It's not like it's a federal offense to play and have fun."

"I guess I'm just a worrywart," she said.

"Yeah," I replied. "Well, you and Mom both are worriers. I just don't know why you're both so worried that something is going to happen. Kids play, they get bumped, it's all good."

"I honestly don't think you worry enough," she remarked.

"And what good would worrying do?" I asked. "Is it going to change the fact that nothing happened? That Grant is totally fine? That the kid was embarrassed and probably got into trouble? No," I concluded. "None of that is going to happen, because worrying does nothing but cause you pain and turmoil and trouble. I have enough of that without looking for more in my life."

"I'm sorry," she said, and I could tell she meant it.

"I know," I replied. "I appreciate you wanting to help, but that isn't going to do it. I'm not going to lose sleep over some kid who accidentally ran into the stroller because in the big picture, it doesn't matter."

"I guess you're right," she said.

"I am," I replied. "I'm sorry if I sound angry, but I'm tired and today has just been amazing, but also really hard."

"Yeah?" she asked. "Why's that?"

"Meg isn't here to share this with me," I said. "That, and the fact that I should have two kids right now, instead of just Grant."

"Oh, no," she said. "I forgot all about that. I mean, I didn't forget, it's just… I'm so sorry I didn't plan something for you."

"No," I said. "I don't need to be reminded of what I could have had. Did we ever tell you the name?"

"I didn't know you had one," she said.

"We had two," I replied. "It was a girl, though, so the boy name doesn't really matter."

"It was a girl?" she asked.

"Yeah," I said. "Grace Katherine."

"Oh," she said, kind of shocked.

"Meg's great-grandmother was a Katherine," I explained. "But she really liked it because of you. You were one of her favorite people."

"She was one of my favorite people, too," Kate said, tearing up.

"Yeah," I said, and we sat there reeling in the memory of what was and the loss of what should have been.

"Whatever happened to the dude that hit her?" she asked after a while.

"I think he died," I said. "Honestly, though, it doesn't matter."

"That sucks," she said, and she sounded angry.

"Why?"

"He should have to pay for what he did to you and Grant," she said.

"He's dead," I said again. "Not much more he can do to pay for it, now is there?"

"But his family should pay or something," she said. "Wasn't he drunk?"

"I have no idea," I said. "Honestly, I don't even care. If I could do something to get Meg back, I would. That isn't possible, though, so I just have to keep on keeping on and moving forward. As they say, looking back is for time travelers."

"I've never heard that before," she said.

"Meg said it all the time," I offered. "She would always tell me that what happened in yesterday's game was over and there was nothing anyone could do to change it. Today was a new day, and we had to look forward to get to where we wanted."

"She was really smart," she said.

"Smarter than me," I agreed.

"Well," she said with a smirk. "That's not that hard to do."

"Rude, much?"

"Rude," Grant said around a mouth full of fish crackers.

Then he laughed that big belly laugh he did sometimes. It was exactly what we needed in that moment. It lightened the mood, and it gave us a little joy in the midst of our sorrow.

～

"COME ON, SLEEPY HEAD," I SAID, PULLING GRANT FROM HIS CAR SEAT when we got back to the condo. "Let's get you into your jammies and into your bed."

Kate had pulled the backpack from the back seat and was waiting at the elevator for us. By the time I got there, Grant was back asleep on my shoulder.

"He really can sleep anywhere," she said.

"Definitely," I replied, shifting him a bit as I stepped into the lift. "He's always been a good sleeper."

"What's your schedule tomorrow?" she asked as we ascended.

"Workout in the morning," I said. "Then prep for the game on

Thursday. Opening day is always fun. You sure you're good to miss this much work to stay through Saturday?"

"Oh, yeah," she said as we stepped out of the elevator. "As long as I head back on Saturday, Mom will have Sunday to get Grant back into the routine for the next week. My boss has been really accommodating with my needs this whole time. Mom's loving having him there all the time, you know."

"Yeah," I said. "I do miss him, but it's nice knowing that he's safe, cared for, and loved in my absence."

Keying my way into my space, we stepped through the door and I dropped my keys in the bowl on the stand next to the door. Moving through the living room, I went to Grant's room and opened his dresser drawer to pull out pajamas. I laid him down on the changing station and pulled his shoes off first, then went about the process of getting him into a dry diaper and pajamas before putting him into his bed. He was drowsy, but was awake through the process, so I spoke softly to him.

With his little fox in his hand, I tucked him into the crib and stepped out the door, closing it behind me. By the time I got to the living room, Kate was fast asleep on the couch, no blanket or anything. I pulled one from the ottoman we had in there and put it over her. She shifted but didn't wake. Smiling, I went to my room to ready myself for bed. The wedding photo on the top of my dresser caught my eye, and I went to it.

"You would have loved today," I said to the image. "Grant was just adorable with all the little things he saw. Every single one of them was his favorite until the next one came along. He's inquisitive, and smarter than any kid I've ever met." I sucked in a breath, then continued, "Take good care of Grace. She's loved, even though we never got to meet her. Tell my granddad that I miss him, too. And your dad. He would have loved to make little wooden things for Grant, and this boy probably would have been carving things by now if he had the chance."

I wiped a tear from my cheek but continued my conversation.

"I wish you could be here," I said. "I don't understand why you had to leave. Why did you not get to stay?"

I waited, hoping against hope that I would get an answer, but just as every time I asked that question in the past, nothing came. Those whispers in the dark, when it was just me and my memories, those were the moments I missed Meg the most. She would have either said something ridiculous or sweet, and either way, it would have been the perfect thing to say. Now, though, I was left with just the memory, the thought of what could have been.

Closing my eyes, I swallowed the lump that grew in my throat and went to the closet to change. No, nothing would tell me why she had to go. Nothing could explain why the vibrant, beautiful, wonderful wife and mother was taken from this earth. She was perfect in every way, absolutely the best thing that ever existed, and she created within her a child and was working on another. Then in some random act that is beyond all sense, she was taken. Just gone. And nothing anyone could do would bring her back.

CHAPTER THIRTEEN

*L*ucy...

"This is stupid," Rayne said. "Why can't you just tell us where we're going?"

"Don't you like surprises?" Thomas asked.

I'd picked my daughter up from my parents' house that morning and we were heading into downtown for my big surprise.

"No," Rayne complained. "They're usually stupid and involve me being embarrassed. Actually, I really hate surprises."

"Party pooper," Thomas said.

"Jerk," Rayne replied.

"Kids," I warned. "I know you don't like surprises, Rayne. This, however, is something your dad set up for us. He did it last year, and I felt like it would be wrong of us to not go and do it, even though he isn't here."

"Dad set this up?" she asked.

"Yup," I replied. "It was something he'd always wanted to do, so he scheduled it last summer. He didn't want to do it before now because he told me it was supposed to be the start of a great tradition."

"Well," Rayne said. "His timing sucks. He should have just done it before he died. Then we could actually remember him with this instead of doing something he wanted to do without him."

She'd been salty for weeks and I hadn't really figured out what was up with her. I just left it alone, deciding that if I didn't engage, maybe she'd get over whatever mad she had going on. That hadn't happened, but I was hopeful that this little trip, and the other things I had for them from their dad, might tip her over the edge and move her back to the happy girl I'd known six months earlier. Unfortunately, that little girl, and the little boy that was Thomas, were no more. No, those two innocent kids were gone, and here we had two wizened and scarred individuals who would never be the same.

"The stadium?" Thomas said, his eyes growing big.

"Come on, Mom," Rayne whined. "I don't want to do some stupid baseball thing. That was Dad and T's thing, but it wasn't my thing."

"Humor me, Rayne," I said. "Yes, your dad and brother loved baseball, but so did you. I have so many pictures of you being all kinds of excited coming to the games. And I love it, too. In fact, one of the first dates your dad took me on was to a baseball game. Did you know that?"

"Really?" Thomas asked. "That's the best date idea ever."

"That's the most boring date idea ever," Rayne complained.

"Well," I said, pulling into the parking garage. "This was something your dad set up. I plan to enjoy myself. Rayne," I continued as we got to the person taking money for parking, "you can choose to be happy or you can choose to be angry, but the choice is yours. This is what today is about, and it's all on you as to how you react to it."

"Cash or card?" the attendant asked.

"Card," I said, handing my card over to her.

She swiped it through her little handheld machine, then handed me a receipt, saying, "Put this on your dash. Level four."

"Thank you," I replied, moving ahead and around the corner up into the structure.

We wound our way around a couple of turns before finally reaching the fourth level where another attendant with a baton waved us around and toward the other end of the building. After I'd parked, I turned the car off and turned around to look at both kids.

"I miss your dad," I said. "I miss him so much it hurts to even think about. But," I continued. "I want to remember the things he loved. I want to remember all the promises he made to us, the things he said we'd do when we were older. We all lost someone, and each of us lost a different version of the same man. I can't know what it's like to lose a father, but neither of you can understand what it means to lose a partner in life, either. I think we need to give each other a little grace and maybe, just maybe, we'll find some happy here."

"You're such a sap," Rayne said, smirking.

"But she's right," Thomas said.

"Then, let's go," I said, turning back around and opening my door. "We've got a stadium to explore."

"WELCOME TO THE CASCADES' FIELD," THE BUBBLY YOUNG WOMAN said. "I'm Paisley and I'll be showing you around our beautiful stadium today. Unfortunately," she continued, "there are a few places we aren't going to be able to see. With tomorrow being opening day, and with the teams already in town, the clubhouses are going to be off-limits to us. Almost everything else is up for us to view and learn. Is this your first time at the stadium?"

"Nope," Thomas said. "We love it here."

"Then you probably know a whole lot about it, right?"

"It's been a few years since we did the tour last," I interjected.

"Then we'll start at the beginning," she said.

Ryan and I had done a date at the field one year for our anniversary. He had scheduled everything. First, we stopped at the field for a tour, then it was a fancy lunch at the Space Needle, and after that, a baseball game, with a stay at the Edgewater Hotel on the waterfront. It had been a wonderful weekend, and this was bringing back all those memories.

"The stadium was first conceived in 1991 by architect James Wyatt," she began as we stood in the team store where all the tours started. "His vision was embraced by the Cascades' leadership and they moved ahead with a vote to build it just south of the old King Dome site. I think you two are too young to remember that one, but I bet your mom does."

"Gramps used to take me there when I was a kid," I said. "Those were great memories."

"And the memories keep coming," she continued. "It took two full years of construction before the stadium was ready to embrace its fans and the team that would fill the seats. One of the unique features of the stadium is the fact that fans could purchase bricks that would be used along the outfield concessions area. As you walk that area, you will see many names, but if you're looking for one in particular, you can use one of the many kiosks to find it.

"If you'll follow me," she continued, as she made her way to the stairs in the store. "We'll head up to the upper level and begin our tour within the stadium there."

We walked up the staircase to the upper floor of the store where we again stopped.

"We have several items that are on the higher end for sale up here," she said. "Including game-worn jerseys, signed baseballs, bases from specific games, and even lineup sheets from the dugout. If you're a collector, this is one of the best places to come to find that one thing you were looking for."

"Mom," Thomas said, pulling on my sleeve. "Can we get a ball signed by Ichigo?"

"Not right now," I replied. "Let's do the tour and see what we see. When we're done, we can look through the store and see if there's anything we want to take home."

"There are a multitude of gift and souvenir ideas within the store," Paisley said. "I'm sure you'll find just what you want. Here we are at the top of the staircase coming up from the *Home Plate* entrance. And right there," she said, pointing, "is the brilliant sculpture with one thousand bats tumbling around and around. They're made of both resin and aluminum and were one of the first pieces that was commissioned for the stadium. It's the first of many pieces of art we'll find throughout the stadium today."

She turned and walked down the giant staircase toward the main level of the stadium, and we all followed suit. Rayne looked at me with her eyebrows up, then tipped her head toward the young woman who was leading us around. I looked at her questioning, but she just shrugged and sighed heavily.

"Here," the woman began. "You can see the beautiful likeness of the Cascade Mountain range that matches the one in the team's logo. Around the outside are signatures from the entire team from the 1993 season. When the stadium opened in July of that year, every player was given a plaque that had their signature on it in front of the team logo as a memento of the part they played in the team's history, as well as the historic opening of the stadium."

"This is so cool," Thomas said, looking at all the signatures. "This was before either of us were born, Rayne."

"Yeah," my daughter replied. "It's almost as old as Mom."

"That's right," I quipped. "I'm older than dirt, so it makes sense that I'm older than the stadium."

Try as she might, Rayne couldn't hide the smirk from my comment, and it made me warm to the fact that she just might be getting over her mad.

"Next," the guide said. "We'll head up to the suites and press boxes."

"Can we talk into the microphone for the stadium?" Thomas asked.

"Unfortunately, that system is shut down unless there's an actual game," she said. "The only announcements that come out over any of the speakers during non-game times are emergency announcements, and we don't want to hear any of those."

"True," I said.

CHAPTER FOURTEEN

*J*onathan...

"I can't believe you've got me out here doing drills," Beckett said. "This is my last free day before the season starts."

"Mine, too," I replied. "But Coach said I was in charge of your training, so this is what we're doing."

"Why isn't anyone else here?"

"Oh," I replied. "They'll be here, just not yet. It's the last day to prep for the rest of the season. What you do in practice becomes what will happen in the season. Let's go."

I didn't wait for any more complaining, just turned and headed out to the field. It was still early, so the stadium was pretty much empty and quiet. These were the times I loved. When I could commune with the baseball spirits and embrace the newness of each season. Coach knew I had a routine that kept me connected to where I was from, as well as to ensure that I knew where I was going, and he had asked that I include the rookie in this with me. I'd been hesitant, as it was something sort of sacred to me, but Coach said he wanted me to work with the kid to get him to understand the history of the game, the truth beneath the turf, the connection we all had with the past, and how it would propel us into the future.

"Wait up," he called from the dugout.

"Keep up," I replied. "I'm older than you. That shouldn't be a problem."

The kid was young, but he did have talent. I'd seen it throughout the spring, and if he could stay focused and stay out of trouble, he just might make something of himself. Who knew, maybe he'd even pull some sort of award this year.

The bucket of balls was heavy, but not so much so that they were unmanageable. My mitt was tucked on top of the balls in the bucket and I held a bat in my other hand. The goal was to get him used to coming out every day, doing something that would improve his game, and learning discipline. We'd learned to get along all right during the spring, but it had been a fight in the beginning. Maybe with time spent learning, he could see that I could be a resource for him, someone he could look up to, even. It was either that, or he'd burn out like a shooting star; fast, hot and gone before anyone got a good look at him.

"You know," he said when he'd caught up to me in the outfield. "For an old man, you're pretty quick on your feet."

"For a punk-ass kid," I returned, "you're pretty slow."

"But look at me," he crowed, walking backward in front of me toward the outfield and holding his hands out as if he were a fine specimen. "All the ladies love this. I gotta beat them off with a stick."

"Well," I said, looking him over. "The ones that are going for you are probably dogs, so all you gotta do is throw a stick and they'll all run after it."

"Ha, ha, very funny," he said. "At least I get some attention. You've been single for too long and should be back out there looking to at least get some tail. I mean, come on, you'll go blind if you keep on the way you're going."

"I've been just fine," I said, annoyed already. "This was supposed to be a time when I taught you about finding your center, the place where you are most attuned to the game. It's not about your love life. Not something I need to hear about, at all."

"If you'd get laid—" he began.

"Nope," I replied. "That is so not a conversation I'm going to have with you."

"Dude," he said. "I know you're old, but they've got pills for that sort of thing."

"Seriously?" I asked. "Do you wanna do well in this league, or are you more interested in fucking some bullpen bunnies? Cause if you want the latter, then get the fuck off my field. I don't have time for your shit, and I've just about had it with your attitude."

"Jesus," he said. "I'm just screwing with you. Can't you even take a joke?"

"Not when it's at the expense of my practice time," I replied. "You may have raw talent, but that'll only get you so far. If you don't put in the work, you're gonna burn out and be a has-been before you even get started."

"Bro, chill," he said.

"No, bro," I barked back. "Either get with the program or get out of my way. There ain't no in-between."

"You know what," he said. "Fuck you, and fuck Coach for making me your little pet project. I am great, better than you ever were, and I don't need your fucking woo-woo shit to get me there. I'm doing just fine, thank you very much. Enjoy your time communing with the ghosts of the past. You're gonna be joining them soon enough."

With that parting shot, he turned and walked back to the dugout. I could hear him muttering under his breath, but honestly, I was glad he was gone. This was the day before the first official game of the season, and I didn't need his attitude or his shit to mess with my head.

I set the bucket of balls down, dropped the bat next to it, and started doing some stretches. Thinking about how the spring went, I knew I had to be able to perform, or this may actually be my last season with Seattle. While I loved the city, there were so many memories tied to Meg that it might be a better option for me to move on.

Jogging across the outfield, I ran through everything that happened earlier with the kid. Sure, he was an asshole, but he was also really talented. I began to wonder whether he resented the fact that I was here without that kind of natural talent. The fact that I was about average when it came to my swing meant I had to put in extra effort on defense. Usually, when I was sent into a game, it was for a defensive substitution, and my skills were good enough to get me a gold glove award a few years ago when I ended up playing fairly steady at second base.

Maybe he didn't like the fact that I could play multiple positions. My usual spots were middle infield, which included the shortstop position Beckett played. Coach had put me in to replace him a few times in the spring, especially early on. He'd always made some smart-ass comment to me when Coach told him he could sit out the rest of the game, but I'd never paid it much attention.

After I'd done my stretching and jogging, I picked the bucket of balls back up, along with my bat, and headed back to the clubhouse. For some reason, there were people standing on the warning track just outside the visitor's dugout. While tours were common at the stadium, they usually didn't happen if we were at the park. It was early, though, so maybe it was the last one of the day, and they were just finishing up. The group was small, and my curiosity was piqued, so I detoured and headed toward the group instead of directly to the dugout.

CHAPTER FIFTEEN

*L*ucy...

"Now that you've seen most of the stadium," Paisley said as we walked out of the Diamond Club area, "what has been your favorite part?"

"I love the press box," Thomas said. "I wanna be a press person when I grow up. That way I can see all the games."

"I gotta say," Rayne added. "The suites were really cool. How many people can be in one of those?"

"They can host parties up to thirty people," the young woman explained. "And all the catering is included in the price."

"We could do my birthday here," my daughter said to me. "I mean, it would be pretty cool to do that, don't you think?"

"We'll have to wait and see," I replied.

We stepped out onto the field itself as we talked, Paisley mentioning all the amenities of renting a suite, and really doing a great job of upselling it.

"Mom, look," Thomas said as we stepped onto the dirt.

I turned to look at the outfield where he was pointing and saw a player or coach out there, a bucket of balls sitting on the turf.

"What did I say, T?" I asked him.

"If we see any players, they're working and we can't interrupt them," he moaned.

"Exactly," I replied.

"Oh dear," Paisley said as she stepped onto the dirt behind us. "There weren't supposed to be any players on the field at all today."

"Guess someone didn't get the memo," I quipped.

"Let's finish our tour here," she said. "Then we'll head in on the other side of home plate to head back to the team store. Please be sure to stay on the warning track and not go onto the grass. That's a rule for anyone on the field who isn't a player."

"He's coming this way," Thomas said, eyes wide with excitement.

"As you can see," Paisley tried, but my son was distracted by the player that was making his way in from the outfield.

"He's old," Rayne said as he got to the infield area.

"Let's head toward the backstop," Paisley said, trying to usher us away from the player, but he seemed determined.

"Hey," he said as he got close enough for us to hear him. "You guys on a tour?"

"I'm so sorry," Paisley said. "We didn't realize you were doing your workout on the field. We'll just be heading back up and you can continue with your work."

It was obvious she was flustered, but the player seemed unbothered by our presence.

"It's totally fine," he said. "I was just finishing up. How's it going slugger?" he asked, tussling Thomas's hair.

"It's really great now that I get to meet a real-life player," my son gushed. "What's your name?"

"I'm J," he said. "What's your name?"

"I'm Thomas," he said. "Most folks call me T, though."

"Good to meet you, T," the man said, then turned his attention to my daughter. "And you are…"

He left the question unasked but insinuated that he wanted her name.

"Rayne," she said, folding her arms over her chest.

"Like the weather we get around here, eh?"

"Ha, ha," she said, unamused. "Like I haven't heard that one before."

"Well," the player said, dropping his hand he'd had out to shake. "It's a pleasure to meet you Rayne the mysterious."

"She's just mad because she's a girl and doesn't like baseball," Thomas said, very eager to be part of the whole conversation.

"Some girls don't like sports," the player said. "Some do. Nothing wrong with either one. I'm Jonathan," he said, stretching his hand out to me.

"Lucy," I replied, taking his hand.

He looked familiar, but I wasn't sure why. Likely it was because I'd seen the team play for years. His hand was warm and there were a few callouses, but it wasn't as rough as I thought it might be.

"Absolute pleasure to meet you," he said, holding my hand a little longer than may be considered polite. When he dropped it, he asked, "You guys from around here?"

"We live in West Seattle," Thomas said.

"Thomas," Rayne chastised. "We don't tell strangers where we live."

"You are quite right," Jonathan said. "But West Seattle is a pretty big area, so I think you're safe." He winked at her and she blushed and looked away. "I was just meaning whether you were from the area or were in from out of town, though. Is this your first trip to the stadium?"

"We come here whenever we can," Thomas said, nearly busting out of his shoes with energy at meeting a player on the field. "Do you know Ichigo?"

"Thomas," I said. "I'm sorry," I offered Jonathan. "My son kind of has a one-tracked mind when it comes to the player."

"I don't blame him," Jonathan said. "Ichigo is one of my favorite players, too."

"Really?" Thomas asked, eyes wide.

"Oh, for sure," Jonathan said. "It's really fun to play behind him. It's like we get a break from actual play because he's so good."

"We really should—" Paisley began, but Jonathan cut her off.

"You guys have any baseballs?" he asked.

"Not with us," T said.

"If you don't tell," Jonathan said in a conspiratorial tone, then looked around the stadium as if he were afraid he'd get caught. Once he'd finished, he pulled a couple of baseballs from the bucket he had with him and handed one to each of the kids.

"This is so cool," Thomas said, staring at the ball in his hands. "Can you sign it?"

"I don't have a pen," he said. "Do you have one?"

"Me?" I asked.

"Yeah, Mom," Rayne said, glaring.

I rummaged through my small purse but didn't have any pens in it.

"Sorry," I said. "I don't have one."

"Ma'am," Jonathan said to our tour guide, who had been struck silent by the conversation between my family and him. "You have a pen?"

"What?" she asked. "Me? Oh, no, I don't have anything, actually."

"I'm sure I can scrounge one up in the clubhouse if you guys wanna wait," he said, looking at me.

"As long as Paisley says it's fine to wait, then I'm fine with it, too," I replied, looking at the employee of the stadium.

"We do have a little bit more to see in the stadium," she began, but looked at Thomas and gave in. "But we can wait."

"Perfect," Jonathan said. "Hey, T. You wanna go to the dugout?"

"Oh," Paisley began.

"Just the dugout," Jonathan interrupted. "And only as long as your mom says it's fine."

"Please," Thomas begged.

"Stay where I can see you," I said. "And follow directions."

"Yippee," Thomas crowed.

"You wanna come, too?" Jonathan asked Rayne.

"Nope," she replied.

"All right," he said. "Shall we make our way to the dugout?"

"Let's go," Thomas said.

"It's not allowed—"

"He's with me," Jonathan said. "That makes it okay."

"Fine," Paisley said, clearly frustrated and feeling a bit put out by this whole derailment of her tour. I sort of felt sorry for her if I were honest with myself.

"God, Mom," Rayne said when the boys were out of earshot.

"What?" I asked.

"Why don't you just rip your clothes off and jump on him?"

"What are you talking about?"

"*It's fine if you take my son to the dugout,*" she mimicked. "*I'll just stand here and fawn all over you.*"

She'd pushed her hair behind her ear and batted her eyelashes while saying that.

"Was I too polite for you?" I asked.

"You could at least pretend you missed Dad," she snapped. "Sure, you said that in the car, but one look at a baseball player and you're all over that hurt and ready to move on."

"Rayne Nicole," I barked. "I was polite. It's what adults do. I am not fawning over anyone, not jumping into a relationship with anyone, and not just forgetting your dad. If I could have him back, I would do whatever it took to make that happen. But I can't. I can't change the past, can't bring him back, and can't make it hurt less that he's gone. I'm trying my hardest to just get through the days. I don't need you coming at me like I'm doing something wrong."

"But you're throwing yourself at that guy," she said.

"How?" I asked. "How was being nice to him, letting your brother have a moment of goodness, and being polite, throwing myself at him?"

"You just were," she sobbed, and there it was.

She was missing her dad, knowing that he wasn't here to do the fun thing he'd planned for us, and she had to get through it with all of us. I pulled her to me and wrapped her struggling body in my arms. She was stiff, tried to push away, but then finally broke down and clung to me as she sobbed. I looked over her head to see the tour guide with a confused look on her face. Closing my eyes, I shut her, and the rest of the world out, and just held my girl as she fell apart.

CHAPTER SIXTEEN

*J*onathan...

"Your friends call you T?" I asked. "Why's that?"

"My dad didn't want me to be called Tommy," he said. "Said it was a childish name, and he wanted me to have an adult name."

"No Tom, either, then?" I asked.

"Nah," he said, shrugging. "He said it was either Thomas or T, nothing else. Apparently, Mimi called me Tommy when I came home from the hospital, but he said it wasn't my name and it wasn't allowed."

"Good for him," I said. "Sometimes as parents we have to be tough on our own parents."

"Yeah," he said, as if he understood the complexities of adult relationships. "Papi and Mimi call me T, now."

"Where is your dad?" I asked as we came close to the dugout on the first base side of the stadium.

"Oh, he died," Thomas said, and I was shocked and nearly stumbled.

"I'm sorry," I said.

"It's okay," he replied. "He's been dead a while. He set this up for us, though, so that's cool, right?"

"That's really cool," I said, but had to run things through my brain to figure out how we got here from where we started the conversation. "Well," I said as we got to the top step of the dugout. "This is the dugout."

"This is so cool," he said, and looked excited to be here.

"Coach sits right there," I said, pointing with my bat at the bench along the top of the dugout steps. "Watches every single pitch, hit, and throw. He's gotta make sure he knows what's going on every minute of the game."

"Can I sit there?" he asked.

"Absolutely," I replied. "You sit and wait there while I see if I can find a pen to sign the balls for you and your sister."

"Okay," he said, climbing up onto the bench seats. "If you see Ichigo, can you ask him for an autograph, too?"

"I'll see if he's here," I said, then ducked my way into the clubhouse.

The hallway wasn't too long, but I sped my steps up so I didn't keep everyone waiting on me. When I turned into the locker area, I saw the Guardian sitting in a chair near his locker.

"Hey, Strawberry," I called, using the other meaning of his name.

"Hai," he replied.

"Got a kid that wants your autograph," I said, knowing he understood English fairly well. "You good to sign a ball for him?"

"Hai," he said again.

"Cool," I said. "Lemme find a pen."

I went over to the desk outside the coach's office and saw there were several Sharpies sitting on its top. I picked one up and took it with me back to the locker area.

"Think fast," I said, tossing the pen across the space between me and the other player.

He snatched it out of the air without any problem, then I tossed a ball to him. He quickly signed it, then threw it back to me, followed by the pen.

"Thanks, man," I said.

He simply smiled and nodded. I grabbed a couple other balls out of the bucket I had and quickly signed each of them, tucking the pen into my back pocket for later. Retracing my steps, I went back up the hall and out to the dugout where Thomas was still waiting.

"Hey, T," I said, and he turned to me. "I found something you might want."

I handed him the ball and his eyes grew big. It was obvious that it was signed by the Japanese closer we had for the team.

"Really?" he asked, and I nodded.

I didn't have but a moment to react when he launched himself from the bench seat and into my arms. Thankfully, I was able to catch him without dropping the other two baseballs I held in my hands.

"This is the coolest thing ever," he mumbled into my shoulder.

"I'm glad he was here," I replied, still holding him.

I wasn't sure exactly what to expect, but I heard him take a deep breath, then raise his head off my shoulder.

"You good?" I asked as I set him on the top step.

He sniffed and nodded his head, wiping the side of his face with his sleeve.

"You need a minute?"

He nodded, keeping his back to the field and his family. Once he'd gained his composure, I tipped his head up by his chin.

"It's okay to cry," I said. "Real men know how to show emotions. It's the fake ones that tell people that men can't cry."

I could see him struggling to regain his composure, so I just watched him, waiting right alongside him. It didn't take long before he was back to the smiling kid I'd seen just a few minutes earlier.

"I got these, too," I said, holding out the other two balls. "It's just my signature, though."

"That's cool," he said, still sniffing.

"Shall we go back to your mom and sister?" I asked.

"Don't tell them I cried," he said.

"Wouldn't dream of it," I replied as he turned around.

The walk back to the other side of the infield was silent. The three women were standing close, and it looked like the employee was uncomfortable. She was standing a few feet away from the other two. While the mother was facing toward us, the daughter was looking at her mom.

"Hey, Rayne," Thomas said. "Look what I got."

I was surprised at how quickly he had recovered from his earlier emotions but was thankful as well. When the girl turned around, I could see that she had been crying. I looked to the mother, questioning, but she just shook her head.

"Let's see, T," the mother said, holding her hand out.

"He got me a baseball signed by the Guardian," Thomas said.

"That's really nice," she said, and I could see she was appreciative.

"Just happened to be here," I said. "I also signed a couple other ones for them. If you want, Rayne, you can throw it at me."

She looked at me, clearly confused.

"I mean," I fumbled. "If you don't want it, that is."

"It's fine," she said, but was so quiet I had to strain to hear her.

"Thank you so much," the mother said. "I really appreciate you taking time out of your day to be kind to my kids."

"Absolutely no trouble at all," I said. "You guys coming to any games this weekend?"

"Can we, Mom?" Thomas asked.

"I hadn't told them yet," the mother said. "But that was the other thing Dad did. He got us season tickets for the year, so we'll be here all weekend."

"Oh my God, really, Mom?" Thomas nearly shouted.

"Yep," she said. "And we're staying in the city tonight so we can be here bright and early tomorrow morning."

"If you'd like," I said, seizing the opportunity. "I can get you some passes to get into the stadium before it opens to the public. One of the advantages us players have if you're interested."

"Mom," Thomas said, jumping up and down. "Can we do it? Please?"

"I wouldn't want to impose," she began.

"Nonsense," I replied. "It's one of the perks, and I am happy to be able to offer it to your family. Shall I have three or four?"

"Four," she said. "My dad's coming with us."

"Great," I said. "Can you handle that?" I asked the employee who had simply been standing to the side, clearly uncomfortable with all that was going on between the rest of us.

"Umm," she said.

"Hang on," I said, pulling a piece of paper out of my back pocket. It was the list of drills I'd planned to run the kid through, but it seemed useless now. I also pulled out the pen I'd stuck in there earlier and handed it to Lucy. "Why don't you write your name down," I said. "I'm terrible with names, so this will help out. Oh, and write down where your seats are. I'll see if I can find something for you all before tomorrow's game. It's gonna be kind of crazy before the game, but if you're gonna be here all weekend, I'll see if I can meet with you later on."

"Okay," she said, taking the paper and pen from my hand.

"Would you be okay with me having your number?" I asked. "Only to make sure you know where to go and what to do when you get here to get in."

"I mean," she hesitated.

"If you're not comfortable, I totally understand," I said.

"No," she said, scribbling it down. "Here."

She handed the paper and pen back to me, then tucked her hair behind her ear. I couldn't be sure, but it looked like she was a bit uncomfortable.

"I'll text you where to go to get your entry," I said. "Once I've done that, I'll delete your number, if that makes you feel better."

"No, no," she insisted, looking right at me. "It's just, well, no, it's fine."

She was flustered, I could tell, and I felt bad about that.

"Tell you what," I said. "I'll text you to get the tickets, then once you're here and text me that you got them and are in, I'll delete your number. That way you know I won't be bugging you at all or anything. I'm sorry, this is awkward."

"It's totally fine," she said and reached out, putting her hand over mine on the paper.

I looked at her then and could see that she was really trying to not cry or something, and I honestly didn't know what to do.

"Okay," I said.

"Thank you," she said, patted my hand, then pulled it away. "I think we need to finish our tour, right?"

"Yes," the employee said, clearly ready to be anywhere but where she was standing.

"Thank you," Thomas said. "I am so happy I got to meet you."

"Same here, kiddo," I replied. "You, too, Rayne."

"Whatever," she said without a backward glance.

I stood there for a minute, waiting to see if Lucy would turn around again, but she didn't, just walked away with the tour guide leading the way. The question was, did she give me her real number, or was she just being polite. I guess I would find out once I got my phone and sent a text. But first, I had to do some planning. Honestly, I had no idea whether it was even a thing to give a family pass to someone who wasn't family. I mean, Kate had a pass, and she could bring Grant with her, but they were family. I wondered whether it would be the same with Lucy and her kids.

CHAPTER SEVENTEEN

*L*ucy...

"Seriously, Mom?" Rayne said as we got to the car.

"What?" Thomas asked.

"Rayne," I warned.

"Mom's done with being sad about Dad," she said. "She's ready to move on, and it looks like she's set her sights on this poor guy."

"That makes no sense," he said.

"Didn't you see her?" she asked. "She was giving him her number and everything."

"That's so we can get into the game early tomorrow," Thomas argued.

"Oh, yeah," Rayne said. "That's what they pretended it was about, but I know she's just gonna go meet him at some trashy hotel and hook up. God, Mom, you're horrible."

"Rayne," I barked. "That's enough. Your brother is right. He asked for it so that he could make sure that we got into the game early tomorrow. I would think you would be appreciative of him being kind, but I guess you just don't care about that."

"Whatever," she said as she climbed into the back seat.

"Mom?" Thomas questioned.

"She's just upset," I said, not really sure what else I could say. "Get in and we'll go to our hotel where we're staying tonight."

He climbed into the back seat next to his sister, but she'd put her headphones in and was looking out the window, clearly angry at the world once again. Tonight was going to be a long night, and the weekend looked like anything but pleasant.

～

"FOR REAL?" ANDREA ASKED.

"Yeah," I replied.

I'd finally gotten the kids to sleep, then slipped out of the hotel room with my phone and headed down to the bar in the hotel. When we'd checked in, I had sent a text to my best friend asking her if I could call her later.

"So," she prodded. "Did he text you?"

"No," I replied. "But he probably didn't get a chance to get the answers to his questions, either, so…"

"Rayne was pissed about it, though?"

"Oh." I laughed. "She was so pissed. Like, you would have thought I'd jumped him right there in the middle of the stadium with everyone around."

"What is she so upset about?"

"She thinks I've moved on from Ryan and have already planned a future with this Jonathan guy," I said. "Like, the dude was being nice and offered to get us in early, which you would think she'd be happy about because she absolutely hates waiting in lines. But no, she's gotta be pissy about it and bite my head off the first chance she gets."

"I'm assuming this guy is young," she said.

"Not really," I replied. "He looked to be close to my age, maybe a little younger. He wasn't one of those twenty-something kids, that's for sure."

"Then what's her problem?"

"I think she's just missing her dad," I said. "This was something he planned, and now he isn't here to do it with us. I think this is really hitting her hard that he's gone. I mean, it's been hard, but this is just somehow the most real it's been for her, I guess."

"You holding up?"

"I mean," I began. "I'm sitting in a hotel bar talking on the phone with my friend while my kids are asleep upstairs and wondering what exactly I'm supposed to be feeling."

"Yeah," she said. "But how are you, really?"

"I don't know," I said. "Honestly, I think it would be nice to be noticed. But then again, it's only been six months, so it's way too soon to even think about a relationship or anything."

"But you wanna get laid, right?"

I damn near choked on my drink.

"Girl," I said. "That is so not what this is about."

"Come on," she said. "If you're gonna be hanging out with baseball players, you gotta know that I'm gonna try to live vicariously through you."

"Stop." I laughed.

"Don't tell me you didn't at least think about it for a minute," she said. "When I said it, your mind went there, didn't it?"

"Not gonna lie," I said.

"See." She laughed. "You know you wanna get down and dirty with one of those boys. I don't blame you, either."

"What are you talking about?" I asked. "Marco is a great guy."

"But he doesn't make millions of dollars a year," she said.

"If he's a good guy, he's a good guy," I said. "Doesn't matter whether he's your average Joe or a billionaire."

"But," she said. "It's much nicer to cry in a Mercedes than on your bicycle."

"True," I said. "But I'm not hurting for money right now, so I think I'll just stick to being appreciative of what he's offered and not go looking for trouble."

"Trouble is fun." She laughed.

"True," I replied. "It's also sometimes a headache."

My phone buzzed, and I startled.

"What's up?"

"Sorry," I said. "Phone just buzzed."

"Bet it's the boy, and he's gonna hit you up," she said.

"You are incorrigible," I replied. "But I should check. You know, just to be sure and all."

"That's my girl," she gloated. "I'll let you go. Sleep well and have fun tomorrow. I know it's gonna be amazing."

"As long as Rayne doesn't stay pissy," I replied. "Sleep well."

"'Night," she said, then ended the call.

I pulled my phone from my ear and saw that I did have a text message. I opened up the app and saw that it was a number with an area code that was definitely not from Washington, so figured it must be him.

Lucy, it's Jonathan. I need your seat information to get you set up to get in early. Text it when you can. Sorry it's so late.

I typed out a return message with our seat assignments to him and thanked him for being so kind to us.

No problem. You'll go to the press entrance off 4th Street. Just show them your tickets and let them know you're a guest of Jonathan Bridge. They should get you in no problem.

The name sounded familiar, but I couldn't figure out why. I quickly typed my response.

Thank you again. I really appreciate your help. I will text you when we get there to let you know we're in.

I hadn't expected a response, so was pleased. Of course, it would be nice to thank him in person. He responded quickly.

I probably won't have my phone because of BP, but I'll see if I can spot you in the stands. Might not get a chance to say anything until after the game, though. If you don't mind sticking around.

I was surprised to see that response, so typed one back.

We will definitely stick around. Want to thank you in person.

I was feeling much better about this chance encounter and finished my drink and headed back up to my room determined to make tomorrow an amazing day.

CHAPTER EIGHTEEN

*J*onathan…

I got the last text from her and was thankful I could do something nice for them. It wasn't much, but I had already set in motion some other goodies as well. By the time I got home, I was beat. Practice was good today, and I felt like we were shaping up to have a great year. Coach was still pissed about Beckett ditching me for my early morning routine, but I was a bit glad he wasn't there. That probably would have spoiled the whole thing.

I tossed my keys into the dish by the door and saw Kate sitting on the couch.

"Good practice?" she asked.

"Except for the idiot kid who tried to ruin it," I replied. "Met a family that were there doing a tour, though."

"Oh yeah," she said. "Don't they usually do those when there aren't games and stuff?"

"Usually," I replied, plopping myself down at the other end of the couch. "But we're not normally there as early as I was today, either, so I think they didn't think there would be a problem."

"What was it you said about the rookie?"

"Yeah," I replied. "Coach wanted me to work with this new kid and try to get him a little more contained than he's been so far. Wanted me to run him through my drills for pre-workout. He was being a little bitch, though, and told me to go fuck myself, so I just did what I normally do before the season starts."

"He told you to go fuck yourself?"

"Yeah," I said. "He thinks he's God's gift to baseball and God's gift to women, apparently. He had a few issues right before Spring Training, and I thought we'd gotten him out of that pattern, but it seems to be that he just hid it well. He's probably gonna end up with a suspension or something early in the season. I mean, I hate to see him go down like that, but his attitude needs some serious adjustments."

"Boys," she said. "They're stupid and I throw rocks at them."

"But not me," I countered.

"You're a man," she said. "Boys are the ones who think they know things, think they're hot shit, and need to be knocked down a time or two in order to ensure they know that women are the better gender."

"Won't argue with you there." I laughed.

"Because you're smart," she replied.

"Grant go to bed good?" I asked.

"That kid is amazing," she said. "I just run the routine and he goes with it. Bath, jammies, cup of milk, and his little show, then it's off to bed and he just stays there. How did you train him to be so easy to manage?"

"Not me," I said. "That was all Meg. She was the absolute best mother, ever."

The tears welled up, and I realized I wasn't over her, yet. Not that I ever would be. Sometimes I wondered whether I'd ever get past being alone, being without my absolute favorite person in the world. Having Grant as a reminder was both a blessing and a curse.

"Go to bed," Kate said. "You're tired, and you're emotional. You need sleep for your big opening day tomorrow."

"Yes, Mom," I replied, but it was true.

I was tired, and that always made me more emotional than normal. I went to my room and got on with the routine of getting ready for bed. Just like every other night, I looked at my wife's picture, the one from our wedding where we were so in love and so sure that we were going to be spending hundreds of years together. One crash changed all of that, and it still bothered me.

"How do I go on?" I asked the photo, not for the first time.

Of course, there was no answer.

"Did I do the right thing today?" I asked, shifting gears. "I mean, was what I did the right thing? That little boy doesn't have a dad, and that broke my heart. I thought about Grant, and how he doesn't have a mom, either. At least, not someone here that can hold him and love him in the here and now. I did what I would want someone to do for him, and it was such a simple little thing, too. Sure, I have some other things, but this was just one thing."

I didn't expect an answer, but when Kate spoke from the doorway I startled.

"She would be proud of you," she said.

"You think?" I asked, very unsure of myself in that moment.

"Absolutely," my sister confirmed. "You have a heart that's bigger than anyone I know. If you did something for someone, then it was the right thing."

"I just don't know," I replied, turning and sitting on my bed. I patted the edge in an invitation for her to join me. "This kid was just so nonchalant about his dad being dead that I didn't really know how to respond."

"Maybe it's been a while," she offered. "Could be that he's been gone so long that this is his normal, and no big deal."

"I mean, I guess," I said. "But he also said his dad set it up for them, so that sounds like it was something that was new to him, too. Like, I don't know how the tickets work, but if they have them, then it wasn't just something that was done years ago."

"Unless," she interjected, "they've been doing this for years, and the first time it was set up by the dad, so the kid thinks it always has been."

"Sure," I said. "I can see that logic. But the girl was crying. Not really sure what that was all about, but she definitely looked upset. So did the mom now that I think about it."

"People grieve in their own time," Kate said. "Some move through the process quick, while others can take years. Remember Meg talking about when her granddad died?"

"Yeah," I said.

"She said that her mom went through it pretty quick," she said. "Even though it's been years, she was still moved when something reminded her of her dad."

"Man," I said "That's right. Her granddad died before we even met, but she would still get teary when she saw something that reminded her of him."

"So," she surmised. "The boy may have moved through it quick, but the girl is still in the throes of emotions from it."

"And the girl is older," I agreed. "She may have more memories than he does. Maybe the baseball stadium was something that was special to her but wasn't a big deal to him. That could be why she was so upset."

"There you go," she said, patting my arm. "Now, get some sleep. I want to see you play tomorrow, or at least look amazing out there."

"Not a starter," I said. "I don't think I'll play. Then again, if Beckett keeps his shit up, I may end up on the field at shortstop for him."

She laughed and said, "Then you can thank him for giving you the chance to play on opening day."

"Petty," I said. "But I'd do it."

"Goodnight," she said, standing. "Sleep well. And don't dwell on this. It'll make you crazier than you already are."

"Very funny," I said, but she was right. I needed to focus on tomorrow and what might happen. In order to do that, I needed to get some sleep. Especially if Beckett held true to form and did something stupid, which was highly likely.

CHAPTER NINETEEN

*L*ucy…

"This is stupid," Rayne said, and I struggled to not roll my eyes at her. "I mean, there isn't even a line out here. Why do we have to be here so early?"

"I think it's great," my dad said. He'd driven in from his place to meet up with us so we could all sit together. "I was never a line person, myself, so the fact that we can get in without one is wonderful."

"And we'll get to pick the best spot for us to watch them do batting practice," Thomas added.

"Baseball games are boring," she said. "They're long and nothing happens. And now, we have to be here an extra couple of hours on top of it."

"Rayne," I said. "I understand that this isn't your favorite thing to be doing, but your brother, your grandfather, and your mother are all wanting to enjoy our day. Is there any way you can look at it as a blessing to be with us?"

"The only reason we're here is because of Dad," she said. "And he isn't even here with us, so it's just stupid that we're here at all."

"Quit being a party pooper," Thomas said.

"Whatever," she said, folding her arms across her chest.

I could tell it was going to be a long afternoon and evening. I just hoped she would find something to enjoy while we were there.

"This is for press only," a man said as we finally found the door Jonathan told us to go to.

"We were told to come here," I said. "We're guests of Jonathan Bridge."

"Tickets," he said, holding his hand out.

I pulled out my phone and showed him the electronic tickets I had. He scanned them with his handheld device, then waived us to the desk behind him, saying, "Check in there."

We all walked into the small space with its nice floor, fancy furniture, and expensive-looking artwork on the walls. It was amazing how quiet it was in this small space. The crowd outside had picked up some, and people were starting to line up near the entrances. I was thankful that we were able to find a decent place to park in the garage when we got here. Dad had picked us up at the hotel so we only had to bring one car and only pay for one parking spot.

"Welcome to the Cascades Stadium," the young man behind the desk said. "How can I help you today?"

"We're guests of Jonathan Bridge," I said. "My name is Lucy Fallon."

"Let me just check," he said, clicking on his computer at the desk. "Ah, yes," he said finally. "Looks like you already have your tickets, right?"

"Right," I said, holding out my phone one more time.

"Fantastic," he said. "Here are lanyards for each of you. This will allow you to be in the Diamond Club area prior to the gates opening. Once the gates open, the door to the stadium will open up and you can make your way to your seats. Do you know where you're sitting?"

"I think so," I said.

"Let me see," he said, holding out his hand. He looked at the ticket that was on my screen and then pulled out a map of the stadium. "You're going to enter the stadium through the Diamond Club, here," he said, pointing on the map. "When you're there, you'll take these stairs up to the main concourse and follow it around this way, toward the first base dugout. Look for your section number, and when you reach it, you'll go down the steps a few rows to your row."

"You catch that?" I asked, looking at my dad. He was the one who knew the stadium better than me, even though I'd been several times. Dad just had a way of following directions.

"Got it," he said, smiling.

"Great," the man said. "If there's anything else I can do for you, please let me know."

"Thank you so much," I said, then followed my dad and the kids as we moved into the club section we were told to go through.

The moment we stepped in, I felt completely out of place. Everything in there was high end. I'm talking plush couches and fancy drinks and people dressed like they were in boardrooms rather than at a baseball game.

"I feel weird," Rayne whispered to me.

"Me, too," I replied. "But we were invited, and we have these lanyards, so we're fine."

"It's just so fancy," she said.

Her eyes were wide as she looked around the space. I glanced over and saw Thomas had the same expression of wonder on his face. Dad was looking impressed with everything around him, and seemed to fit right in.

"Sure is a nice space they have here," he said. "Be a shame to miss out on all this when we did get invited here."

He walked up to a bar that was set back against one of the walls. It was as if he were right in his own element, while the kids and I were like fish out of water.

"I'll take a Blue Moon," he said to the bartender.

"Right away," the man behind the bar replied and got busy pouring my dad's beer.

Once it was done, he handed it over. My dad had pulled out his wallet and held a card out for payment. The man swiped it through his machine, then handed the card back to Dad.

"Receipt?" the man asked.

"No thanks," Dad replied, then turned and walked back to us. "I could get used to this," he said with a big smile.

"I'd love to say I felt the same," I replied. "But I feel completely out of my element."

The space began to fill up a bit more, and we found our way to a table where we could all sit down. I'd grabbed some popcorn for the kids, as well as drinks, and I was sipping on a glass of wine. I knew they sold wine at the stadium but was always under the impression that it was served in plastic glasses. This was an honest to goodness wine glass, and I was a little excited, yet completely overwhelmed.

In what seemed like an eternity, we sat in that space with all the other people until the doors to the stadium were finally opened to us. I looked at my watch and realized we were still about an hour before the rest of the stadium would open.

"Let's go," I said, once most of the folks that were heading into the stadium had moved out.

The light from the stadium was bright as we exited the club and stepped out right behind home plate. I mean, it was right there, on the other side of the netting they had up behind it. The players were so close we could almost touch them. I looked around, wondering whether I would be able to spot Jonathan, but I couldn't make out who any of them were.

Following my dad, we made our way up the steps toward the walkway that ran around the top of the seats on the main level. Ryan had picked out some pretty good seats for us, so we would have to climb the stairs, walk around to our aisle, then go back down more stairs to get to the row we were seated in. Both kids were taking in the arena with wide eyes, and I had to admit that it was pretty cool to see it all decked out for the first game of the season.

Fans were coming in from most of the entrances by the time we made it to our seats, though none were down along the edge of the field yet.

"Can I go down there?" Thomas asked, pointing toward the field.

"What for?" my dad asked.

"See if I can get some autographs," he replied.

"Pretty sure the players don't have time to sign your stuff," Rayne said.

"I see them signing stuff all the time," Thomas argued.

"Tell you what," I said. "You and I can go down there and see if we can get an autograph while Gramps and Rayne sit in the seats."

"Let's go," he said, bouncing on the balls of his feet.

CHAPTER TWENTY

*J*onathan...

"What'cha looking for?" Cote asked me.

The second baseman had been with the team a couple of years and was a really good player. He was also very kind and willing to help out damn near anyone around him.

"My sister is coming with my son," I said, although that was somewhat of a lie. Well, it wasn't a lie, actually. My sister was coming with Grant, but I wasn't looking for her. I was looking for Lucy and her kids, hoping to catch a glimpse of them before the game.

"Don't you know where they're sitting?" he asked. "I would assume they'd be in the family section."

"Oh, yeah," I said absently. We were standing behind the fencing they had up in front of second base, working on our turns. "I think she said she was gonna come down to the edge of the field, though. Thought I might see here there."

"Good deal," he said. "Wanna head that way or are you good doing a couple more turns?"

"What?" I asked, completely not paying attention to my teammate. "Oh, no. I'm gonna head up and see if I can get a few swings in before they pull this shit off the field."

"Cool, cool," he said.

Watching the player in the batting cage, I walked toward first base, then stood behind that guard before wandering up toward the cage myself.

"Jonathan," I heard and turned toward the stands. Changing my trajectory, I wandered over to where I saw Lucy and her son standing at the end of one of the aisles.

"Hey, buddy," I said to the kid. "You guys made it."

"Yeah," he said. "Gramps is up with Rayne because she didn't want to come down."

"You were able to get in without any problems?" I asked Lucy.

"Yes," she said. "Thank you so much."

"Absolutely not a problem," I said. "I found some stuff for you guys."

"Really?" Thomas asked, eyes wide.

"Nothing fancy," I added. "Just some stuff they had around for this year's promotional stuff. I was able to grab a couple of things. I've got them in my locker, but I can meet you guys after the game and give them to you. Does that work?"

"Mom," Thomas said, looking pleadingly at his mom. "Can we? Please?"

He drew the last word out, almost begging with that one word.

"I'm sure we can hang out after the game," she said. "Thank you again. It was so kind of you to do this for us."

"I'm just glad I stumbled into you guys," I said. "It's always good to meet people who are kind."

"Yes," she said. "You've been very kind, and I really do appreciate it. This has been—"

"Hey," Beckett said, coming up to me. "Thought you said we weren't supposed to fraternize with the fans."

"Beckett," I warned.

"Just making sure you don't get into trouble." He laughed, then went into the dugout.

"I'm sorry," she said. "We should probably let you get back to your work."

"It's fine," I replied. "He's just mad at me."

"Why?" Thomas asked.

"Long story, bud," I said. "Look forward to seeing you after the game."

"Same," she said.

"Hit a home run for me," Thomas said.

"I'm not starting today," I replied. "But, if I get in, I'll do my best."

"Yay." He jumped up and down, shouting.

"Play well," Lucy said.

"Thanks," I replied, then stepped into the dugout myself.

I'd barely made it into the locker room down the hallway before Beckett ambushed me.

"You're banging her," he said.

"The fuck?"

"I can see it," he gloated. "You talk all this good shit about being better than me, but you're out there banging bullpen bunnies just like I did. Not so professional now, are we?"

His taunting was not something I wanted to deal with, so I simply ignored him.

"Ha," he laughed. "I knew it. You sure talk a good game, but you're just as guilty as every other player."

"I am not doing anything of the sort," I said, although I knew that arguing would be futile.

"Leave him be," Cote said. "That's his sister."

"Dude," Beckett said, drawing the word out.

"Not funny, kid," I retorted, continuing to my locker.

"If it's your sister, maybe I should be the one banging her," he said.

"That's enough," Coach said, coming between my fist and the kid's face. "Beckett, get your shit together and get to the outfield station. J, chill."

I turned around and pulled my uniform out of the locker, bent on ignoring the kid for the remainder of the game if at all possible. Once he'd stepped away, I turned to the coach.

"Keep him away from me," I said. "He's gonna say something that will cross the line more than he already has, and I'm not going to be responsible for the outcome."

"I'll put Huffman on him," Coach said.

"That'll do," I replied, knowing he had less compassion and a much shorter fuse than I did. If the kid started to have a go at him, I wouldn't be surprised if Huffman knocked him out with one blow.

CHAPTER TWENTY-ONE

*L*ucy...

The number of games I'd been to in my life, between coming as a kid with my dad, and continuing the tradition with Ryan, I'd never made it to an opening day. I mean, I'd seen it all on television, but it was something altogether different in person. They rolled an actual red carpet out from the centerfield fence to the infield, and they introduced everyone. First, the coaching staff, then the players who weren't starting, and finally the starters. Both teams were introduced, which I thought was a classy thing to do.

Of course, Thomas cheered as loud as he could the whole time, but especially when they introduced Jonathan. Rayne seemed to finally get a little more into it once things started moving along, but she was much more subdued. Dad looked as if he were in heaven, sitting at the other end of my family, cheering for the players as if he were as young as them.

When the game finally started, after all the pomp and circumstance, it moved along at a quick pace, neither team getting any player on base during the first several innings. Rayne began to complain that it was boring, but my dad, somehow, taught her how to keep score on the scorecard we'd gotten with the program we purchased before the game.

He was showing her meticulously how to tally each at bat, what the players did when they hit the ball, and how the out was made. He'd shown me when I was younger, but I never quite caught on. Rayne seemed to be very interested in it, though, and was paying close attention to the game.

By the time the seventh inning stretch came around, I was ready to move my body. They'd only been playing for a couple of hours by that time, but as baseball games went, it was pretty fast. In the bottom of the inning, our leadoff batter, the second baseman, was up to bat first and he swung at the very first pitch they threw at him, hitting it high and deep and over the fence on our side of the field.

The stadium erupted with cheers, my family included. We watched as the player went around the bases, pumping his fist in the air the whole way. It was as if it were the game winner, but we still had a few innings left to play.

"Mom," Thomas shouted. "Did you see that?"

"I sure did," I shouted back to him.

The rest of the game was mostly like the first part, with no one getting on base, and the players just getting out each time at bat. When the top of the ninth inning came around, everyone in the stands were on their feet. Thomas wasn't happy that they didn't bring the Guardian in to finish the game, but he was happy they won.

After everyone was done cheering, the stands started to empty. We stayed in our seats, hanging out, waiting for the rush to thin out. It was something that my dad always did. He said it was better to sit in the stands than sit in the car wasting gas, and I had to agree. By the time the space cleared out some, we were able to move toward the field where we were going to meet up with Jonathan.

"There he is," Thomas said as we got closer to the field.

"Hey, guys," Jonathan said.

"That was awesome," Thomas shouted. "This is Gramps."

"Pleasure to meet you," Jonathan said, sticking his empty hand out to shake my dad's. "Rayne," he said, nodding at my daughter, who promptly folded her arms over her chest. It had become her stance of choice, lately. "I got a few things for you guys," Jonathan continued, holding out a couple of bags to the kids.

"Thanks," Thomas said, looking into his bag.

I bumped Rayne's shoulder after she stood there a while, until she finally said, "Thanks," as well.

"I didn't see you out there," my dad said.

"That's one of the drawbacks of being a utility player," Jonathan replied. "Not a ton of time on the field in the early games, especially when the team is playing like they did today."

"It was a really good game," I said.

"Here," he said, passing me an envelope.

"Thanks," I replied, tucking it into my purse that was slung over my shoulder.

"Well," he said. "I gotta get in and shower. Hope you guys enjoy your stuff."

"Thank you again," I said.

"Absolutely," he replied, then turned and headed down into the dugout.

"Mom, look," Thomas said, pulling a bobble head from his bag.

"Let's leave it all in the bag," I suggested. "At least until we get to the car. Don't want to lose anything."

"Oh, right," he said, stuffing it back into the bag.

"Looks like we should be able to get out of the garage pretty quickly, now," Dad said.

"I hope so," I replied. "I'm just glad we're staying downtown. I hate fighting traffic back to the house after games."

While the walk to the garage was fairly quick, there were still several cars in the lot lined up to get onto the freeways, so we did have to sit and wait. Once we were out of the garage and onto the side streets of the city, it was less crowded.

"That was the player you met yesterday?" Dad asked when we were on the street.

"Yeah," I said. "He's the one who got us into the club area and got us in early."

"He seems like a nice kid," Dad said.

"I don't think he qualifies as a kid," I replied. "He's probably my age."

"You're still my kid," Dad retorted. "I can call him a kid, too."

"Sure, Dad," I said. "Whatever makes you happy."

We drove in silence to the hotel, where my dad dropped us off with the kids and their bags of goodies from the game. We all hugged him goodbye, then headed up to our room. By the time I got the kids settled in to sleep, I was wound up again, so decided I'd see if I could read a little. Then I remembered the envelope that Jonathan gave me. I rummaged through my purse and found it, taking it back to bed with me, along with my book that was in my suitcase.

I wasn't sure what to expect when I pulled a folded note out of the envelope with my name neatly printed on the outside.

Lucy,

I was pleased to meet you and your family yesterday. Your son was such a breath of fresh air with his enthusiasm for his favorite player, as well as his obvious love of the game. I hope that the gifts I found for them weren't out of line. I just wanted to ensure they had something to remember today with in a tangible way. Your son mentioned that your husband passed away. I am so sorry for your loss. I hope that my asking him about his father didn't cause him any additional grief. Please accept my apology if it did.

I recently lost my wife, so I understand some of the struggles you're facing and know that mentions of the lost family member can bring up many difficult memories. I would love to meet up with you and talk about the common thing we share and learn what you have done to move forward. This is probably not something you expected, so I completely understand if you're hesitant. Maybe we could meet for lunch or dinner some time and see how we can help each other move forward through the journey we're both facing. If you're not comfortable with this, I completely understand, and will not at all take it personally. If you are at all interested in comparing notes, so to speak, I

*would be very happy to talk with you. Again, there is no pres-
sure for you to say yes. I just want you to know that I'm here
and available if you are interested. You have my phone number,
but in case you have deleted it, I have put it on this note. I look
forward to hearing from you if you're interested.*
Sincerely yours,
Jonathan Bridge

I blinked, sniffed, and wiped tears from my eyes. No one had ever offered something as sweet as this man was doing, and we had just barely met. I reread the note several times, wanting to see if there was anything in it that felt out of bounds or like it was a pressure kind of thing, but nothing stood out. The only thing that was clear was that this kind man was willing to get together and talk about our mutual grief and how we were dealing with it.

In a spur-of-the-moment decision, I picked up my phone and shot off a text. There was likely no way he would respond tonight, with as late as it was, but I wanted it to be there when he woke up. I wanted him to know that I was interested in getting together to discuss this horrible thing we shared. I was surprised when my phone indicated a response.

**Whatever works for your schedule will likely work for mine, as
long as it isn't during a game, or while I'm out of town.**

I looked at the response, then realized that I should probably have checked to see what the schedule for the team was. Instead, I simply offered an option. I was going to be staying in town through Monday, even though the kids would be going back to my parents on Sunday after the game for school next week. I had a meeting with the bureau Monday morning, but it was late enough that a late dinner would definitely be doable.

**Would Sunday after the game work? I'm in town until Monday,
with the kids going to my parents on Sunday evening.**

I waited, wondering whether he'd respond, but then saw the little dots at the bottom of the message thread indicating he was typing an answer.

Sunday works great. Game will probably be over around 5, so with travel and such, we could do dinner say, 7 or so? Is that too late for you?

While that was later than I normally did dinner, it wasn't so late that it would be awful. I responded that it would work fine, and asked whether he had a place in mind, or if he would like me to find somewhere.

If you like Italian, I have a place in mind. It's called Zoppa's, and it's on the northern end of Seattle.

I hadn't heard of the place but did a quick search on my phone and found it right away. It looked like a quaint little mom-and-pop-type of restaurant, which I loved going to. After reading their menu online, it looked like it would be a delightful place to meet.

That looks like a wonderful place. I'll meet you there at 7 on Sunday.

With that set up, I put a reminder into my phone, with the address so I could get directions when the time came as well. My phone buzzed with an incoming text, so I opened it.

Perfect. Olissio and Adriana are wonderful people. I'm sure you will enjoy their food. I'll make a reservation for us.

That was unexpected. I didn't realize that he knew the owners, who were listed on their website. It made me wonder how often he went there.

Great, thanks.

I plugged my phone into the charger on the nightstand between my bed and the one the kids shared, then pulled out my book. Flipping it open to the bookmark, I started reading, hoping that something would help me sleep tonight.

CHAPTER TWENTY-TWO

*J*onathan...

"Hey," Kate said as I walked in the door.

"Hey, yourself," I replied.

"Sorry we had to leave early," she said. "Grant was being a cranky kiddo, and I didn't want to have to worry about him not sleeping tonight."

"No problem," I said, dropping my keys in the dish by the door. "When did you go?"

"Beginning of the fifth," she said. "You guys won, though. Got to watch the rest of the game once we got home."

"Oh yeah," I said, hanging my coat in the closet. "Mickey hit a bomb in the bottom of the seventh. Only hit tonight off their starter."

"What's the deal with starters going all the way in game one?" she asked.

"Yeah," I said. "Not normal for game one, but we'll take it. Normally we're lucky to get six or seven, but Sammy was killing it and I think Coach felt like it would be a disservice to him to pull him, even for Strawberry."

"Why do you call him that?" she asked. "Isn't his nickname the Guardian or something?"

"Something." I laughed. "His name actually has both meanings. Someone found out that the female meaning for Ichigo is strawberry, while the male is guardian. We decided to start calling him Strawberry for fun and he loved it. Not sure why, but he's super laid-back and willing to go with the flow, so it's nice."

"You guys are awful," she said, though she was laughing.

"I mean," I began. "We're all assholes, so it shouldn't surprise you."

"But you could be nicer," she insisted. "He's not even from here, so you shouldn't screw with him like that."

"Are you kidding?" I asked, plopping on the other end of the sofa. "That dude is the biggest prankster in the clubhouse. He will do damn near anything to get a laugh, sometimes."

"Still," she insisted. "You could be nice sometimes."

"Oh, we are," I said. "It's just fun to screw with him. It's sort of like when I would do things that would annoy you growing up. Same kind of thing. We're a brotherhood, sort of, as messed up as it is."

"Except," she began, "you'd stick up for me and fight anyone else screwing with me."

"True," I replied. "But we'd do the same for him. If it was another team that was screwing with him, we'd clear the benches. We can mess with him, but no one else can."

"I mean…" she shrugged.

"So," I said. "What was up with Grant tonight? He seemed fine when I left."

"Mom said she thinks he's teething," she explained. "Said this was about the time you started with your two-year molars, so Grant is probably following suit."

"Poor little guy," I said. "Did I have anything to give him for it?"

"I did," she said. "Mom packed some baby Tylenol and that numbing stuff to put on his gums. Worked like a charm for a while, but then he was cranky once we were in the stands. I didn't want him to get too worked up, so decided to pack it in and bring him home."

"Good call," I said.

"Yeah," she replied. "He ate a big dinner when we got home, even after snacking like crazy at the field. I think he's gonna have a growth spurt."

"You sure you don't want to just move up here and stay with us?" I asked.

"Not giving up my life," she said. "Besides, you're gone half the year anyway."

"I know," I replied. "I've been thinking about it a lot, lately, especially with you guys up here. Wondering whether I made the right decision to come back to the team."

"Stop it," she barked. "You are not going to give up everything you dreamed of just so you can be a stay-at-home dad. I know you're hurting, and that you miss Grant when you're not around, but this is not going to help anything. Besides," she added. "Mom is loving the whole being a gramma and spoiling him."

"I just wish I could keep him here," I said. "I know it's the right thing for him, but it is so hard to not have anyone. I feel so alone."

"I'm sorry," she said, reaching her hand out to me. "I wish I could stay up here, do the whole nanny thing and all, but I have a life I worked hard for down in Rosedale, and I don't want to give it up."

"And it's selfish of me to try to make you," I agreed. "Why does life have to be so hard?"

"Because it sucks," she said. "There isn't any rhyme or reason behind it. Have you gone to any support group meetings?"

"I don't have time," I said. "I've gone to the team shrink, and he's given me some good things to do when I start to spin out of control, but it's just not easy sometimes."

"You ever start to feel like you can't handle it, I want you to call me," she said. "Day or night, I don't care. I know it's hard for you to reach out, but I need to know that you're gonna look out for yourself. Grant can't lose both parents."

"It's not like that," I countered. "I just sometimes wonder what I could do to make this more bearable. I suppose I could hire a nanny and keep him here, but that feels wrong."

"Mom would kill you." She laughed, lightening the mood some. "Seriously, though, she would much rather him stay with her than have him raised by a stranger. Your schedule doesn't allow for that kind of thing."

Just then, Grant started crying, hard. I was up and in his room before I even registered I needed to move.

"Hey, buddy," I cooed, picking him up. "What's wrong?"

He just sobbed, hugging my neck hard. I rubbed his back, whispering that it was all going to be okay while silently cursing myself for thinking of doing anything other than what was best for my boy. I just had to figure out what that was, and how it looked in my life.

CHAPTER TWENTY-THREE

*L*ucy...

"Bye, Mom," Thomas said with a hug.

"Yeah," Rayne said with her own hug. "Have fun tomorrow."

"It's a meeting," I said. "Nothing fun about it."

"If you need anything, you just give us a shout and we'll be happy to help," my dad said after hugging me, too.

"Thanks, Dad," I said. "Shouldn't be a problem, but I really appreciate you and Mom taking the kids for the night."

"We love having them," he said as they got their things to head out the door. "You just relax tonight, deal with the bureau tomorrow, then come home after that."

"I will," I replied.

I hadn't told them I was going out to eat with Jonathan. I didn't want to give Rayne anything else to be mad about. Once they were out the door, I jumped in the shower to clean up. It wasn't a date, that was for sure, but it would be rude to smell like the ballpark in a nicer restaurant. By the time I'd finished my shower and found something to wear, it was later than I wanted, so I grabbed my keys, phone, and purse, and headed out the door.

The drive was uneventful, and I actually arrived earlier than my navigation said. I parked my car near the door and climbed out. Walking into the restaurant, I noticed how small and intimate it was. While that would normally not be an issue for me, it felt a little bit awkward for the type of meeting we were having.

"You must be Lucy," a woman said when I stepped inside. "Jonathan said you should be here shortly. He's waiting for you over here."

I followed her through a handful of other patrons to a back table where Jonathan was seated. He stood and pulled a chair across from him out, allowing me to sit down before pushing the chair in.

"Thank you," I said.

"Of course," he said.

"Shall I bring you some wine?" the woman asked.

"None for me," I said.

"Just water for tonight, Adriana," Jonathan said. "If you can give us a minute, we'll be ready to order."

"No rush," she said, moving away from our table to stop and talk with other customers.

"This place is so tiny," I commented.

"But the food is to die for," he replied. "Meg found this place when we first moved up here, and it really has been the best place for quiet dinners. Keeps us away from the fans in downtown."

"I bet you get a lot of folks coming up to you," I said.

"Sometimes," he replied. "Most are harmless, but there is always that one that just doesn't understand that we're people with private lives, too."

"So," I said, changing the subject and picking up the menu that was on the table. "What's good here?"

"Everything," he replied. "Seriously. I don't think I've ever had anything that wasn't absolutely perfect."

"That's a glowing report." I laughed. "Let me see, what do I feel like tonight?"

"Make sure you leave room for dessert," he said. "They make the best cannoli's in town."

"Good to know," I said.

It didn't take long to find exactly what I was looking for. Manicotti with an Alfredo sauce was my all-time favorite Italian dish, and they actually had it without having to do the special request to change the sauce.

"That smile tells me you found what you wanted," he said.

"Sure did," I said, setting the menu on the table.

"Looks like you're ready," the woman who had seated us said, appearing out of nowhere.

"Ladies first," Jonathan said, holding his hand out to indicate that I should order.

"I'll have the Manicotti with Alfredo," I ordered.

"Soup or salad?" the woman asked.

"Oh," I said, not realizing that was part of the meal. "Do you have minestrone soup?"

"Only the best in town," Jonathan said. "Just like everything else here."

"Jonathan," the woman said. "You compliment too much."

"It's true," he said. "Honestly, I haven't had any better Italian food anywhere on the road, either. I think you've spoiled me."

"You deserve it," she replied, and she was blushing. "You want your usual?"

"You know it," he said.

She walked away, and I looked at the man across the table from me.

"What?" he asked.

"Sorry," I said. "I just... I don't know. That was one of the kindest things I've ever seen, the way you complimented her and her restaurant."

"I've been doing this baseball thing a long time," he said. "I've been to so many food places that I know what's good and what isn't, and this is the best food I've ever had. Hands down."

"I'd think you would have eaten at five-star restaurants all over," I said.

"I have," he replied. "Still, this is the best. I would eat here every day if I could."

The woman returned with our soup, along with a basket of breadsticks, and our water.

"If you need anything, just give a holler," she said. "I'll be back soon with your food."

"Cheers," Jonathan said, holding up his water glass.

"You know it's bad luck to toast with water, right?" I asked him.

"Really?"

"Something Ryan said all the time," I explained. "You can toast with anything, as long as it isn't water. Not sure why, can't remember, but it was something he always said."

"Guess we'll have to toast with our soup, then."

"Absolutely," I replied, taking my spoon, and filling it just a little bit, then holding it out to him.

He did the same, then we tapped our spoons and put them in our mouths.

"Oh, man," I said. "This is so good."

"Told you," he replied.

The conversation lagged as we enjoyed our soup, and before we were even finished, Adriana was back with the main course. Swapping our soup bowls out for the plates with our meals, we continued to enjoy the quiet company and good food.

"How long?"

"I'm sorry, what?" I asked.

"Since your husband died?" he asked.

"September," I said.

"Really?"

"Yeah," I replied. "How about you?"

"September as well," he said. "But it seems like it's been forever since I held her."

"It does," I said. "I heard it gets better, though."

"I don't know how," he confessed. "Every day seems to be harder than the last. Like, how can I continue on without her. She was my better half, and I don't say that lightly."

"Maybe it just gets easier to hide the pain," I said. "From others, but also from ourselves."

"But we shouldn't have to," he countered.

"No," I said. "We really shouldn't have to. Then again, we do have others we have to think of as well. My kids can't see that I am so broken I don't want to get up in the morning."

"I'm fortunate that I don't have to try to hide that from my son," he said.

"Why's that?"

"He's staying with my mom right now," he replied. "She watched him the tail end of last season, then jumped at the chance to keep him during this season. I was honestly thinking I'd take a year off."

"Why didn't you?"

"I need the distraction," he said. "Keeps me from absolutely losing my mind."

"Being alone," I began, then had to stop and swallow. I took a sip of my water before beginning again. "It's hard to do. I don't have a job I go to, nothing to distract me from the fact that I still have a closet full of clothes I need to go through. There's an office in my house that I haven't been in since he died. I know I should be going through those things, but I just can't make myself do it."

"Afraid if you do," he began, "that means he's really gone?"

"Exactly," I replied. "If his stuff is still there, then there's a slight possibility that he might come home. That this could all just be a nightmare that I'll wake up from."

"Except it's not," he said.

We'd both put our forks down, hadn't continued to eat, and somehow we'd reached across the small table between us and grasped hands. I looked down, my left hand grasped by his right, and just stared.

"Sorry," he said, moving to pull his hand away.

"It's fine," I said, gripping it tighter. "I think we both could use some comfort right about now."

He raised his eyes to look at me and I was struck with how familiar they were. It was as if I'd seen them a hundred times before, except we'd just met.

"What?" he asked.

"You just look familiar," I said. "Probably because you've been with the Cascades for years and I somehow remember seeing you on TV."

"That's probably it," he agreed, but there was an edge to the way he'd said it, like he didn't believe that for some reason.

We stayed like that, our hands clasped and looking at each other, for what seemed to be an eternity before the waitress came back to ask if we were finished. I'd lost my appetite somewhere in there, so said I was done. I didn't have a way to take the leftovers home. Honestly, I wish I could have. Jonathan was right that it was the best food to find here in the city.

"I should go," I said once she was gone.

"Why?"

"Got an early meeting in the morning," I lied easily. "Need to be sure I'm up for it."

"Let me at least walk you out," he offered, standing with me. "I wouldn't feel right if I let you go out there alone."

"Thank you," I said, picking up my purse from the back of the chair.

He'd dropped a couple of hundred-dollar bills on the table without even seeing the check, and I was a bit surprised.

"Tips are important," he said quietly when he saw me looking.

I simply nodded, not trusting my voice. The last few minutes had made me uncomfortable, but in a strange way. I didn't have a problem with Jonathan, though. In fact, the exact opposite was the case. I felt entirely too comfortable with him, and that made me uneasy.

CHAPTER TWENTY-FOUR

*J*onathan...
"Thank you again," I said as she got into her car.

I waited until she locked her doors and started it up before I walked across the parking lot to where my car was, opening the door and climbing in. I took a deep breath and let out a huge sigh. Something happened in that restaurant, and I wasn't sure what it was, or whether it was a good thing or not, but I didn't really want to analyze it too much.

The short drive home to my condo was quick, and by the time I was opening my door, I was doing the thing I didn't want to do.

"What am I doing?" I asked the empty space.

I didn't expect an answer, and probably would have jumped sky high if there had been one. Honestly, I wasn't sure exactly what happened in that restaurant, but there was some sort of connection between Lucy and me, and I wasn't sure it was a bad thing.

Since I'd already showered at the park, I didn't need to do any of that before heading to bed. Lying there, I ran over what had happened in the last couple of hours. Dinner was going well until I asked her how long she'd been without her husband. That was the catalyst to the conversation that led to us holding hands in mutual support. For me it was a little different, in that I had already cleaned out most of Meg's things, especially her personal things. I couldn't handle them being here. Even the photos were sometimes too much, but I knew I needed them around, especially when family came up.

The flood of memories from that day six months earlier were thrust upon me and I was overcome with all the emotions. Some of them I knew were there, just under the surface, waiting for a chance to be released. Others were newer, and very strange. I didn't want to look too closely at them for fear of what they would reveal. Instead of trying to fight it, I let my emotions take over completely, allowing myself to actually feel all the things I didn't want to feel. The horror at the fact that my beautiful wife was gone, that my son would never really remember her at all, and that nothing I could ever do would bring her back.

Giving in to them, I sobbed. For all the things I'd lost. The future that was supposed to be assured to me. My daughter that I would never get a chance to meet in this lifetime. The mother of my son, who would grow up without her wonderful and caring love for him. Absolutely everything that was taken from me in a moment that couldn't be changed. If I could, I would reverse time and go with her to that appointment. Maybe, just maybe, I would have been the one to have died. I would be fine with that because it would mean that Grant would have a mother. That Grace would be here, living and thriving. But it wasn't meant to be, and that was the worst thing. They weren't meant to be here now, and I didn't know how to go on without them.

"You look like shit," Beckett said when I stumbled into the locker room.

"Feel about the same," I replied, tossing my stuff inside my space.

"What the hell did you get up to last night?"

"Bad dreams," I replied, not at all wanting to have a conversation with this kid about my life and the loss and the shit I was dealing with the night before.

"Should have found a woman to drown your sorrows in," he suggested.

"Shut up, Beckett," I replied, then walked away from him.

Whatever Coach was thinking, putting our lockers next to each other was a bad idea, and I was about to remedy it right now.

"Hey, J," Coach said when I walked up to his door.

"Something has to change," I said.

"What's up?"

"That kid or me," I said. "One of us has to move. I can't put up with his bullshit any longer."

"Damn," Coach said. "I was hoping your demeanor would rub off on him, not the other way around."

"Well," I said. "Something's about to rub off on him, and it's likely going to be my fist."

"Hold up," Coach said. "What is this really about?"

"What do you mean?"

"You've been rumbling around the locker room with a big-ass chip on your shoulder this year," he explained. "Now, I know you had a shit ending to the season last year, and that your family has been ripped up bad, but you were doing great during the spring. So, I ask again, what is this really all about?"

"Fuck," I said, running my hand down my face. Of all people, I figured my manager understood what had been going on with me the last six months.

"You need a day?" he asked.

"No," I said.

"You need to play?"

"Something," I replied.

"Ask Huffman if he's good with a day off," the coach offered.

"Outfield?" I asked.

"Can't put you at second," he said. "That's just too close for comfort when it comes to your other issue. You go see if Huffman is good with a day off. If he's fine with it, have him tell me and I'll put you in the lineup."

"You know he's gonna say no," I said.

141

"Just ask," he replied, then turned away from me as if the conversation was completely over.

I turned around and walked back to the main area in the locker room and right over to my friend.

"Coach said to ask if you're good with taking the night off," I said.

"You need to play?" he asked.

"Kinda," I replied.

"I'm good with it," he said, patting me on the shoulder.

Never, not once, had anyone asked another player to take a day off if they weren't hurt or struggling, especially in the first week of the season. Yet, here I was, asking for my friend to take the bench so I could work out my issues between the chalk lines. Fuck, I needed to make an appointment with the team shrink. There were some serious things going on inside me, and I really did need to get through them.

"Coach said you have to tell him," I said.

"No prob," he replied, making a beeline for the coach's office.

Meanwhile, I headed over to my locker to get into my warm-up gear and get out on the field. The sooner I got changed, the sooner I'd be away from the punk at the locker next to me.

"Seriously," he said when I got there. "You have got to do something. You're funking everyone's shui right now."

"You keep talking and your shui is gonna be the least of your worries," I said, then turned my back on him.

Get changed, get on the field, get into the cage, something had to be done, and I just had to work it out. Maybe beating the shit out of some balls in the batter's box would help. Yeah, that might be just what I needed.

CHAPTER TWENTY-FIVE

*L*ucy...

"Thank you for coming in, Mrs. Fallon," the agent said.

"You said it was important," I replied.

Ryan hand been retired for three years, but there were still a handful of cases that he was consulting on. They'd called to ask that I come in and discuss things, just to see if he'd left any information at the house before he died. He'd actually been in the office that morning, dropping a few things off.

"If you don't mind, I would appreciate it if you would go over the notes Ryan left." he said. "None of us can decipher them. We thought he may have had some sort of code or something, and you would likely be the only person who might know what it was."

"I don't know anything about a code," I said. "But I'm happy to look and see if I can make sense of them. But aren't they secret? Should I really be reading these notes?"

"We trust your discretion," the agent said. "Besides, they're just notes related to what he saw. None of that is admissible in court, just helpful for our other agents in the field."

"Okay," I replied.

The stack of papers they set in front of me in that office was massive. I swallowed my fear and dug into them. Seeing Ryan's handwriting triggered me more than I expected, and I found myself missing the little notes he would leave for me in the house. Always something silly or simple but left with love and devotion as well.

What I expected to take a couple of hours turned into nearly the whole day. They brought me some lunch, but otherwise left me to take notes on what they wanted to know about what he had written. By the time I was leaving, I was stuck in rush hour traffic trying to get home.

My phone rang on the way home but I ignored it. Nothing was worth answering a call while I was driving. It was something that Ryan had been insistent on, and something I agreed with wholeheartedly. He'd seen too many deaths related to people who couldn't be bothered to just leave the phone alone while on the road.

"Mom," Thomas shouted when I walked in the door.

"Hey," I said, giving him a hug.

"You're here," Mom said, coming from the kitchen. "Thomas, will you set the table, please? Rayne is finishing up her homework. Why don't you go unpack?"

"Thanks," I said, picking up my suitcase and taking it up to my room.

When I passed Rayne's door, she was sitting on her bed, reading.

"Hey," I said, poking my head in her door.

"Oh," she said, looking up from her book. "I didn't know you were home."

"Just got here," I said.

"How was today?"

"Hard," I admitted, stepping into her room. "Seeing your Dad's handwriting on all the notes was more than I could handle. I didn't think it would be that—"

"Emotional?" she asked.

"I guess that's the word I'm looking for," I said. "I'm gonna unpack. Grams has dinner almost done."

"Okay," she said, sticking a bookmark in her book and laying it on her bed.

I went to my room and wheeled my small bag into the closet.

Looking around, I realized that I should probably start removing some of Ryan's things from there. I didn't need them all, but I wasn't sure I was ready to be done with them, either. Nothing needed to happen today, though, so I simply stuffed the bag in there and figured I'd deal with it in the morning.

~

"YOU'RE SERIOUS," ANDREA SAID TO ME WHEN SHE STEPPED INTO MY closet the next morning.

"Absolutely," I replied.

Noah was in a playpen in my room with a handful of toys to keep him occupied while we took on the task that was Ryan's clothes.

"I figured starting here would be the least painful," I explained.

"For who?" she asked.

"I just need some help in figuring out what I should donate and what I should hold on to," I said. "I'm afraid to give any of it away."

"Let's start with his suits," she said, taking control.

Within a couple of hours, we had sorted through all of his clothes, putting them into categories that would be easier to manage. All of his suits were put into a big trunk I had in the attic and taken back up there. Eventually, I would have to make a decision about what to do with them, but for now they were safe up there. Dress shirts were in another box, while his ties were in a much smaller one. Underwear and socks were thrown out. No one wants used ones of those, so no need to do anything with them. We'd even checked with the homeless shelter in town and they told us they weren't able to take them, so out they went.

His t-shirts were another thing altogether. He had ones that he absolutely loved, and there was no way I was going to part with them. What I would do with them, I didn't know. I just wasn't ready to do anything, so another box was filled up and moved to the attic. By the time it was nap time for Noah, we'd done a ton of work and I felt like I had made much better progress than what I would have been able to do alone.

"Let me know if you want me to come over again," she said when she headed home.

"I will," I replied. "And thanks. You have no idea how much help this was."

Closing the door, I turned around and headed back upstairs. Between the physical effort of doing the sorting and moving, and the emotional impact of seeing how empty the closet was without Ryan's things, I was done for and thought I'd go ahead and take a nap myself before the kids got home from school.

When I stepped into my room, I could see that my phone was ringing, so I rushed to the nightstand to grab it before the call went to voicemail but was too late. When I opened the phone, I saw that Jonathan had been the one to call, so went to see if he left me a message. It took a couple of minutes, but it finally registered a message. Clicking play, I listened to his voice.

Lucy. It's Jonathan. Wondering whether you were open for lunch sometime this week. I know our dinner was a little awkward, but I would really like to meet up with you if you're willing. Give me a call if you want to. No pressure.

No pressure, he said. Except there was pressure. Meeting with someone and comparing notes was a good thing, especially with the fact that we'd both lost our spouses so recently. But was I ready to meet him? What if what I felt, he did, too? I was only six months out from losing my husband and here I was thinking about meeting up with another man. Except it wasn't really like that. Or maybe it was, and I just didn't realize it. Would meeting up with him disrespect Ryan? Would it make me a bad wife? I honestly didn't know what I should do, so I did the only thing I knew. I called my best friend to let her make this decision for me.

CHAPTER TWENTY-SIX

*J*onathan...

I disconnected the call and wondered whether what I just did was the right thing to do, or if I just made things more awkward between us. Honestly, either one of those things could be true. If she called me back, I would take it as a good sign. Unless, of course, she just called to yell at me and tell me how horrible I was. I didn't think that was the likely response, though.

Instead of waiting for a return call, I got on to the other things I had to do before heading out to the stadium. Yesterday had been rough, but somehow, being on the diamond helped. I made sure to thank Huffman for giving up his spot to let me deal with my own demons, and boy were they large and terrifying. The benefit was, we won, and I played as good as I ever had before.

Gathering up my laundry, I picked up my keys and phone and headed out to the dry cleaners. Meg had always done this for me and knew what could be just thrown into the washer and what had to actually be sent out for cleaning. I just didn't have time to deal with trying to figure it all out right now. On the road, it was simple. Throw everything into a bag and when we landed at a hotel, send it all out first thing. By the time we were ready to leave, we had everything back and ready for the next town. At home it was a different story. I didn't have a laundry service in my condo, so I had to actually take things out to the cleaners myself.

My phone rang just as I stepped into the elevator, but when I went to answer it, the service was gone, and so was the call. By the time I got to the garage and had service again, I had a voicemail. Dropping my clothes in the trunk, I climbed into the driver's seat and hooked my phone up to the sound system as soon as I'd started the car. When I pulled out of the garage, I had enough service to pick up the message.

Jonathan, it's Lucy. I'm not sure what you're wanting, but lunch would be good. I'm pretty open but have to do it in time to be home when the kids get home from school, so it would definitely have to be a lunch date. I mean, not a date, just... oh, never mind. Yes, I'll have lunch with you.

I hadn't thought about it as a date, but then again, maybe it was. No, I wasn't ready for that. Meg was still too fresh in my mind. It was just a meeting of two people who lost their partners, working out the difficulties that came along with that.

By the time I got to the cleaners, I wasn't sure what I wanted. Part of me wanted to move on, be with someone. But a bigger part of me couldn't do that to Meg, or Grant. No, I needed to make sure that Lucy knew this wasn't a date, just a meeting. After dropping off my laundry, I hopped back in my car and made the call back to Lucy.

"Hello?"

"Lucy?" I asked.

"Yeah," she said. "Sorry. I didn't see who was calling."

"That's fine," I said. "So, lunch. Are you available Friday?"

"I am," she said. "But, like I said, I have to be home in time to get the kids."

"What time is that?"

"I pick them up at three," she said. "So, if we're meeting in Seattle, I would need to leave by no later than two."

"If we met by noon, that should give you enough time, right?" I suggested.

"Oh, for sure," she said. "You want to meet in Seattle?"

"If that works for you," I said. "I don't want to put too much pressure on you or make it more difficult for you."

"It's fine," she said. "Do you have a place in mind?"

"Nothing fancy," I said. "Unless that's what you want."

"No, no," she said. "I'm all about casual."

"There's a place in the market that sells crepes," I offered.

"We love that place," she said. "But I won't be able to tell Rayne we went there. She'll get so jealous."

"Great," I said. "Meet you then."

"Absolutely," she said. "My treat this time."

"I feel a little weird about you paying," I confessed. "Just doesn't feel right."

"And if I insist?"

"I guess I shouldn't argue," I said. "But it still doesn't feel right."

"Well," she said. "You're just gonna have to get over yourself, then."

"I suppose," I said. "See you then."

"See you then," she said, then disconnected the call.

This is not a date.

No matter how many ways I said it, though, it felt like one, and I wasn't sure whether it was a good thing or a bad thing. I started my car and headed back to my condo, pondering the date, or non-date, that was happening in just a few days. When I finally got back into my condo, I decided I needed another mind to ponder this, so I called my mom.

"Hey," she said when she answered the phone. "This is a delightful surprise. Grant just went down for a nap, though, so I'm afraid you won't be able to talk to him."

"That's okay," I replied. "I actually wanted to get your opinion on something."

"You are not going to retire," she said. "That is not going to fix anything."

"That's actually not what I was calling about." I laughed. "But, good to know where you stand on that issue."

"As long as we're clear," she said, and her lighthearted nature was back in her voice. "What's troubling you?"

"I met someone," I began.

"Jonathan," she chided, but I interrupted her.

"It's not like that," I explained. "There was a woman at the field the day before opening day with her kids. Turns out her husband died recently, and we struck up a conversation."

"I thought there was a rule about interacting with the fans," she said.

"There is," I confirmed. "But this is something different. We went out to dinner on Sunday night after the game. It was going fine, just kind of talking around the subject, until I asked her how long ago she lost her husband."

"What did she say?"

"September," I offered. "Same as Meg. It got awkward after that, though, so I called and asked if she wanted to maybe do lunch this week to talk about how we're both coping with the losses."

"That's not a bad idea," Mom said. "But you should really be talking to your psychiatrist about this."

"Mom," I said. "I've talked 'til I'm blue in the face to shrinks. I need to talk to someone who is exactly where I am right now. I really think that Lucy and I can help each other heal from our losses. Whatever that looks like."

"Sounds like you've already made up your mind," Mom said.

"I just wanted to know what you thought," I said. "I'm not dating her, just having lunch and talking about our lives and what they look like now."

"If you think it will help, then I don't see the harm in it," she said. "But," she added, pausing to make sure I was listening. "If this becomes something that is no longer comfortable for either of you, I need to know you're going to be brave enough to walk away."

"Are you planning a wedding already?"

"No," she said with all sincerity. "I just know how hurt you are, and all the things you've gone through. I don't want someone else to do that to you. I don't know this woman, so I can't say whether she would be that way, but you should be careful. Fans can say and do crazy things just to get with a player."

"Don't I know it," I said. "But Lucy isn't like that. In fact, she isn't the one who told me her husband died. Her son did."

"She has kids?"

"Two," I said. "Rayne is a teenager, I think, and Thomas looks like he's about eight, but sounds older, so who knows."

"And you feel comfortable with her," she said. It could have been a question, but it sounded like she was just confirming what I felt. "I don't want you hurt. I especially don't want Grant to get comfortable with someone only for them to walk away from him. He's already lost one mother."

"Mom," I said. "We're just talking about loss. We're not dating. Not getting married. And I won't introduce anyone to Grant until I'm really sure."

"Good," she said.

"Thanks for listening," I said.

"Anytime," she replied. "Talk to you soon."

"Soon," I said. "Bye."

After disconnecting the call, I felt better in some ways, but more unsure in others. Was Lucy trying to use me? I didn't think so, but after talking to Mom, I just wasn't sure. I guess Friday would be when I would get some answers.

CHAPTER TWENTY-SEVEN

*L*ucy...

"Come on, Lucy, get it together."

I was standing in my closet in my bra and panties, trying to figure out what I should wear to lunch. It was casual, so definitely not anything dressy. But it was with someone who was somewhat famous, so he might be embarrassed if I wore something sloppy. Ugh, this was insane.

Grabbing a pair of jeans and one of my t-shirts with the Rolling Stones logo on it, I finally got ready to go into Seattle. Parking was going to be a nightmare, but maybe there would be something in the garage by the market. As luck would have it, I found a spot near one of the elevators in the garage. Picking up my purse, I went to the elevator and rode it down a couple of floors to the skybridge access to the market.

While it was still early, I didn't want to be late, so headed straight to the crepe shop. There was already a line forming, so I decided to stand there and wait, hoping Jonathan would show up before it came time to order. Sure enough, he stepped up to me and said hello.

"Thought I'd get here early," I said. "Sometimes lunch can be complicated at these restaurants in the market."

"That was my thought," he said. "Glad we were both on the same thought pattern."

"I figured if you weren't here, I'd just let folks go until you arrived," I explained.

"Solid plan," he replied. "So, sweet or savory?"

"Starting with savory," I began. "But getting sweet for dessert."

"Same," he said as we moved forward in line.

The wait was short, and when we got to the front, we quickly ordered, then found a spot to sit and wait for our food.

"It's way more crowded than I thought," he said.

"You should see it on a Saturday," I countered. "This is pretty tame."

"We'd always come earlier in the day," he said. "Guess that lunch rush really is a thing."

"Oh yeah," I said. "It's usually pretty full here, but lunch and dinner times are the worst times to try to get in. I've had to stand in line for almost an hour before."

"These are good," he said. "But I don't know about waiting that long."

"Which is why we usually come either earlier in the morning," I began. "Or midafternoon."

"Lucy," the guy at the counter said, and Jonathan got up before I could to grab our crepes.

"Thanks," I said when he came back.

I looked at him and he looked at me and then he said, "Dig in."

Doing exactly that, I took a bite of my savory crepe, reveling in the rich flavors within. We ate in comfortable silence, each enjoying our own concoction of meats, veggies, and cheeses. When we'd finished those, we dug into our desserts.

"This is really good," he said.

"Probably my favorite place to eat in Seattle," I replied.

"I can see why," he said.

We sat, letting our sweetness digest, both of us not wanting to dive into heavier subjects. Finally, I decided to address the elephant in the room.

"Let's talk about how we're doing," I suggested. "What we've done to move away from the dependency of grief."

"You sound like the team shrink," he said.

"I've done therapy," I explained. "More than I probably should have."

"The guy I talk to said that you need it until you don't," he said. "So, my guess is that if you're still going, you still need it."

"I guess," I said. "But I feel like if we talk about it, we understand what others don't. It's that been there, done that, kind of thing."

"Except I wouldn't want anyone to have been there," he said.

"Me, either," I replied. "Not even my worst enemy."

"There are days I'm not sure I'll ever get over her," he said. "Like I shouldn't be here anymore because she isn't."

"And yet," I offered. "The kids need us. They need us to remember when they can't."

"But also, to give them new memories," he said. "Things that they will remember that aren't all about the missing parent. It's important to remind them that life moves on."

"I just wish it didn't move on so quickly," I said. "Or without regard to our readiness of it. I just don't feel like we should have to rush ahead when we need to sit and think."

"I'm always wondering whether the rest of the world sees how dark it is without Meg," he said.

"Sounds like she was the light of your life," I said.

"Everything she touched made the world a better place," he said. "My life was so boring before I met her. Nothing she ever did was easy, or simple, but she made it look effortless."

"Where did you meet?"

"School," he said. "We were in the same classes, but she was so far ahead of me it wasn't fair. The woman was brilliant, and I'm not just saying that. She got a full-ride scholarship to come out here from Tennessee, otherwise we'd never have met."

"Full ride?" I asked. "That's impressive."

"Oh yeah," he said. "She was more than smart, she was brilliant. I kind of felt bad when we got married, and she wanted to stay home instead of going to work. Not that I minded, but I felt like she was giving up so much potential."

I watched as his face lit up while he talked about his wife. Everything he said made him glow even more, and it was an amazing thing to watch.

"What?" he asked, and I realized I'd been staring at him.

"Sorry," I apologized. "Just watching you talk about her, it's a beautiful thing."

"I'm sorry," he said. "I shouldn't keep going on and on about her."

"No," I argued. "That's the way we keep them alive. We talk about them, remember them, tell people who never met them who they were."

"I guess you're right," he agreed. "I hadn't thought about it like that, but it totally makes sense."

"She sounds like someone I would have loved to know," I said.

"She always said that strangers were just friends you hadn't met, yet," he said.

"I really like that sentiment," I replied. "Seems like she was right, at least about us. Seems like we've figured out a friendship."

"Yeah," he agreed. "I guess we have, haven't we?"

"I think so," I said.

I pushed my hair behind my ear and he took notice of my wedding set.

"You still wear it?"

"Yeah," I said. "I have his ring, too."

I pulled the necklace that had his ring on it from beneath my shirt to show him.

"I wish I would have thought of that," he said. "Grant would probably want to use that to propose at some point."

"You probably didn't think about it," I suggested. "Ryan and I talked about it a lot before he retired."

"Was he significantly older than you?" he asked. "Because you don't look old enough to retire."

"He was a few years older than me," I said. "But he didn't retire fully, just from the bureau."

"The what?"

"Sorry," I said. "The FBI. I've just always called it the bureau because that's what he called it."

"He was an agent?" he asked. "That's actually kind of cool."

"Not in the field," I replied. "It was mostly an office job, which is pretty boring. Reports and analysis and spreadsheets and the like. Forensic work is not glamorous, despite what you see on television."

"Makes sense," he said. "It's like baseball. It's not all glitz and glamour. Mostly working out, staying strong, lots of time watching film and working with the coaches to get the best out of what you have."

"I imagine there's a lot of work that goes on that most people don't know about," I said. "Probably like any job, I guess."

"Probably," he agreed. "So, how did you two meet?"

"He would come into the coffee shop I worked at when I was in school," I said. "He was there every morning, then started coming in at lunch, too. Finally, one day, I asked him if he wanted to go out to eat or something. He asked about getting coffee and was surprised when I told him I didn't drink it."

"You're from Seattle and you don't drink coffee?"

"Nope," I replied, popping the p at the end. "It does crazy stuff to my body, and I have learned that it's not worth any benefit I might get from the caffeine."

"Makes sense," he said. "I would drink it all the time if it didn't affect my sleep pattern, not that I have one, mind you."

"Yeah," I said. "You work some really weird hours."

"Days, nights, mornings," he said. "Honestly, it's surprising that I get any sleep at all."

"I figured the physicality of the job would help with that," I said. "I know that when I run, I sleep better, so figured that you do a lot physically for your job, so it must help you sleep."

"Once we get into the season, then the patterns start to work out," he explained. "Spring training can mess with it, though, because we have so many games, with split squads and such, and at all times of the day. Rarely do we have night games during the spring, so once the season gets into full swing, mostly we're playing at night. Add in the travel and changes in time zones and it gets all kinds of messed up."

"I didn't even think about the time zone thing," I confessed. "I bet that makes it even harder."

"Especially with a day game on the East Coast after a night game out west." He laughed. "Don't even get me started on the fact that a game that starts at one on the East Coast is a ten in the morning game for us."

"That sounds brutal," I agreed.

"But," he said. "We were supposed to be talking about you."

"A subject I am all too familiar with and don't particularly like to share," I said.

"Interesting to me," he said. "You are quite the woman."

"Thanks," I said, looking down.

"Don't be embarrassed," he insisted. "You are fascinating in that we're both at a similar place in our lives."

"I guess," I said.

"Seriously," he continued. "I could learn a lot from you. The way you have handled being a single parent is better than me, that's for sure."

"Rayne would disagree." I laughed. "She thinks I've done everything wrong."

"Don't believe it," he urged. "You inspire me."

I looked at him and it took me a minute to realize that he wasn't kidding, that he truly felt inspired by me. Whatever I had done to give him the impression I was an inspiration, I couldn't say, but it was nice to see that in his eyes.

CHAPTER TWENTY-EIGHT

*J*onathan...

She was staring into my eyes, and I was both happy and nervous. Lunch had been good, the conversation better, and now we were just sitting there, staring at each other.

"Are you sure we haven't met before?" she asked.

It was a question she'd asked before, and now that we were sitting so close, I felt she might be right.

"I don't remember meeting you," I said. "But then again, I meet hundreds of people all the time, so it is possible."

"Not like at a game or anything," she said. "More like something outside of baseball. I can't quite put my finger on it, but I swear I've met you, and even talked with you before."

"I'm not saying it's impossible," I said. "But I think I'd remember you."

"Out of the hundreds of people you meet on a regular basis, you think you'd remember me," she said. "Why's that?"

"For starters, you're beautiful," I said and watched her face pink with embarrassment. "Don't doubt it," I continued. "You are quite stunning."

"Now you've pushed into fantasy." She laughed. "Pretty I can see.

Even beautiful is pushing it, but stunning is so far out of my looks that it's just not possible."

"I'm serious," I said, and I was. "Even now, with little makeup and in jeans and a shirt, you're gorgeous."

"Stop," she insisted. "You're embarrassing me, and yourself."

"I'm not embarrassed," I said. "I have no issue with calling someone exactly what they are, and you are absolutely beautiful."

She looked me in the eye, and I tried to put everything I was feeling into the responding look. Whoever had made her feel less than beautiful ought to be ashamed, and if it was her husband, then it's probably good he isn't here to continue to make her doubt.

"You really mean it," she finally said.

"Sure do," I said.

It took her a minute, but she finally realized that I was telling her the truth.

"Thank you."

"You are more than welcome," I said.

We sat there, the market bustling around us, but in our own little world, just the two of us. While I didn't want to break the spell we'd woven around us, I knew she had to get back home to pick up her kids.

"You coming to the game tonight?" I asked.

"Yeah," she said. "Ryan got season tickets, so we can go to all the games. I know we can't actually do that, so I've been selling off the ones we can't use. Weekends are definitely doable, though. Not sure who all will be with me, but I know Thomas wants to come. He was so happy with that little bag of goodies you gave him last weekend. Thank you, by the way for that. It was very thoughtful."

"I'm just glad I could find some stuff to give them," I said. "Did Rayne like what I picked for her?"

"She won't admit it," Lucy said. "But she was actually really touched that you thought of her, and that you chose something that wasn't all about baseball and more about her being a girl and a teenager."

"I have to admit, I have no idea what to get for teenage girls," I said. "I kind of just picked things up and hoped for the best."

"Well," she began, "you did great. You'd never know you didn't have a teenage girl at home."

"I'll look for you during batting practice," I said. "If you want, come down to the edge of the field. I'd love to say hi to your kids again."

"Thomas would flip," she replied. "Not sure who all will come, but we'll plan on being there early in order to say hello."

"Do you want me to get you into the club again?"

"That's not necessary," she said. "It was really nice, though."

"It's not a problem," I said. "Just have to let them know. I can make it a permanent thing for you if you want, then we won't have to check each time."

"You are so kind," she said. "If it really isn't a big deal, I would love it."

"No problem," I said. "I'll set it up as soon as I get to the park. Speaking of which, I should really head out."

"Me, too," she said. "Gotta get back to get the kids, then get things ready for tonight."

"See you then?" I asked.

"Absolutely," she replied.

We stood up, and without even realizing it, we hugged each other. She was shorter than me, but not nearly as short as Meg, who barely stood above five feet. Lucy's head came up to my shoulder, just under my chin. I held her close, closing my eyes to just enjoy the feeling of her. Before I was ready, she pulled away.

"Sorry," she said, a blush rising up her cheeks.

"For what?"

"Should have asked before I just hugged you," she apologized.

"Did you see me complaining?"

"But it was presumptuous of me," she explained.

"I liked it," I whispered into her ear, moving close again.

"Me, too," she said, and it was pleasant to hear that.

"Okay," I said. "Gotta run. See you tonight."

"I've got a couple of things to pick up," she said. "See you tonight."

I turned and walked away, up the ramp toward the higher level of the market, and through the press of the crowd that had steadily grown. I was looking forward to tonight for more than just the game, but I was also worried that I was becoming attached to someone who might not be interested in more than just a friendship. The thing was, I wasn't sure exactly what I wanted from this, either. I guess time would tell, and that began tonight.

CHAPTER TWENTY-NINE

*L*ucy…

    I'd lied. I didn't have anything to pick up at the market.

    No reason to rush out of lunch, except things were getting a little too intimate for my liking. Oh, sure, he was wonderful to talk to, very nice to look at. And the way he hugged me, that was a little too much of what I probably shouldn't need.

    Except I did need it. I needed that close contact with someone. The hug, the closeness, the… everything. Andrea was going to have a field day with what I had to tell her, and maybe she was right. Maybe I did just need to get laid and get it over with. But I didn't want that. I wanted something more than just a good roll in the hay, and there may be something like that with Jonathan.

    To hell with it. I walked over to Tenzing Momo, which was right next to the crepe shop, and perused their scents. My friend had recently gotten into making all sorts of fun things, like bath bombs and soaps, so she would appreciate my gift. Selecting a handful, I checked out and headed back to the garage to get my car and head home.

    By the time I got out of downtown, I had to head straight to the school to pick up the kids. Unfortunately, that meant that I wouldn't be able to hide my purchase from the market.

"You went without us?" Rayne demanded.

"I had an errand and stopped to pick something up for Aunt Andrea," I replied.

"But you were at the market," she insisted. "You got crepes, didn't you?"

"I ate with a friend," I said. "You were in school. I couldn't very well take you with me, now, could I?"

"Of course you can't do anything special for me," she growled.

"What do you want me to do?" I asked. "I can't stop being who I am, and I can't give up everything that might make you upset."

"It's one thing," she insisted. "You should at least be able to give me one thing that's special to me."

"Am I supposed to not go to Seattle without you?" I asked. "I do have other things I do that don't involve you. I have meetings I have to go to, friends I meet, other things that do not revolve around you. Contrary to your insistence, the world does not begin and end with you."

"You really hate me this much?"

She sounded hurt, and I understood that, but I was not about to put my entire life on hold until she figured herself out.

"I get that you're upset," I consoled. "But you have to understand that I did not do it to hurt you. It just happened to be where it worked best for us to meet."

"Whatever," she said, but there was a strain in her voice.

"I'm sorry," I said.

"No, you're not," she barked back, then stuck her headphones in and proceeded to ignore the rest of the world.

"Can we go tomorrow?" Thomas asked, and I wasn't sure what he meant. "To the market and get crepes?" he explained.

"I think we can make that happen," I said, smiling at the fact that he almost always had an answer to ease the tension.

"See, Rayne," he said to his sister, but she completely ignored him.

The short drive home was tense, and I'd barely gotten the car in park when Rayne was out, rushing to the front door to go inside.

Thomas followed slowly behind her, and I took my time to gather the rest of my things before making it up to the door.

Sitting next to the door was a small bouquet of flowers with a card in them. I picked it up and brought it into the house. It had been a while since I had flowers delivered, so I didn't think anything of it until I opened the card and saw another note from Ryan's former coworker.

I am still watching you.

The handwriting was unmistakable, and I simply set it back down and picked up my cell phone.

"Hey," Andrea said when she answered.

"Is Marco home?" I asked.

"Not yet," she replied. "Why?"

"Got another note," I said.

"Shit," she said. "I'll send him over when he gets home."

"I'd rather come there," I replied. "I have other things to discuss."

"That's right," she drawled. "You had a date."

"Something like that," I agreed.

"I'll text you when he gets home," she said.

"Thanks," I replied, then hung up.

I took the flowers, dumped the water out, put the vase in the trash in the garage, and the flowers into the yard waste. The box they'd been housed in went into the recycling.

"Kids," I shouted, but only Thomas came in. "Where's your sister?"

"I think she's in her room," he replied.

"Stay here," I said, then went upstairs. "Rayne," I said through her closed door. Nothing. I knocked, then said, "I'm coming in."

When I opened the door, I saw her sitting on her bed, holding a small teddy bear, one I didn't recognize.

"Where did you get that?" I asked.

"Found it on my bed," she said.

"When?"

"Just now," she said.

I grabbed it, tossed it back on the bed, and grabbed her hand.

"Come on," I said, then pulled her from her room.

"What's going on?" she asked, stumbling behind me.

"Not now," I said, continuing down the stairs. "Thomas," I shouted toward the kitchen. "Come on. We need to go, now."

"Mom," Rayne said, and there was an edge to her voice. "What's going on?"

"Just a minute," I said, holding my finger up to my mouth to shush her.

Her eyes went wide, as she knew that I meant we could be heard, which obviously made her more than just a little uncomfortable. I grabbed my keys, walked out the door with the kids, locked it behind me, and we walked right over to our neighbor's house.

"Mom," Rayne said, but I put my finger to my mouth again.

"Hey," Andrea said when she opened the door, then saw the confusion on Thomas's face, the fear on Rayne's and the pure rage on mine. "Come through the garage," she said, closing the door in our face.

We went back down the walk to the driveway and walked up to the garage door that was slowly rumbling up on the chain from the automatic opener. Once it was fully up, we stepped inside, and Andrea pushed the button to close it again. She was holding her finger to her lips just as I had done before, and I knew she was going to do a quick check for bugs of any kind on us.

The kids had been told that if either Ryan or I put our finger to our lips, that meant we weren't sure whether there were listening devices around. The fact that our neighbor was also in the security field, and that Andrea was giving the same signal, made them even more nervous. She walked out to us, waved one of her husband's gadgets around us, similar to what they do when we went to the stadium, and then gave the signal that all was clear. Following her into her house, we sat on the couch, the kids fidgety.

"What's up?" she asked once we were settled.

"Rayne got a teddy bear," I said. "She found it on her bed. It wasn't there when we left this morning."

"That son of a bitch," she muttered, pulling out her phone and dialing. "Hey," she said once whoever was on the other end answered.

"Any chance you can bring home some equipment to do a search?" Another pause as whoever was on the other end, likely her husband, answered her question. "It's worse."

Rayne looked at me, both confused and afraid. She didn't want to ask the question that was going through her brain, but I could see that she knew the answer was true. Someone had gotten into our house and left that bear on her bed. I had never wanted my kids to fear the world. Their dad did a good job of keeping the scary things away from them when he was working with the bureau, but this wasn't from one of those jobs. This was someone he'd met after he left there.

Now, because of some idiot's obsession with me, they were going to have to deal with the scary things in the world that I never wanted them to know about.

"He'll be home soon," Andrea said after disconnecting her call.

"I'm so sorry I have to bring you into this," I said.

"Nonsense," she replied. "You guys want some snacks?"

"Mom," Rayne said, her voice trembling.

"It'll be okay," I lied. "Uncle Marco will help us out, and then we'll be good to go."

"Please don't lie to me," she said. "I know that something's up, so just tell me."

"Hey, T," Andrea said to my son. "Let's go see if we can find some cookies."

Thomas looked at me and I nodded. Scaring one kid was going to be bad enough. I didn't need both of them knowing that there was a stalker after me.

CHAPTER THIRTY

*J*onathan...

"You're sure in a good mood," Huffman said when I stepped up to my locker.

Coach had moved things around so that we were next to each other and Beckett was across the room from us.

"Nice afternoon," I admitted.

"Good to see," he said. "You deserve happy."

"Thanks, man," I said, then got to changing for batting practice.

I knew I wasn't playing today, so was just planning to get some stretching and field work in before the actual practice started. I headed out to the field and was doing my stretches when the kid came up to me.

"You finally get laid?" he asked, then laughed and walked away.

"Fucking punk," I muttered, walking toward the outfield.

This kid was going to make me do things that weren't very good for me or my career. Maybe, if I avoided him long enough, he'd get the hint and leave me alone. I probably wasn't that lucky, though.

By the time I had my fill of shagging balls in the outfield, the fans had started to enter the ballpark. I headed toward the dugout, watching the stands to see if I could pick out Lucy. It wasn't until I got closer that I could distinguish her from the rest of the fans who had gathered near the end of the dugout. She was next to the edge, her son beside her, and I could see him waving madly toward me.

"Hey, slugger," I said as I got closer.

"Hi," he said. "I'm so happy you're here and we get to see you again."

"Same here, buddy," I said. "Hey," I said to Lucy, looking above her son's head.

"Hey, yourself," she said, and she blushed a bit, which was a surprise, but not an unpleasant one.

"You okay?" I asked.

"I'll manage," she replied, but I could tell that something was off.

I wanted to ask her what was going on, but the throng of fans surrounding her made this so not the place to do it.

"Are you playing today?" Thomas asked.

"Not today, kiddo," I said.

"Bummer," he replied.

"I will eventually," I said. "It's the nature of the game. Well, I gotta go get ready. You guys cheer us on, okay?"

"I will," the kid said, his smile so bright it was heartwarming.

I looked at Lucy and hopefully signaled with that gaze that she could talk to me about whatever was going on with her. Maybe I'd send a quick text once I was changed. I waved to them both, then plodded down the steps and headed down the hall to the locker room.

"That your fuck buddy?" Beckett said as he passed me in the hallway.

"If you know what's good for you, you'll shut your damn mouth around me," I countered.

"Come on, old man," he jested. "Any time you wanna take a swing at me, I'm all yours."

"Fuck you," I barked, then made a beeline away from him and toward my locker.

"Don't worry about him," Huffman said when I got to my locker. "Team has your back."

"You guys shouldn't have to fight my fight," I said.

"Not just your fight," he replied. "Punk-ass bitch has been barking up everyone's tree, and we're all getting a little sick of him. One of these days he's gonna find himself without anyone on his side, and it ain't gonna be pretty."

"'Preciate it," I said. "But—"

"Nope," he said. "Not your call. Team is one unit. When someone steps out of line, it screws the whole team over. Ain't gonna tolerate that."

"Thanks," I said.

Pulling my phone out, I shot a quick text off to Lucy, just to let her know I was here for her if she needed someone. Once that was done, I changed and got ready to ride pine and watch the game.

By the bottom of the third, we were up five to nothing and their pitcher, Brinkman, started buzzing players inside after he gave up a home run to Kelly. Beckett was leading off the inning, so we were all on the top step, waiting to see if he could figure out how to find the ball with his bat. He'd struggled the last couple of days, but somehow had connected well in the first.

The pitcher wound up and let the ball go, and we all watched as if in slow motion as it took a curve and tailed into Beckett, hitting him square in the numbers as he turned his back. The kid threw his bat down and charged the mound, the rest of us backing him up by rushing the field. Even though he was short, he had a hell of a punch, and landed one right on their pitcher's chin before he could even realize what was coming. The dude went down, and Beckett climbed on top of him, punching him in the head over and over again.

By the time we got to the infield grass, the rest of their team had emptied the dugout as well, and we all started pulling our own players off the other team. It lasted just a few minutes, but when all was said and done, the kid had been ejected, their pitcher had been ejected, and both benches were given warnings. I was honestly surprised that the managers weren't thrown out as well, but it was early in the season, so maybe that would have happened if we were in June.

"That son of a bitch threw at me," Beckett was shouting as we drug him off the field.

"J," Coach shouted when we got to the dugout. "Take first. You're in at short for the kid."

"Sure thing," I said, dropping into the dugout myself to grab my helmet.

I walked out to first base, stretching both my arms and legs on the way, getting loose to be able to move when another hit happened.

"What the fuck is with that kid?" Sacramento's first baseman asked me.

"He's all kinds of hot and bothered," I replied, but didn't elaborate. I was the last person who should be asked about the mindset of that kid.

"That was a little over the top," the first baseman said. "Especially this early in the season. He knows he's gonna have a bullseye on him, right?"

"He's a kid," I said, as if that explained everything.

Honestly, though, I wasn't even sure what to do about him. My plan was just to play the rest of the game, keep my head down, and hope like hell we got out of it without anyone else getting beaned. It was always a gamble, though, so we would see how we fared. I was, however, going to have a serious talk with the kid, and there was going to be a come-to-Jesus moment when he realized that his actions had consequences. If he was gonna go off like a loose cannon, no one was going to help him out.

CHAPTER THIRTY-ONE

*L*ucy…

Andrea had come with us to the game, bringing Noah with her, so Marco could do what he did best at my house. He'd checked our phones before we left, so we knew they were clean. I just hoped that by the time we got home, everything was gone and we were safe.

We'd left the game early when Noah began getting cranky. He was a really good baby, but loved his routines, so that made it an early night for us. Honestly, though, I was glad. I loved going to the games, but sometimes I needed to be home, and this was one of those times.

"He said to come in," Andrea said as we pulled into the drive. "He's got some stuff he wants to talk to you guys about."

"Mom," Thomas said, but Rayne cut him off.

"Uncle Marco knows what he's doing," she said.

"He does," I reiterated. "And he'll be able to help keep us safe."

"Who's doing this?" he asked.

"Not something you need to worry about right now," I said.

We walked into the house, and Marco was at the kitchen table with several devices in a box. He looked more than just a little concerned.

"Lucy," he said. "I think we need to talk before we talk to the kids."

"Kids," I began, but Rayne said, "We'll help Aunt Andrea with Noah."

"Thanks," I said as they followed my neighbor up the stairs to the nursery. Once they were out of earshot, I turned to Marco. "Spill," I said.

"Sit," he insisted. "You're gonna need to."

"Shit," I replied, sitting next to him at the table.

"These," he said, showing me some small devices from the box on the table, "are like the ones I found in both the master bathroom and the guest bathroom, as well as the one the kids use."

They were so small, so innocuous looking, but I knew immediately that they were cameras.

"It gets worse," he said, and I looked at him. "Your modem has been tapped, so everything you're doing online is being watched."

"How long?" I asked, wanting to know exactly what this asshole was up to.

"Hard to say," he confessed. "But my guess is quite a while. The security system also had an additional password on it. It was obviously not something you did, as it was an external request."

"How did he—"

"Hold up," Marco said. "We're just getting started."

I sighed, knowing this was gonna be a long night.

Marco continued to tell me about all the security risks he found in the house, and how he thinks Captain Clueless got in. It was more than just a little frightening, and by the time he was done, I was convinced that I needed to just burn the whole house down and start new some-where else.

"Kids are in the guest room," Andrea said when she came down a couple of hours later. "Figured it would be best if they just spent the night. You can go over to the house and Marco can walk you through what needs to happen tonight, or you can crash here and we can do it in the morning."

"I'd rather go tonight," I said. "I don't want that asshole to think he's won. I want him to know that I know what he's doing and he won't get away with it."

"About that," Marco said. "I have an idea."

He then laid out a plan that was more than just efficient, but devious in how it would play out. The only problem was that I would have to live there with cameras and work really hard to pretend I didn't know they were there. It would be hard, and I'd have to make sure that the kids didn't know too much, or they'd give it away. If things went as Marco recommended, though, we would catch him in the act and would be able to get him put away for a long time.

"You ready?" he asked once he'd told me the whole plan.

"Absolutely," I replied. "I miss Ryan but knowing that you're here to help when shit like this happens makes me appreciate your friendship."

"I wouldn't have it any other way," he said. "You're family. Just because there isn't shared blood doesn't make it any less true. It's what I would expect someone to do for me and mine, so I have no problem doing it for you."

"You have no idea how much I appreciate this," I said.

"And when you get back, we can talk about your date," Andrea said.

"Oh God," I said. "I totally forgot about that."

"That doesn't sound good," she said.

"No," I replied. "It was good. I just don't want to think about Jonathan and Captain Clueless at the same time."

"Fair enough," she replied. "But we are gonna talk about it."

I just laughed and got up, walking with Marco out their front door and down the walk, making our way to my house that somehow didn't feel safe any longer. This was going to be rough, but it was necessary, so I'd do whatever it took to make sure that he didn't get away with this.

CHAPTER THIRTY-TWO

*J*onathan...

"Can you tell us about that last play?" the sports announcer asked during the post-game interview.

"Just watching each other's back," I said. "We're a team, and we need to think not just about ourselves, but how our actions will affect others on our squad."

"What are your thoughts on their pitcher hitting Hennings in the third?"

"Not something I want to talk about," I admitted. "Emotions run hot inside the lines, and sometimes we do things we realize aren't in our best interest. As I said, we're a team, and what one of us does affects all of us."

"Good luck in tomorrow's game," she said.

"Thanks," I replied, then turned and headed into the clubhouse.

While I didn't mind talking with the press, sometimes they asked questions that shouldn't be asked. Hopefully, what I said was within the right theme of what the management was going to spin on this disaster the kid had brought about.

"Bridge," the manager called from his office when I stepped into the locker room.

"Yeah," I replied, moving closer.

"Nice job on the interview," he said. "Perfectly said without throwing the kid under the bus."

"While I'd love to trash him, even I know that sometimes we let our emotions run us into the ground," I admitted. "Maybe he'll learn from this and go forward with a better sense of how a team works."

"I sure as shit hope so," he replied.

I left his office and headed to my locker.

"Apparently, the kid got upset and went home." Huffman laughed. "Guess he can dish it out but can't seem to take it."

"Doesn't surprise me," I replied, pulling my jersey off.

"I hope this doesn't come back to bite the rest of us in the ass," he said.

"You and me, both," I replied, then pulled the rest of my uniform off to head to the showers.

Letting the spray run down my back, I thought about what had happened earlier in the day. Lunch with Lucy was wonderful, even if it was cut short because of schedules. Spending time with her, though, was exactly what I had needed in that moment. The hug was wonderful, and I felt like I might need another one, especially after tonight's game.

I finished up my shower, headed back to my locker, and dressed to head home. When I turned my phone on, I saw there was a text from Lucy. I decided to check it out when I got to my car. I didn't want to have to listen to anyone else when I read her words, and there were still quite a few players in the locker room.

The walk to my car seemed to take longer than usual, so by the time I arrived, I was anxious to read her words.

We had to leave early. Baby got fussy. We're going to the market tomorrow if you want to join us. No pressure.

Did I want to join them? Absolutely. But should I join them? Had she told her kids that we'd met outside of the couple of times at the stadium? I didn't know the answer to that, and so I thought I'd sleep on it and see how I felt when I got up in the morning. Starting the car, I shifted it into gear and headed home to my empty condo. While the drive wasn't long, it seemed to take forever to get there.

I parked, walked to the elevator, rode it up, unlocked my door, dropped my keys in the dish, and was almost to my bedroom when the phone rang. I answered it immediately.

"Hello," I said.

"It's not too late, is it?" Lucy asked.

"Nope," I replied, flicking the light in the bedroom on and kicking my shoes off in the closet. "I was just coming home."

"Oh, good." She sighed. "I know I sent you that text about meeting tomorrow at the market, but I don't think that's a good idea."

Her words were rushed, as if she didn't want to stop or get interrupted saying them.

"That's cool," I said, sitting on the edge of my bed. "I wasn't sure if your kids knew we'd met, so figured I'd text you in the morning and make sure you were good with it."

"What?" she asked, and it was clear she was distracted. "Sorry, yeah, no, they don't know. It's just that something has come up for me, so I need to be a little more cautious as to where I go and who I meet."

"Is there anything I can do?" I asked.

"Oh, no," she said. "It's all covered for now. I'm actually going to be in the city for something else, and the kids aren't gonna be with me. I promised Rayne that I wouldn't go to the market without her again, at least for a while."

"Ah," I said.

"Yeah," she said, still distracted. "So, just wanted you to know so you didn't plan anything."

"That's totally fine," I said. "Are you sure you're okay?"

She gave a deep sigh, and I could tell she was tired, but it wasn't a physical thing.

"I'm not okay," she finally said. "It's more than I want to talk about right now, but I may need an ear and a shoulder, if you're willing."

"Sure thing," I said. "We're heading out of town on Sunday after the game, though, so if it doesn't happen this weekend, it'll have to be a virtual shoulder for you to cry on."

"Oh, crap," she said. "I totally didn't even think about that. You probably have so many things to do to get ready, you don't need my drama right now."

"Hey," I said, cutting her off before she could continue. "I'm not worried about it. I've been doing this so long it's second nature packing for a road trip. I want to be here for you."

It was a confession I wasn't sure was real until the words were out of my mouth. I really did want to be there for her, in any way she needed. And while it surprised me some, it didn't feel like it was a forced thing.

"You do?" she asked.

"Yeah," I confirmed. "I really do. I know we don't know each other very well, and haven't even known each other for long, but I feel like we have a really good connection, you know?"

"Yeah," she said, and she was fully into the conversation now. "I guess I've just been a little off-kilter lately, so I think my brain is kind of derailed."

"That's reasonable," I said. "You wanna talk now?"

"It's not really a good time," she said, then I heard a man's voice in the background and something inside me reared up that I wasn't expecting. "I gotta go," she said. "I'll call you tomorrow morning if that's okay."

"Any time after ten is fine," I said.

She disconnected the call, and I had to examine what was going on inside me. In those few moments, something had changed, and I wasn't sure whether she had felt it or if it was simply something inside me. I blew out my breath and stood up. There was no way I was going to get to sleep with these thoughts running around in my head, so decided I should get to packing. One less thing to do tomorrow.

CHAPTER THIRTY-THREE

*L*ucy…

"I gotta go," I said to Jonathan. "I'll call you tomorrow morning if that's okay."

"Any time after ten is fine," he replied, then I disconnected the call.

"Sorry," Marco said.

"No problem," I replied. "What did you need?"

"I wanted to tell you I'm tapped into the feed from the cameras," he explained. "When he connects, it'll trace it back to its location and we'll have him."

"Can I do anything about it?" I asked.

I knew Ryan had dealt with this type of thing when he was on the job, and he and Marco had talked a lot about it when they first moved in a few years before that. I'd never talked specifically about anything like this, but he'd given me, as well as the kids, some good plans if anything happened like this, thus the signal with the finger on our lips. Never in my wildest dreams did I think I'd have to have someone search my house for bugs and cameras or put a trace on them to find the creep who installed them.

"For right now, we'll just keep an eye on them," Marco said, "Make sure you keep your doors locked and do an update with your security system. Do it in person, though, not through their website or on the phone. If you do it either of those ways, he'll be able to get the new access codes, and we don't want that."

"I'll go there on Monday," I said. "This is just ridiculous."

"It is," he said. "I'm sorry it has to be this way for now, too. I don't feel safe with you being there alone."

"I don't either," I agreed.

"Who is this guy to you?"

"He used to work with Ryan," I said.

"At the bureau?"

"No," I said. "He's Captain Clueless."

"Oh, shit," he said.

"Yeah," I replied.

"Do you think he had anything to do with Ryan's death?"

That shot me cold. Could he have done something to Ryan? They said that he had an aneurysm, but there wasn't any indication that it wasn't something to happen naturally.

"I guess I shouldn't have asked that," he said.

"It just got me thinking," I said. "I guess another stop I'll have to make on Monday is with both the bureau and the doctor."

"God," he said. "I am so sorry to make you think all these things. Andrea tells me I need to read the room and know when to shut the fuck up, but I never thought I was doing anything like this. I am so sorry."

"It's fine," I said, even though it was worrying me more now. "I'll get some answers on Monday. In the meantime, though, I need to get some packing done. I'll call my mom in the morning and see if we can stay there this weekend."

"Tonight, though, you're staying with us," he insisted.

"Oh, yeah," I agreed readily. "No way am I staying in my house tonight."

"Good," he said.

"Thank you," I said. "I really appreciate everything you and Andrea have done for us."

"We're family," he said. "See you in the morning."

"Goodnight," I said as he stepped out of the living room and headed up the stairs.

While the couch wasn't the most comfortable place to sleep, I wasn't sure I was going to get much anyway. I shot a text to my mom, letting her know we needed a place to stay for the weekend and asking if she would mind handling the kids on Monday morning so I could get some answers to the questions running around in my head. I knew she wouldn't see it until the morning, so I didn't bother to wait for an answer. Then I sent a text to Jonathan. I had been short with him on the phone earlier, and I wanted to apologize. He replied right away, thanking me for the text, so I sent him another asking if he was up for a call. When he said yes, I dialed his number.

"Hey," he said when he answered the phone.

"Sorry," I said

"Don't be," he replied. "You obviously have some things going on. I get that."

"I kinda just need to vent a little," I said. "If you don't mind."

"Not at all," he replied. "I told you before, I'm happy to be a shoulder for you."

"But you have a game tomorrow," I said.

"Not till six," he said. "I've got plenty of time."

"I don't want to overwhelm you," I explained. "There's a lot going on, and I kind of need someone to dump on. I don't want to ruin what we've got started here with all my baggage."

"Babe, we're good," he said, and the term of endearment hit me a little hard.

Swallowing, I unloaded. I told him about how Ryan had warned me about George, that I was never to be alone with him, what he'd done previously and gotten away with, and that he was worried about any interaction I might have with him. I explained why I cut him off earlier, that it was because I was talking with my neighbor about what was going on at my place, and how we'd found the cameras. We were just waiting for him to make a move to access their feed so we could link it to him. How I wasn't going to stay at the house until I had a chance to talk to the authorities on the next steps that I might need to take, so I was going to be staying with my mom.

By the time I'd finished with everything that had been going on in the last couple of weeks, I was exhausted.

"I'm sorry," I said, finally. "I really just needed to get it all out and see if I was as crazy as I thought."

"You're not crazy by any standards," he said. "In fact, I think you're holding it together better than most people."

"Thanks," I replied genuinely. "I just didn't realize until I started laying it all out how screwed up this situation was."

"If you need a place to stay," he said. "Somewhere that he doesn't know about, you can stay with me. The kids, too."

"I can't ask you to do that," I said.

"You didn't," he replied. "I offered. I'm gone starting Sunday night, so if you and the kids want to crash at my condo, I'm totally fine with it."

"You're trusting a near stranger to have access to your home?"

"We haven't known each other very long," he admitted. "The thing is, I trust you. Something in my gut is telling me you're a good person, someone I could spend time with. Someone I can trust."

"I just…" I began but stopped. What did I say to that? There was something in the way he said he could spend time with me that made things fuzzy in my head.

"Hey," he said. "Feel free to say no. I know it's a bit soon to give you a key to my place, but it's there if you want or need it. You don't have to commit today but talk it over with your friends and family and see if it's something you want to do."

"I really appreciate that," I said, and it was true. "You have been so kind to me and my kids, I don't even know how to thank you."

"Just keep doing what you're doing," he said. "I'm here for you if you want, but I won't pressure you."

"I might take you up on Sunday night," I confessed. "I have to go to the bureau office Monday morning, and also have to go to my security company. If I go straight from my house, George can follow me, but if I'm already in the city, he won't know where I am."

"Just a thought," he said. "Have you checked your parent's house for bugs or cameras?"

"Oh my God," I said, realizing that I could have unwittingly given him access to their house as well.

"Check tomorrow," he said. "You should probably get some sleep, though."

"Yeah," I replied. "Although I'm not sure how well I'll sleep after everything that's happened today."

"Dream of baseball," he said. "That's what I do when I can't sleep. I think of what it would be like to play in the World Series. Works like a charm every time."

"I'll see if that helps." I laughed.

"Good to hear you laugh," he said.

"You've lightened my mood immensely," I replied.

"Then you should get some sleep," he insisted.

"You, too," I replied. "See you tomorrow night?"

"You bet," he said.

"Good," I said. "I could use some good in my life right now."

"I'm happy to supply good to you," he said. "I'll bring a key and a fob for the elevator, as well as an access card for the garage. I'll put it all in an envelope with a card with the address on it. This way you have it if you need to use it."

"You are too good," I said.

"Nah," he replied. "I'm just trying to be helpful."

"Well…" I said, then paused. This was moving pretty fast, whatever it was that we had going on, and I didn't want to jinx it or push it too hard.

"Hey," he said. "We're good."

"Yeah," I said. "I guess we are."

CHAPTER THIRTY-FOUR

*J*onathan...

Everything was in a manilla envelope with Lucy's name on it and was sitting under some stuff in my locker. I figured I'd keep it there until I talked to her. There was a sheet of paper with the address and unit number as well as the space that was available for her to park, along with the code for the security and how to turn it on when she was staying. I put the key to my place and the fob for the elevator, as well as the card for the garage. I hoped she'd take me up on at least staying tomorrow night. I would feel better knowing she wasn't in her house with all that security equipment there watching her. It sounded like her neighbor was on it, though, and at least looking out for her. I was really happy about that, too.

"What's that for?" Beckett asked when he saw the envelope.

"None of your damn business," I replied, stuffing it behind a couple of other things where it couldn't be seen.

"Thought you said you didn't hook up with fans," he goaded. "Looks to me like you're doing some of that shady shit you harped on me about."

"You know what," I began, but Kelly stepped between me and the kid.

"Get your fucking face out of here," he growled. "You're on everyone's shit list tonight, so you best be sitting your ass down and shutting the fuck up. Got it?"

Our designated hitter was a tank and scary when he was being nice. When he turned on the intimidation factor, he was over-the-top terrifying.

"Yeah," the kid bit back. "Well, fuck the lot of you. All of you can fuck all the way off."

He stormed over to his locker and I had to tuck my head down to keep from laughing at him. Grant wasn't as much of a tantrum thrower as that kid, and he was barely over two.

"You good?" Kelly asked me.

"Yeah," I said. "Thanks."

"Anytime," he replied, then moved further into the locker room to his assigned space.

I turned back to my locker and sighed. Not for the first time in the last few hours, I wondered if I was doing the right thing. Somehow, though, it seemed right. I sent a text to Lucy letting her know I had the envelope with all the details for her, and that I wanted her to have it just in case she decided to take me up on my offer.

I changed and headed out to the field to run my drills and do some batting practice. Even though I didn't play every day, I still tried to keep myself in as good a shape as possible. You never knew when someone was going to need to be pulled for either a day off, an injury, or like last night when the punk-ass kid decided he was in charge of everything and the whole world was out to get him, and that every slight was a personal attack.

Shagging balls first, I then headed to the batting cage to hit a few and get my rhythm going. After each pitch, I looked over to the dugout, or more specifically, the stands right next to it, to see if I could see her. Somehow, in the last week, I'd become very connected to her, and it was a little unreal.

After my allotted time in the cage, I picked up my mitt from the ground outside and made my way to the dugout, scanning the crowd along the sideline. Lucy wasn't there, and I sort of felt hurt by that fact.

When I got to my locker, I pulled out my phone and powered it on, hoping to see a response to the text I'd sent.

I can pick up the packet after the game.

I was relieved to see a response, so I quickly typed one back to her, then went about changing into my uniform. It was amazing how much of a lift those few words gave me.

"Good news?" Huffman asked when he saw my smile in the dugout.

"Yeah," I replied, not wanting to elaborate further.

The game went by slower than I wanted, but that probably had more to do with what might be happening after the game than anything else. We'd lost, but it was close up to the end. Then, in the eighth, the Houston team got on a roll and not even the Guardian was able to escape the punishment. No one wanted to talk to the press, but the coach took the baton for the team, taking all the blame on himself, when really it was just a bad day at the ballpark.

I grabbed the envelope and headed back out to the dugout and around the corner to meet Lucy. She was there, but was alone, so I was a bit confused.

"Where are the kids?" I asked.

"Thomas had to go to the bathroom, so I sent him up with my parents," she explained. "Rayne is staying with a friend tonight."

"I see," I said. "Well, this has the address and all the instructions on how to get into the garage and the condo. It's also got the key and fobs to get you where you need to go. If you get stuck or anything, you can text me. We'll be in Anaheim until late Tuesday night."

"Do I need to not be there when you get back?"

"Oh, no," I said. "It's totally fine. Just send me a text and I'll be sure to be quiet when I come in. There's a guest bedroom with a queen bed, and the couch is comfortable, if the kids don't want to sleep in the same bed. You can take my room."

"Are you sure?" she asked. "I mean, if you come home, where will you sleep?"

"I can take one of the couches," I said. "Wouldn't be the first time."

"Your wife kick you out often?"

She said it with a laugh, so I think it was more teasing than anything else.

"Meg sometimes didn't sleep well," I explained. "And she hated being woken up every single night when I'd come home late. It was easier to just crash on the couch until she and Grant were up, then go to the bedroom to finish out my rest."

"I guess that's a good thing." She smiled. "It's good to know what works best for everyone. I know when Ryan was out of town, I never slept well, so he'd come in and climb in bed as soon as he was home. He didn't go out of town often, but when he did, I needed to know he was home and safe."

"Feel free to use the place the whole week if you need to," I said. "I should be home through next weekend, then back out on the road again. I'm happy to let you use it any time I'm gone."

"I really appreciate this," she said.

"Absolutely," I replied. "You should be able to feel safe, and if I can offer that to you, I'm happy to do so."

"Thanks," she said.

"Ma'am," one of the building crew said. "I'm going to have to ask that you exit the building. We're closing up."

"Oh, I'm sorry," she said. "Talk to you soon."

"See you around," I replied, then watched her walk back up the stairs.

My guess was her parents and son were already ushered out, because I never saw Thomas. I was just glad that I could offer her a safe space, somewhere she could go and not be worried about who was watching her.

When I finally made my way back into the locker room, I had to pass by Beckett.

"Setting up your next hookup?" He laughed.

"You do know you're an asshole, right?"

"Of course I am," he said. "That's why everyone loves me."

"Fuck you, man," I said and walked past him. I didn't have the mindset to listen to his shit any longer.

The drive home was quiet, and when I walked into the condo, I took a look at the place as if I were seeing it for the first time. It was clean, picked up, and no one would assume a bachelor lived here. We had a service that came in once a week, usually on Wednesdays, so it had just been done. I should probably let Lucy know if she was going to be here a while, but then thought better of texting her this late.

I went to my closet and pulled out my travel bag, leaving it by the front door. Since tomorrow's game was earlier in the day, I knew I would need to get everything ready to go so I didn't forget anything. There was always an extra charger in my bag, along with a toiletry kit that lived there. I'd replenish it every month, just so that nothing would run out while on the road. Sure, we could pick things up, but buying toothpaste from a hotel was more expensive than I wanted.

One more game on the homestand, then a quick trip to California for two days before coming back home. Having Wednesday off would be nice. I'd be able to get caught back up on a few things. Maybe Lucy would be willing to meet me for lunch again.

CHAPTER THIRTY-FIVE

*L*ucy...

"What's that?" Dad asked when I caught back up to them.

"Jonathan said we could stay at his place while he's out of town," I explained.

"Really?" Mom asked.

"Yeah," I said. "We've been talking a bit. He lost his wife last year, too. It's been nice to have someone I can talk to who understands what I'm going through."

"That's really nice," Mom said.

"Isn't this a little soon?" Dad asked. "I mean, you just met the guy. How do you know he's not a serial killer or something?"

"Very funny, Dad." I laughed. "I feel pretty confident that he is absolutely not a killer of any kind."

"You can also stay at our place," Mom offered. "I mean, if you want."

"I appreciate that, Mom," I said. "I'm just going to play it by ear and see how things go. Marco has things pretty well locked up at home, but I need to brief the bureau on Monday. If I stay at Jonathan's, then I'm already here in town."

"Solid plan," Dad said. "But look in his closet and see what kind of skeletons he's got hiding in there."

"Pretty sure that's not a literal saying, Dad." I laughed.

"Good to hear you laugh," he said.

Thomas had been up ahead of us the whole walk but had stopped at the top of the escalator and waited.

"You guys are slow," he said.

"We're old," Dad said. "We gotta take little steps so we don't fall over and break a hip."

"Mom's not that old," he countered.

"She's gotta make sure we're steady as we go." Dad laughed as he stepped onto the escalator with my son.

Mom and I stepped on after him, and I looked around the stadium, noting how empty it was. It was a little eerie, but also kind of cool.

The drive to my parent's house was uneventful, and we all headed in to get to bed. I'd pick Rayne up tomorrow from her friends, then we'd go home to pack before heading to the game. I honestly wasn't sure how Rayne would take the news that we'd be staying at Jonathan's place. That, and the fact that we'd been talking for the last week, might just bring back the tempest that she'd allowed to slow in that same time.

~

"YOU'RE SERIOUS?" RAYNE SAID WHEN I PICKED HER UP.

"I am," I replied.

"This is just not cool, Mom," she said. "Like, I know you need to move on at some point, but Dad's been dead less than a year. The least you could do would be to pretend to care that he's gone."

"Rayne," Thomas tried.

"I don't care what you think," she said. "You're only happy because you're getting to spend time with a baseball player. I don't want to."

"He's not going to be there," I said.

"What?" Thomas asked.

"He leaves after today's game for California," I said. "He'll be gone a couple of days and said we could stay there until Uncle Marco figures out what's going on. We probably won't even be there at the same time."

"Whatever," Rayne said. "Can't I just stay with Gabby? That would be so much easier."

"No," I said. "I haven't had a conversation with her parents, and I don't want to run the risk of having something happen to them because of what's happening to us."

"What about Grams and Gramps?" she asked.

"Grams has an appointment tomorrow morning, and Gramps has to take her," I said. "They said that we could stay there, but I don't want to do that. I wouldn't feel good bringing the crazy to their house. It's bad enough that we've done that already."

Rayne turned her head away from me and plugged her earbuds in, shutting me and the rest of the world out, once again.

The ride home was quiet, but I could tell she was really upset. She slammed her door as soon as she was in there, then turned on her melancholy music to drown out whatever feelings she had. Thomas set about packing up a bag so we could have them in the trunk before the game, and I did the same.

I wondered what his place would look like. Would it be trashed like some single guy or would he have it nice and neat? The truth was, it could go either way. After I'd packed my suitcase, I went to the kitchen to pack some snacks and breakfast stuff for tomorrow morning. Thinking about breakfast, I thought I'd send a text to Jonathan and make sure he had milk and some staples. I'd hate to get there and not really be able to make anything.

Do you have milk? Eggs?

He texted back pretty quickly that he had that, and if I needed, there was a grocery in the next block that was open twenty-four hours a day so I could grab something quick in there.

With that settled, I put the grocery bag by the door next to my suitcase. Thomas had his there already, but Rayne was still up in her room being moody.

"Rayne," I hollered. "I need you to get down here. We have to go."

The music stopped, and I heard her open her door, then she slammed it shut again and came stomping down the stairs, suitcase in hand.

"This is ridiculous," she snarled. "I don't see why we can't just stay home."

"I've told you why," I said. "It's what we have to do right now."

"Fine." She sighed and stood by the door.

We stepped out, and I locked up behind us, pushing the button on the key fob to open the trunk. I'd stuck the envelope into the front of my suitcase but had already programmed Jonathan's address into my phone so we'd be able to get to his place easily. Of course, Rayne would probably take it to mean that I'd been there before.

Once at the stadium, we went through the gates and met Dad inside.

"You guys eat?" he asked.

"Not yet," Thomas said.

"Hungry?"

"Always," I said, looking at my son.

"What?" he asked. "I'm a growing boy."

Dad and I laughed, but Rayne simply scowled at us. We picked up some hot dogs at the concession stand, then headed to our seats. Thomas begged to go down to the field, but it didn't look like anyone was practicing. At least, not our team, so I made him stay with us. He complained but settled rather quick.

The Cascades won big today, and Jonathan even got to play in the outfield. Thomas begged again to go down after the game.

"They have to fly out right after the game," I explained. "I don't think anyone will be coming out. I'm sorry."

"Only because you want to see your new boyfriend," Rayne interjected.

"I don't think you understand what your mom is going through," Dad said. "It's good that she's found someone who has gone through the same thing in order to be able to talk about it."

"Wait, you've been talking to him?"

I sighed, but not because I was angry with my dad. No, I was angry with myself for not letting the kids know that a friendship had been growing between Jonathan and I over the last week. It was hard to explain exactly what it was that was going on between us, but I didn't want to define it.

"I have," I confessed. "He's been a really good listener."

"You sure he's not lying just to get into your pants?" she asked.

"Rayne Nicole Fallon," I admonished. "Just because two people are friendly, doesn't mean that anything romantic is going on between them."

"I didn't say romance," she cried. "I said you two were gonna have sex. It's what you want. I saw it when we first met him. You thought I was stupid, but I saw the way you looked at him."

She stomped away from us, arms crossed over her chest, and I noticed the slight hitch in her step and the shake of her shoulders. God, I was such an idiot. I should have explained what was going on. The problem was, I honestly didn't know.

When we arrived at Jonathan's condo, it was easy to find the parking spot, and then use the things he gave me to get into the elevator and up to his place. The door opened to a good-sized living room with a kitchen to the right. It was clean and seemed very well organized, and not nearly as sterile as I'd anticipated. Then I remembered that he'd shared the home with his wife and son.

"He said there's a guest bedroom," I told the kids. "Why don't you guys go put your suitcases there, then we can have a quick bite to eat before bed."

"Okay," Thomas said, heading down the small hallway to the left.

Rayne followed him, rolling her bag behind her. I set the things I'd brought for dinner on the counter in the kitchen, leaving my bag to take to the master bedroom for later. We had a quick dinner and then I sent the kids to bed.

Walking into the master bedroom was a bit uncomfortable, but I was pleasantly surprised to find the bed made and the room clean. The pictures on top of the dresser of their wedding and another with the three of them at a beach somewhere were a little hard to look at, but it just showed me what kind of a man he truly was. I went into the bathroom to clean up, then climbed into bed to sleep. Tomorrow was going to be busy, and I'd have to be up earlier than usual to get the kids to school.

~

MONDAY MORNING ARRIVED EARLY, AND I GOT THE KIDS UP AND OUT to school before coming back into the city to meet with the bureau. I explained what was going on with the house, and who I thought it was. Marco had kept the notes so I could bring them with me. I wanted to get rid of them, but he insisted.

"And you're sure it's him?" Agent Richards asked.

"I can't be sure," I explained. "But he started sending me notes. Before that, it was just the flowers and gifts. I assumed they were from Ryan, but when that first note was there, I became worried."

"You did the right thing," he said. "We'll have someone check your place out in the next week or so. Do you have somewhere to stay in the meantime?"

"I do," I said. "I have a friend who is out of town that is letting us stay at his place."

"Is it secure?" he asked. "Would this man know where you were?"

"I feel pretty confident that he wouldn't be able to find us," I said. "But we're being careful, just the same."

"Good," he said. "Like I said, we'll have someone out to check things out later this week."

"Thank you," I said, then headed out to get the kids.

Tuesday went much easier, as I simply went to the security company to ask about getting a change on the passcodes for the system. They'd argued that I should have done it online, but I explained that there was an issue with my internet security. When they tried to have me do it in their app, I again told them I was going to change it with them in person due to security concerns. Finally, I got the code changed, and had them put a lock on any additional changes —no changes were to be made except by me and in person.

When we made it to Jonathan's after I'd picked up the kids from school, we had dinner and made it an early night. Both of them had homework, and then we watched a movie before heading to bed. I tossed and turned, trying to find a comfortable way to sleep, but it just didn't seem to want to work. Finally, I got up and grabbed the sleep gummies out of my bag. I hadn't had to use them for a while, but they had been a godsend right after Ryan died. If I hadn't had that extra push, I think I probably would have been awake for days at a time, only crashing when my body could no longer function. Hopefully, I'd be able to sleep well tonight.

CHAPTER THIRTY-SIX

*J*onathan...

"You got another pussy in Anaheim?" Beckett asked me when we were getting off the plane Sunday evening.

I ignored him, choosing silence over the millions of things I wanted to say to him. Now was not the time to get physical with him. No, I needed to keep a cool head. Eventually, he'd figure out that he was a fucking idiot and that he would be losing more than he'd gain by keeping up with this train of thought.

By the time we made it to the hotel, I was beat. I had received a text from Lucy saying they were going to stay at my place, which made me happier than it probably should have. I crashed hard when I got to my room and was up early and ready for the day to begin. It was our first trip out of town, and it was a short one, which was nice. The other nice thing was we stayed on the West Coast. We'd be here for two games, home through the weekend, then we'd start our first big road trip, heading to New York, Baltimore, and down to Dallas before coming back.

"You good to play third?" Coach asked when I stepped into the clubhouse late Monday morning.

"Sure," I replied. "What's wrong with Mitch?"

"Said he pulled something in the last game," Coach said. "I think it's just a case of coming back to the team that traded him away in the off season."

"I'd think he'd wanna play and show them what they're missing," I said.

"Me, too," Coach replied. "But it is what it is."

"Thanks for the heads-up," I said, then went to my locker to get ready for drills.

I hadn't been at third yet this season, but did play there some last year, so it shouldn't take long for me to get back into the swing. Being this close to Beckett, knowing we had to work well as a team, was a struggle. But I had to hand it to the kid. Once we were between the chalk lines, he was in his element and played better than most anyone I'd been on the diamond with. Maybe, just maybe, he would make it in this league after all.

Between the flight, the short night, and being on the field for a full game, I was beat when we finally made it back to the hotel after the game. I had my phone in my hand when it buzzed.

You up? Can I call?

I hadn't heard from Lucy all day but was concerned when she sent this text.

Sure. I'm at the hotel, so call any time.

My phone rang almost right away, and I answered.

"Hey," I said.

"Thanks for letting me call," she replied.

"You okay?"

"Not really," she said.

"Want to talk it out?"

"I don't know," she confessed. "I feel like I shouldn't burden you with all of this."

"I don't mind," I said, and meant it. "Sounds like you could use that shoulder right about now."

"Are you sure?"

I sighed. I was tired, and should probably go to bed, but I'd listen to her, give her a way to vent, and space to figure things out.

"Absolutely."

"It's just been a long day," she said. "I went to the bureau and talked with an agent there about what's going on. He said he'd be sending someone to my house later this week. Tomorrow I have to go to the security company and get my passcodes changed and put a note in my file to not let anyone change anything without an ID and in person. Nothing over the phone or online. The kids are cranky. Well, Rayne, mostly. Thomas thinks it's so cool that we're staying at your place, which is really nice, by the way."

"Thanks," I said, trying to give her space to purge.

"I just wish I didn't have to do this," she whispered.

"Neither do I," I replied. "But you need to keep yourself and your kids safe. That's the most important thing."

"I know," she said, and I could hear the weight of her world in those two words.

"Breathe," I said. "Deep in, to the count of three, then hold to three, then out to three."

She did as I suggested, the deep breath in as I counted, then I counted again, then could hear the relief when she let it out slowly.

"Better?"

"I think so," she said. "Thanks."

"Absolutely not a problem," I said.

"Not just for that," she added. "But for being so kind to me, and to the kids. For letting us stay here and letting me unload on you. It's probably not fair, but I really do appreciate it."

"I'm happy to help," I said. "I'm just glad we've made this connection and you have a safe place to be."

"Me, too," she said. "I don't know what I'd do without you."

"I'm here for you," I said, and meant it.

"I should probably let you go to sleep," she said. "You played tonight. Nice game, by the way."

"Thanks," I said. "I should probably hit the sack. You should, too. You've got things to do tomorrow as well. I'll be home tomorrow night, late. I'll crash on the couch."

"That will work," she said. "The kids are fine in the guest room. I just hate that you have to give up your bed."

"Like I said, I'm used to it," I replied. "And it's comfy."

"If you're sure," she hedged.

"Go to bed, Lucy," I said. "You need to sleep and stop worrying about everything that you can't control."

"Goodnight," she said.

"Sleep well," I replied, then ended the call.

I don't know about Lucy but I crashed immediately after I hung up and plugged my phone in. I must have been more tired than I thought.

MITCH WAS READY TO PLAY TUESDAY NIGHT, SO I WAS RIDING PINE once again. Honestly, though, it was probably for the best. I had dreams that were completely inappropriate about a beautiful woman who was quickly becoming very important in my life.

"You dreaming about that pussy waiting back in Seattle?" Beckett asked when he sat next to me in the dugout after the bottom of the first.

"You have no tact," I barked at him. "And no class whatsoever. Maybe you should just sit at the other end of the dugout and leave me alone."

"Ah." He laughed. "Guess that phone sex thing didn't work out too well for you, then."

"I swear to all that's holy—"

"Beckett," Coach barked. "Get up here."

"Better luck next time." He laughed as he went over to the coach.

"Hey," Huffman said, taking the spot Beckett held earlier. "You doing okay? You look a little down or something."

"Just tired," I said. "And a bit confused about some stuff, but it'll work itself out. These things usually do."

"You need someone," he began, "just let me know. If you need Beckett to get a pounding, though, there's gonna be a line."

I laughed, deep from my belly, and it was something I really needed. We ended up winning again, and it was a joyful flight home.

The bus took us to the field where we all picked our cars up to head home. While it was a good time, I was tired.

Keying my way into the condo, I saw that the alarm was set for stay, so I reset it, dropped my keys in the dish by the door, then made my way into my room, shutting and locking the door behind me. My closet was big enough for me to drop my bag and undress. I hung my jacket up, unbuttoned my shirt, and dropped it in the hamper while toeing off my shoes. Slacks and socks were next to go into the hamper, then I walked to the bathroom to pee.

The bed was warm, and I slipped under the covers, snuggling up to the woman in it. I wrapped my arm around her middle and stuck my nose into her hair and took a deep whiff.

Not Meg, I thought and froze. No, this was Lucy, warm and safe in my bed. The bed I promised to avoid when I got home tonight. Before I could extract myself, though, she scooted back against me, and I was not man enough to back out. The feel of a warm body next to me was something I hadn't had in more than half a year, and I decided to indulge, just this once.

We both had clothes on, and it was an innocent mistake. Either she knew it was me, or she was completely unaware, but I wasn't going to deny myself this small pleasure. I just prayed it wouldn't screw everything we'd built over the last week. Tomorrow would figure itself out, but as tired as I was, though, I just crashed, and hard.

CHAPTER THIRTY-SEVEN

*L*ucy…

Mmm, he's so warm. His heartbeat is steady and strong under my ear, and the firm chest is exactly how I figured it would feel. Holding me close against his side, that arm could probably break me if he wanted. Instead, though, I feel protected, like the world can't find me tucked so close to him in the dark.

His stomach is tight, ridges where the muscles contract, and just above his naval the hair starts. I follow it down, feeling him suck in a breath as I edge closer to his boxers… if this is a dream, why isn't he naked.

He chuckles, the rumble deep in his chest, and I can hear it in my ear, muffled.

"It's not a dream," he said, and I froze.

"Oh God," I whispered, pulling my hand back, but he snatched it and kept it on his stomach.

"I don't mind," he whispered, and I stiffened.

"I'm so sorry," I said, trying to pull away.

His arm tightened around me, holding me where I was. He let go of my hand and ran a finger across my brow, pushing my hair behind my ear, then tilted my face up to his. The room was dark, just a small light coming from the bathroom.

"I don't mind if you don't," he said.

"I shouldn't want this," I confessed, and he chuckled again.

"Why not?" he asked.

I stopped to think about it, and he was right. Why shouldn't I want this. I was a single woman, although only for a few months. He was a single man, also for only a few months. Maybe, just this once, I'd do what Andrea would do and just go for it. For a brief moment, maybe I wouldn't feel so alone.

"Kiss me?" I asked.

"With pleasure," he replied.

He took his time, slowly descending toward me, giving me every chance possible to stop this. But I didn't want it to stop. I needed this, even if it was just for this moment. His lips were so soft, the whiskers around them bristly, but not terrible.

After just a chaste kiss, he pulled back, waiting, I guess, for me. I moved closer and pressed my lips against his and he moved into it, pressing firmer, opening slightly, and I responded in kind. The first fleeting flick of his tongue into my mouth was perfect, just like he seemed to be, and I slid my tongue against his, caressing it inside my mouth. He moaned and shifted to his side, wrapping the other arm around my back, pulling me tight against him.

His hand moved up my back to the back of my head, holding it in place as he devoured my mouth, claiming it for himself. I gave willingly, wrapping my arm around his waist, pulling him into me. God, I wanted him so bad, and I threw away every thought that popped in, trying to make me stop.

He pulled back, both of us breathing heavy.

"You're sure," he said, but it was almost a question.

"I need you," I replied, confessing my weakness to him.

His hand slid down my back, over my tank and to the waistband of my panties, his eyes watching me in the dark for a reaction. I did the only thing I could and followed suit, my hand moving down his back, then pushing at the material covering him. His breath hitched and he shifted, pushing his hand up inside my tank, lifting the material higher and higher, pushing it up until it was bunched under my armpits.

Sitting up a little, I let him push it up off my free arm and over my head. I finished the job, pulling it the rest of the way off and tossing it aside.

The sun was coming up. I could tell because the room started to lighten a little, the light just barely creeping around the curtains. Finally, I could see him, and the look he gave me made my chest seize.

"You're beautiful," he said.

I couldn't talk, so I simply leaned back down and kissed him again. In this moment, right here and now, I let go of everything. His hand slid inside my panties and pushed them down over my ass, further and further until he pulled them off and tossed them off as well. Shifting, he removed his own boxers and then pulled me tight against him, kissing me with less control, as if he was afraid I'd stop this at any moment.

But I didn't want it to stop. I needed this, needed him, needed to feel loved and cared for and that I wasn't lost in this sea of sorrow any longer.

He traced lines down my back as we kissed, his hand smoothing down and down, finally pulling my leg up over his hip. I could feel his warmth and desire, his cock solid and long between us and I pushed in, trying to get closer. His hips moved and the friction of his length sliding between my folds set things moving at a faster pace.

I slid my hand between us and grabbed him, holding him tight as he pulled back and hissed.

"Yeah, baby," he whispered. "Just like that."

Building a rhythm, I stroked him from base to tip, slow and steady, just feeling every inch of him. His hand pushed on my hip, laying me back. I continued to hold him, and his hand slid around the front of me, sliding through my wetness, teasing me higher and higher. I sucked in a breath, shivering with each movement.

"You good?" he asked, and I simply nodded my head.

My hand became quicker, moving swiftly up and down him, his

hips moving in time with my hand. His finger slid inside me and I gasped. He froze.

"Don't stop," I breathed. "Please, don't stop."

It'd been too long since I'd felt desired, and this man who seemed more than perfect was playing me like a fiddle, stroking inside me, his thumb on the sensitive nub. My breathing was shallow, coming in quick pants, and I'd given up trying to keep him satisfied while he was giving to me. His head dipped, and he took one of my nipples into his mouth. The scruff on my breast, along with his warm, wet mouth around my nipple, sent me over the edge. I moaned in satisfaction, trying desperately to keep my volume down.

"That's it, baby," he whispered, his breath on my wet breast adding to the pleasure.

"I want you," I said, reaching back around to grip him again.

"I don't have any condoms," he confessed.

"It's okay," I replied. "Can't get pregnant."

I was having a hard time forming thoughts with the want inside me and I pulled him closer.

"Please," I begged, needing to be filled with someone again.

Shifting, he put his weight on top of me, leaning in to kiss me again.

"You're sure," he asked, his mouth on mine.

"Please," I begged, and his hips pressed to mine.

He reached between us, shifting himself to tease my opening and I gasped. It'd been too long, entirely too long, and I couldn't get him in me fast enough. Slowly, meticulously slow, he slid inside me and I moaned.

"You feel so good," he said in my ear, pressing himself to me as he filled me.

Slow and steady, an even rhythm, we moved together. With every thrust he added more of his cock to me, and I lifted my hips to bring him further and further inside. We were a team, moving together to give each other the pleasure we'd likely both been missing. Reaching down, he pulled my leg higher on his hip, giving him that much more space to get a better angle. It was just right as he rubbed right along the spot inside me and pushed me over the edge one more time.

It was like I was flying, higher and higher, and I could feel his frenzied movements quicken as he found his own release. Panting, he collapsed on me, his weight a comfort in the post climax, grounding me in the moment. Then his breath hitched, and I felt him shift.

"Don't go," I said, holding him.

"I just need a minute," he replied, shifting off me, but keeping me close at the same time.

We caught our breath, slowing the breathing down some, and held each other.

"You good?" he asked.

"Very," I replied, still holding him.

"Mom," I heard from the door, with a light knock.

"Oh shit," I whispered. "Just a minute," I said, louder to my daughter.

Jonathan kissed my forehead and slid off me more. He looked at me, clearly asking what I wanted, but I didn't know what that was, and I was afraid he was going to see rejection in my eyes. Another kiss on my lips and he slid out of bed, picking up his boxers, and walked to the bathroom. Before he shut the door, he turned and put a finger to his lips, showing me that he would be quiet so I could deal with Rayne.

"Mom," she called again. "Are you getting up?"

"Yeah," I replied. "Give me a minute."

"Okay," she said, and I could hear her move away from the door.

I sat up, pulling my tank top from behind me and slid it over my head. I couldn't find my panties, though, and I was completely embarrassed about what just happened.

Padding to the bathroom, I knocked quietly. He cracked the door open and looked out, then opened it fully.

"You good?" he asked again.

"I'm sorry," I replied.

"For what?"

"That probably shouldn't have happened," I said.

"I'm glad it did," he replied, and I looked up at him. "Really," he offered.

His smile wasn't really a smirk, but it was a satisfied look, and I realized that this was actually a really good thing. I smiled in return, then stepped closer. His hand came off the door, and he wound it around my waist, pulling me to him, then dipped his head down to kiss me, long and luxurious. I got lost in the moment, trying to memorize every moment of this.

"Mom," Thomas called from the door and we broke apart, breathless once again.

"I'm coming," I called. "Go have some cereal."

"Okay," he called back.

"I'll stay in here until you're gone if you want," he said.

"Yeah," I replied. "Probably a good idea."

He stepped out of the bathroom so I could go in and do my morning routine. When I came out, he was curled up, back to me, and I could see the slow rise and fall of his chest, his eyes closed. I stood there for just a moment and wondered whether this could actually work, the two of us.

With a deep breath, and a large sigh, I rummaged through my bag and pulled on some clothes, then grabbed my brush to tame my hair, pulling it into a ponytail. I walked out of the room, closing the door behind me, and headed to the kitchen to face my kids.

CHAPTER THIRTY-EIGHT

*J*onathan...

I stretched, reaching over to the other side of the bed, but it was empty. I was disappointed, but not completely surprised. Her scent was still here, in my bed, and I could still feel the way she felt, under me, around me, so responsive to my touch, craving me, begging me, wanting me.

Rolling over, I looked at the clock. It was just after ten, so I got up and headed back to the bathroom. I was half tempted to not shower, just so she could stay with me throughout the day. Flipping the light on, I relieved myself, then walked back into the room. Her panties were tucked under the side of the bed, but everything else of hers seemed to be gone. I picked them up and listened, just to make sure I was alone, then walked out of the room and down the hall.

The guest bed was made. The kitchen was clean, and nothing remained of her time here, and that bothered me more than it should. I grabbed a glass of water and downed it, then headed back to the bedroom and grabbed my phone.

Lucy: I'm sorry about this morning. I shouldn't have done that.
Lucy: If you want to cut contact, that's fine.
Lucy: I hope you won't, though. Call me if you want.

Three separate texts, several minutes between each of them, like the thoughts popped up in her head randomly. I sighed, then sat on the bed to dial her up. The phone rang, then went to her voicemail, and I wondered if she was avoiding my call.

"Hey, Lucy," I said. "I'm not sorry about this morning. If you're uncomfortable, I get it, but I want to talk."

I hung up before I could say anything else that might come across as desperate. I wasn't, except, maybe I was. She felt right, next to me, in my arms. It was nice to come home and find her in my bed. To wake up to her wanting me. The sex was tame, but only because I was mostly asleep, and I think she was nervous.

"Fuck it," I said, getting up and going to the closet.

I grabbed the laundry from my travel bag, along with the rest of the stuff in my hamper. I left her panties on a shelf in my closet, figuring I'd get them back to her at some point. Patty would be here soon to clean, so I took my bag and headed out to do some errands.

As I drove to the cleaners, I pondered what life would look like with Lucy in it. Would she want to move to my place? Probably not, since the kids were in school. Besides, I wouldn't want to uproot them, or her, to meet my needs. But maybe she didn't want to be together. Maybe this morning was loneliness and grief trying to find an outlet, and that she didn't see us that way.

By the time I got home, Patty was already there, cleaning away. I avoided her as much as possible, but she found me in the guest room at my desk.

"Mr. Bridge," she said. "I found something in your closet. Wanted you to know in case there was an issue."

"What was it?" I asked.

"Well," she blushed.

She was almost as old as my mom and had been our housekeeper for years. I insisted that Meg not lift a finger once we found out she was pregnant with Grant, and Patty had stayed on long after. Suddenly, it dawned on me she probably saw Lucy's panties and I realized her embarrassment.

"I'm sure it's fine," I said. "I'll just go have a look."

Getting up, I strode to my closet and there they were, sitting where I left them. Patty was behind me, and I thought she was watching to see what I would do with them. I tried to figure out the best way to handle this, but simply shoved them into my pocket and walked out. Maybe it was because she and Meg had such a close relationship that I was uncomfortable with the fact that I shared my bed with another woman, but I honestly didn't know.

Today was supposed to be an off day, but I needed to get this pent-up nervousness out, and there was no better way to do that than spending time in the batting cage, so I headed to the field to get a workout in. It was still early enough in the day that I probably wouldn't run into any of my teammates there.

"Look what the cat drug in," Beckett said as I walked into the cages below the stadium. "Get enough beauty sleep?"

"Shut up, Beckett," I barked, moving to a cage further down than the one he was in.

It didn't take long to get the machine set up to pitch to me, and before I had too much time to think about things, I was swinging away, pounding out my frustrations and confusion on the balls that were coming at me at a high rate of speed. I spent a good couple of hours working through hitting, then headed back into the locker room. With it not being a mandatory practice day, only a few of the players were at the park, along with a handful of coaches. Everyone loved the occasional day off at home we got so rarely, and most were taking advantage of it.

"Hey, man," Huffman said. "You good?"

"Yeah," I replied. "Just working on some things."

"You see the little shit got mandatory drills today?"

"Oh yeah?" I asked.

"Apparently," he continued, "Coach didn't like his attitude in Anaheim, so he's gonna work him until he's worked his shit out. Couldn't happen to a nicer guy."

He laughed, then pulled his bat out of the locker and headed toward the cages I just left. I hadn't known Beckett was going to be here, or I might have chosen another avenue for getting my frustrations out. Just as I was grabbing my clothes to head to the showers, he walked in. Of fucking course, that's when Lucy's panties decided to fall out of my pocket, right in front of him.

"Don't screw the fans, Bridge." He laughed. "It's not good for the team."

"You know what," I barked. "You don't know shit, and you know absolutely nothing about my life. Why don't you just go do your homework while the rest of us grown-ups move on with life. Some of us know how to handle the world around us. We also know that the world doesn't owe us shit. Something you might do well to remember."

I snagged her panties, threw my shit in my bag, and left the facility. Being there was more work than it was worth, and I didn't want to be around that little shit any more than I already had to. I'd shower at home where I could have some privacy.

CHAPTER THIRTY-NINE

*L*ucy...

"Why was the door locked this morning?" Rayne asked as we got into the car.

"Must have accidentally pushed it when I shut it last night," I lied.

I was just thankful that Jonathan had the forethought to lock it when he got home. Without taking a shower, I could still smell him on me, and it wasn't exactly upsetting. Honestly, I just wanted to try to figure out where we went from here.

After I dropped the kids off at school, I headed to the house. The bureau was going to be sending someone out that morning, so I wanted to be there when they arrived. Pulling up to the house, though, I could see that they were already there. Andrea came out of her house when I pulled up, toting Noah with her.

She waved at me as I parked on the street in front of the house.

"I see I'm late to the party," I said as I got out of the car.

"They actually got here super early this morning," she said.

"Why?"

"Probably should ask them," she suggested, nodding her head in the direction of the police that were on the scene.

Walking up the drive, I noticed the door was wide open, but something was off about it. It wasn't until I got to the porch that I saw the frame was shattered and there was broken glass and wood strewn around the entry.

"Ma'am," a detective said when I got to the front steps. "I'm going to have to ask you to stay outside for now."

"This is my house," I said, hoping there wasn't as much damage as what appeared by the door.

"I understand that," he said. "But this is a crime scene and we can't have you contaminating it."

"A crime scene?"

"Ma'am," he said. "I'll send someone out to talk to you. Would you mind waiting with your neighbor?"

"Oh, sure," I said, still confused as to why it was a crime scene.

I made my way back down the drive and over to where Andrea stood with Noah.

"Did they show you?" she asked.

"No," I said, now more worried than I was before. "What happened?"

She lifted her chin, pointing at the officer that was coming my direction. As he stepped closer, she moved away, but I wanted to pull her back for the moral support.

"Mrs. Fallon?" the officer asked.

"Yes," I replied.

"There seems to have been a miscommunication between you and your boyfriend," he said.

"I don't have a boyfriend," I said, looking him in the eye. "My husband died in September. He was an agent with the FBI."

"My apologies, ma'am," he said. "Someone contacted the police department to do a welfare check on you, stating that you had not been seen in a couple of days and that they were worried. He said he was your boyfriend."

"What is his name?" I asked, my blood running cold.

"He said his name was John Bridge," he replied. "We did a trace but were unable to find him from the call he made."

"So, you kicked in my front door?"

"Ma'am," he said. "When we receive a credible report, we must act on it."

"But you didn't call me," I said. "I was not contacted at all. You could have done a welfare check without breaking down my door."

"There were signs of a struggle inside," he said. "That's why we took action. We didn't want to leave an injured person, or a person in distress, inside the location."

"What signs of a struggle?" I asked, growing concerned.

"If I could see your ID," he said, holding his hand out.

I pulled my driver's license from my purse and handed it to him. He looked at it, then stepped away from me to call the information in. I turned to look for Andrea, but she must have gone inside with Noah. By the time I turned back, the officer was coming back to me, my license in his outstretched hand.

"If you'll come with me," he said, turning toward the house.

"Do you mind if I make one call first?" I asked.

"Not a problem," he replied, then stepped away from me.

I pulled up the number to the Seattle field office for the bureau, waiting for them to answer.

"Seattle field office, Federal Bureau of Investigation," the receptionist answered. "How may I direct your call?"

"I would like to speak with Agent Richards," I said.

"Who may I say is calling?"

"Lucy Fallon," I said.

"One moment, please," she replied, then the awful music that almost every hold system had began to play.

"Mrs. Fallon," Agent Richards said when he answered the phone.

"There's been a change," I said, without waiting for the niceties.

"Can you elaborate?" he asked.

"I'm not sure," I said. "I came home to find my door bashed in and the police here."

"I'll be out within the hour," he said. "Let me talk to the officer in charge."

"Sure," I said, walking over to the man who had been talking to me earlier. "FBI," I said, handing him my phone.

"Hello," he said, then paused. "Officer Jameson," he replied to whatever question was asked of him. "Yes, sir," he continued after a short pause. "I'm happy to make sure you get a copy of our reports."

There were a few other bits, but I didn't listen. I just kept thinking that I was glad I wasn't home, that the kids weren't here to see this, and that we had somewhere we could stay if this kept up. Then I thought about Jonathan, and how he likely wouldn't want my crazy at his place, especially if his son was going to be there.

"Ma'am," the officer said, handing my phone back to me. "If you'll come with me, I can escort you through the house."

"Thank you," I said, taking my phone and following him.

As I walked in the door, I looked to my right and saw my living room was trashed. The couches were turned over, the lamps and picture frames broken. Even the photos on the wall had been pulled down, and the walls themselves were covered in graffiti saying horrible things.

"Oh, God," I whispered, covering my mouth with my hand.

"I'm sorry," the officer said as he walked me further into the house. "It seems the master bedroom and the office were hit the worst. We'll look at the office on this floor before heading upstairs."

I followed him back to Ryan's office and almost fell to my knees. His desk was broken in several pieces, and the awards and certificates, as well as his diplomas and accommodations that had been hung on the wall were now in pieces amidst the rubble. I gripped the doorframe for support, trying like mad to keep from losing my shit.

"Are you ready to see the bedroom?" the officer asked.

"Not really," I confessed. "Might as well get it over with, though."

We walked up the stairs, and as we passed the kids rooms, I peeked in them. Nothing seemed out of place, so I asked about it.

"The kids' rooms seem fine," I said.

"Doesn't appear they were the target," he said. "Brace yourself," he added before we got to the door to my room. "This is really bad."

I took a deep breath, then nodded. I could do this. I was strong. I was capable. I was able to defeat any foe.

I was also very wrong.

The room was not just trashed, it was absolutely destroyed. It didn't look like anything at all was spared from some sort of destructive force. *YOU ARE A WHORE* was spray painted on the wall above the bed in bright red, and I had to swallow several times to keep from throwing up. Turning away, I stepped toward the stairs.

"Mrs. Fallon," the officer said as he followed me. "Do you know who might have done this?"

"Did you find the cameras?" I asked.

"No, ma'am," he said. "No security equipment was here except the alarm system, which was armed. We called the company, and they told us that it hadn't been used since yesterday around noon. It was recently changed to allow only you to have an access code, and that all changes were to be made in person. We aren't sure how the alarm could still be activated, as no one was inside. I assume you didn't do this to your own home."

"Absolutely not," I said. "I need to go outside."

Walking as fast as my legs would carry me, I went down the stairs and out the front door, pausing once outside to take a deep breath, letting it out in a gush.

"Do you have any idea who might have done this?" the officer asked again once he caught up to me.

"George Warde," I stated. "He's been stalking me for about six months, only I just now found out about it in the last couple of days."

"So," he began. "No report of this stalking is on file?"

"Unfortunately, no," I replied. "But my neighbor can vouch for what has been going on. Marco was going to meet with me and the FBI today to discuss what to do about the cameras he had set up in my house."

"Like I said, we did not find any cameras," the officer explained.

"He probably came to remove them," I offered. "That's probably when he trashed the house. What I don't understand is how he got in without setting off the alarm."

"That is a concern," the officer agreed. "Do you have somewhere you can stay? At least for a little while, until we get the house taken care of?"

"I have both family and friends nearby," I replied.

Just then, a blue sedan pulled up with federal plates and I knew the bureau had arrived. Two men got out of the car. One I recognized, the other I didn't.

"I'm Agent Richards," the agent I recognized said. "This is Agent Smith."

"Officer Jameson," the officer said, reaching his hand out to shake the agent's.

"Lucy," he said, once he'd finished that formality.

"Hey," I said. "Not exactly what I expected to be showing you when you came."

"Not at all what I wanted to see, either," he replied. "Ryan was a good man, and you deserve better than this."

"Will you walk us through?" Agent Smith asked the officer.

"I'm gonna stay out here," I said. "I've seen enough."

"That bad?" Richards asked.

"Worse," I replied.

Andrea stepped out of her house, saw me with the agents, and headed in our direction.

"Marco's on his way," she said when she got closer.

"Thanks," I said.

"Come on inside," she said. "Unless you need her."

"Not right now," Richards said. "Go on in and sit down. You look like you're gonna fall."

"Thanks," I said. I seemed to be saying that a lot.

I followed Andrea into her house and she gave me a hug once the front door was closed. She held me for a minute, then it hit me and I broke. I started to sob and nearly dropped to the floor. Somehow, she managed to maneuver us to the couch where I absolutely lost it.

"Why?" I kept asking, but there really wasn't any answer that made sense.

Nothing I did was deserving of this, absolutely nothing. Why did he decide now, of all times, to destroy my house, my life? What would that accomplish in the grand scheme of things? I couldn't find any answers, and honestly, I didn't think there were any.

CHAPTER FORTY

*J*onathan…

By the time I made it home, Patty had already left, so I didn't have to deal with that uncomfortable situation again. Honestly, I didn't know why she still came, what with it just being me. I paid her well, though, and had no need to drop the service, even if once a week wasn't actually needed. She deserved a bonus, though, after today's mishap. Hopefully she didn't think poorly about me.

I jumped in the shower after dropping my bag on my bed. Letting the water run over my body, I thought back over the last week or two at what all had changed in my life. New seasons always meant changes, but not everything was baseball related. No, Lucy was the biggest thing on my mind, and I honestly didn't know what was going to happen with her, or where it might go, if anywhere.

This morning was very nice, and I had to admit, coming home to her in my bed was a pleasant notion, one I could get used to in a hurry. When I finished my shower, I toweled off and put my workout gear into the bag to take back to the stadium the next day, knowing I had at least a couple more sets that were clean there, and this one would be washed with the rest the next time the crew did laundry for the team.

Not wanting to be cooped up, I dressed and headed out to the market to pick up supplies for the next few days until the team headed out again on Sunday for the first long road trip. Getting some chicken and veggies, along with a few staples for the house, just in case Lucy wanted to hang around. The only thing that wouldn't keep if she didn't were the veggies, but that was a small price to pay in hoping she'd be back.

Walking in the door, I tossed my keys into the dish and set the bags on the counter in the kitchen, putting the perishables away in the refrigerator and freezer. I shelved the dry goods, folded the reusable bags, and put them by the door to take back to the trunk when I went back down. With nothing left that was urgent, I went back into the guest room where my desk was and opened the laptop to watch some film the coaches had sent.

As soon as the machine powered up, the lock screen showed an image of Meg, Grant, and me, the last time we were all together on Alki Beach. It was right after I got back from the last road trip before she was killed, and the last day off we had together. I sat there and stared at it, mesmerized by her eyes, so bright, along with her smile. Grant was the spitting image of her, and it was clear that they were mother and son. The only piece of me he seemed to have were my eyes.

It happened quick, and I wasn't prepared for the emotions to steamroll me the way they did. Whether it was real or imagined, I felt like I'd betrayed her, taken something that was so beautiful and tarnished it by sleeping with Lucy in our bed.

"I'm sorry," I whispered, unable to put any force into my voice.

The tears started, and I wasn't sure when, but they were falling steadily, rolling down my cheeks, spilling onto my shirt, and I simply let them.

"What have I done?"

It wasn't a question that could be answered, at least not by me. Had what I'd done, what I'd allowed, tarnished my love for Meg? Had I sacrificed the lifetime I'd built with her for a moment of pleasure? Would she be mad at me?

The screen faded to black as I sat there and wept for the life I should have had. The one that was stolen from me in an instant.

CHAPTER FORTY-ONE

*L*ucy...

    "And this is everything you remember?" Agent Richards asked for the millionth time.

"That is what I know about him," I replied. "He worked with Ryan at the school. I only saw him a couple of times at events there. It wasn't until the funeral that I actually spoke to him."

"I was there," Andrea added. "He was not too good about taking a hint to take a hike, but somehow I convinced him."

"Because you're amazing," I said.

"The devices that were there were pretty sophisticated," Marco added, getting us back on track. "And they were hooked up to Lucy's Wi-Fi directly. I did the best I could at trying to find a connection to his system, but it was bouncing all over the place."

"He's in the cyber security department at the college," I said.

"How many devices total?" Agent Richards asked Marco.

"I found at least thirteen," he said. "But I think that there were also some in some nanny cams within the kids' toys and such. We know of two that he put in there for sure."

I just kept shaking my head, wondering whether this was all a nightmare, or some sort of cruel joke. Except it wasn't. This was my life at the moment. I jumped when my phone rang.

"Shit," I muttered, then picked up the call.

"Mom," Thomas said. "The school said we have to wait in the office for you to come get us. What's going on?"

Agent Richards had suggested that I call the school and let them know there was a security issue, and that the kids needed to stay in the office instead of coming home.

"They said some guy was here asking about us," he continued.

"What?"

"Yeah," Thomas said. "The secretary said he told her he was there to pick us up."

"Did she get a good look at him?" I asked, my heart going to my throat.

"Said he was a friend of Dad's," Thomas said, and I heard a wobble in his voice.

"Just stay there," I said. "I'll come get you."

"Rayne doesn't want to stay," he said.

"Is she there?"

"Yeah," he said, then I heard him pass the phone over, and Rayne came on the call. "What?" she asked.

"Something has happened," I said. "I need you to not go anywhere until I get there."

"You're kinda overdramatic, Mom," she said.

"I'm not even dramatic enough," I said. "Something happened at the house. It's a crime scene. You can't go anywhere until I get there. It isn't safe."

"A crime scene?" she whispered over the phone.

"Yeah," I replied.

"I'll take you," Marco said.

"Uncle Marco is going to bring me there, then bring us back here," I told her. "Tell the secretary that we're coming and will be there soon."

"Okay," she said. "Are you okay?"

"Not at all," I replied. "But we'll get through it."

"I love you," she said, and it was the first time she'd uttered those words in a really long time.

"I love you, too," I replied. "I'll see you soon. Do *not* leave the school with anyone."

"I won't," she said.

"Good," I replied, then disconnected the call.

"We can wait on the rest," Agent Richards said. "We'll be here a while."

"Someone tried to pick up my kids," I said, and he paled.

"I'll get the security tape sent to you," Marco said.

"Thank you," Agent Richards replied. "I'll leave you for now and get to work on what we know. This will all work out, Mrs. Fallon. I promise."

"Thanks," I replied, using the same term I'd used most of the day.

Marco led me to his big SUV, chirping the locks when we got close, and opening my door for me to climb in. He went around the front and climbed into the driver's seat.

"It's gonna be okay," he assured me. "We'll get this all sorted."

"I really appreciate your help," I said. "I know you have your own job and things you have to do, but—"

"Nope," he said, cutting me off. "We're family. We stick together and help each other out when we can. It's what I would expect you to do for us if the situation were reversed."

"Thank you," I said, again using those words.

The drive to the school was fairly quick, and we pulled up in front and parked. Marco got out with me, taking in everything around us as we walked into the building. When we got to the office, Thomas nearly launched himself at me, hugging me tight.

"Hey," I said. "We're here. It's all good."

"Mom," Rayne said, a catch in her voice.

"It's good," I said, not wanting to get into anything more here at the school.

Marco had walked up to the desk and had asked about getting the footage from the security system to the bureau so they could analyze it and see if they could catch George in the act. I simply held my kids, waiting for him to be done.

"Ready?" he asked a short time later.

"Yeah," I said, then grabbed both kids by the hand, one on each side, and we walked out of the school.

The ride home was silent, and when we pulled into the cul-de-sac, I heard the kids take in a quick breath.

"Mom?" Rayne asked, her voice shaky.

"It'll be fine," I said. "We'll get it all figured out."

When Marco parked, I climbed out first, and the kids followed. Andrea had come out of her house and was ushering us inside, away from the handful of neighbors who were watching us.

"I'm going to die," Rayne said once we got inside.

"Not if I can help it," I replied. "My job is to keep you safe. That's exactly what I'm going to do."

"Mom," she said. "There are cops all over at our house. What is going on?"

"The person who has been watching us…" I began. "He broke in."

"But you didn't get a call," she interrupted.

"He's in cyber security like your dad," I said. "He's gotten into our security system. I don't know why or how, but he decided that last night was a good time to come in and trash the place."

Both kids sucked in air. Thomas was shaking as well.

"He didn't do anything in your rooms," I added, so they would feel at least a little more secure. Or at least that's what I hoped it would do for them. "The living room, kitchen, Dad's office, and my bedroom were all really bad. I don't want you guys to have to see that, so we're gonna hang out here until we figure out what we're doing."

There was a knock on the door and I jumped, both kids doing the same.

"It's Agent Richards," Andrea said. "He said he'd be over when you got back."

She opened the door and let the agent in.

"Hey, kids," he said when he saw them sitting in the living room.

"Hello, sir," Thomas said, sounding braver than I knew he was.

"Why?" Rayne asked.

"That's the million-dollar question," he replied. "And that's what I'm here to try to figure out. Did you see the man who came in to try to pick you up?"

"I didn't," Thomas said.

"Nope," Rayne agreed.

"Okay," he replied. "They sent me the footage, and our analyst has pulled out some stills from it. I'm going to ask if you recognize anyone. I want to do this with each of you by yourself so I know whether he's been in contact with any of you, and so you don't feed of each other's reactions. You understand?"

I nodded, then looked to my kids who were looking to me for guidance.

"Can Andrea sit with them?" I asked. "Just in the room so they aren't alone?"

"That's fine," Agent Richards said. "But I'm gonna need you to be absolutely still when I bring up the footage."

"I can do that," she said. "Let's sit in the kitchen to do it. This way we're away from everyone."

"Lead the way," the agent said.

"Thomas," I said, but Rayne interrupted.

"Let me go first," she said. "I should go first."

"If you want," I replied.

"I do," she said, then walked after Andrea and the agent into the kitchen.

"Mom," Thomas said after she'd gone. "What's gonna happen?"

"I'm not sure, yet," I said. "We'll get everything figured out."

"I don't want to move," he said, and there was a hitch in his voice. "It's not fair that we have to move."

"We won't move," I said, determined to give the kids back their security.

"But what if—"

"Not gonna be a problem," I said. "We're strong, we're brave, and we're fighters. I'm not going to let anyone ruin our lives. Got it?"

He nodded, his head bobbing faster than it probably should. It didn't take long before Rayne was coming back.

"Your turn," she said to Thomas.

I squeezed his hand as he got up, and he turned and gave a wane smile.

"How did it go?" I asked my daughter as she sat on the couch.

"He said I shouldn't say anything," she said.

"True," I agreed. "But you can tell me if it went well."

"I mean," she hedged, but didn't say more.

"We'll get through this," I said, trying to convince her just as much as I was trying to convince myself.

Thomas came out of the kitchen, Andrea right behind him.

"Your turn," she said, looking at me.

"Did you look?" I asked her.

"Nope," she said. "You go first, then I'll go after."

Standing, I hugged my youngest, then walked into the kitchen.

"Ready?" Agent Richards asked.

"As ready as I can be," I said, sitting at the counter in my friend's kitchen.

"I'm going to show you the stills that I showed the kids," he said, holding his phone in front of me.

He swiped each image, slowly, giving me time to look at them all. I shook my head. This wasn't right. It was supposed to be George, Captain Clueless, the man who had been tormenting me for more than half a year. But this didn't look like him.

"Can I see them again?" I asked.

"Sure," he said, swiping the other direction on his phone, showing me the grainy images in reverse order once again.

"I'm sorry," I said, looking up at the agent. "I don't know if that's who I thought it was or not."

"It's all right," he said. "Nothing wrong with not being sure. I'd hate for you to be absolutely sure, only to find out that you were mistaken. Eyewitness testimony is flawed at best. These images aren't the best, either, so it isn't a problem."

"But this means he'll get away with this," I complained, feeling the panic rising in me.

"Depends on what they find at your house," he said. "Would you ask Andrea to come back?"

"Sure," I said, getting up.

I couldn't shake the feeling that this guy was going to get away with this. That he was going to be able to continue to stalk me, watch me, inside my own house, and that there wasn't anything I could do about it.

CHAPTER FORTY-TWO

*J*onathan...

The phone ringing jolted me awake.

"Hello?" I answered without looking.

"You don't sound good," my mom said. "You feeling okay?"

"Yeah," I lied. "Just ended up taking a nap at my desk, which isn't very comfortable."

"I would think not." She laughed. "I wanted to check in on you. Haven't heard from you since your first road trip. How did it go?"

"We won both games," I said. "So there's that. I didn't play, so nothing new there. Just working out, keeping myself ready for when the coach needs me."

"I was thinking of coming up in a few weeks," she said. "Grant has been asking for you, so it might be nice to bring him up."

"That sounds great," I said. "I'll have to check the schedule, though. I can't remember how long the next road trip is, or when we'll be back. I also have a friend who has been crashing at my place a little."

"Oh, yeah?" she asked.

"Yeah," I said. "She had some issues with her place, so her and her kids were here this week."

"She?" Mom asked, clearly looking for more information.

"It's not what you think," I said, although I wondered if that were true. "She's the widow I told you about. I guess there's a dude who used to work with her husband who has been making some waves. I wanted to give her a safe place to be."

"You have always been too nice," she said.

"It was the least I could do," I said. "Honestly, I'd let her move in and I could find another place if it made her safe. She told me some of what this guy did and it's really scary. I don't want her kids to be stuck in that kind of situation."

"As long as you're being careful," she said. "Check your schedule and let me know what you think would be a good weekend to come up. We could also come up during the week if that's easier for you."

"I'll let you know," I said. "And, Mom," I began.

"Yeah?"

"I love you," I said.

"I love you, too," she replied. "Now, get to work."

She disconnected the call, and I had to laugh. It was one of the things she'd always say to me when I would talk to her throughout the year. She'd ask how the games were going, how I was handling the sporadic playing, and whether I was getting enough exercise outside of playing. I'd assure her that everything was fine and that I would let her know if there was an issue.

I looked at my phone and saw that there was a missed call from Lucy, and a voicemail from her. I pulled up the voicemail and let it play.

"Jonathan," she said, and sounded a bit on edge. "Things have gotten a bit weird here, and I don't want to put you in danger, so I'm going to cut contact for now. It has nothing to do with this morning, I promise. I just need to be sure that I don't do anything that will get you hurt. I'll call you when I can."

While I didn't know her well, I could still hear the edge of fear in her voice, the slight shaking on certain words. Whatever was going on in her life was tearing her up, and she wouldn't let me in to help, which was frustrating. I didn't need anyone to keep me safe, I could do that on my own. I decided to send a text, just on the off chance that she might get the message.

Jonathan: Be safe but let me know how I can help. I'm not worried about me, but I am worried about you. Keep me posted.

Whatever it was that was going on with her, I needed to know she was safe. I couldn't explain why, but there was a need there. Something instinctual that made me want to protect her and her kids. Problem was, I didn't know how I was going to do that. She knew where I lived, but I had no idea where she was. I did, however, know her last name, and the kids' names. Maybe I could figure out where they went to school and find them that way. The more I thought about it, though, the more it sounded as if I were the stalker she was trying to get away from. I guess the only thing I could do would be to wait and see if she came to the game tomorrow night.

I got up from the desk and had to try a couple times before I could get my legs to cooperate. Apparently, sleeping in this chair was not a good idea.

Instead of watching film as I'd planned, I decided to go for a run around Green Lake. It was warm enough, by Pacific Northwest standards, so I changed into shorts and a t-shirt, grabbed my keys and phone, along with my headphones, and headed out the door. The drive out to the lake was nice, and since it was a Wednesday, in the middle of the day, parking was readily available. I parked and pocketed my key, stretching before heading out to run around the lake.

By the time I made my second trip, I was feeling the burn in my legs, but I pressed on, knowing that soon I would get that euphoria feeling I always did near the end of a long run. I was breathing heavy when I made it back to my car and unlocked it. That was when I noticed a note tucked under the wiper. I pulled it out and climbed into the car, tossing it on the seat next to me.

I grabbed the note when I got out in my garage and flipped it open as I stepped into the elevator.

*She's mine. You can't have her. There is nothing you can give
her that she actually wants. Give up and move on.*

I couldn't get to my condo soon enough, and by the time I was locked inside, I was beginning to shake. Picking up my phone, I dialed Lucy, but the call went straight to voicemail without ringing. I didn't want to leave a message, but then remembered that she had said her husband had worked for the FBI. I did a search for the local office in Seattle and found the number and dialed it.

"Federal Bureau of Investigation, Seattle office, how can I direct your call?"

The woman was polite, but I honestly didn't know exactly what I was supposed to do about this.

"I think I need to talk to someone," I said.

"What is the situation, sir?" she asked.

"I have a friend whose husband used to work for you," I began. "She recently told me that she's been having some issues. I got a note on my car when I was out for a run today, and I think it might be related."

"Please hold," she said, then clicked whatever button she used and I heard that boring music that was always playing on hold.

"FBI," a man said. "Agent Smith. How can I help you?"

"I'm not exactly sure," I said. "I told the woman who answered the phone that I got a note on my car and it might have something to do with a friend."

"Sir," he said, sounding annoyed. "Notes on cars don't usually warrant a call to the FBI. Perhaps you should toss the note and get a new girlfriend."

"Don't you even want to know what the note said?" I asked, getting annoyed.

"Fine." He huffed, as though humoring me was wasting his time.

I read the note, word for word, and when I finished, I heard the agent sigh again.

"Like I said," he reiterated. "You should find a new girlfriend."

"Don't you even want to know my friend's name?" I asked, getting more upset by the minute.

"Not really," he said. "Look, you probably have a girlfriend who already had a boyfriend or husband and he's just warning you off. Best walk away now and be done with it."

The phone line disconnected, and I was left with dead air.

"Fuck," I muttered, knowing something was up. I just didn't know what to do about it.

CHAPTER FORTY-THREE

*L*ucy...

The day was long, longer than I wanted, and by the time the police and agents were done at the house, I was ready to just crash.

"The kids are upstairs," Andrea said. "They were both really tired, so I told them to rest in the guest room. I think they were asleep before their heads hit the pillows."

"I kinda feel the same way," I said. "I keep fluctuating between anger and fear, back and forth, over and over again."

"Have you eaten anything?"

"Actually," I said, just as my stomach growled.

"I'll get you some toast," she said, going to the kitchen.

"You holding up?" Marco asked as he came downstairs with Noah.

"Best as I can," I said.

"Do you have somewhere to stay?" he asked. "You can totally stay here if not, but—"

"I don't know," I said. "They may want me to be put up in some stingy hotel or something."

"More likely they'll have you stay with friends or family," he countered.

"I just don't want to put anyone out," I said, feeling like I was more problems than I was worth.

"Here you go," Andrea said as she brought in the toast.

Marco had put Noah on the floor with some toys and he was happily babbling to himself in his own little language. Oh, to be young and have no worries in the world.

"I didn't get a chance," Andrea began, "but how was the stay?"

"What stay?" Marco asked as he stepped in from the kitchen after grabbing a beer.

"I stayed at a friend's house overnight," I said. "Actually, I was there from Sunday to this morning."

"And…" Andrea pushed.

I could feel the blush raising up my throat and coloring my cheeks.

"I know that look." Andrea smiled.

"I'll let you two chat," Marco said, making a beeline for the front door. "I'll be outside if you need me."

He walked out the door, closing it behind him.

"Girl," she said, looking at me in a knowing way.

"He was gone until sometime in the middle of the night last night," I said, looking to the stairs to make sure the kids weren't going to be coming down and hear me.

"But he came home in the middle of the night," she coaxed. "I take it he didn't sleep on the couch."

"No," I confirmed. "He slipped into bed at some point. I don't know when, though, because I didn't wake up."

I stopped, hoping that what I'd given her was enough, but knowing she'd pry the rest out of me. Sure enough, she gave me the look, the one that gets me talking about everything I don't want to talk about.

"I woke up snuggled up next to him," I confessed. "I thought I was dreaming because he wasn't supposed to be there. I realized it wasn't a dream when I got to the waistband of his shorts."

"Please tell me he's ripped," she gushed.

"You are awful." I laughed. "And yeah, he is."

"Go on," she said, waiting impatiently for the rest of the story.

I laughed and continued. "I must have said something about it being a dream because he laughed," I said. "Told me it wasn't a dream. When I tried to pull away, he grabbed my hand and kept it where it was, right at the top of his waistband."

I paused, glancing once again at the stairs.

"They're dead to the world," she said. "I promise."

"God." I sighed. "I can't do this."

"I'll get wine," she said. "That will help lubricate things. Red or white?"

"I probably shouldn't," I said, but she replied with, "Nonsense," and floated into the kitchen, coming back with two glasses and a full bottle of Moscato. "You are awful," I said.

"Here," she said after pouring a glass. "To help steady your nerves."

I took a sip, then another larger swallow, before setting the glass down on the coffee table. Noah had crawled over and was pulling himself up, so I rethought my location and put it on the table behind the couch, a little more out of the little man's reach.

"Okay," she said, after taking a healthy drink herself. "Let's get back to the dream that wasn't a dream."

It took me a while, but I finally told her everything that happened that morning, including almost getting caught by the kids.

"That would have been a total buzz kill," she said.

"And would have made things a whole lot more complicated," I agreed.

"But was it good?"

"You are horrible," I said, blushing once again.

"That's not a no." She laughed. "So," she continued after another swallow of wine. "Are you gonna see him again?"

"I honestly don't know," I said. "I don't want to get him wound up with Captain Clueless at all. That wouldn't be fair to him, and I can't ask him to do that to himself or his kiddo. I would hate it if something happened to him."

"Has he called?" she asked.

"I honestly don't know," I replied.

I pulled my phone out and realized that it had somehow been

turned to do not disturb. When I took that off, it lit up with a handful of text messages and a couple of missed calls. There were a couple of voicemails as well. I pulled that up and listened.

Lucy, Jonathan said. *Call me when you get this. It's important.*

His voice was curt, almost rude, but there was something there. I looked at the text, which had come in much earlier in the day, as well. This voicemail was left just a little while ago. I decided I should probably call him, that would be easier than doing everything by text.

"Lucy?" he answered.

"Hey," I said.

"Are you okay?"

"What do you mean?" I asked, concerned with the sound of his voice.

"Are you okay?" he reiterated.

"I'm fine," I said. "Why?"

"Thank God." He sighed. "I was worried about you, and when I couldn't reach you, I got even more scared."

"What are you talking about?" I asked.

"I got a note," he said. "Someone left it on my car when I went for a run today."

"Oh, shit," I whispered. "What did it say?"

"It was a threat," he said.

"Against you?"

"Yeah," he replied. "Said I should leave you alone. Are you sure you're okay?"

"Jonathan, I need that note," I said. "Is there a way I can get it from you?"

"I can bring it to you," he said.

"I don't want to put you in danger," I replied.

"Lucy," he said. "What is going on?"

"I'm so sorry," I said. "I didn't mean for any of this to spill over onto you. You shouldn't have to deal with all of this. It's all my fault."

CHAPTER FORTY-FOUR

*J*onathan...

"It's all my fault," she said, and I could hear both the fear and the worry in her voice.

"Where are you?" I asked.

"I'm at my neighbor's house," she said. "I don't want to put you out—"

"Would they be okay with me coming over?" I asked.

I needed to see her, needed to convince myself that she was safe. There was a muffled sound, then she came back on the phone.

"Andrea said it was fine," she said, then rattled off the address.

"I'll be there as soon as I can," I said. "Don't worry about it."

"Be safe," she said, and I wondered whether it was something I really had to worry about.

"I will be," I replied. "See you soon."

I disconnected the call, then grabbed the note along with my wallet and keys and headed out. My GPS gave me clear instructions on how to get to the house, and it didn't take long, even though it felt like hours had passed. When I pulled up, I could see caution tape around the house next door to the address she'd given me, so I assumed that was her house. There was a man standing in the front yard, putting some golf balls around.

"Can I help you?" he asked when I parked.

"I'm here to see Lucy," I said.

"Who are you?" he asked, and I could see that he readied himself for a fight. He was a big guy, but even if he weren't, I didn't think I could have taken him on. There was that sense that he knew how to use his body to his advantage, and I didn't want to find out just how powerful he really was.

"My name is Jonathan Bridge," I said. "She was staying with me the last couple of nights."

Just then the front door opened and Lucy came barreling out.

"Jonathan," she sobbed as she got to me. "Are you okay?"

I gathered her into a hug and held her, then pushed her back to arm's length to look at her. Seeing her again did something to me, especially with the worry in her eyes.

"I'm fine," I said. "You good?"

"Yeah," she said, then turned back toward the house. "Come on. You can meet my best friends."

We walked up to the yard, and she introduced me to Marco, who had been putting in the yard.

"Nice to meet you," he said, sticking his hand out. "I appreciate you helping Lucy the last couple of days."

"Not a problem at all," I replied. "I was actually really glad to help."

He led us inside the two-story house to a woman on the couch and a little one on the floor. The kid looked to be pretty young, maybe a year or so.

"Andrea," she said. "This is Jonathan."

The woman stood and stuck her hand out to shake, saying, "Nice to meet you."

"Pleasure," I replied.

"We'll leave you two alone," she said, picking up the baby and giving her husband a look that indicated he would follow her or be doomed.

"Did you bring the note?" Lucy asked as soon as they were out of the room.

"I did," I said. "I called the FBI, but they blew me off."

"Who did you talk to?" she asked.

"Don't remember," I said. "But he seemed to think that I was just screwing some woman who was married and her husband was telling me to get lost."

"God." She sighed. "I hate the way they assume things sometimes."

"It was a little odd," I replied. "I mean, I've never called them, but you would think if someone was calling, they may want to at least pretend to care."

"Let me call Agent Richards," she said, pulling out her phone. She dialed and waited for them to answer. "Agent Richards, please," she said, then paused. "Lucy Fallon," she responded to what I assumed was a question on who she was. "Hey," she said when whoever she was waiting for answered. "He's left a note with my friend," she said, then paused. "Sure," she added, then handed the phone to me.

"Hello," I said into the device.

"My name is Agent Richards," the man on the other end said. "Lucy said you got a note."

"I did," I said. "I called you guys, but didn't know who to talk to, so they just brushed me off."

"Typical." He huffed. "Can you read it to me?"

I pulled it out of my pocket and read it to him, then looked up to see Lucy turning white as a ghost. Grabbing her, I pulled her to my chest, wrapping my arm around her. I could feel her shaking with what I can only imagine was either fear or rage.

"Did he sign it?" the agent asked.

"Nah," I said. "Just what I read. It was in a plain envelope tucked under my wiper when I left Green Lake."

"And have you had any run-ins with anyone recently?"

"Besides one of the players on my team," I laughed, "there's been nothing."

"This sounds more like who we've been dealing with," he said. "But I'd like to get that note if you wouldn't mind."

"No problem," I said. "I have no need for it, and if it will help keep Lucy safe, I'm all for that."

"Thank you for bringing it to our attention," he said. "You can leave it with Lucy or her neighbor and we'll get it the next time we're out there."

"Sure thing," I said. "Anything else you need from me?"

"We may need to have you come in and give an official statement," he said. "But that can wait for now."

"That's fine," I said. "Anything I can do to help. Did you need to talk to Lucy again?"

"If she doesn't need me, I'm good to go," he said.

I looked at Lucy, and she shook her head, so I said, "I think we're good."

"I'll be in touch with Lucy to get that letter and set up a time for you to give a statement," he said. "Thank you for your help."

"Sure thing," I said, then the call disconnected.

We'd managed to sit on the couch, and she was tucked up against me. I set the phone on the table in front of the couch and held her.

"You good?" I asked after a while.

"I'm so sorry," she said, and her voice was rough. "You shouldn't have to deal with this."

"Hey," I said, tilting her head with my finger under her chin. "I'm in this, now. You need to be kept safe, and I'm good with helping out on that front."

"I'm just so embarrassed," she said, looking away.

"Nothing to be embarrassed about," I replied. "You don't have to do this alone. I'm here, of my own accord, and have no problem shouldering whatever weight you can't carry."

She sniffed, then pulled back, looking at me again.

"Jonathan?" I heard Thomas ask from behind me.

"Hey, buddy," I said, looking over my shoulder.

"How did you know where we live?"

I laughed and said, "Your mom sent me the address. I thought I'd come check on you guys."

It was clear he had just woken up, which I thought was odd for late afternoon. But, judging from the tape around their house, and the stress that Lucy seemed to be shouldering, I figured whatever had happened had caused them to be exhausted.

"You're so nice," he said.

"I try," I replied.

"Where's your sister?" Lucy asked.

"She's still asleep," he said as he made his way around the couch to sit on the loveseat that was next to it.

"Hey," Lucy's friend said as she poked her head out of the kitchen. "I've got some dinner going. You can stay if you'd like, Jonathan. I don't know if you can eat what I made, but you're free to stay."

"Much obliged," I said, rubbing Lucy's back, trying desperately to give her my strength. "I can eat darn near anything."

"Good," she said. "Thomas, would you help me?"

"Sure, Aunt Andrea," he said, then got up to go help her with whatever it was she needed.

"I don't know what to do," Lucy said once Thomas was gone. "I can't go home because the place is a wreck and I don't want the kids to see it—"

"You can come to my place," I offered. "Stay as long as you want."

"I can't do that to you," she said.

"I wouldn't offer if I wasn't serious," I replied.

"What's he doing here?" Rayne asked as she came down the stairs.

"Hey, Rayne," I said.

"Mom," she said, ignoring me.

"He got a letter from the guy," she said.

"Great." She huffed. "Is he after everyone?"

"That's what we're hoping to find out," she said. "Agent Richards will be back over pretty soon to look at the note. We'll see what he has to say."

"What's for dinner?" she asked.

"Ask Aunt Andrea," Lucy said. "She's in the kitchen."

The girl walked that direction, going to wherever it was that everyone else had gone.

"You doing okay?" I asked.

"Why does everyone keep asking me that?" she asked. "No," she continued. "I'm not doing all right. My house has been trashed, my family is scared, and I'm being stalked. What part of that sounds like a good time?"

"I'm sorry," I said. "I know you're overwhelmed. I'm here for you, though."

I wasn't sure what it was about Lucy, but I felt the need to be there for her. Whether it was a shoulder to cry on, someone to hold her when she was down, or someone to share a bed with. I was in it for real, and it seemed so odd that it was so sudden.

"Why are you here?" she asked. "Why do you care?"

"I honestly don't know," I confessed. "It could be just that you're in a rough spot. Or that I understand what you're going through. Does it really matter?"

"I mean," she began, but Rayne called from the kitchen that dinner was ready.

"You sure you want to stay?"

"I do," I replied. "This will be a good way to get to know your friends, too."

She stood up, then held a hand down to me. When she didn't let it go when we walked to the dining room, I wasn't sure what to think.

CHAPTER FORTY-FIVE

*L*ucy...

I dropped his hand just before we rounded the corner into the dining room, not wanting to give Rayne any additional worries, and not wanting Thomas to get too excited. I also wasn't sure exactly where this thing between us was going to go. This morning seemed like years ago, and the fact that he was actually here was impressive.

Still, I didn't want to get my hopes up, but also didn't want to put false expectations on Jonathan. Dinner was quiet, with Noah being the most vocal. Of course, what do you expect from a baby. About halfway through, though, there was a knock on the door and we all tensed.

"I'll get it," Marco said, getting up from the table.

"It might be Agent Richards," I commented as he went past.

"Lucy," Marco called from the other room.

I got up, dread weighing my steps, and went in that direction. Jonathan got up and followed, knowing he had the note the agent would want.

"I have some news," he said. "Is now a good time?"

"It's as good as any," I said, then turned to see that both kids were standing at the portal to the rest of the house, watching.

"Mom," Rayne said, looking fearful for the first time.

"Come on," I said, knowing neither of them would be able to eat or pretend that there wasn't something going on in here.

We all sat down, crowded as it was, and waited for Agent Richards to give us information on what was going on.

"Can I see the letter?" he asked Jonathan.

"Oh, yeah," he said, standing up and pulling it out of his pocket.

Agent Richards looked it over, nodded, then stuffed it into the binder he had with him.

"We think we have identified the man who attempted to pick up your kids," he said, pulling something out of the same folder. "Can you tell me if you recognize this man?"

I looked at the pictures he handed me, trying to see if any recognition came to me, but it wasn't there. Whoever this guy was, I didn't know him, which made things even worse. If it had been George, I would have at least had some answers. But this guy, this kid, really, because he didn't look like he was much older than about twenty, was no one to me.

"Can I see?" Rayne asked, holding her hand out.

I passed the photos to her and she and Thomas looked them over.

"I don't know him," Thomas said.

"Me, either," Rayne agreed.

Jonathan had looked at them when I was holding them, and he added that he hadn't seen him before, either.

"We'll look into him," the agent said. "And we'll check out this note as well. Where did you say you got it?"

"I was on a run at Green Lake," Jonathan said. "When I got back to my car, it was under the wiper."

"And you didn't see anyone around?"

"Oh, yeah," he said. "There were a lot of people around, just no one next to my car."

"I see," Agent Richards said.

"Do you know who this guy is?" Marco asked, handing the photos back to the agent.

"We're running his face through some software to see if we can get a match," the agent said. "Until then, I suggest you all stay safe and together if possible. Do you want me to set up a hotel for you and the kids?"

I looked to Jonathan who gave me a nod, letting me know he was good with whatever choice I made.

"I think I have someplace," I said.

"Good," he replied. "If you need anything, let me know."

"I will," I replied.

"Are you gonna catch him?" Rayne asked as the agent stood up.

"That's my job," he said. "I'll do my best to keep you safe and find out who is doing this. In the meantime, though, you should pay attention to your surroundings."

"Thank you again," I said, ushering the agent back to the door.

"I'll call you with updates," he said, then stepped outside.

"What did I miss?" Andrea asked as she stepped into the living room with a freshly washed baby.

"They have better pictures of the guy who tried to pick the kids up," I said.

"You guys staying here?" she asked.

"I'm not sure," I replied. "I need to call my parents."

"Grams and Gramps could come get us," Thomas said. "We could stay with them."

"Let me figure some things out," I replied.

I wasn't sure I wanted to put my parents in the line of fire of this guy. Also, not knowing who this other guy was made things even more terrifying. Add to that, what was going on with me and Jonathan, and you had a recipe for disaster I wasn't sure I wanted to be part of.

"Hey," Jonathan said. "You can do this."

The confidence he implied was kind, but he had no idea what people were capable of. After seeing what George did to my house, I was really scared. I didn't want to put anyone else in danger.

"Can I sit in your office?" I asked Marco. "Make some calls and figure things out?"

"Absolutely," he replied. "Take your time. We're here if you need us. You can stay with us, go somewhere else. If you need to, you can even switch cars with us."

"I was thinking the same thing," Jonathan said. "If you drive mine, it may be harder for the guy to find you."

"He found you," I replied. "Just give me a little bit. I'll be back."

I walked into Marco's office, which was so similar to Ryan's, and shut the door. All I wanted to do was fall apart, but I had to stay strong. I had to do whatever I could to keep my family safe. I pulled out my phone and dialed my dad.

"Hey, kiddo," he said when he answered.

"Dad," I replied. "I need your help."

CHAPTER FORTY-SIX

*J*onathan...

Lucy closed the door behind her and all I wanted to do was open it up and wrap her in my arms and keep her safe. It wasn't my place, though, so I let her do whatever it was she thought she had to do.

"Why are you here?" Rayne asked me once her mom was gone.

"Rayne," Andrea warned.

"No," the girl replied. "I need to know what is going on with you and my mom. Are you guys screwing?"

"Wow," I said. "I don't even know what to say to that."

"You are," she said. "I knew it. That's all you want from her is to get into her pants and screw her. You know my dad only died a few months ago, right?"

"I do know that," I said. "Your mom and I have been talking over the last couple of weeks by phone. My wife died just a few months ago, too, so we've been talking about how to get over the loss. Your mom still loves your dad, and probably always will."

"That isn't keeping you from screwing her, though," she said, and I could see the tears building in her eyes.

"Rayne," Thomas said, but she was having none of it.

"Why don't you go fuck someone else?" she shouted. "I'm sure there are plenty of women who would do it with you, so why do you have to be fucking my mom."

"Rayne Nicole Fallon," Lucy boomed.

I hadn't even heard the door to the room open, but there she was, standing just inside the living room. Rayne stormed off, but not before I saw the tears starting to fall. I had no idea what just happened, but Lucy took off after her daughter up the stairs. Marco and Andrea seemed just as shocked as I was with what the girl said.

"Jonathan," Thomas said, and I could see the conflict in his face.

"It's gonna be okay," I lied. I had no idea whether anything would ever be okay again for this family.

"But is she right?" Thomas asked.

"What is going on between your mom and I is just that, between us," I said. "We have a lot in common, and we're finding it helpful to talk to each other about that kind of thing."

How was I supposed to explain to this boy that his mom and I had been bumping uglies, but only once, and it just sort of happened, and that we hadn't talked about where things would be going from here?

"Hey, T," Andrea said, drawing his attention from me. "Your mom is really having a hard time, and Jonathan is being a really good friend to give her a safe space to share her emotions. Remember how Rayne was when your dad first died?"

"Yeah," Thomas said.

"It's like that," she said. "Your mom can't just go screaming through the house, slamming doors, pretending nothing else matters. She had to be there for you and your sister, to help you guys work through what was going on with you. Now it's her turn, and Jonathan has been helping her with that."

"You have?" he asked me.

"She's been helping me, too," I replied. "It's hard to know how to go through this sort of thing. Your mom and I have talked about what we feel, what we're afraid of, and how we move forward. It's really hard, but she's been really helpful for me. You know, I have a little boy, too. He's much younger than you, though. Your mom has helped me see how I can help him deal with his mom being gone. I don't know if I could have gone through this without her."

The confession was true. We'd had long conversations about how to help the kids get past the loss, but it had also been about how we were supposed to move forward, too. While we hadn't actually talked about a relationship, one sort of had developed. It was frightening how fast it moved, but at the same time, we were moving at the pace that worked for us. I would never tell someone to get into a relationship less than a year after their spouse died, but Lucy and I had become friends first, and that was always the best foundation for any good relationship.

"It's okay if you want to date my mom," Thomas said. "I like you. Besides," he continued with a smile. "We'd be able to go to all the baseball games we wanted if she was dating you."

Andrea laughed at the boy and I just sat there and looked at him. Yeah, I could date his mom. That wouldn't bother me at all.

CHAPTER FORTY-SEVEN

*L*ucy...

"Rayne," I shouted as she stomped down the hall.

She tried to slam the door to the guest room, but I caught it before it closed.

"Mom," she cried, and she was truly crying now. "How can you do this to Dad?"

"I don't know what you're talking about," I said.

"Him," she shouted, pointing out the door. "Why do you have to do that?"

I took a deep breath and held it, counting slowly to ten, then let it out through my mouth. This conversation wasn't supposed to happen. Hell, I didn't even know what was going on with Jonathan and me. Finally, I decided that truth would always be the best option, so I sat down on the edge of the bed she'd thrown herself on.

"Rayne," I said. "I need you to listen to me."

She turned a bit so she was facing me and I could see the anger and confusion on her face and it broke my heart.

"I love your dad more than anyone in the world," I said. "I miss him so much it's not even funny. There is nothing I wouldn't do to get him back. But that isn't possible. He will never be back here, and I can't change that. You may think that you know everything there is to know about losing him, but you lost someone very different from who I lost. He was your dad, and no one will ever take his place. I would never ask you to look at anyone as your dad, because that would disrespect both him and you.

"You need to know that absolutely nothing will change if I decide to have a relationship with Jonathan," I continued. She sucked in her breath, but I forged ahead. "We have been talking. We have had dinner. But we are not dating. Neither of us is at the point where we want to do that right now. At least I'm not. We haven't even had a conversation about dating or what that would look like."

"But we stayed at his house," she complained.

"Because he's a nice guy," I countered. "He knew things were getting creepy and wanted to give us a space where we could be in case we needed it. That's it."

"But you slept in his bed," she said.

"Would it have been better if I slept on the couch?" I asked.

"Well," she hemmed, but didn't elaborate.

"He said we could use his place for the couple of days he was out of town," I said. "We did that. When we left, I made sure that it was as clean, if not cleaner, than when we got there. That's what good guests do. I don't want to overstay our welcome with Marco and Andrea, and I don't want to put Grams and Gramps in danger. It's also not fair that we bring this man to your friends or Thomas's friends. This is why I agreed to stay at his place."

"Why can't we just go to a hotel or stay at home?"

"It's not safe to be at home," I said. "You didn't see it, but the place is unlivable. I wouldn't want you to see what that man did to our home, so it's better that we find an alternative."

"Are we gonna stay with him again?" she asked. "And if we do, are you gonna sleep with him?"

"Tonight," I began, "I was gonna see if you and Thomas can stay with Grams and Gramps. That's why I called them. They're gonna come and get you guys and take you up to the cabin. It's safer there, hopefully, and then I can figure out what to do about the guy."

"Where will you stay?"

"I don't know," I confessed. "I may ask that the bureau put me up in a hotel, or I may stay with Marco and Andrea, or I might go stay at Jonathan's. That isn't a decision I've made yet, and it isn't something I've figured out. My main goal is to make sure you and Thomas are safe. That's what's most important to me."

"I don't want you to die," she said.

"I'm not gonna die," I replied.

"Dad didn't think he would, either," she added.

"You're right," I said. "I might die, but I'll do whatever I can to keep that from happening. This is what I've been trying to do. Will you do me a favor and trust me?"

"I don't want you to die," she said again, and that's when the tears started again.

She crumpled onto the bed and I pulled her into my lap, holding her close as she absolutely lost it. I rocked her back and forth and let her get it all out. Telling her to hush, that it wasn't that big of a deal, or that she should get over it, wasn't something I wanted to do, and also not something I believed. She just needed to work it out.

Once she'd settled, I brushed the hair from her face and kissed her forehead.

"I'm sorry," she said.

"Nothing to be sorry for," I replied, holding her close.

"Why is this happening to us?"

"Because someone believes they're entitled to something they have no right to have," I said. "It's the same reason that people steal things. They want it, they don't care who they hurt to get it, and they don't care about any consequences."

"Do we have to go to school?"

"I'm going to call them in the morning," I said. "I'll tell them you're going to be taking a break, and that we may be back before the end of the year, but we aren't sure yet."

"What about my friends?" she asked.

"I know it's gonna be hard," I said. "But I'm gonna need you to not call them. In fact, we're gonna leave our phones with Uncle Marco. I'll get you a burner phone to have in case something happens, but if you want, you can text your friends and let them know you'll be gone for a while. Just don't tell them why, okay?"

"What should I tell them?"

"I don't know," I said. "Maybe tell them you're traveling and will be back with them when you're back. Make it interesting."

"I can tell them a great-uncle died." She smiled. "That we were left with a castle and we have to go and work on it before we can do anything else. That we have to leave tonight in order to get there and get everything switched to our names."

"That sounds like fun," I said. "They probably won't believe you, though."

"Because they would believe my mom has a stalker who is threatening to kill us," she said. "Not sure which one is less believable."

I laughed and hugged her one more time, then asked, "We good?"

"We're good," she said. "I'm sorry, too. For what I said."

"I know you're upset," I replied. "It's hard to go through all of this and not be a little crazy."

"Yeah," she said. "I don't like this kind of crazy, though."

"Neither do I," I said. "Not at all."

"Will you tell Jonathan I'm sorry?"

"I think that's something you should do," I said. "But you don't have to do it right now if you don't want to."

"I really don't," she said.

"I'll let him know you'll apologize when you see him again," I said.

"Thanks, Mom," she said.

I left her with her phone and headed downstairs. This next conversation was going to be interesting, and not in a fun way, either.

CHAPTER FORTY-EIGHT

*J*onathan...

I'd stepped out into the front yard after Lucy took off after Rayne. I didn't want to leave, though, because I really did want to talk to Lucy about what was between us. The neighborhood was quiet, no one going down the streets. It was just the way a suburb should look. Then I saw him. If I hadn't been looking, I probably would have missed him, but he was there, on the other side of the street, standing behind a tree, looking right at me.

What should I do? Should I call out to him? Let him know I saw him? Or pretend he wasn't there and call the cops on him? The door opening behind me made me jump and turn around to Lucy standing there.

"Hey," she said as I turned to her.

"Let's go inside," I replied, almost pushing her into the house. Once the door was shut, I said, "There's someone watching."

"What?" she asked. "Who? Where?"

"Some guy," I replied. "He's across the street. I don't know who he is or why he's there, but I don't think he knows I saw him."

She pulled her phone out of her back pocket and dialed.

"I think he's here," she said once whoever was on the other end of the line answered. "We're all locked inside," she continued after a moment. "I don't know what he's wearing," she said, then said, "Hang on."

She handed the phone to me and I put it to my ear.

"Hello?" I asked.

"Mr. Bridge," the man said. "Did you see him?"

"I saw someone," I clarified. "I can't be sure who it is, though. It's pretty dark out already."

"Does he know you saw him?" he asked.

"I don't think so," I said. "But I can't be sure."

"Just stay inside," he ordered. "I've got someone en route."

"Thanks," I said.

"It's my job," he replied.

"I still appreciate it," I said.

He disconnected the call, and I handed the phone back to Lucy just as Marco came into the room.

"He's here," I said.

"Shit," Marco said under his breath. "What do we do?"

"They said to stay inside," Lucy said. "I think they're sending someone."

"He said someone was on the way," I confirmed.

"When are your parents supposed to get here?" he asked Lucy.

"Crap," she said, then dug her phone back out and dialed.

"Hey," she said when they answered. "Can you guys hang out at the grocery store on the main road?" She hesitated, then added, "I don't want you to come yet. There's been something that's happened." Another pause, then, "We're safe," she said. "I just don't want you to come quite yet. Not until Agent Richards gets here and figures out what's going on."

There were a couple of other directions, but then she ended the call.

"This is a nightmare." She sighed.

I reached out to her, and she came to me, folding into my arms as I held her, being the solid ground she could use to shore herself up with.

We stayed that way for a while, her just absorbing the strength I didn't know I had. When a knock sounded on the door, she jumped.

"I got it," Marco said, and I noticed he'd armed himself, a holster under his arm.

He looked out the peephole and then opened the door.

"We looked," the young man who stepped inside said. "Didn't see anyone around. My guess is he's gone."

"Thanks," Marco said.

"We'll stick around for a while," he offered. "At least until you guys figure out what you're going to do. Richards said we were on duty for tonight."

"Sure thing," Marco said, then the man stepped outside and Marco shut the door.

Lucy already had her phone out and was telling her parents to come on over, and that we were at the neighbor's house. When they arrived, the kids grabbed their bags and headed out the door. Rayne wouldn't look at me, but I wasn't worried about it. She had a lot to go through, and I wasn't hurt by her accusations. Honestly, I was just glad she hadn't hit me or yelled any more. Once they were gone, Lucy looked at me.

"Would it be an imposition to stay with you?" she asked.

"No problem whatsoever," I said, and it was true. "Do you need to get anything from your house before we go?"

"I don't want to go in there at all," she said.

"Do you want me to go get something?" I asked, wanting her to be comfortable.

She just shook her head, and I could see the weight of the day pushing her down.

"Okay," I replied. "Let's get you out of here. Do you want to move your car or is it fine where it is on the street?"

She looked to Andrea who was holding her little one and said, "Is it okay to leave it there?"

"Give me your keys," the other woman said. "I'll make sure the guys get it for that detailed review. I've got all your phones, too. Jonathan," she said to me. "Would you be comfortable giving me your number? This way I can get in touch with Lucy until we get her some burner phones."

"Not at all," I replied, rattling off the digits.

"Hold up," she said, then pulled out her phone. "Here," she said, handing it to me after unlocking it. "Just call yourself. That way I have yours and you have mine."

"Good thinking," I said, taking the phone and doing just that. "Here," I said, after I'd taken care of adding the numbers. "You ready?" I asked Lucy, and she looked at me dazed.

"Take good care of her," Marco said, coming up behind his wife. "She's family."

"I know the feeling," I said. "I'll make sure she's safe. Thank you for a great dinner. I just wish we could have met under better circumstances."

"You and me, both," Andrea said. "We got you," she said to Lucy, wrapping her in a one-armed hug, keeping the kiddo out of the way.

"You guys are the best," she said.

"Don't you know it." Marco laughed as he gave her a hug as well. "Thank you," he said to me, shaking my hand.

"Happy to help," I replied. "I just wish I could make a bigger difference."

"I think you're doing the best thing in the world," Andrea said. "Now, take her home and make sure she's safe and feels loved."

"I'll do my best," I agreed, wondering whether Lucy had shared what happened this morning with her friend. The look she gave her, though, said she had.

"Come on," I said, pulling Lucy toward the door.

She picked up her bag that was still likely packed from her last stay at my place and we walked out to my car. I opened her door and let her get in, then dropped the bag into the trunk before rounding to my door. The drive to my place wasn't long, but by the time we got there, Lucy looked like she was ready to be done for the day.

"Come on," I said as we stepped inside. "Let's get you a warm bath and to bed. Everything will look better in the morning. I promise."

CHAPTER FORTY-NINE

*L*ucy…

"Everything will look better in the morning," he said. "I promise."

I wanted desperately to believe him, but he hadn't seen the things I had. George had gone off the deep end, worse than any subject my husband had ever dealt with. The things he wrote on my walls, the damage he did to my house, the fear he put into me. No, this was not a normal person. This was someone who should be feared, and I didn't think Jonathan knew how afraid I was right now.

He walked me through his space without turning on any lights. It made sense that he knew how to get around. I imagine he used to come home and not turn on any lights after games, knowing that the light might wake his family. It gave me a pain to remember that he didn't have his wife any longer, and that his son was away from him because of his job.

We stepped into the master bedroom and he dropped my bag by the closet, continuing his walk to the bathroom.

"Hold on," he said in a hushed tone, then stepped in.

I caught the flick of a lighter of some kind and the room grew more illuminated as the candle caught.

"Do you want some help?" he asked, and I wasn't sure exactly what I wanted.

I stood there mute, just staring into the space and he pulled me to him, hushing me as he rubbed his hands up and down my back. Not for the first time, I broke down, letting the fear and anger and everything else just pour out of me.

"Why?" I managed to get the word out in strangled tones, but there wasn't an answer.

He stepped back from me and pushed my jacket down over my shoulders, letting it fall to the floor behind me. He turned and put the plug into the tub, starting the water. Turning, he gathered my shirt. He began to lift if off, slowly bringing it up my body.

"Arms," he whispered, and I raised them, obeying him, not knowing what else to do.

Once my shirt was off, I reached behind to unhook my bra. I let it fall from my arms. He then worked the belt and button at the top of my jeans, pushing them, along with my panties, down over my hips. I kicked off my shoes, then let him slide the pants over my feet, pulling my socks with them. I stood there, naked, in his bathroom.

"Come on," he said, turning me toward the tub.

It was over halfway full already, and I saw that he'd put some sort of oil or bubbles in it, as it frothed under the tap. He held my hand and kept me balanced as I stepped into the tub. I turned to him, not wanting to let go of his hand.

"Join me," I said, and he looked at me, questioning. "Please," I begged.

"Okay," he said, letting go of my hand so he could remove his clothes.

We hadn't seen each other naked, just felt what we could that morning. His back was strong as he dropped his shirt on the floor with my clothes. Kicking his shoes off, he unbuckled his belt and shoved his pants and boxers down. When he turned to me, I took in a breath. He was beautiful, like one of those statues at the museums we went to on the school trip just a month or so earlier.

As he drew nearer, I moved to the side, shutting the water off so it wouldn't overflow with our bodies displacing it. He stepped into the tub, turning me so my back was to him, then pulled us both down into the warm water. Leaning back, he wrapped his arms around my waist and I sighed, feeling him strong against my back.

"Just relax," he said, swiping my hair back around my shoulder. "I'll take care of you."

He pressed his lips to my neck, then my collarbone, then along to my shoulder, and I couldn't help but moan. With everything that had been going on in the last few days, I hadn't taken the time to relax at all, and the warm water, and warmer body behind me, made this feel so right.

We stayed like that for some time, him holding me as I relaxed in small ways. His hands began to rub against my stomach, slow circles at first, then lower and lower still, until he reached the hair at my pelvic bone. I put my hand over his and pushed it further down until he was right at the apex of my thighs. There wasn't much room in the tub, but I found a way to open my legs, allowing him access to my sex. He took that invitation for what it was, and delved between my lips, caressing slowly as I relaxed that much more.

His mouth stayed on my shoulder, sucking and biting in inter-changing moments, as his other hand moved up, caressing, then squeezing my breast. Between the warm water, and his hands moving on me, I let myself go. Let myself feel the enjoyment he was bestowing on me. I could feel him growing hard behind me and he had to shift slightly before continuing to massage me.

He'd worked me up, growing more and more needy until he slipped a finger inside me and I groaned.

"That's it, baby," he murmured against my shoulder. "Just relax and let me please you."

I took the invitation he gave me and pulled my knees up, giving him more access to me, allowing him to push even deeper into me with his fingers, having added a second digit to the first. In and out, slow and steady, with his other hand massaging my breast, occasionally tweaking my nipple between his finger and thumb.

"Come on," he whispered in my ear. "Let go. Let everything go and just enjoy."

My eyes were closed, just feeling him wrapped around me, his fingers inside me, and I did as he said and just let go. It took but a moment, and when I fell, it was like lightening coursing through my veins, fissures running through me to spark at the edge of my skin. I stayed there, in that moment, for what felt like forever. When I came back to myself it was to him praising me, something I didn't know I needed.

He moved out from inside me, shifting again behind me, and I could feel his need pressed against my back. I shifted with him, trying to turn around, but there just wasn't room in this small space.

"I need you," I whispered, afraid I'd sound as desperate as I was.

He shifted again, standing up, and I watched as the water ran off his body in ripples and I felt jealous of how it caressed him.

"Come on," he said, holding a hand down to me.

I stood, still a bit unsteady from my earlier climax, and he helped me out of the tub first, coming out after me. He grabbed the towel off the bar next to the tub and wrapped it around me, rubbing me with the soft fabric.

"You good?" he asked.

"Yeah," I said, allowing him to care for me.

Once I was dry, he took the towel and dried himself, then hung it over the bar where he'd gotten it from, guiding me slowly toward the bedroom. He blew out the candle and we were plunged into darkness, me unsure where I was going.

"I've got you," he said, his arms wrapping around me from behind as he guided us through the dark to his bed.

My eyes grew a bit more accustomed to the darkness, the night-light from the bathroom, giving just enough for me to see where I was. I sat on the edge of the bed after pushing the sheet and blanket away. He cupped my cheek with his hand, his thumb running over my lips in a slow, smooth rhythm. I reached up, running my hands up his thighs, along his hips, and moving to the front of him where I found his cock hard and ready. With slow movements, I ran my hand up and down its length, gauging its measure. It was long and smooth in my hand as I ran it up and over the head before moving back down to the base.

His thumb continued its sweep across my lips, though the rhythm stuttered here and there as my hand moved along him. Slowly, I moved toward him, licking the head of his cock before taking it into my mouth. He sighed, holding very still, as if to not shatter this moment we'd created.

Warm, with a slight salty taste from the fluid that had leaked out already, I let my mouth work up and down as he moaned, his hand moving back toward the back of my head. He didn't grab my hair, didn't try to guide me, didn't force me at all. He just held his hand there, holding my hair back away from my face.

I was deliberate in my movements, in and out, bobbing on him as it were, and I could feel him stiffen even further, moaning his pleasure throughout.

"Stop," he said, using his hand to pull me back off of him.

I let him slip from my lips and looked up at him, the light more than enough for me to see he was looking down at me. He pushed my shoulders back, gently encouraging me to move further onto the bed. I did as he suggested, leaving room for him to join me. Climbing in, he slid down to lie next to me, once again caressing my face.

"You're so beautiful," he said, then leaned in and kissed me.

It was slow at first, just a chaste touch of his lips to mine. I leaned into him, kissing him deeper, parting my lips, swiping my tongue across the seam in his, and he opened, allowing me to explore his mouth with my tongue. His arm went around my back, pulling me up against him, then his hand moved lower, to the globe of my ass, moving down to bring my leg up and over his own hip.

He was so warm, so strong and solid next to me, and it was something I had missed desperately. Reaching a hand between us, I gripped his length, stroking it up and down, then moving it so it was nearer my entrance. I rubbed the head of his cock between my lips, back and forth until it found purchase and slipped in, just the head.

"Oh, God," he groaned against my lips, moving his hips to move in and out of me in short strokes. "You feel so good," he moaned.

CHAPTER FIFTY

*J*onathan...

She was so warm, so wet, and I thought I might lose it from entering her. I'd had to stop her from sucking me off, for fear I would lose all control. Now, with my length slowly pushing inside her, and her body snug against mine, I was sure I wouldn't hold out much longer. I tried to take it slow, small movements, getting deeper and deeper into her, but she was needy, and I didn't want to deny her anything.

"More," she begged, and I gave it to her, focusing on her voice, her eyes, the need I saw there, rather than what her body was doing to me.

Her eyes fluttered shut once again, and I watched as pleasure wrote its story across her face in beautiful ways—her bitten lip, the way she sighed with each thrust, the sharp intake of air as I bottomed out inside her. I held myself there, deep within her beautiful body and watched as she reveled in the feel.

"You good?" I asked in a hushed tone.

"Very," she replied, letting her eyes open slightly to look into mine.

I moved again, pulling out just a bit before pushing back inside her, and once again, she let herself go in the pleasure of the moment, sighing with the movement. The pace was slow, intentional, with the purpose of bringing her to that miraculous place of falling without leaving her body. She'd done it once in the tub, and I wanted to get her there again before letting myself enjoy my own release.

Pulling her leg a little higher, I changed the angle, and she gasped as I pressed further in. I held still, letting her settle, then began to move again, sliding in and out of her in slow, cautious strokes, wanting her to get to the top of the hill and fall over just one more time. She leaned back from me, giving me access to her breasts, and I took advantage, dipping my head to take one of her nipples into my mouth, flicking my tongue around the tip, then sucking back with just a bit of teeth to add that edge of the pain-and-pleasure combination.

We were new at this, and still figuring everything out, but it seemed we had enough knowledge to know what was working, and this was it.

"Oh, God," she whispered, squeezing me with her pussy. "Yes, just like that," she continued.

I did as she asked, keeping my rhythm the same while still sucking on her tit. Her breathing increased and I could feel her rising to that wonderful place at the top of the fall. With her hands in my hair, she pulled me from her breast, then crushed her mouth onto mine and I let go, increasing my speed and finding my own release.

Panting as we came down, she shuddered in my arms, the last of the euphoria leaving her body. I ran my hand up and down her back, and down over her ass, as I held her in that post high world we'd entered.

"Jonathan," she whispered against my chest, and the sound of my name on her lips did something to me I hadn't expected.

"I'm right here, baby," I said, a bit strangled. "I'm not going anywhere."

～

I SUCKED IN AIR AS SHE RAN HER HAND ACROSS MY ABDOMEN.

"Sorry," she said, sleep in her voice.

"Nothing to be sorry about," I replied. "What time is it?"

"Six," she said.

I groaned, not wanting to think about the fact that I hadn't gotten near enough sleep. She moved to sit up, but I held her where she was, not wanting to lose this connection.

"Don't go," I said, and it sounded more desperate than I'd have liked.

"Just have to pee." She giggled, and I released her.

There wasn't any light in the room, except the night-light from the bathroom, but I watched as she slid out of the bed on the other side, then padded around to go into the bathroom. She shut the door and I must have dozed off because the next thing I knew it was lighter out, probably closer to the time I usually got up.

I reached across the bed only to find it cold and empty. Running a hand over my face, I slid out of bed and made my way to the bathroom, needing to get that out of the way before trying to find Lucy. When I finished, I threw on some shorts and headed out into the condo, hoping she hadn't left. I was pleased to see her in the kitchen, cooking something that smelled really good.

"Whatcha making?" I asked, and she jumped.

"Holy crap," she said, a hand to her chest in what I assume was an attempt to get her heart rate to slow down. "You scared the crap out of me."

"Sorry," I said, sliding onto one of the stools at the bar at the island of the kitchen. "You sleep okay?" I asked.

"I really did," she said. "Which is surprising considering everything that's going on."

"Yeah," I replied. "Have you heard anything?"

"I don't have a phone," she said as she flipped whatever was in the pan on the stove over.

"Oh yeah," I replied, feeling stupid. "Did you want to call anyone?"

"Wouldn't mind checking in with Agent Richards," she said. "Let me just finish this and then I can call, if you don't mind me using your phone."

"Not at all," I replied. "Anything I can do to help?"

"Nope," she said as she plated whatever she'd been making onto two plates. "I hope you don't mind I took the initiative."

She set a plate in front of me and my mouth dropped open.

"Where did you find all of this stuff?" I asked.

"Your kitchen is surprisingly well stocked," she said. "There were a few things that were expired that I set on the counter over there," she added, angling her head in that direction. "But you had most everything needed to make a decent breakfast."

There was an egg scramble of some sort with a few different meats, as well as toast and the drink of the gods, coffee.

"I don't know how you take your coffee," she said. "So it's black. Do you want sugar or milk?"

"Some milk would be good," I said, and she turned and grabbed it out of the fridge, handing it to me to add to my mug.

"Come, sit," I said, patting the stool next to me.

She came around the counter and sat next to me. That's when I realized she was just wearing my shirt from the day before, and I had to admit that it looked sexy as hell on her.

"Dig in," she said, and I realized that I'd just been staring at her. "It'll get cold, and it's no good that way."

She shoved a forkful of the egg mixture into her mouth and I watched as she pulled the fork out slowly, and damn if I didn't get a little chub going.

"What?" she asked when she noticed.

"Sorry," I said, turning and adjusting myself. "Got a little distracted."

She giggled and when I looked back at her she was grinning, but also blushing like crazy.

"You're cute when you blush," I said, and she replied, "Eat."

Doing as she bid, I took a fork full of the food on my plate and savored the mixture of flavors she'd blended together.

"This is really good," I said.

"It's perfect for when you need protein," she said. "And I kinda do."

That pink rushed up her neck and to her cheeks once again, and I couldn't help but ask, "What do you need protein for?"

She choked on her bite but swallowed it down finally.

"Burned a few calories last night," she admitted, getting even redder.

"Ah, yeah," I replied. "That we did."

I reached out and caressed her cheek and she turned into my palm, looking at me.

"You doing okay?" I asked, hoping she understood that I meant with what happened between us and not everything else that was going on with her.

"Yeah," she replied. "Thank you."

"For what?"

"For not letting me be alone last night," she said. "I really needed someone to be with and to try to forget about everything for just a little while."

"I'm more than happy to be your distraction," I said, and meant every word.

She sighed and looked back at her plate and I could see that she'd lost her appetite.

"Hey," I said, bringing her attention back to me. "It'll all work out. I'm sure of it."

"What makes you so sure?" she asked, and I could tell she was asking about everything else and not us.

"Because you're braver than anyone I've ever met," I said. "I don't know anyone who could deal with what you've gone through and still end up standing."

She sniffed and the first tear rolled down her cheek. I hadn't even noticed that they'd been building in her eyes. I pulled her to me, bringing her into my lap, and it had nothing to do with sex and every-thing to do with being a solid point she could depend on. Letting her get her bearings, I simply held her.

"Thanks," she said, sniffing again. "Mind if I make that call?"

"Not at all," I replied. "Come on."

I led her to my room and unplugged my phone, unlocking it so she could make her calls while I left her alone. I went back to the kitchen and finished my breakfast, then cleaned up. I didn't want her to feel like she needed to do everything, especially since she cooked for me. That was something I hadn't expected but was pleasantly surprised to have.

Once the kitchen was put to rights, I looked down the hall to see if she'd opened the door. Since she hadn't, I decided to step into the guest room and pull up some film to watch until she had taken care of her business. It wasn't anything I needed to interrupt.

CHAPTER FIFTY-ONE

*L*ucy...

"Mrs. Fallon," Agent Richards said as he got on the line.

"I thought I would check in," I said. "Since I don't have a phone right now, I wanted to see if there was anything you needed me to do."

"Right now, we're just waiting on some responses to our requests for subpoenas," he said. "Once we get those back, we can do some additional digging."

"Did you ever figure out who it was that was trying to pick up my kids?" I asked.

"Facial recognition hasn't come back," he said. "But I'm hopeful to get some answers either today or tomorrow. Are you somewhere safe?"

"I am," I replied, and felt it was the truth. "Kids are also safe with my parents."

"Good," he said. "Stay out of public for right now," he continued. "I think that's gonna be the best course of action. I don't want to have to put you in a safe house, even though that might be the safest. It's just not that easy to get it set up, so if you've got somewhere you can be, that'll be the best."

"Any idea how long we'll have to stay in hiding?" I asked,

wondering whether it would be best to stay here, or go join my kids at the cabin.

"No clue at this point," he said. "You should stay hidden through the weekend if possible, though. Is that doable?"

"I think I can make that happen," I said. "I'll ask the friend I'm staying with if I can stay till then. I know the kids will be fine with my parents, too, so I don't need to worry about them."

"They didn't take their phones with them, right?" he asked.

"We left them all with Andrea and Marco," I replied. "Didn't want anyone to be able to track us."

"This friend isn't them, then?" he asked.

"No," I replied. "It's someone I recently met."

"Do you trust them?"

"Actually," I replied. "I really do. They've been more than accommodating for me and even let me and the kids stay here earlier this week."

"That means he may know where you are," he said.

"Oh, shit," I said. "I didn't even think about that."

"Is this the man who I met yesterday?"

"Yeah," I said.

"The one who got the note?"

"Crap," I said. "I didn't even think about that. I guess he may know where I am."

"He might," Agent Richards said. "But, if it's a secure building, you may be fine."

"I'll talk to Jonathan," I said. "He'll know whether it's secure or not. I mean, I had to use a key card to get into the garage, then a fob to call the elevator. Does that seem like it might be secure enough?"

"It might," he said. "Give me the address and I'll have my team check it out."

I gave him the address, and he thanked me, said he'd check it out, and then disconnected the call. With a deep sigh, I took the phone with me out into the hall. Jonathan wasn't in the kitchen, but after a bit I found him in the guest bedroom on his computer.

"Here's your phone," I said. "The agent asked me something I didn't know how to answer."

"Oh, yeah," he said. "What's that?"

"He asked how secure the building was," I said. "I told him that I had to use a key card to get into the garage, then a fob to get into the elevator, but I wasn't sure whether it could be accessed any other way."

"There's a front door," he said. "But it's also locked. You have to have either a key or a fob to get in."

"I gave him the address," I explained. "Hopefully he'll be able to figure out if it's good enough. He was worried because apparently George knows where you live."

"That makes sense," he said. "Since he followed me to Green Lake and left me that note. Plus," he continued. "You were here with your phone, and if he had a tracker in it, he could follow you. I don't think he'll know which unit we're in, though. Do you feel safe here?"

"I do," I said. "But I don't want you to get stuck in any of this crap."

"Why don't you let me worry about me," he said.

"You wouldn't have to worry about any of this if you hadn't let me stay," I countered.

"But if you hadn't stayed…" he said. "We wouldn't have…"

He let the word hang there, without adding the things we'd done. It was true, we wouldn't have done anything, but I don't want to think about having had to miss out on that.

"Would you give that up?" he asked.

"No," I said.

"Me, either," he said. "I have some work to do. Do you want to check on your kids?"

"My parents didn't take their phones," I said. "I can call the cabin phone, but I'm not sure they'd pick it up."

"Well," he said. "Feel free if you want. You got anything else you need to do today?"

"Absolutely nothing," I said, then remembered. "I actually have to call the kids school," I added. "I totally forgot that they don't know where the kids are."

He handed me back his phone, and I dialed the school, letting them know the kids would be out at least through Monday, and maybe longer, too. I also asked if they had any other people come in looking for the kids, which they didn't.

"All good?" Jonathan asked when I handed his phone back.

"I think so," I replied. "Mind if I take a shower?"

"Not at all," he said. "Want company?"

I thought about it, which apparently wasn't the right thing because he said, "Go on."

"I mean," I hedged, unsure what to say.

"I'll let you get in there and get clean," he said, but the look in his eye told me he was thinking all the dirty thoughts and I can't say that I was upset about it.

"Give me five minutes?" I asked.

"Oh," he said. "So, you do want company."

I smiled, then turned and headed to his room.

CHAPTER FIFTY-TWO

*J*onathan...

Since the start of the season, I had moved back to Seattle, to my empty apartment. Met an amazing woman. Helped give that woman a refuge to use when I was out of town, only to come home and forget she was here. Shared my bed and my body with her. Received a threat to stay away from said woman. Been interviewed by the FBI. And was now getting ready to share a shower with this woman. This was absolutely not what I expected to have happen to me to start the year.

If someone had told me this was what was in store for me, I would have laughed in their face. Instead, I was looking forward to what the next few days, weeks, and months might hold for me. Checking the time, I had just enough to share this shower with Lucy, and a little more, before having to head into the stadium to get ready for the game.

As I stepped into the bedroom, I could hear the shower running. I undressed and threw my stuff into the basket in the closet before going into the bathroom. While it wasn't a huge shower, it was bigger than a standard one, which was one of the things we had wanted when we were looking for a place to live. The room was filled with steam, and I could hear Lucy humming some tune, but I didn't recognize it.

"Ready for company?" I asked, not wanting to just step in.

"Sure," she replied, and I could see her move a little further under the tap at one end.

I stepped in at the other end, making sure the shower head at that end didn't spray the rest of the bathroom. She was absolutely gorgeous, and I didn't even try to hide the fact that I was looking at her. My body's reaction to seeing her was obvious, and she blushed as her eyes trailed down my body. When her eyes came back up to mine, she smiled, and the blush deepened.

"Is this weird?" she asked.

"Is what weird?" I countered.

"This," she said, using her hand to indicate the two of us. "I mean, we've known each other for what, a couple weeks? Does this seem like it's going too fast?"

"Do you think it's going too fast?"

"I don't know," she confessed.

"Did you want to slow down?" I asked.

She looked down, likely unsure how to answer that. I stepped closer, placing a hand on her shoulder and said, "Hey."

When she looked up at me, I could see something there, in her eyes.

"I don't know what to do," she said, and I knew that was hard for her to say.

"We can do whatever we want," I said, hoping I wasn't going to lose her in that moment. "We can keep going, or stop, or whatever else feels right."

"But," she began, then swallowed. "What if it's too fast, or a rebound, or something? What if this," she asked, waving her hand between us again, "isn't gonna work out?"

"Why wouldn't it?" I asked.

"I don't know," she said, her voice cracking.

"Do you want it to work out?" I asked. "Because I do."

She'd looked down after her confessions but snapped her eyes back up to me at the last statement I made.

"You do?"

She sounded incredulous, like it was a preposterous notion that I would want to stay with her.

"I really do," I said, tilting her head up.

I closed the space between us slowly, giving her all the time in the world to look away, turn away, step out, push me back, or even slap me. None of those things happened, though. Instead, she closed the gap between us and crashed into me, her lips on mine, her standing on tip toe to reach me. Her arms wrapped around my neck, and I encircled her with my own, pulling her flush against me.

Time stood still, or rushed by, I didn't know which. All I knew was that this woman in my arms was exactly what I had been missing the last few months. I was built to share my life with someone. Meg was the first to fill that role, but Lucy was settling into it rapidly, and I didn't even want to think about what that meant about me, about us. The only thing I knew was I didn't want to be apart from this woman if I could do anything about it.

She pulled back from the kiss, both of us gasping as we tried to desperately catch our breath.

"We're really doing this," she said. "You and me."

"I'm in," I said, looking in her eyes. "I know it's soon, that we don't know each other well, but it just feels right. You feel right."

"You do, too," she said.

I watched as she swallowed again, like it was a struggle, and then she sniffed.

"You good?" I asked.

She nodded her head but wouldn't answer me.

"Hey," I said, tipping her chin so she looked at me again. "Are you good?"

Again, she nodded, then croaked out a simple, "Yeah."

"You want to just shower?"

"No," she answered quickly, then slapped her hand over her mouth, her eyes wide, her cheeks growing pink again.

"Me, either," I said and leaned into her.

She pulled me faster than I intended, and before I knew it, I had her pushed up against the wall of the shower, my lips on her, my tongue in her mouth, doing what I intended to do to her with my dick soon enough. Breaking from her lips, I laid light kisses down her neck, across her shoulder, then slowly moved down her body. She wasn't under the spray, but I was, so I worried a bit about her staying warm enough, but she didn't seem to mind. The lower I got, the more she moaned, her fingers in my hair, holding me to her, pushing me lower and lower until I was kneeling before her.

My hands were on her hips and I moved them lower, spreading her legs apart so I could reach my ultimate goal. She opened for me beautifully and I kissed the hair right above her clit. She shuddered, but held onto my head, not letting me go anywhere else. I darted my tongue out, flicking the sensitive nub at the apex of her sex and she gasped. When I looked up her body, she was staring down at me and it damn near did me in. To have someone look at me like that, the trust that was in her eyes, the love I saw there, it was something otherworldly. I continued to watch her as I licked her again and her eyes fluttered shut, her head leaning back against the tile.

With my arm, I shifted her leg, so it was up and over my shoulder, giving me better access to the rest of her. I licked her up and down, sucking on her clit with each stroke, adding a finger once she was more than just wet from the shower. She sighed as I did, and I could feel her squeeze my finger with her pussy, holding me fast where I was. Sucking her clit into my mouth, I shifted my finger, doing a bit of a come-hither motion and felt the rough patch just inside her, and watched her eyes grow big, looking down at me once again. I hummed against her and her head fell back again with the most delightful moan.

I kept up my work, pushing a second finger into her as she loosened for me, all the while sucking and licking her. When I felt the tightening of her around my fingers, I knew she was close, and I didn't want to interrupt her climax.

"Oh, God," she moaned, her fingers tightening in my hair to the point of almost being painful, but I didn't let up.

Once she'd come back to herself, I removed my fingers, and she sighed with a slight shiver. I held onto her, keeping her steady in the aftermath until I was sure she could stand by herself. The water had grown cold, so I shut the taps off, pulling the curtain back, grabbed a towel, wrapped it around her.

"You didn't," she began, but I kissed her to stop the complaint.

When I pulled back, she smiled at me, and I returned it readily. I rubbed the towel up and down her, drying her off best I could, then pulled her in and kissed her forehead before turning her to the bedroom.

"I'll be there in a minute," I said, and she stopped, but then continued on into the room.

I closed the door, figuring I'd take care of myself, then get ready for the drive into the stadium. It didn't take long for me to find that release, then I cleaned up and left the bathroom. Lucy was sitting on the edge of the bed, still in the towel, and she looked up when I stepped out. I'd grabbed a pair of boxers on my way into the bathroom, so was at least wearing those when I came out.

"Hey," she said, looking at me. "You need me to…"

"Nah," I said. "I'm good. I have to head out. Do you want me to leave my phone for you to use in case anything happens? I would feel really bad if you were here without a phone."

"You don't mind leaving it?" she asked.

"Not at all," I said. "Like I said, I'd feel weird if you didn't have one and something happened."

"If you're sure," she said.

I leaned over her on the bed and kissed her, letting myself linger there for a minute before pulling back.

"I want you safe," I said.

"Thank you," she replied. "You don't know how much this means to me."

"The feeling is mutual," I replied. "Gotta get ready to go, though. You do whatever you need to do for the rest of the day. I'll be quiet when I come home in case you're asleep. You good with me climbing in bed with you."

"I'd be offended if you didn't." She laughed.

"Good," I said, then turned and stepped into my closet.

Pulling out a button-up shirt, slacks, socks and a jacket. Once I was dressed, I came back out to find her under the covers, the towel on the floor next to the bed, sound asleep. Poor thing was plum worn out. I set my phone to vibrate and plugged it in on the night stand next to the bed, then shut the lights out and went to work.

CHAPTER FIFTY-THREE

*L*ucy...
When I woke up, I was disoriented, but quickly realized where I was. There was a buzzing from behind me, so I rolled over to see a phone lit up on the nightstand. I pushed the covers off and picked the phone up to see that it was an unknown number in the phone. Then I realized that this was Jonathan's phone, so wasn't sure whether I should listen to voicemails or anything. Then I realized that under the phone was a note from him.

> *Lucy,*
> *Password for the phone is 1717, my number twice. Feel free to check messages or use it to text or call whoever you need to. Be home probably by midnight, but maybe sooner.*
> *Jonathan*

He was very trusting with his phone, but I wasn't about to give him a reason to not be. I saw that the call had registered a voicemail, so I used the password he gave me and opened the phone up to listen to the message.

This is Agent Richards. I have some information. Please give me a call when you have a chance.

He left his direct dial number, so I returned the call.

"Agent Richards," he answered.

"Hi," I said. "It's Lucy Fallon. You left a message that you had some information."

"I do," he said. "Looks like we have a name for the person who was trying to pick up your kids. Do you know anyone named Taylor Tomlinson?"

"It doesn't sound familiar," I said. "But then again, it could be someone I met one time. Honestly, at this point, nothing would surprise me about what's going on."

"Not to worry," he said. "Once we get more information on him, I'll touch base with you again. Will this number work to call you?"

"For now," I said. "I'm not sure exactly what I'm going to do going forward, but for now, you can get to me through Jonathan's phone, or through Marco and Andrea. I think you got those numbers, too, right?"

"I do," he said. "Should I call here first? Or them first?"

"For now, here," I said. "If anything changes, I'll let you know."

"And you're staying somewhere safe, right?"

"I'm still at the address I gave you before," I said. "Did you check it out?"

"Hang on," he said, and I could hear him clicking keys on a keyboard. "Yeah, that is a pretty secure building. My only concern is that he was able to get past your security system, so he may have the skills to get into the building. Just don't answer the door to anyone, don't order anything in, and stay inside if at all possible."

"That's my plan," I said.

"Are you alone?"

"Right now I am," I said. "But Jonathan is still in town, so he's here when he's not at work."

"So, at night you're not alone," he said.

"Well," I replied. "He works odd hours. He's a baseball player, so he's gone right now, but said he would probably be home about midnight."

"Okay," he said. "I guess that will have to do."

"I feel pretty safe here," I said. "I have the door locked with a deadbolt and no one knows I'm here, so I should be good. If someone comes to the door, I'll just be silent and wait for them to leave."

"He may try to break in," Agent Richards said. "So be sure to put something in front of the door, at least during the day."

"You really think he'll go that far?" I asked and could hear the panic in my voice.

"I don't think so," he said. "But I'd rather be safe than sorry."

"Guess I'll see what I can do, at least for the moment," I said. "Anything else you need from me?"

"Not right now," he said. "For now, just stay put and stay safe. I'll call back if I get any new information."

"No response to the subpoenas?" I asked.

"Not yet," he said. "But those things take some time sometimes. We should have something by the weekend."

"Good," I said. "I really want this to be over."

"I don't blame you," he said. "If there is anything new, I'll let you know."

"Thanks," I said, then disconnected the call.

I wanted to call Andrea, see what she had heard, but I didn't really want to risk him getting this number, so I held off. I looked at the phone in my hand and realized that it had been a few hours since I last saw Jonathan. Then the warnings that Agent Richards gave about how George might try to break in got the better of me and I went to the dining table and pulled one of the chairs over to the front door, wedging it underneath the handle. I would move it before I went to sleep tonight.

With that little security thing taken care of, I walked into the kitchen to find something to eat. It had been a while since breakfast, and with the nap, I was getting really hungry. After I made something light, that leftovers would taste good for the next couple of days for me, I went to the living room area and looked for the remote. I figured if I was gonna be here for a while, I better figure out something to do, and watching TV sounded like something that would use as little brain power as possible, yet still be entertaining.

CHAPTER FIFTY-FOUR

*J*onathan...

"Hey, J," Huffman said as I walked into the locker room.

"What up?" I asked.

"You didn't stay long yesterday," he said.

"Didn't need to," I replied. "Also didn't want to deal with the child."

"I know that." He laughed. "So, what did you get up to?"

"You know." I shrugged. "Just normal day off shit."

"Cool, cool," he said. "Loving that the Dragons are coming in for the weekend. They're always a good time."

"For sure," I said.

The Houston team were competitors, like most every other team, but they always seemed to be at the top of our division. Being in the west, we had an uphill climb every year, and never seemed to make it over the last hurdle to get to the big series. We'd played in some post-season games, but that elusive ring and championship always seemed to be just out of reach. Houston never seemed to have that problem.

"Let's get this thing," Beckett said as he walked in. "Hurwitz is gonna be my bitch tonight."

"'Cause you did so well in Anaheim." I laughed. "Better get your tee ready to go, kiddo."

"Fuck you, Bridge," he said, then slunk away toward his locker.

"God, that kid," Huffman said.

"Agreed," I replied.

I was a bit earlier than normal, but it wasn't so much so that it was noticeable. By the time I got suited up and headed out to the field, it was like I hadn't left the field. Something about the miles of green grass, the dirt of the infield, and the chalk to hold it all in was magical, a place where anything can happen and you never knew whether it would be a good day or not, but as long as you were on the field, it was better than most.

"HOLY SHIT," MITCH SAID AS I CLAPPED HIS HANDS AT HOME.

Coach had put me in to get some work in the outfield, and to give Rothman a break. He'd done something to his quad in Anaheim, and even with the day off, he wasn't quite back to his best, so Coach gave him an extra day to rest.

"Nice hit," Coach said as I stepped into the dugout after the rest of the guys who had been on base went down the steps.

I got high fives and head slaps all the way down the line. Even Beckett seemed to be in good spirits. By the time the game was over, we had beat the current leaders by a score of eleven to two and had handily smacked their ace starter out of the game by the second inning.

"What got into you guys tonight?" Jenn, one of the announcers asked in a post-game interview.

"Just hitting on all fronts," I replied. "Seems like we've figured out what we want and how we want it. Always good to be in this type of situation early in the season.

"I was sitting dead red," I explained. "With a three oh count, you kind of have to. You know they have to throw a strike, and with the bags juiced, he had nowhere to put me. It was like seeing a beach ball come flying in and I just swung and connected."

Just then, some of the guys poured the entire Gatorade bucket over me, damn near drowning me. Jenn had just enough time to get out of the way to keep from getting drenched herself.

"I'll let you go get cleaned up," she said.

"Thanks," I replied, heading into the dugout and down the hall to the locker room.

My night wasn't over, though. I barely got into the room and there were reporters angling for my attention, asking me about the hit, about the game, about how we managed to get the Dragon's star pitcher out so early. By the time we got all of the reporters moved to the press room, I was exhausted. I hit the showers, rinsing the sticky sports drink out of my hair and off my body, then pulling on my street clothes.

As I was heading out, Coach caught me and asked, "What got into you tonight?"

"No clue," I replied, but it was a lie.

"Whatever it is," he said. "Keep doing it."

"Plan on it," I replied, and that was the God's honest truth.

I walked to my car and climbed in, starting it up to head home and to Lucy. It was weird to be this excited, but at the same time, it felt right. Everything about being with her felt right. I pulled into the parking garage under the condo and walked to the elevator, using the fob to allow me access. The trip up took longer than it should have, but it was all a matter of perception. I pulled out my keys and opened the door, stepping in to see her sitting on the couch, the post-game show still playing on the local sports station.

"Hey," I said, and she turned and smiled.

"Nice hit," she said as I dropped my keys in the dish by the door.

"Couldn't miss it," I said as I strode toward her. "It was right there, thrown right in my wheelhouse. All I had to do was swing."

I plopped down onto the couch next to her and she scooted closer.

"I'm surprised you were up," I said, raising my arm so she could tuck herself into my side.

"Kinda couldn't sleep," she said and I could sense the tension in her.

"Oh yeah?"

"Talked to Agent Richards," she said. "He has a name for the guy who tried to pick the kids up."

"Anyone you know?" I asked.

"No." She sighed. "Never heard the name before."

"Well," I said. "They'll get it figured out. Did you get a chance to call your kids? Or your friend?"

"I didn't want to risk your number getting picked up," she said. "You know, in case he was monitoring their phones or something."

"I'll see about getting you a burner phone," I said. "At least until they figure out what is going on. That way you will always have one with you."

"Not planning on going anywhere," she said. "Agent said I should stay put, not go out, not order in, not let anyone in except you."

"Guess that means it's just you and me for a while," I said and couldn't help the smile that pulled at my lips.

"Guess so." She smiled up at me.

I closed the distance between our lips slowly, allowing her to stop it if she wanted, but she didn't. She closed her eyes as I got close, then sighed when our lips met. My hand went to her face, caressing her cheek as we kissed, then slid it down and around the back of her head, holding her to me as I deepened it. Her arms went around me, one around my neck and the other around my waist as she moved to sitting on my lap.

I hadn't noticed what she was wearing, but as my hand moved down her back and under the edge of the shirt she had on, I realized she only had panties on underneath, I slid my hand inside, cupping her ass. She shifted, moving just so over my cock which was getting stiffer with every move she made.

Pulling back, I looked into her eyes and asked, "Bedroom?"

"Or here," she replied.

"Your call," I offered, and she sat back and began unbuttoning my shirt.

She closed the distance between our lips once more, keeping just enough space between our bodies so she could continue to unbutton me. When she reached my belt, she worked that free, then undid my pants, reaching inside my boxers to grab my cock. I moaned as she gripped it, stroking her hand awkwardly between us.

When she broke the kiss, she whispered, "Too many clothes," and pulled her shirt over her head, then pushed at my own, shoving it down my arms. I was effectively trapped there, at her whim, and she smiled down at me from her perch in my lap. She hummed, then scooted off my lap, using her hands to pull my pants down. I tried to help but could only shift my body weight so it wasn't on them.

I hadn't even taken my shoes off, and she had me nearly naked in my living room. She shimmied out of her panties as I sat there and watched, helpless to do anything else, and I rather liked the position she'd put me in. Climbing back on my lap, her knees on either side of my thighs, she kissed me again, rubbing her slit up and down my length at the same time, and I was in heaven. Her hand slid down my chest, then between us, as she grabbed me and worked me against herself. As she found purchase, she slid down, excruciatingly slow, over me, kissing me all the while.

Once I was seated deep inside her, she began to shift her hips, using her own body to give her that feel good she was looking for. It wasn't doing much for me, but I honestly didn't care. If it was making her feel good, I was all for it. She pulled one of her hands from my face and slid it down between us, using her fingers on her clit to get her that much closer. She pulled her mouth back and looked up, eyes closed, as she just enjoyed herself. I had enough movement that I was able to bend down and take one of her nipples in my mouth and she gasped, then thrust her chest further forward, allowing me to ease back a bit, which was nice for my neck.

Her moans and movement continued as she rose higher and higher, finding that peak that would let her fall, plunge into euphoria, and release all the tension I was sure she had in her body, and I was here for it. If all I was here for was to give her the space to be free, from the worries and shit that life had handed to her, then I could do that. I felt her clench, tightening around me, and I watched as she erupted into a million pieces around me. It sucked that my arms were trapped and I couldn't catch her when she came back together, but I was there for her the only way I knew how to be.

"I got you," I said, struggling against my binding, finally pulling one arm out of its sleeve, wrapping it around her. "You're free."

CHAPTER FIFTY-FIVE

*L*ucy...

I floated, watching galaxies being torn apart and reformed in a beautiful cacophony of light and sound. All the while, he held me, rubbing up and down my back, laying kisses along my neck, pulsing inside me and under me. After an eternity, I came back to myself and fluttered open my eyes, looking up into the brilliant snow blue of his and smiled.

"You are exquisite," he whispered, planting a kiss on the side of my mouth.

In that moment, everything was perfect. No one else existed, nothing mattered but the two of us together. I could have lived there forever. I don't know how long we stayed there, but he finally shifted and I could see the slight pain on his face.

"Oh, God," I said, sitting up. "Are you okay?"

"Just need my other arm," he said, and I looked down at him.

Somehow, in my haste to have my way with him, I had trapped him on the couch. He'd gotten one arm free, the one that had been caressing me, but the other was still halfway in the sleeve of his shirt and pinned to his side. I shifted back, and he sucked air in between his teeth.

"Up first, please," he said, and I realized that he was still inside me and still hard.

"Sorry," I said, lifting myself up and off him, which was another moment I just had to close my eyes and enjoy.

He pulled his other arm free, and I felt him shifting his legs under me. I turned around and looked behind me and realized that I hadn't even bothered to get his pants all the way off, and he still had his shoes on, which he was in the process of removing.

"Just trying to get a little more comfortable," he said.

"Oops." I giggled and slid off his lap and onto the blanket I'd left on the couch.

He pulled his shirt from behind him and tossed it on the pile of his other clothes on the floor, then turned to me and gave me that devil may care smirk of his and I melted even more than I already had.

"My turn," he growled and moved toward me, closing the distance between us, capturing my lips with his and devouring my mouth.

I lay back on the couch, using the arm rest for a pillow and he followed, putting his body weight on me, pressing me deeper into the cushions of the couch. His hands slid up my side, slowly and sensually, and I shivered under his touch. I slid my arms around his neck, pulling him to me even more. When he slid his hand back down my body, sliding my leg up and around his waist, I was in the perfect position to accept him into me, and he slid in without any resistance.

He hummed against my mouth and I smiled, enjoying his pleasure. Shifting up off me, he grabbed my hands in his, pushing them up and over my head where he gripped them in one hand while running his other down my arm, down my body, caressing me with more than just his hand.

"So beautiful," he said, his eyes moving down to where he entered me.

He moved back, watching himself slide in and out of me in slow, rhythmic movements, and I was caught with how amazing he felt, but also how amazing he looked. His hand slid back up my body to my breast, cupping and squeezing it.

"So exquisite," he whispered, watching his hand move along me, and seeing how my body responded to his touch.

His hand went further up, caressing me along the way.

"Do you know what you do to me?" he asked.

I couldn't speak, just shook my head.

"You destroy me in the best way," he said, continuing his slow and steady sliding in and out of me. "You take me apart and make me new each time we touch, each time we kiss, each time we make love. I am absolutely taken in by you."

He increased his speed just that much more, along with going deeper inside me. I arched my back, unable to reach up to touch him, but wanting more contact than what we had. Bending low, he pulled one of my nipples into his mouth, licking, flicking with his tongue, sucking, then adding teeth just enough to get me even more aroused.

"Yes," I whispered, begging him with my body to continue what he was doing.

"You like that?" he breathed along my skin.

"Yes," I said. "Very much, yes."

His chuckle sent sparks through me and I writhed underneath him, trying desperately to get to that pinnacle of pleasure so I could topple over into the bliss that awaited on the other side.

"That's it," he said, low and deep, continuing his slow pace. "Come for me, baby."

He'd moved away from my body, but the hand that was not wrapped around my wrists moved between us and found that bundle of nerves at the apex of my sex and he pressed against it, then started a slow and steady circular motion, round and round, winding me up and up, higher and higher.

"Let go," he said. "Come apart for me, baby."

And just like that I did, bursting into a million shattered pieces, and it was amazing. There weren't words to describe what it felt like, and I didn't want to try. He picked up his pace, faster and faster, in and out until he, too, fell off the cliff and into his own release.

Collapsing atop me, he released my hands, and they found their way around him, tangling in his hair as I held him to me. We stayed there for a while, both of us trying to remember how to breathe properly. Finally, he pushed up, looking down into my eyes, and I saw something shift. He blinked it away, but it had been there. I didn't have a name for it, but I imagine it was something similar to what had flashed through mine.

Lowering his lips, he took mine in a chaste touch, almost as if he were afraid I'd break if he pushed too hard. My hand caressed his cheek when he pulled away and he turned and placed a kiss in my palm. It was so intimate, even more so than us sharing our bodies, and it made my breath hitch.

"Come on," he said, pulling out of me slowly. "Let's get cleaned up and to bed."

I nodded, following suit, allowing him to pull me up from the couch. I wobbled a bit, but he steadied me with his hands on my hips. Once my footing was solid, he turned, but reached back and grabbed my hand, pulling me behind him toward his room. He set me on the toilet and told me to pee, then left to do something, I didn't know what.

By the time he came back, I was done. He pulled out a washcloth and got it wet with warm water, knelt in front of me, pressing my legs apart slightly as he washed me, cleaning up the mess we'd made of ourselves.

"My turn," he said, turning me toward the bedroom.

I walked in and found all of our clothes sitting on the floor next to the bed, the bedding pulled down so we could climb in. I figured I'd deal with the clothes in the morning, especially since I didn't have anything else to do, and crawled under the covers. He joined me pretty quickly after, sliding between the sheets. He clicked off the bedside lamp, then settled, reaching for me in the dark.

Moving closer to him, I tucked myself into his side, his arm wrapping around me, pulling me even closer, and sighed. With my hand on his chest, I could feel the steady beat of his heart. Thump thump, thump thump. It lulled me to sleep, and I crashed into the darkness without even thinking about what the next day or even the next minute held. Nothing mattered but the steady beating of his heart under my palm and in my ear.

CHAPTER FIFTY-SIX

*J*onathan...

Stretching, I found my bed cold and empty once again. This was something I wasn't going to get used to, at least I didn't want to get used to it. I got up, went to the bathroom to get the morning started, then threw on some boxers, just in case there was a reason. The clothes at the end of the bed were gone, but her suitcase was still sitting by the closet. Walking out, I could hear her soft voice talking, and I wasn't sure whether she was alone or what, so I was slow to enter the living area of my condo.

"He's still asleep," she said into my phone. "As soon as he gets up, I'll ask him to bring me over."

She was sitting on the couch, her back to me, and I could see her profile, the phone on the opposite side of her. I leaned against the wall, crossing one foot in front of the other, folding my arms across my chest. I could look at her all day.

"I will," she said. "Thanks."

Pulling the phone away, she disconnected the call and turned, nearly jumping off the couch.

"Shit," she whispered. "You damn near gave me a heart attack. Why do you need to sneak up on me like that?"

"I didn't mean to," I said, and looked her over.

Wearing my shirt once again, I wondered whether there was anything on underneath. I stalked over to her and her eyes went wide when I wrapped my hands around her face, pulling her to me and planting a kiss on her lips. It didn't take long for her to melt into me, her own arms wrapping around my neck over the back of the couch.

"Good morning," I mumbled when I pulled back.

"Morning." She smiled, blush rushing her cheeks.

"Who was on the phone?"

"Agent Richards," she said and my heart plummeted.

"He wants to see you," I said. It wasn't a question, but she nodded just the same. "When?" I asked.

"As soon as possible," she replied. "But I need a shower."

I looked over at the clock on the stove and realized that we had plenty of time for a quick shower and for me to get her to wherever it was she needed to go and still make it home before I had to head into the stadium.

"I've got time," I said, winking.

"Umm," she hummed, looking away.

"Hey," I said, turning her eyes back to me. "What's wrong?"

"It's just..." she paused and her cheeks colored a bright pink. When she didn't continue, I looked more forcefully at her, trying to get her to trust me. Finally, she said, "I'm a little sore is all."

"No worries," I said, pulling back. "I'll help you get cleaned up, nothing else. Come on."

I held my hand out to her, and she took it, coming around the end of the couch and walking with me to the bedroom. I unbuttoned my shirt a little, then knelt before her, continuing to open the shirt. Once it was done, I pushed it away, laying a kiss between her belly button and the hair at her pelvic line, then looked up.

She placed her hand on my cheek, caressing it, and I just sat there, amazed that this beautiful woman was even here. I stood up slowly, then leaned down, kissing her softly, gently, then pulled back.

"Ready?" I asked, and she nodded.

I turned her toward the bathroom and walked behind her. She

dropped my shirt along the way, and I did the same with my boxers. I turned on the water, getting it warmed up, and made sure there were towels available for afterward, then slid the curtain back to allow her to get in first, following behind.

Stepping under the spray at the opposite end, she got her hair wet. I pulled the shampoo out and poured some into my palm, then stepped closer to her as she turned around. With my hands full of suds, I started massaging it into her hair, rubbing it through the long locks, ensuring that each strand was thoroughly clean before stepping closer, encouraging her to tip her head back to rinse it.

While she did that, I wet my own hair, using the remaining suds to get it clean as well. Then I pulled out the body wash, lathering it along her skin, caressing each curve, taking care to not take advantage of what I was doing for my own benefit. I couldn't help my body's reaction to hers, growing stiff the more I touched her.

She noticed and began to return the favor of lathering me up, paying extra attention to my hard cock, using slow, deliberate strokes to bring me closer and closer to climax.

"You keep doing that," I choked, "and I'm not responsible for the natural reaction of my body."

"Let me do this for you," she said, adding, "Please," to the end.

The way she looked at me, the need I saw in her eyes, was more than I could handle, and I pressed my palms on the wall behind her, moving my body closer to her as she continued to stroke me. We weren't touching, but we were as close as we could be without it. The shower ran down my back, she was covered in suds, and she stroked me, slow and steady, watching my face as she did.

There was so much intimacy with this act and I was humbled that she would do this for me, give me pleasure without wanting any of her own. My breathing became ragged, stuttering with each stroke until finally I felt that tingle at the base of my spine right before everything went bright and I exploded in her hand. When I caught my breath again, I looked down, and she was staring at me. Her beautiful brown eyes full of light, gold flecks flashing through them. I hadn't realized how much life there was in them until this moment. Honestly, we didn't really know that much about each other.

Leaning down, I placed a chaste kiss on her lips, then pulled back.

"Is this okay?" she asked, and I looked back at her, surprised. "Us," she continued, waving her hand between us. "Are we good for each other?"

"You're certainly good for me," I said, rinsing the suds and my own seed from me. "Do you not feel the same?"

"I don't know," she said, stepping into the spray and rinsing herself off. "I don't want to put too much pressure on you. I also don't want to rush into something just because it feels good and safe, either."

"So far," I began, but had to swallow. "I think we're good for each other. We know what we've been through and can relate in such a way that many others can't. So, until something happens that we can't handle, I think we're good."

"But," she said. "How will this work?"

"Do we need to have everything figured out right now?" I asked.

"I mean…" She shrugged.

"Come on," I said, turning the tap off and opening the curtain. "Let's get dressed and head to the bureau. We can work on whatever else we need to as things come up."

She nodded and took the towel I wrapped around her, stepping out of the tub, and out of the bathroom before I had a chance to help dry her off. It felt like she was pulling away, and I didn't like that feeling. Quickly, I dried off, but by the time I got to the bedroom she was done and pulling on jeans, already having put on a shirt.

"Hey," I said, standing there in a towel.

"We're gonna be late," she said without looking at me, then stepped out of the room.

"Fuck," I mumbled to myself. I wasn't sure what had just happened, but I didn't like it at all.

CHAPTER FIFTY-SEVEN

*L*ucy...

The ride to the bureau was brutally quiet, aside from the small directions I gave him on how to get to the building. I think I screwed everything up in the shower, and I didn't even know why I had those questions going through my head. Once we were checked in, with our visitor badges pinned to our chests, we were escorted to a conference room and instructed to wait for Agent Richards. Tension was running high, and the room was thick with things that hadn't been said.

"Hello," the agent said as he came into the room. "Thanks for coming down."

"Sounded like you had new information for us," Jonathan said, and I could hear the strain in his voice, though I doubted the agent caught it.

"Turns out," the agent continued as he sat down with a folder full of papers, much thicker than I was expecting. "The man who was trying to pick up your kids was told that the kids in question belonged to one of his professors."

"No," I whispered, waiting for the rest of the bad news I knew was coming.

"You are correct," the agent said. "George Warde had sent one of his students to your kid's school with instructions to see how good the security at the school was. He was told that the professor was worried that someone would try to kidnap his kids, and he needed to be sure they were safe while at school."

"What is with this guy?" Jonathan asked.

"It appears he has become obsessed with Lucy," the agent replied. "And it didn't start with the funeral."

"Wait," I said. "What? That's the first time I actually met him in person."

"But he has known about you for a while," the agent returned. "Your husband had several pictures of you in his office when he was teaching there. George would often meet with him to discuss class schedules and common students, which is a completely normal thing for teachers to do. The problem came when he started to get a little bit pushier, asking specifics about you."

"I had no idea," I whispered.

"Which is how he wanted it," the agent explained. "The trip that Ryan made into the office the day he died was regarding this issue. With the new quarter starting, he wanted us to do a little digging on his colleague, find out if there were any red flags that might be a reason for him to go to the head of the department for reprimands in his record at the very least, but perhaps even dismissal. I had our techs take another look at the accident and they found some discrepancies."

"What accident?" Jonathan asked. "I thought he died of a brain aneurysm."

"He did," the agent said. "But he never would have had one if he hadn't crashed the car. Because he hit his head so hard when he crashed, it caused the aneurysm to occur. It was originally thought that there was a defect with the airbags, but it turns out that those had been tampered with and didn't deploy properly. It is tragic that the driver of the other vehicle had to become collateral damage for George's retribution."

"Oh, God," I whispered, tears filling my eyes.

"When was this accident?" Jonathan asked, and all of a sudden, my stomach plummeted.

"September nineteenth," the agent said. "Why do you ask?"

I watched as Jonathan went pale, and I knew, right then, that my husband had killed his wife. There was no way that could have been any clearer than what I saw on his face.

"What was the name of the other driver?" I asked, even though I knew the answer. I watched Jonathan, hoping beyond hope that what I was thinking, and what he was obviously thinking was wrong, even though I knew we both knew the truth.

"Let me see," the agent said, filtering through the stack of papers in front of him. "Here we go," he said, pulling some report out. "Looks like her name was Margaret Bridge. Wait, isn't that—"

"I'm gonna be sick," Jonathan said, rushing from the room.

"That was his wife," I explained after finally finding my voice. "Ryan killed his wife."

CHAPTER FIFTY-EIGHT

*J*onathan...

All I wanted to do was scream, but I couldn't do that. Not here. I crashed through the bathroom door and into a stall, dry heaving at the bowl. We hadn't had time to fix anything for breakfast, not even coffee, so there was nothing in my stomach to get rid of, even though my body tried desperately.

"Fuck," I shouted at nothing, then punched the stall wall, shouting it again. "Fuck, fuck, fuck, fuck, fuck."

This could not be happening. There was no way this was real, no way that we could be this tied together in this cosmic shitstorm of reality.

"Jonathan," I heard from the open door.

I didn't answer. I didn't know what to say to her. There was nothing I could say. Her fucked-up life had cost me Meg, and there was nothing that could be done to undo it. Logically, I knew it wasn't her fault, and yet, somehow, I still blamed her.

"Jonathan," she said, this time from right behind me. "I didn't know," she whispered, and I felt her touch my shoulder.

I jerked away, turning on her, and I realized that she felt completely at fault for this, but she was not to blame.

"I'm so sorry," she sobbed, and I couldn't stop myself. I gathered her to me and we both just stood there, both of us sobbing. "I'm so sorry," she continued through her crying. "I didn't know. I didn't know."

We stood there in the men's bathroom, both of us crying for the horror that had been done to us, neither of us to blame for it.

"Oh," someone said as he came in, then turned around and walked back out.

"Oh God," she said, but I didn't let her go.

It took a few minutes, but finally we both settled ourselves and I felt like we could breathe again, so I let her go, but kept a hand on her shoulder.

"I'm so sorry," she said for the millionth time and I just squeezed her shoulder.

"It wasn't you," I said. "You didn't do this."

"But—"

"No," I said firmly. "You were not responsible. Whoever this asshole is, I want him to pay for what he did to both of us."

"How can you even look at me, though?" she asked.

"Oh, baby," I said, caressing her cheek with my thumb. "You are the best thing to happen to me since that day. I would give anything to have Meg back. I know you feel the same way about Ryan. But I wouldn't want to give you up now. Not when I realized that there is still something worth living for."

She stared at me and all I could do was think that Meg knew I needed someone, and she must have known that Lucy did, too. She must have coordinated everything between us so we found each other, and I couldn't be happier.

"Let's go," I said when another man stepped into the bathroom.

We walked out, hand in hand, and went back to the conference room we'd been in before.

"I didn't know," Agent Richards said as soon as we walked into the room.

"Of course you didn't," I said. "The question now is what do we do with this information."

"Well," the agent said. "There are several things we need to corroborate, but I think with what we have, we may be able to put this guy away."

"Good," I said. "He needs to be somewhere he can't hurt anyone else."

"We should be able to do that," the agent said. "Do you two need anything else right now?"

"I would like to be able to go home," Lucy said.

"That may take some time," the agent replied. "But I'll see if I can put a rush on the cleanup process."

"You sure you want to go back?" I asked.

"It's been our home since the kids were tiny," she said. "I don't want to lose anything else to him. It won't be easy, but I think I can make it work."

"Then let me help you," I said.

She looked at me confused and asked, "Why would you do that?"

"You gave me new life," I replied, and it was true. "Let me do that same thing for you."

"It may be awhile before it's safe for you to be there," the agent said. "We're not yet at a point to be able to arrest him."

"Even for the accident?" I asked. "Or the break-in?"

"We don't have any definitive evidence it was him," the agent replied.

"What about that kid?" she asked. "The one who tried to pick up my kids."

"It's a he-said, she-said situation," the agent said. "Trust me, we're working on things. Right now, we just need you guys to stay safe and out of the limelight. Can you do that?"

"My job kind of puts me on the radar," I said.

"What is it you do?"

"I'm a member of the Seattle Cascades baseball team," I replied.

"Oh," he said. "Ryan always liked baseball."

"He's the reason we met," Lucy said, looking at me in a way I wasn't sure how to interpret.

"I think you'll be safe," he said. "But if you want, we can give you a detail."

"That is the last thing I want," I said. "I'm not a superstar, just your average Joe, so I should be good."

There was no way I wanted babysitters following me around everywhere. That was not the life I signed up for, and I didn't want to have to deal with it if at all possible.

"That's fine," he said.

"Should I keep the kids out of school for a while longer?" Lucy asked.

"I would," the agent replied. "In fact, if there's somewhere out of state you can go, that would be even better."

"They're out of town right now," she said. "I'll see what we can figure out."

I had ideas, but I didn't want to discuss them with the agent right there. I didn't know how much he knew about our relationship, and I wasn't even sure what the relationship was, but I did know that I wanted to spend as much time with her as I could. We thanked the agent, then went out and got into my car. I drove us back to the condo, not wanting to say anything until we were there. Even then, I wasn't sure whether I should broach the subject or not.

When we pulled into the garage, I parked the car and shut it off.

"You good?" I asked her.

She'd been quiet the entire ride back, short as it was, and I wanted to know what she'd been thinking.

"I don't have anywhere to go," she said, her voice trembling. "We have money, but I wanted to save it for the kids for college. If I have to, though, I'll use it to keep them safe."

"Would you let me help?" I asked, and she turned to me, unshed tears filling her lower lashes.

"Why would you help me?" she asked. "I'm the reason your wife is dead."

"Oh, no," I said, reaching my hand up to brush the tears that began to roll away. "It isn't your fault that he became obsessed with you. You said you never met him before the funeral, so how could you have known?"

"Ryan should have told me," she replied. "Should have warned me that this was going on. Prepared me for what has been happening."

"Babe," I said, unbuckling my belt and reaching further over. "You did nothing wrong. This asshole feels entitled to you, and that is on him. He is to blame for everything that has happened."

"Because of me," she whispered.

"Come on," I said, clicking her seatbelt to let it release. "Let's go up and talk this out in more comfort."

She nodded and let the belt withdraw back into its housing. I got out and walked around the car, opening her door for her, a hand down to help her out. She held onto me as we walked to the elevator, the whole ride up to my floor, and into the condo, and I relished in the fact that she was finding strength in me when I felt so very weak. Maybe we would get through this and find our own happily ever after.

CHAPTER FIFTY-NINE

*L*ucy...

He was so kind, so forgiving, I wasn't sure whether it was real or imagined. What were the odds that we would come together after this strange and tragic connection from so long ago? I'm sure they were astronomical, something I would never be able to compute, but it still felt weird that we'd found each other. I don't think I'd noticed before, but there was a picture of him with Meg and his son right by the front door.

"This is your son," I said, waiting as he locked the door behind him.

"Yeah," he said. "That's Grant and Meg. We were at Alki Beach right before she was killed. We took a bunch of pictures and she printed them all up. They were sitting on the desk and my mom got them all framed up for me to have scattered around the house."

"You look so happy," I said.

"We were," he replied. "She was going to go get her ultrasound the next morning. I had an early call time with the team, so wasn't able to go with her. Day games are like that."

"She was pregnant?"

"We were having a girl," he said, then swallowed. "Neither of them had a chance."

"I'm so sorry," I said.

"Hey," he said, squeezing my arm. "None of that."

"I don't know how this is supposed to work," I confessed. "It's like a nightmare that I'm afraid I can't wake up from."

"Except you are awake," he said. "And everything just sucks."

"So bad," I replied.

"I have about an hour," he said. "Do you want to call the kids?"

"Not yet," I said. "Until I know something, I don't want to get them worried or excited."

"So," he began, moving us to the couch. "I have an idea, and I totally would understand if you don't want to do it, but I think it might be worthwhile for you to at least think about."

"Why does this sound ominous?"

"Honestly," he said. "I have to check with some people first, but I wanted to see if you would be interested before I got things moving."

"Should I be worried?"

"I hope not," he said. "My family lives in Salem, Oregon and I'm sure that this asshat would not have any idea where they are, so I thought maybe, if you wanted, I'd see if they would be cool with hosting you for a little while."

I stared at him, completely taken off guard by his offer.

"If you're not comfortable," he began, "I am fine with that, too. I just wanted to give you an option."

"So," I said, then stopped, the gears in my head running through everything. "Would I just stay with them?"

"I have a house down there," he said. "You and the kids could stay there for a while. It is just that it's on the same property as my parents, so they would be right there, too."

"And you'd just let us live in your house?"

"I let you stay here," he replied. "And you're staying with me now, so I don't see an issue."

"I don't know." I shook my head. "It just seems like…"

"Like what?" he asked after I hadn't continued.

"I don't know," I reiterated. "Just weird, I guess?"

"I've rented it out as an Airbnb before," he said. "We wouldn't have to tell my parents or sister who you were, just someone who was renting the place."

"But how would we get there?" I asked, actually thinking this might be something that would be okay.

"Yeah," he said. "Guess you couldn't drive your car. I mean, I don't use mine much, and I am going on a long road trip in about a week."

"I don't want to put you out," I said, but he stopped me.

"Whether we like it or not, we're together in this," he said. "I rather like that thought."

He liked that we were in this together. That was unexpected but felt right as well.

"I feel like you're getting the short end of all of this." I laughed.

"How so?"

"Well," I said. "There's the obvious collateral damage issue."

"Which is not your fault," he interrupted.

"Yeah," I said. "But then, you have people you don't really know staying with you. You're offering your car and your house to us, and what am I giving you?"

"If you don't know how you have helped me, I can show you," he said.

He wiggled his eyebrows up and down and I couldn't help but laugh. Honestly, I couldn't remember the last time I laughed, and it felt good.

"Do you have time?" I asked, warming to the idea.

"You sure you're not still too sore?"

"I think I can manage." I smiled, and he leaned toward me, closing the little distance there was between us on the couch.

His kiss was swift, chaste, and he sat back up like he'd been shocked.

"Hey," he said after pulling his phone out of his pocket and answering it. "No, I'm up. Had some stuff to do but am getting ramped up to head into the stadium."

I didn't want to interrupt his call, so went to stand, but he grabbed my arm and kept me next to him on the couch.

"Well," he said, looking at me. "I have company right now." There was another pause, then he said, "It's someone I just met."

I wasn't sure who the call was with, but it was obviously someone he knew well.

"Yeah," he said. "I'll call you tomorrow."

Staring at him, I waited.

"That was my sister," he said. "She was thinking of coming up this weekend. Since we're not sure what's going on, I didn't want that to happen. I don't want Grant up here until that guy is taken care of."

"Oh God," I said. "I don't know what I'd do if anything happened to him."

"Yeah," he said somberly. "I was on the phone with Meg when she was killed. I don't know what I would have done if I'd lost both of them."

"Losing Ryan was the hardest thing I ever went through," I said. "If I were to lose the kids as well, I don't know that I would survive."

"Exactly," he said.

We sat there, likely both contemplating the same terrifying thought of losing our entire family.

"You said you can't have more kids," he said, and the shift in gears threw me for a minute.

"Oh," I said. "I forgot I told you that."

"Can I ask why?"

"I ended up having to have a hysterectomy," I said. "Apparently, my body hates me and tried to kill me shortly after Thomas was born. He was just a little guy when I went for a follow up appointment and my OB was concerned with some of my numbers. The best option was to have the surgery, which was fine since we were pretty sure we were done having kids."

"That's scary," he said.

"Meh," I replied. "It was not fun immediately after the surgery, but I am really thankful now. There are parts to being a girl that just plain suck, and most of those are gone for me now, so…" I shrugged.

"That's wild," he said. "But extremely convenient for me."

There went those eyebrows again, and all I could do was laugh. That was, until he captured my mouth with his, pulling me into his lap. I went willingly, loving the way we worked together, how passionate he was, and how much more alive I felt in his arms.

CHAPTER SIXTY

*J*onathan...

By the time I made it out of the condo, I was running farther behind than planned. I would still make it to the stadium before the crowd started to get too wild, so there was that.

"Look who finally showed up." Beckett laughed, already changed to hit batting practice. "Thought you weren't supposed to be fucking the fans."

"You need to learn to shut your pie hole," Huffman said, then turned to me. "So," he said, looking for an answer as to why I was so late.

"Just had a few unexpected errands popped up," I said. "Figured out what happened to Meg, though, so there's the bonus."

"I thought she was hit by a drunk driver or something," he said.

"It's a long story," I replied. "Not something I wanna get into here, though. Prying ears and all that."

"For sure," he said. "No worries. You need a shoulder, I'm here."

He walked away and headed out to the field. I took my time getting dressed, remembering the way Lucy had felt in my arms, and I realized that she really was my perfect match. Honestly, extra innings in baseball were a pain, but finding a chance to keep playing in real life, that was worth it.

"Was worried I'd made a mistake putting you in the lineup," Coach said as I stepped up to the batting cage.

"Just a little snag in my morning," I replied. "Nothing to worry about."

"Good," he replied. "'Cause I need your head in it tonight. Mike has a fever and has been hurling all morning. I'm gonna need you on second, maybe through the weekend."

"Damn." I whistled. "Not contagious?"

"Probably," he said. "His kids came down with something and he caught it from them on the day off. His wife called me and apologized something fierce, but I told her I understood. Kids carry so many germs it's amazing they even make it to their teenage years, let alone adulthood."

"Yeah," I said. "Grant was always coming down with something every time he went on those play dates Meg took him to."

"It's cause they're always putting shit in their mouths." He laughed. "Get in there and get ready. I want you on it tonight. The Anglers have been killing it so far, and I honestly think they're probably the team to beat for the eastern division, which means we'll have to go through them if we expect to get those championship rings we're pushing for."

"And we all want those." I laughed, then took my bat and replaced Huffman in the cage to do some practice swings.

Getting the start was always a treat, and I would take advantage of it every time it was offered to me.

~

"HOLY SHIT," BECKETT SAID AS HE CAME OFF THE BAG AT SECOND. "That was fucking amazing."

"We do seem to work well together," I said. "Too bad it doesn't spill over into real life."

This was the third double play we'd turned behind our starter, Sammy, and it was only the fifth inning.

"Hey," he said as we made the trot to the dugout. He tossed the ball into the stands, then dropped down the steps and turned. "I'm sorry I've been screwing with you. I know it's shitty of me to keep on it."

"Yeah," I said. "It is pretty shitty, especially since we're supposed to have each other's backs."

"I know," he said. "It's just that some shit came up with my mom and I kinda feel like if I don't blow off steam it's gonna mess me up more than it already has."

"Hey, kid," Coach called. "You're on deck. Get your helmet and get out there."

"On it," he said, turning away from me.

Somehow, in that small moment, the kid who had been the bane of my existence this whole year became a decent human being, and it kinda threw me. I gathered my gear and stuffed it into the cubby where my helmet was and sat on the bench.

"You good?" Huffman asked as he plopped down next to me.

"Yeah," I said. "Beckett seems like he's finally pulled his head out of his ass, though, so I'm not quite sure what to do with that information."

"Don't worry." He laughed. "He'll be back to his shit talking before the game is over."

"Probably," I said.

The rest of the game flew by, and we ended up turning a record six double plays, which is absolutely unheard of. Strawberry came in and saved it for us in the top of the ninth because, while we were on fire in the field, we couldn't figure out how to hit a damn thing, Huffman's home run in the bottom of the eight being the only run we made.

"Hey, Jonathan," Jenn said as we walked off the field after the last out. "You and Beckett seemed to be on the same page out there."

"It's the first time we've worked together in a game this season," I said. "But he's a good player, and when you're on like we were defensively tonight, things just seem to all fall into place."

"Is it true that the two of you have had some issues this season?"

"Every team has some growing pains when new players come in," I said. "We get through it and figure out how to work together. That's what we did tonight."

I knew it wasn't what they wanted to hear, they wanted the gossip, but I didn't feel like throwing him under the bus, especially after what he said earlier.

"Nice game, J," he said as he walked off the field.

"Back at you," I replied, then turned back to the sports announcer.

"I guess it was all rumors," she said. "Anyway, nice night."

"Thanks," I said, then turned and headed into the dugout to walk back to the locker room. "Hey, kid," I shouted when I got closer.

"What's up?" he asked.

"Thought I'd let you know," I said. "Jenn asked about our beef. I told her it was the simple growing pains of new players."

"Really?" He seemed surprised.

"It's true," I said, lying a little. "Any time a new player comes in, things shift. It's the way of the game."

"Thanks for the heads-up, man," he said, and seemed really happy I'd told him.

"Anytime," I replied, then went to my own locker to get out of my uniform and into my street clothes.

I really wanted to get back to Lucy, and I wasn't at all ashamed to think that. Saying it out loud, however, might not be the best option. But that time would come, for sure.

"Bridge," Coach called when he came into the locker room.

"Yeah," I replied.

"Got a call for you," he said, pointing to his office.

While getting calls at the stadium wasn't unheard of, it was certainly rare on game days, and especially after the game, so I was confused. My first thought was that it was Lucy, and she was in trouble.

"Line three," Coach said then stepped out of the office to give me privacy, I guess.

I picked up the receiver and pressed the button for line three, then said, "Hello."

"You think you're so smooth," the man on the other end of the phone said. "With your fancy words and your baseball playing skills. You don't get to keep her. She's mine."

The line went dead, and I just stood there. Before I could even think, I clicked another line and dialed my cell number, praying that Lucy would answer it. After two rings she did.

"Hello?" she asked.

"Lucy," I said.

"Jonathan," she replied.

"Is the door locked?" I asked. "If not, get it done now. And stick something in front of it to keep it from being able to be opened. Then call the FBI agent and let him know that the dude just called me at the stadium."

"Wait, what?" she asked, and I heard the fear in her voice.

"Is the door locked?" I asked, then gave her a chance to respond.

"Hang on," she said, and I assumed she was getting up to check the door. "Door's locked, and I flipped the little extra thing onto it, too."

"Good," I said. "Can you put something next to it or something that would keep it from being broken down?"

"Let me put a chair under the knob," she said, and I again heard movement as she did what I asked. "Okay, there's a chair under there now. How will you get in?"

"Don't worry about me," I said. "I want you to hang up and call that agent. Tell him that I got the call from the dude and ask him what we should do."

"What did he say?" she asked.

"Doesn't matter," I replied. "Just let him know that he called the stadium, and that I took the call in the manager's office. He'll know what he needs to do. I'll stay here and wait for them if that's what they want to do."

"How will you know?" she asked, and I was growing frustrated.

"Lucy," I said firmly. "Call him. Tell him what I said. He'll figure out what to do and I'll stay here and get changed. I won't leave alone, but I want to make sure you're safe first."

"Okay," she said. "I'll call him. If I call this number that's on your phone, will I be able to reach you?"

"I don't know what number it is," I replied. "But you can try it and see. Just tell them that you need to talk to a player about his family and they'll route it in here. I'm assuming that's what the guy did to get the call to me."

"I'm sorry," she said.

"Not a problem," I replied. "I want you safe. Call that agent. Please."

"Okay," she said. "I love you."

She disconnected the call before I even had a chance to process what she'd said. Were we there, yet? Honestly, it didn't matter. What mattered was that she was safe. I stepped out of the office and Coach could tell something was wrong.

"What's up?" he asked.

"Are there any cops around?" I asked.

"I'm sure I can find one," he said. "Are you all right?"

"Not at all," I replied, and it was the God's honest truth.

CHAPTER SIXTY-ONE

*L*ucy...
I disconnected the call and then went in search of the card Agent Richards had given me. When I found it, I tried to dial, but messed up at least three times before I got the number right.

"Federal Bureau of Investigation, Seattle Field Office, how may I direct your call?"

"I need to speak to Agent Richards right away," I said.

"I'm sorry," the receptionist said. "He isn't in the office at this time."

"You need to get this call to him," I said. "My name is Lucy Fallon and my stalker just contacted my friend at the stadium and threatened him. I don't feel safe."

"Ma'am," the woman said. "If you are in immediate danger, I am going to need you to dial 911 and speak to your local police precinct."

"Agent Richards has been working with them on my case," I said. "He told me to call him if anything changed. I need to reach him."

"I'll see if I can reach him," she said. "Your name."

"Lucy Fallon," I repeated, then spelled it out for her.

"Please hold," she said, and that horrible music they played came from the receiver.

"Lucy," Agent Richards answered.

"Jonathan said he got a call at the stadium," I rushed out. "He said he wanted to make sure I was safe and told me to call you."

"Hold on," Agent Richards said. "When did he get this call?"

"I don't know," I said. "I assume it was just a few minutes ago. He said he just got it when he called me."

"Did he say what the person said?"

"He said he didn't want to worry me," I replied. "He said he knew it was George, though."

"Okay," Agent Richards said. "Are you safe?"

"I'm at Jonathan's condo," I said. "I have the door locked and a chair stuck under the handle."

"Good," he said. "Do you know the number that was called?"

"Hang on," I said, pulling the phone from my ear and putting it on speaker. "I have the number Jonathan called me from, but I don't know if that's the number that was dialed."

"Why don't you give me that," he said. "It will be somewhere to start at least."

I rattled off the number to him and he said he'd look into it.

"What should I do?" I asked.

"Stay put," he said. "If you can reach Jonathan, ask him if he can get in touch with the police from where he is and make a report with them."

"I can try to call him," I said. "But he wasn't sure whether it would work."

"Why don't you try," Agent Richards suggested. "I'll see what I can do from here and we'll figure something out. Do not under any circumstances open the door, even if it's the police."

"You think he would try that?" I asked, fear crawling up my spine.

"At this point, I wouldn't put anything past him," Agent Richards said. "It's better to be safe than sorry, so stay put and don't open the door for anyone but Jonathan or me."

"I won't," I said.

"If I get more news, I'll call you on this number," he said. "If the police show up, or anyone else who says they're an authority figure, give them my cell number and have them call me. Better yet, just tell them that you need their number, then call me and I will call them."

He gave me his number but had to tell me twice because I mixed everything up. Finally, when I got it down correct, I said, "Thanks."

"Lucy," he said. "You will get through this. We've got you."

"Thanks," I said again, then disconnected the call.

Flipping back through recent calls on Jonathan's phone, I pushed connect on the number he'd called me from.

"Cascades Stadium," a woman answered. "How may I direct your call?"

"I need to talk to Jonathan Bridge," I said. "I'm family."

"Ma'am," the woman said. "The players are not able to be contacted through this line. You will have to try to call him directly on his cell. I'm sorry."

"I have his cell," I said. "He just called me from this number and said I could reach him. He said to tell you I'm family, and you'd be able to reach him."

"I'm sorry," she said. "We aren't able to reach the players during a game."

"The game is over," I said. "He called me from the coach's office and told me to call him back. Can you at least try?"

"What's your name?"

"Lucy," I said. "Lucy Fallon."

"And how are you related to him?"

Oh God, how did I answer that.

"Umm," I stammered. "I'm his girlfriend."

"Sure," she said.

It certainly didn't sound like she believed me, but she put me on hold and I heard the radio station that played the game coming through the phone.

"Lucy?" Jonathan said when he picked up the call.

"Jonathan," I said. "Thank God. I talked to Agent Richards, and he's gonna look into see what he can figure out. He told me not to answer the door to anyone except you or him. He also said you should try to talk to police to see if they could help you, but he wasn't clear on what they should be helping you with."

"I talked to one of the officers that was working the game," he said.

"I have the agent's phone number," I said. "He said to have them call him."

"Well," Jonathan began. "I just told him that he should hook up with the FBI. He didn't exactly seem interested, but he did take my name down."

"Can you come home?"

"Yeah," he said. "I was just waiting to see if you called. I'll head out now and be there soon."

"Be careful," I said. "I don't want you to get hurt."

"I'll be fine," he said.

"Just be careful," I reiterated. "I can't lose you, too."

"I will," he said. "I promise."

"See you soon," I said, and he disconnected the call.

The only thing left was to sit and wait and worry. I'd done enough of that when Ryan was on the job, but this was somehow different. This time I knew the person who was out to get my people, and he had shown that he was not above killing someone to get what he wanted. I just couldn't figure out why he wanted me.

CHAPTER SIXTY-TWO

*J*onathan...

I stepped out of the coach's office and he looked at me and asked, "What do you need?"

"I'm not sure," I said. "I need to go home, but I'm not sure if it's safe."

"You want someone to go with you?"

"I don't want to put anyone out," I said.

"Nonsense," he replied. "Stay here."

He walked away from me and toward the locker room. I sat in one of the chairs in his office, dropping my head in my hands and blowing out my breath. I hadn't been this worried since I heard the accident with Meg. Thinking about that just made my blood boil more. This douche canoe had ruined not just my life, but Lucy's as well, and he didn't seem all that bothered by it. He just kept on messing with her, and the only reason he was messing with me was because I was with her.

"Let's go," Huffman said as he stepped into the coach's office.

"Where?" I asked, and noticed he was still in his uniform.

"Home," he said. "Grab your shit, we're heading out."

"I can't ask you to—"

"Nonsense," he said. "We're family. We take care of our own. Now, get your shit so we can go."

I didn't feel like arguing any further, so I headed to my locker and started to grab my stuff.

"Give me your keys," Beckett said.

"What?"

"Your car keys," he added. "Dude needs to see you leave the garage. Maybe he'll follow your car."

"Seriously?"

"Dude," he said and looked at me.

"Fuck," I said. "You guys think it's that bad?"

"You went to the cops," Huffman said.

"And you look like you're ready to scream," Beckett added. "We got you."

I pulled my keys out of my jacket pocket and pulled the car key off the ring, handing it to Beckett.

"You screw it up..." I said, but didn't bother to finish the sentiment. I think he understood the unsaid words.

"Don't worry about it," he said, turning and heading out of the locker room and toward the garage.

Somehow, in the last few hours, he'd turned himself around to a decent kid, and I didn't want to think too much about it. I had enough worries on my mind right now. It didn't take long to get my shit. Most of it didn't matter, but I needed my wallet and keys, as well as my shoes. I could change them in the car on the way. I didn't want to waste time doing that now.

"Which way?" Huffman asked when we pulled out of the garage.

"Go left," I said.

He had one of those lifted trucks with a long bed and double doors, a crew cab kind of thing I think they called it. I'd never been into trucks, just needed something to keep my family safe, which is why I had gone with a classic sedan. Huffman was single and almost always on the prowl, or so he said. I just figured he'd never found the right girl.

Either way, his red truck was something that was flashy and showy and drew a crowd. Exactly the opposite of what I wanted right at that moment. It roared as we left the garage, and several people who were walking around the stadium turned to look. Thankfully, his windows were tinted and no one could see inside.

I directed him which way to turn, taking some back streets and round abouts just to make sure we weren't being followed. Finally, I had him pull up to the front of the building and we sat there.

"What are we waiting for?" he asked.

"Wanna see if there's any reason I should wait to get out," I replied.

"Give me your keys," he said, turning the truck off.

"What for?" I asked.

"Just give me the damn keys, dude," he said, holding his hand out.

I handed them over, showing him which one got you into the building. He climbed out of the truck and walked up to the door, sticking the key into the lock and opening it up. When the door opened, he turned to the truck, and I looked around. No one was on the street, so I climbed out and went past him into the building.

"Here," he said. "You want me to go up with you?"

"If you wouldn't mind," I said. "You are much scarier than I am."

He laughed, hit a button on his key fob that made his truck horn honk, then shut the door behind him.

"Lead the way," he said, and we walked across the empty lobby to the elevator.

The ride up was fine, but when we got to my floor he said, "Hold up," and stepped out first, looking down the hall. "Okay," he said. "Coast is clear."

I led us to my door and knocked but didn't hear anything on the other side. Knocking again, I said, "Lucy, it's me. Open up." Again, no answer, and no movement. Then I heard a chair being moved, and she opened the door, bursting through and into my arms, sobbing.

CHAPTER SIXTY-THREE

*L*ucy...

After I hung up with Jonathan, I pulled a couple of towels from the bathroom and put them along the bottom of the front door to keep light from seeping out. Then, I found a post it in his office and put it over the peep hole in the door. When I felt like no light was leaking out of the condo, I sat on the couch and stared at the door. I didn't know how long it would take him to get home, but I didn't want to miss anything.

I must have dozed off because when a knock came, I bolted awake. Thankfully I didn't scream or anything. Walking as quietly as I could I went to the door, switched off the light for the living room, and cupped my hands around the peep hole before pulling the post it off. I looked out and saw Jonathan with another player. Only reason I knew it was another player was because they were both still in their uniforms.

It took entirely too long to get the chair unhooked from under the knob and the towels out of the way before unlocking the door and opening it. I couldn't stop myself, I just rushed through and into Jonathan's arms and the reality of the situation hit me and I lost it.

"Hey," he said, smoothing a hand down my back. "Let's get you inside."

"You good?" the other player asked.

"Yeah," he said, the rumble under my cheek soothing somehow. "Thanks, man. I appreciate you helping out."

"Absolutely," he said. "I'll get your keys to you tomorrow."

"Thanks," Jonathan said, steering me into the condo. "See you then."

We moved into the condo further and he shut the door behind him, locking the deadbolt. Pushing me away a bit he looked at me.

"I'm so sorry," I sobbed.

"You're safe," he replied. "I've got you. I am not going to let anything happen to you. We will get through this."

I broke further, just letting the tears run down my cheeks as I stood there.

"Come on," he said. "I need a shower, and I think you could use one, too."

I nodded, and he put his arm around me. I stopped as he was moving down the hall and went back and shoved the chair under the doorknob again. That little extra security was something I really needed right at that moment, and he seemed to understand because he simply waited for me to do it.

He turned the faucet in the tub up to a very warm temp, then plugged the stopper as it began to fill. Flicking the lighter he had in there, he lit the candle that was on the back of the toilet and I watched as it flared, mesmerized by the flicker of the flame. Shutting the light off in the bathroom, he then came to me and held me to him, kissing the top of my head. There was something about being in his arms that relaxed me, and I could just let him be in charge.

Slowly and meticulously, he helped me out of my clothes, only stopping to add something to the tub which filled the room with the relaxing scent of lavender. Once I was naked, he helped me into the tub, which was a bit too warm. I turned down the temp on the faucet until the water cooled just enough that I could sit without burning myself, then turned it completely off.

He slid in behind me and wrapped me in his arms. Sitting in the warm water, the scent of lavender in the air, and him wrapped around me, I felt like I could actually breathe again. I relaxed with each moment we sat there. He didn't push me, didn't ask questions, didn't demand anything. No, he was simply there for me, as a solid stone to lean against, somewhere for me to find refuge.

It started slowly, just a sweet kiss on my shoulder, but grew with every kiss he gave me. The more he kissed, the more I craved him, and it was sooner than he probably expected, but I pushed myself forward and turned around, water sloshing in the tub but not spilling over the sides.

"Make me forget," I begged. "Make everything else go away, even for just a little while."

He paused, but only for a moment, just long enough to ensure I was really asking him, and then he moved closer, cupping my cheek, kissing my lips, caressing my back. It escalated rapidly to him pulling me to a standing position and turning me back around. He pulled the plug on the tub, then turned on the water, getting it hot, and turning the showers on.

While I wasn't sure exactly what he was going to do, I knew he would help me leave this crazy scared place I was and find that blissful fall he'd brought me to time and time again in the last week or two. He'd wrapped an arm around my waist, pressing himself into my back as he kissed and sucked on my neck. His other arm was stretched out in front of us, pressing against the wall of the enclosure. Moving me, his feet between mine, he walked me up to the wall and pinned me between it and him, the cool tile doing amazing things to my body.

"You tell me to stop," he said, but I replied, "Don't stop."

"You say the word, though," he said. "I will stop."

I simply nodded in agreement, wanting him to bring me to a place of escape. He did not disappoint, either. The hand that had been against the wall swept down my side, then slid in front of me, pulling my hips back before reaching between my legs and sliding between my folds, slicking in my own juices as he worked me up and up. He plunged a finger inside me, and even with the awkward angle, it set me off and I groaned and ground into him further.

His cock was at my back, strong and sliding between my ass

cheeks in a way that was erotic and naughty and exactly what I needed. The hand that was around my waist moved up and grabbed my breast, squeezing it hard, his finger and thumb tightening on my nipple, pulling it away from my body, eliciting another groan from me.

"You like that?" he asked, deep and right next to my ear.

I nodded, but he pulled a little harder and I squeaked out, "Yeah."

"Good," he said, then wrapped his lips around my earlobe, sucking and then biting the tender flesh. "You taste so good," he continued between nibbles.

Suddenly, without warning, his hand was gone from my breast and he'd backed away from my body slightly. Then he nudged my feet further apart with his knee and removed the other hand from inside me. I mewled at the loss, but it was short lived when he pushed my ass cheeks apart and nearly knocked me over by putting his tongue right there, lapping at my asshole. His finger returned, just from a different angle, inside me, his thumb rubbing against my clit in quick motions.

All the sensations were nearly overwhelming, and I pressed my cheek against the tile, holding onto it for dear life, as I came apart above him without any warning. I shuddered and spasmed, trying desperately to find something to hold on to and keep me upright, when he was just there, turning me around and gathering me into his arms, holding me as I fell back to myself.

"Mmm," he hummed against my neck, allowing me to find my bearings without rushing me.

He was still hard against my abdomen, and I desperately wanted him inside me. I reached down between us, grasping him and he sucked in air through his teeth. His head rested on my shoulder as he worked to keep his breathing even. I stroked him slowly from base to tip, giving a twist when I reached the end before moving back toward his body.

"God," he whispered against my skin.

The water was starting to cool, and I knew we needed to get out, but I just didn't want to lose this moment.

"Come to bed," he said, turning off the tap and looking into my eyes. "Let me make love to you and show you exactly how I feel."

My eyes flicked between his, looking for the lie, but it wasn't there. Tears sprang up once again, and I let them fall.

"Hey," he said, knuckling one away as we stood there in the empty shower. "What's wrong?"

"I don't know," I admitted. "This feels like it's too good to be true."

He pulled me forward, kissing my forehead and gathering me to him. I could feel him reaching behind me and heard the shower curtain pull back, then felt the warm towel against my back as he worked to get me dry. I let him minister to my physical needs in that moment as I let my emotions settle themselves out. I didn't want to feel, didn't want to doubt, didn't want to even try to think of what was going on or where we would go from here. None of that mattered in this moment, and I tried desperately to forget everything.

That's when we heard it. I jumped from the loud pounding on the door and may have even screamed a little bit.

"Stay here," he ordered, but I gripped his arm, not wanting him to go into a dangerous place for me. "I won't open the door until I know who's out there and what they want."

He grabbed the other towel off the rack and wrapped it around his waist, then left the bathroom. I could hear shouting coming from the front, but I was frozen in fear. The shouting got louder, and I slid down the wall of the enclosure and sat on the floor of the tub, the towel wrapped around me my only protection.

When it grew quiet, I was even more worried. What had happened? Was Jonathan all right? Should I go out there and see what is going on?

"It's all good," Jonathan said as he came into the bathroom and I was just a mess. "It was Agent Richards. He wanted to make sure I made it home. He's in the living room if you're up to talking. He has some news."

I was shaking, both from cold and fear, and he came to the tub slowly, crouching down next to it.

"Come on," he finally said when I didn't move to go to him. "Let's get you into something warm and we can talk. I'll make you some tea to warm you up from the inside, too. Okay?"

He beckoned me with his outstretched hand and I reached out and grabbed it for the lifeline it was. He pulled me to my feet and helped me over the lip of the tub, then grabbed another towel to dry me off quickly. After that, he helped me into some sweats he pulled out of his drawer and threw a t-shirt over my head and a hoodie he grabbed from the closet. I was about as put together as I was likely to get in that moment, so he walked with me out to the living room.

"Sorry to disturb you," Agent Richards said, standing from the couch as we entered.

"It's fine," I replied.

"We executed a search warrant on both the home and office of George Warde," he said. "Unfortunately, he was not at either location."

"What does that mean?" Jonathan asked.

"He's on the run," Agent Richards said. "Where he is, we don't know. We have alerted customs and TSA, as well as sending his picture to train and bus stations in the greater Seattle area. His car was left behind, as well as all the electronics we knew about."

"He's gonna get away with it," I whispered, crushed.

"No," Agent Richards said. "He has nowhere to go. We have the upper hand."

"If he saw you," Jonathan said. "I mean, when you searched his place, will he hide out? What's his plan?"

"We aren't sure," Agent Richards said. "Right now, we have people watching both his home and office. The school has been advised that if he comes in, we are in a position to arrest him with what we found."

"You found something?" I asked.

"Actually," he said. "We found a lot. I can't really get into what we found because of the nature of this case, but I can tell you that once we arrest him, he will be going away for a long time. Of that, I am sure."

It was as if a weight was lifted off my shoulders at the fact that this guy would be going away and wouldn't be able to hurt me any longer. I looked over at Jonathan and he was staring at me, watching for my reaction, I guess. I smiled and squeezed his hand.

"I'll let you two go," he said. "I knew you would want to know this sooner rather than later. Stay vigilant, but you should be safe soon."

CHAPTER SIXTY-FOUR

*J*onathan...

"Good night, folks," Agent Richards said as I shut the door to my condo.

I looked over at Lucy who was still sitting on the couch and wondered what she was thinking.

"It's really almost over," she said when she saw me staring.

"I think so," I replied. "How are you doing?"

"I don't know," she confessed. "I'll feel better once they catch him, but at least there is some light at the end of the tunnel."

"For sure," I said. "You ready for bed? Or do you want to stay up for a while?"

She stood up and smiled. Even in the very oversized clothes, she was just this sexy woman walking toward me and I couldn't help but smile myself. Her pace was slow and steady, sensual in the too big sweatshirt and sweatpants, her bare feet and face the only places I could see skin, but it was more than enough to get me going. When she got to me, she reached out and grasped my hand, then gave it a tug, and walked backward toward the bedroom.

I swear to God, I'd follow her anywhere if she kept looking at me like that. Once we got there, I stepped closer to her, my hands going to the hem of the sweatshirt. I pulled it up over her head, then reached down to pull the t-shirt off as well, then shoved the sweatpants down and watched as she stepped out of them. She pulled at the towel I had around my waist and let it loose to fall to the floor.

There we were, just the two of us, and she smiled again. The light was on in the closet, and the hall light was still on, but that was the only light in the room. Shadows showed me all the curves her body had, and I wanted to kiss every single one of them. I moved closer to her, and she closed the space between us, wrapping her arms around my neck, her body pressed against mine.

"Love me," she said and kissed me.

She'd been the instigator many times, but this felt different. It felt as if she was truly giving herself to me, and it was so damn sexy I didn't even think of arguing with her. I slid my hands down her back, cupping her ass and lifted her. She instinctively wrapped her legs around my waist and I took the few steps left to the bed where I set her down, then climbed in with her, laying on top of her, not breaking the kiss at all.

We kissed until we were breathless, and when we came apart, she slid her hand between us, grabbing me and shifting me so that I was lined up with her entrance. I moved slowly to enter her, but she lifted her hips up, pulling me inside her. Up for the challenge, I moved my own hips forward and pressed all the way to the base, staying there for a moment. My arm was pressed on the bed next to her, and I used the other to run my hand along her hairline, simply staring at her.

"What?" she asked in hushed tones.

"I can't get enough of you," I whispered back. "I don't ever want to lose you."

She blinked, then reached a hand up and wrapped it around the back of my neck and pulled me to her, saying, "You won't."

Her kiss was fierce and passionate and seemed like she was saying everything words couldn't in that moment. My response was just as complete, telling her that she would always be mine.

Slowly, I began to move in and out of her, wanting to take my time and make this moment last. Everything she'd been through in the last couple of days were things I didn't want her to think about. No, I wanted the only thing on her mind to be the way we moved together, the way I felt inside her, the way I loved her.

It could have been minutes, or hours, or days, but we took our time, enjoying the feeling of our bodies connected, loving each other physically in a way that was so intimate and perfect. When she burst into a thousand pieces, I held her so she had a safe place to come back together, and I didn't give myself the chance to take that fall until she'd found her own footing again.

When we were both spent, we fell into a deep sleep, holding each other close.

IT WAS STILL DARK WHEN I FELT HER MOVE FROM THE BED. I GRASPED her hand, but she pulled away. I must have been exhausted because the next thing I knew it was growing light and she was tucked into my side again. I kissed her forehead and shifted, needing to answer mother nature's call. She gripped me tight, obviously not wanting me to leave.

"Gotta pee," I said, then she let me go.

I was quick, and when I came back, she was fast asleep again. I picked up my phone and realized it was later than I thought. I threw on the sweats that were on the floor next to the bed and headed to the kitchen to get coffee going and see what I had in the way of food to make for breakfast.

"Hey," she said about half an hour later when she came into the kitchen in my t-shirt.

"Coffee?" I asked, holding my cup.

"Please," she said, reaching out to me.

I poured another cup and pulled out the milk from the fridge. She doctored it up to her liking, and I put the milk back. She stepped close to me, around the mug in my hand, and went on tip toe to kiss me, then went around the island to sit on a stool on the other side.

"What's the plan for the day?" she asked.

"Not sure," I replied. "I have to be at the stadium by about two, but I'm available for most anything before that."

"Did you get any calls?" she asked, and I knew she wanted to know if I'd heard that George had been captured.

"Nothing yet," I said. "But it's early."

Just then, my phone rang and a Seattle number came up that I didn't recognize.

"Hello?" I said into the phone.

"Mr. Bridge," the man said.

"This is," I replied.

"Agent Richards," the agent said. "I have some good news."

"Hang on," I said. "I'm putting you on speaker because Lucy is here with me."

"Good morning," Agent Richards said through the speaker.

"Good morning," Lucy replied.

"We lucked out," he said without further delay. "We were able to add him to the no-fly list, and he was picked up at Paine Field, trying to board an outbound plane. If he'd been going through Sea-Tac, we'd have missed him."

"You have him?" Lucy asked. "He's in custody?"

"As we speak," Agent Richards said, and I could hear the smile in his voice. "There are several things that will have to happen before everything is all said and done, but for now, you are safe."

"So," I said. "She can go back home? Resume her life?"

There was a bit of hesitation in my voice, I knew, but it was mostly because I had grown fond of having her in my space. We hadn't talked about what would happen when they found the guy, or what our future would look like.

"Her home is still considered a crime scene," he said. "But that should be cleared up soon. I'm going to ask that they make it a priority. You've been through enough and I don't want to delay any more."

"Thank you," Lucy said.

I watched her as she spoke, and it was almost as if she didn't want to believe it. This nightmare was finally going to be over, and she could go back to whatever her life had been before we met.

"I've got a few more calls to make," Agent Richards said. "But I wanted you to know we had him in custody and that you were safe."

"Thank you," I said.

"Have a good day," he said, then disconnected the call.

Lucy stared at me, like she wasn't sure what to say.

"You good?" I asked.

"I don't know," she said. "It feels great to know that he's locked up, but at the same time, nothing is ever going to be the same again."

"I get that," I said. "I mean, I don't know everything you've been through, but I know you've been tense and I've seen the worry on you, so I'm glad he's where he can't hurt you now."

"Can you take me to Andrea's?" she asked. "I wanna get my phone and call my mom and dad and let them know what's happening, then I wanna go get my kids."

"Yeah, sure," I said. "Let's get dressed."

She set her coffee cup down after taking a quick sip and walked back to the bedroom. I shut the machine off and took a drink of my own, then pulled out a couple of travel mugs from the cupboard so we could take it with us.

When I got to the bedroom she was standing there staring at the bed. I came up behind her and wrapped my arms around her waist and asked, "What'cha thinking?"

She sniffed and stepped out of my grasp, then turned to me.

"I don't know where we go from here," she confessed. "You and me, what do we do about us?"

"Not something we need to figure out right now," I said. "Let's get you dressed and back to your own neighborhood. Then you can go get your kids. If you want, you guys can stay here tonight, and for as long as it takes for them to get your house back in shape."

"I didn't even think about that," she said.

"One step at a time, baby," I replied. "Let's start with getting you to your people. After that, we'll figure the next step out. Okay?"

She sniffed again, then went over to her suitcase to grab some clothes. I went into the closet and pulled off the sweats, pulling on a pair of jeans and grabbing a shirt and socks. When I came back to the bedroom, she wasn't there, but then stepped out of the bathroom wearing a similar outfit, jeans and a t-shirt. She'd pulled her hair up into a ponytail and must have washed her face because it was bright and shiny pink. I patted the bed next to where I sat and she joined me.

"We'll get through this," I said. "I'm not going anywhere."

Looking up at me, she smiled.

"Thank you for taking care of me," she said.

"You showed me that my life wasn't over," I replied.

When we got to the door, I picked up my keys and realized that my car key wasn't on it. That's when I remembered that Beckett took my car to throw anyone off my scent.

"Shit," I said.

"What?" she asked.

"My teammate has my car," I replied. "We thought it would help to keep anyone from following me last night."

"What do we need to do?" she asked and I could tell she was at the point where making decisions was outside of her ability.

She'd been through so much, I didn't blame her.

"I'll order an Uber," I said. "We can take it to your place and pick your car up there. You can bring me back, or I can come back myself in the Uber."

"I can bring you," she said. "I'd ask you to come with, but it's gonna take most of the day."

"You still have the key to my place?" I asked.

"Yeah," she said.

"Good," I replied. "You can text me when you decide where you're gonna stay, and if it's here, you can let me know if I should sleep with you or on the couch. I assume the kids don't know about us."

"Yeah, no," she said. "I will probably just head to the cabin and stay there tonight, then come home in the morning."

"Okay," I said. "Uber is on the way, so let's head down."

She grabbed my hand and held it the whole way down, as well as the ride to her friend's house, and even when we went up the walkway to their door. Maybe they knew, but I didn't want to assume. I'd love to tell the world, but I wanted to wait until she was ready. Of course, we still needed to talk about us and what was next for us, so that was a conversation we would have to have later. I'd wait, though.

CHAPTER SIXTY-FIVE

*L*ucy...

"Oh my God," Andrea said when she answered the door, then stepped out and pulled me into a tight hug. "Are you okay? What's going on?"

"Inside," I said, and she pulled back and stepped into her house, opening the door so we could go inside.

"Dish," she said after she shut the door.

"They got him," Jonathan said when I just stood there. "He's in custody and he isn't likely to be getting out any time soon."

"Thank God," she replied. "How did you find out?"

"I'll tell you all about it," I said. "But I wanna call the kids."

"Oh, sure," she said. "Let me go get your phone."

She went to the office on the main floor and opened the door. I saw Marco sitting at the desk, but he was on the phone, so she just stepped in, kissed his cheek, then came out with all our phones.

"They're fully charged," she said. "But they've been off since you left. Might take a minute to get them back on again."

It seemed to take forever for it to boot up, and when it did it started buzzing from a slew of text messages, missed calls, and voicemails. I didn't want to even think about what they were, so I just waited while it did its thing then, when it finished, I pulled up the phone app and dialed my parent's cabin number.

"Hello," Dad said when he answered.

"Dad," I said, nearly breaking down.

"Hey, honey," he replied. "I thought you weren't gonna call us."

"It's over," I said. "They got him. I'm coming up there after I take Jonathan home."

I heard my mom in the background asking something and Dad handed her the phone.

"Lucy?" she asked.

"Mom," I sobbed as I sat on my best friend's couch.

"Oh, baby," she said. "It's all gonna be okay. Dad said they got him."

"Yeah," I croaked out.

Jonathan held his hand out and I handed him the phone.

"Hello," he said. "Yes," he responded after a pause. "That's all we know. They have him in custody and he isn't likely to get out any time soon."

Andrea came and sat on the other side of me and I collapsed into her arms and sobbed as she held me. I could hear Jonathan saying things, then heard Marco come in, but it was all just background noise. My friend held me as I went to pieces, finally free of the man who had caused me so much turmoil and pain, the man who took my whole life and turned it upside down, but who also brought me to Jonathan.

That was the most confusing part, too. I mean, I missed Ryan more than anything, but I would never have met Jonathan if he hadn't died, and that was just awful to think about, which only caused me to cry even more.

When I finally settled, having been passed from Andrea to Jonathan, the men had decided that I was in no shape to drive, and that Marco would take Jonathan back to the city, then they would drive me to my parent's cabin and we'd all stay the night. There was plenty of room, and Noah would absolutely love it. Not to mention, my parents would love the opportunity to have a little baby fix in the mix as well.

I kissed Jonathan goodbye as he left with Marco, then helped

Andrea pack up everything they'd need for the overnight trip. It had been so long since the kids were little that I forgot how much stuff a baby took. We laughed at the insanity that had been the last week, and I told her all about everything that happened with Jonathan, even the sex, to which she had said she was jealous, but I knew better. The way Marco looked at her, and the way she looked back, told me that they had plenty of fire and excitement in the bedroom.

Obviously worn out, I slept most of the drive to the cabin, and when we pulled in the kids were right there waiting, hugging me and then taking Noah into the living room of the cabin while the adults sat around the kitchen table. Once again, I told the story of how they had captured George, that he was in custody somewhere, and that for now, everything was safe.

"Did they say who would pay to clean up the house?" Dad asked.

"I honestly am not sure," I replied. "I think that we're probably gonna stay with Jonathan for a few days. At least until we figure out what is going to happen."

"It's that serious?" Mom asked.

"Yeah." I smiled. "It really is."

"Have you told the kids?" Dad asked.

"Told us what?" Rayne asked, coming into the dining room.

"That we're staying with Jonathan for a few days," I said, not wanting to have the larger conversation right then.

"Oh," she said. "Probably because the house is still a mess."

"Yeah," I said, not elaborating.

Honestly, that was going to be the hardest part of this whole thing, now. Explaining to the kids that Jonathan and I were together, that we hadn't figured everything out yet, but that we would make sure that their feelings were considered as well. Man, there was a whole lot still left to do.

EPILOGUE

*J*onathan...

"You guys ready?" I asked the kids.

"I am," Thomas said.

"Me, too," Rayne added, though not nearly as enthusiastically as her brother.

"Let's go," I said, then opened the door to the locker room.

Father's Day was all about family with the team. We had the opportunity to bring our kids to the field, and they got to hang out and throw the ball around with the other players, and the other kids. Grant wasn't old enough, yet, so he sat with my sister and Lucy in the family section of the stands.

"This is so cool," Thomas said, eyes wide.

"None of the guys are gonna be naked, are they?" Rayne asked.

"Not a single one of them," I said. "Come on. You can meet some of my friends."

As we walked in, Huffman was standing next to his locker, which was right next to mine.

"Hey there," he said, looking at the kids. "You guys ready to shag some balls?"

"I am," Thomas said, holding up the mitt I'd gotten for him.

"How 'bout you, angel?" he asked Rayne.

"My name is Rayne," she said, folding her arms across her chest.

"Yes, ma'am," Huffman said. "Well, Rayne, would you like to head out to the field and do a little catch with me and some of the other guys?"

"I guess," she said, but I could see a little pink in her cheeks.

That little tell, I'd learned over the last couple months, was the only thing that outwardly showed that she was embarrassed. It didn't happen often, but when it did, boy was it clear.

"Better watch out," I said. "She'll outshine all of you out there. She's a natural."

She looked at me, growing a little pinker, but smiled. I winked at her, then patted Thomas on the back and steered them toward the dugout and field.

"Wow," Thomas said, drawing the word out. "This is so cool."

"It is pretty cool," Rayne agreed.

"Never gets old, either," Beckett said as he walked around us. "You are absolutely gorgeous," he said to Rayne.

"Hands off," I barked, but she looked at me like she was gonna kill me and I held up my hands in surrender.

If anything, she was likely to be the only person who could put that kid in his place. He'd grown up some since the beginning of the season, but there was no way I'd tell him that. No, I just showed him how much I trusted him by allowing her to trot out into the outfield and shag balls together.

Thomas turned around and around, looking at the stands as they filled up.

"Don't you get nervous?" he asked as he turned another circle.

"You get used to it," I replied. "Come on, let's go say hi to your mom, then head out and grab some balls."

We walked to the space behind home plate where Kate and Lucy were standing with Grant. He waved at me and it was so good to see him. She'd been coming up every couple of weeks, and had become very good friends with Lucy, which just made me all around happy.

"Mom," Thomas said. "Isn't this the coolest thing ever?"

"It really is," she said.

"We're gonna go catch some balls now," he said. "See you after batting practice."

"Have fun," she said.

Thomas walked away, but Lucy called me back.

"Who is Rayne with?" she asked.

"Beckett," I said. "Don't worry, though. He's grown up, and I honestly think she can take care of herself where he is concerned. She put him in his place the moment he spoke to her."

She laughed, and it was such a great sound.

"See you," I said, then followed Thomas to the outfield.

This was what life was all about. Kids playing a game they loved, people watching and cheering them on, and spending time with family, whatever it happened to look like.

NOTE FROM AUTHOR

Images and Blurbs available upon request.
I would ask that you obtain high quality headshots and cover art images directly through me, rather than taking them from either my website or Amazon, however, blurbs are readily available through both places.

ABOUT THE AUTHOR

Born and raised in the Pacific Northwest, CM Kane was fed a steady diet of sports, particularly baseball. Having this love of the game instilled in her at an early age, she found that nothing was better than getting lost in the game. Storytelling was another gift that was encouraged in her youth, and she's taking to the written word to explore a new aspect to the game she loves.

Social Media and Website Links:

Website:
https://www.authorcmkane.com

Facebook:
https://www.facebook.com/AuthorCMKane

Instagram:
https://www.instagram.com/authorcmkane/

Amazon:
https://www.amazon.com/author/cmkane

BlueSky:
https://bsky.app/profile/authorcmkane.bsky.social

ALSO BY C.M. KANE

Seattle Cascades

1. Extra Innings

2. Caught Stealing

3. Backstop

4. Power Hitter

5. Double Play

6. Find a Gap

7. Sweet Spot (Coming Soon)

8. 7th Inning Stretch (Coming Soon)

New Orleans Magicians

1. Choke Up

2. Caught in a Pickle

3. Brand New Ballgame (Coming Soon)

4. Fan Interference (Coming Soon)

5. Flashing the Leather (Coming Soon)

Austin Aces Hockey Club (Shared World)

Power Play

Anthologies

Unnerving: Eclipse

Street Justice (Limited Time)

Fooling Around (Coming April 1, 2025)

Neon Lights & Country Nights (Coming June 1, 2025)

Stand Alone Titles

A Switch in Time